Accidental Paradise
by Eric Grandy

Paperback ISBN: 979-8988533337
Ebook ISBN: 979-8988533344

Cover design: Ginnefine Art

Published by:
Audecyn Books
Upper Marlboro, MD

DEDICATIONS

For Harry Grandy Sr. and Mary Grandy, who didn't live long enough to see their baby boy become an author. I know that you know.

Rhonda, my wife of 35 years, whose unrelenting love, intelligence, support and inspiration made everything possible.

The Worms family. My daughter Marti, my son in law Wolf and my granddaughter Alexandra. My support system and my most ardent fans.

My siblings, Jacqueline Robinson, Harry Grandy, Jr. and Sylvia Williams. I hope you are proud of your little brother.

Rafael Alvarez, my mentor, my friend. This book would not have been possible without your guidance. Thank you.

Eric Addison, the first writer to tell me my story was publishable.

Cherrie Woods, thanks for pointing me in the right direction.

Lynn Candelaria, your chance introduction led to much bigger things.

Black Writers Guild, my resource for information and ideas.

White Marsh Writer's Group, our twice monthly meetings helped hone my writings.

Accidental Paradise

Big Dog and Peaches
Chapter One

Abbotson Elementary School #50 in East Baltimore was just letting out for the day. It was a two story, flat roofed, "L" shaped building, made of boring blond concrete with red bricks for accent. It just sat there as unremarkable as a flipped over pancake. This was a sunny and warm first week of the 1999-2000 academic year and the school yard was choked with first to fifth graders. The bullies were gathered in their usual spot on the playground, huddled together on the monkey bars like vultures in an acacia tree on the African savanna, scanning the herd for victims.

The leader of this group was Earl Jackson, who somehow graduated from this school last year and was now cutting class at Clifton Park Middle to come over and find somebody to terrorize. He and his two homies, Cordell and Meatball, were narrowing down the field when Earl spied her.

"Hey man, there's that Whitaker girl. She think she so much better than everybody else. Won't talk to nobody, won't come out of her house, like she too good to hang out."

The pack started following her with their eyes.

"Yeah, always carrying some books so she got a excuse not to talk to nobody. She think she's sooo smart too, like she in the thirteenth grade or something. Yeah, I know her reeeal good. She live right across the street from me."

Cordell spoke up. "Man, how you know she all stuck up?"

"Cause I tried talking to her and she just shut me down, looked at me like I was snot, you know what I mean?"

"Yeah, I hate that, man. Whatchoo wanna do?"

"Let's twist her a little bit. She got it coming."

LaVern was walking home alone, as usual, and was unaware as the trio began to follow. By the time she noticed, she was surrounded. Earl walked around in front and was now walking backwards, bending down to look directly into her face.

"Hey Miss stuck up. You remember me?"

LaVern knew exactly who he was. He was one of those rowdy, trouble making Jackson boys her parents told her to stay away from. She didn't recognize the other two.

"I know who you are," LaVern said, not breaking her stride. "I'm minding my business so why don't you mind yours?"

Earl feigned a surprised look. "Oh, check it out fellas. Miss stuck up is talking to us regular folks."

LaVern changed direction to go around. She hugged her schoolbooks closer to her body, unconsciously showing fear. Earl adjusted his back pedaling to remain in front of her.

"I th-th-think she scared, Earl," Meatball the stutterer said. "The l-l-little girl wanna r-r-run home."

"I think you right, homie, I think she scared to death."

Earl stopped backpedaling, forcing LaVern to practically bump into him. The circle tightened around her. Earl Jackson bent down inches from LaVern's face.

"Whatchu gonna do now Miss stuck up? Huh?" He worked his head from side to side as he spoke. He never broke eye contact. "Whatchu gonna do?"

She was afraid to look at him. LaVern stood frozen, her eyes cast downward as her tormentor continued to accost her. From out of nowhere, a loud, shrill voice broke the tension.

"EAAARL!"

Earl Jackson looked out over LaVern's shoulder and saw his younger sister, Shaundra, approaching.

"Earl, leave her alone."

He was momentarily confused, but he regrouped quickly. "Why don't you mind your own business little girl. Leave us men alone."

"I don't see no men here. All I see is you and your two sorry assed flunkies."

Meatball was offended. "I ain't n-n-nobody's flunky."

"Whatever!," snorted Shaundra. She put her outstretched palm inches from Meatball's face.

"Why don't you do like I said Shaundra and take your nosey ass on home."

"I ain't going nowhere Earl. Not till you leave LaVern alone."

"You don't even know her. I don't ever see y'all two hanging out."

"You don't have to *see* me doing nothing. She's my friend, that's all you need to know." Shaundra put her arm around LaVern's shoulder.

Earl eyed his sister angrily. "Fuck this shit fellas, let's bounce." The trio of toughs bounded off to victims unknown.

Shaundra, with her arm still draped around LaVern's shoulder, peered into her eyes and asked her if she was alright. She was visibly shaken.

"That was your brother, wasn't it?"

"Yeah, that was him. He wanna be a badass, but I know he ain't shit."

LaVern took a deep breath and let it out, something her father always told her to do whenever she felt stressed. "Thanks for stepping in like that Shaundra."

"No problem, girlfriend. I'll walk you home."

Everyone on Gorsuch Avenue knew the Jackson family. Three boys and one girl, Shaundra being the youngest. All the boys were hoodlums and hustlers, involved in every kind of illegal activity you can name; drugs, gangs, burglaries, gambling. The oldest brother was currently doing time for armed robbery. But, even at age ten, Shaundra could hold her own in that crowd. She had to. Danger and dysfunction were everywhere.

"How come you don't hang out like everybody else?" Shaundra asked.

"My parents won't let me. I have to come home and do my homework right away. Then, I have chores because my mother is a teacher, and my father works at night. I'm the only child and my parents depend on me."

"Oh yeah, that's tough. I see you on the stoop though. You always have a book. You must like to read 'cause you do it a lot."

"Yeah, I do," replied LaVern. She was almost embarrassed to admit it. A love of reading doesn't earn cred on these hostile streets.

"I read sometimes too." She was going to leave that comment hanging right there, but LaVern's face lit up.

"What do you like to read?"

What little reading she did consisted of what Jay-Z and Beyonce were up to or the real reason Lauren Hill switched to braids. Not quite the heady stuff she was sure LaVern was into. She went into diversion mode.

"I like to read all kinds of stuff. But tell me what you like to read first. I bet you have lotsa books."

"My parents buy me books, and I save every one of them. So yeah, I have lots of books. I have my own library."

This fact stunned Shaundra. "You have your own library? Like the Enoch Pratt Library?"

LaVern had never thought of it that way before. "Well, I guess so, but not as many books."

Shaundra tried to envision The Enoch Pratt inside somebody's house. The girls continued their walk until they got to LaVern's steps on Gorsuch Avenue.

"If you come out on your stoop tonight, can I come over?"

"Sure you can," replied LaVern as she bounded happily up her steps. She closed the door, turned and went up on her toes to peer out of one of the three diamond shaped portholes. Shaundra sauntered across the street and into her house. She thought to herself, *hmm... she's nicer than I thought she would be.*

They became close friends. LaVern was still quiet and timid and susceptible to bullying, but Shaundra was streetwise and smart mouthed and didn't intimidate very easily. One day, Shaundra's seventeen-year-old brother, David (aka Sweat) and her were talking on their stoop.

"Why you always hanging around that nerdy ass Whitaker girl, protecting her like you some kind of big dog? She can't be all that."

"Everybody is always trying to mess with her because she won't fight back. It ain't right, David."

"OK Shaundra, I hear you. You got your reasons I guess, but don't back yourself into no corners trying to play the protector." Sweat then headed off down the street with Shaundra watching him. Midblock, he turned around and cupped his hands over his mouth and yelled loud enough for a dead person to hear him. "BIG DOOOG, woof woof" and broke out into this huge, gapped tooth grin. From that point on Shaundra Jackson became known as "Big Dog" or just plain old B.D.

The Whitaker household was quiet, organized and tidy and there was a routine that was closely adhered to. Jacqueline Whitaker was an English teacher at Baltimore City College, a premiere public high school. She would arrive home around 4pm each day and begin making dinner. Freeman Whitaker left for his night shift warehouse job at 8pm. LaVern was expected to begin her homework immediately. For those few hours in the afternoon, the family would talk about their day and eat dinner. It was LaVern's job to wash the dishes. There were quiet activities like board games, reading or watching television. There was reading material in every room, including the bathroom; The Baltimore Sun, National Geographic, cookbooks, works of fiction, and Freeman's prize collection of Black History books, mostly autobiographies of both famous and ordinary Black Americans.

"You must know your history," Freeman always told LaVern. "Whatever freedoms we enjoy today is because some Black person had to get beaten or hung or burned out of their house. It's a disservice to the past to forget it."

LaVern's education was the center point of both parents' lives and as far as Freeman Whitaker was concerned, that included her Black education.

The Jackson household was directly across the street, and the complete reverse. Much like Gorsuch Avenue in general, it was a chaotic, dysfunctional mess, and downright dangerous. There seemed to be a constant stream of nefarious, shady characters, men and women, day and night. The lights were on constantly and it was never quiet. If it wasn't the TV blasting, it was rap music pouring out of every open window or door. When a complaint was lodged, all that had to be mentioned was Gorsuch Avenue and the cops knew exactly where to go. The alcoholic father was nowhere to be found. The few times he did show up, he made matters worse. The mother, Traci, had lost control years ago. She worked as a maid in one of the downtown hotels. Her drug usage was sporadic but debilitating. The house was cluttered and dusty and no one cleaned up. Dishes were grudgingly washed and roaches were everywhere. LaVern was not permitted to enter that house, EVER!

The contrasts didn't end there. Jacqueline Whitaker demanded correct grammar at home, Shaundra's spoke the language of the streets. LaVern was always neat and clean for school. Shaundra was unkempt and disheveled. LaVern was slim and Shaundra was chunky. But their relationship worked.

Every day after LaVern finished her homework, the girls would sit on LaVern's stoop to talk and watch the neighborhood activity. Gorsuch Avenue was a prototypical East Baltimore street; a concrete environment devoid of greenery, accordion-like row houses that went on for blocks, and constant suspicious interactions. Shaundra knew every who, what, why, how, when and where behind all this ceaseless movement. The boy who popped a wheelie on a bike as he passed by; he was returning from the county where he had stolen it. The young girl standing on the stoop opposite; she was sneaking out to be with her gangster boyfriend.

"How do you know all this?" asked LaVern.

"Girrrrl, if you lived in my house, you hear all the dirt. People think I'm sleeping or looking at TV but I'm ear hustling my ass off."

One evening, three older girls from nearby Kirk Avenue worked their way up Gorsuch Avenue. Shaundra knew them and sensed trouble.

"Don't say nothin' to these bitches, OK?"

She eyeballed the group as they strolled up the middle of the deserted street. LaVern started to follow them with her eyes too, even though she didn't know why. Then, the pack noticed them. Shaundra's eyes narrowed.

"Just be cool," she said.

LaVern was now really worried. *Be cool about what? Why?* One of the trio cupped her hands over her mouth and howled,

"Big Dooooog!" Then in unison they all cupped their

mouths and repeated it. "Big Doooog! Big Dooooog!"

Shaundra stood up and yelled, "I got your big dog right here!"

As they continued up the street they let loose with another barrage. "Big Dooooog! Woof, woof!"

Shaundra sat down and continued to gaze angrily as they rounded the corner. LaVern was confused by the spectacle.

"Who's Big Dog Shaundra? What were they talking about?"

Shaundra had never mentioned her earlier conversation with Sweat.

"They talkin' about me, LaVern. They callin' me Big Dog."

"You!? Why were they calling you Big Dog?"

"Ever since that day when Earl and his boys tried to mess with you, people been saying that I'm protecting you, like a big dog. David started it and now everybody calls me that."

LaVern didn't realize she was being protected. Come to think of it, Earl and his home boys never approached her again after that first incident. A million questions whizzed through LaVern's mind. *How often has she come to my aid? Has she been in any fights over me?* She looked over to Shaundra, who was staring straight ahead, deep in thought. LaVern put her arm around her friend.

"Listen Shaundra, I don't care what anybody calls you. You're my friend. My best friend. If I have to, I would fight for you too."

Shaundra was staring at the ground when she allowed a small grin to appear. "Well, I hope it don't come down to that 'cause we both know you can't fight worth a damn."

A smile creased LaVern's lips too. After a couple of minutes Shaundra stood up.

"I gotta go home now, OK?

"See you tomorrow at school, right?"

"You know it."

Despite their regular get-togethers on LaVern's stoop, Shaundra had never been invited inside. This was solely on orders from Freeman. He was familiar with the goings on in that Jackson house and he didn't want any of them bringing their bad habits and foul language into his. But LaVern felt differently.

"I have to ask you something, Daddy."

"What is it, Peaches?"

When she talked, even to her parents, LaVern's eyes were cast downward. Freeman repeatedly tried to correct this flaw. He reached over, placed a curled forefinger under her chin and gently raised her head and repeated his question. With their eyes now locked, she began.

"Daddy, can I invite Shaundra inside one day?"

After asking her question, LaVern's eyes dropped back to the floor. Maintaining eye contact was still a work in progress.

"Why do you want her to come in the house? Don't you two have a good time out on the steps?"

"We do Daddy, but she's my best friend. I want to show her my room, my books and my clothes. We even talked about doing homework together."

"Your mother and I will discuss it and we'll let you know, OK?"

"Yaaaay! Thank you, Daddy. She's not like the rest of her family, you'll see."

The following day, Freeman broached the "Shaundra Jackson" subject. "You know they've been spending lots of time out front after school."

"Yes, I'm aware of that," said a wary Jackie.

"She asked me yesterday if that Jackson girl could come in the house."

"Come inside!? For what reason?"

"Peaches said she was her best friend, and she wanted to show her her bedroom and books and things."

Jackie looked very pensive for a moment. "This is the first time Peaches has expressed a desire to invite any neighborhood child over here. She has never said she had a best friend."

"She even said Shaundra wasn't like the rest of her family."

"I should hope not. But it would be good for her to have a little girlfriend. She stays by herself so much." Jackie seemed to be searching for a silver lining amidst this Jackson "black cloud".

"Of all the people, why one of those Jackson's?" Full of

consternation, Freeman finally relented. "OK, but we should take this whole thing very slowly. I want this to be a positive experience for her."

"Great. Who's going to give her the good news?"

"I'll do it," said Freeman. "Since she asked me, I'll tell her."

Jackie started to walk toward the kitchen when she yelled over her shoulder, "I'm still checking that child for roaches. Friend or no friend, I'm not letting her bring those things into my house."

When Shaundra took her first steps inside the Whitaker home, both parents were there to greet her.

"So, you're Shaundra," said Jackie. "I've seen you around, but this is my first chance to meet you."

"Hi, Miss Whitaker."

"I'm Mr. Whitaker, Shaundra."

"Hi, Mr. Whitaker."

While Shaundra's attention was directed towards Freeman, Jackie eyed her up and down and prayed she wouldn't see something crawling off this child. LaVern was standing right there beaming and grinning like it was Christmas morning. She couldn't hide her delight at finally having her best friend inside her house.

"Well Peaches," said Jackie, "why don't you take Shaundra upstairs and show her your room?"

"OK Mama. Come on Shaundra," squealed LaVern.

As she was being led through the house Shaundra quietly exclaimed, "Wow, your house is so neat and clean and quiet. Not like mine."

The Whitakers stared at each other with a "I hope we didn't just make a big mistake" look.

When Shaundra entered LaVern's bedroom, she was astonished at how bright and tidy and orderly it was. There were no clothes draped over an unmade bed. There were no random pencil or crayon marks or dirty handprints everywhere. Her lamp actually had a lampshade, which matched the curtains, which matched the walls, instead of just a bare bulb. No anger induced holes in the walls. The paint wasn't peeling. Her little wooden study desk was organized with her schoolbooks stacked in a neat pile. And books! Just like she said, she had a small bookcase along one wall that was crammed end to end, top to bottom with books. Shaundra just stood in the doorway in silent amazement. It was all so warm and inviting. She didn't speak for so long that LaVern thought something was wrong.

"Shaundra, are you OK?"

"LaVern, your room, your house, it's all so neat and clean and beautiful."

Then, Shaundra noticed multicolored letters on the wall above the bed, arranged in a semi-circle that out spelled PEACHES.

"I heard your mother call you Peaches. Why do they call you that?"

"My father told me that when I was born, I was all fuzzy and cuddly like a peach. That's about all I know."

"Can I call you Peaches too?"

LaVern thought for a moment. "My mommy and daddy are the only ones who call me that. But you can too if you want to."

Shaundra considered it an honor to be included in such an exclusive group.

In time, LaVern's house became a refuge for Shaundra. The calm, regulated atmosphere of the Whitaker household was in direct contrast to the turbulent and disordered air of the Jackson house. The Whitakers came to view her as a trusted friend for both their daughter and them. When they insisted she abide by their house rules, Shaundra eagerly complied. She helped LaVern clear the table and wash the dishes after dinner. Her grades began to improve due to the Whitakers' unbreakable rule regarding doing homework right after school. She even began staying overnight where they giggled and whispered and talked about boys in the quiet of LaVern's bedroom.

Per her parents' orders, LaVern never visited the Jackson house, but it was obvious why Shaundra gravitated to her home. Even at age ten, Shaundra knew quality when she saw it.

During the summer before LaVern's sixth grade year, Freeman opened a letter from the Felder Academy, a private school in Baltimore. The Whitakers had tried to gain admission for their daughter in the first grade. Not surprisingly, they received a politely worded denial. The next and last acceptance period was before the sixth grade. The letter began…

"It is our sincerest honor and pleasure to inform you that your daughter, LaVern Renee Whitaker, has been granted admission to…"

Freeman blinked. He read it a second time. Then…

"Jackie!"

No reply. Then a little louder, "Jackie!!"

A voice came from the distance. "What is it, Freeman?"

He didn't answer. He just quick stepped it through the living room, the dining room and into the kitchen where he held it up. "You *really* need to read this."

Freeman watched his wife's eyes as they tracked along each line. Then, her eyes widened in astonishment. She looked up at Freeman, then back the letter.

"I knew it, I knew it!" She jumped into her husband's arms, and they shared a long, tight and emotional embrace. "I told you, Freeman. I knew our baby girl belonged with the best. I didn't care what those uppity White folks said."

"You know how this society works," said Freeman, "even when you have the talent, you don't always get the opportunity. I didn't think they would give her a fair shot."

Jackie took a deep breath and exhaled. "We've got to tell her. She's upstairs with Shaundra."

Both parents headed up the steps and entered LaVern's room. The girls were sitting on the floor crossed legged, giggling and talking. Jackie and Freeman stood motionless. They gazed down at their daughter knowing her life was about to change. The two girls stared back, waiting for the grownups to say something.

"Sweetheart, we have some exciting news for you."

LaVern's face lit up. "Oh boy. What is it Mommy?"

"Well baby, you're going to go to a new school next

semester."

LaVern was puzzled. She looked at Shaundra as if she could understand what her parents meant. Then, she shifted her attention back to her parents. She said nothing. Freeman tried to clear up her confusion.

"It's called The Felder Academy and it's a much better school than 50. You'll have better teachers and smaller classes and better facilities."

LaVern lowered her head. "But, I like 50."

Jackie and Freeman looked at one another. They realized that explaining the advantages of going to Felder Academy would not be easy. All LaVern understood was she was going to a strange new school.

"We'll talk some more in the morning," said Freeman. "Everything will be alright Peaches. You two keep playing, OK?"

When the Whitakers walked out, they left two very confused little girls in that room.

"You're going to a new school, Peaches," said Shaundra.

"I guess so," LaVern replied, her head still down.

"That means we won't see each other in class. We won't walk home together either." Shaundra was completely anguished.

"But, my parents want me to go. So I have to."

Both girls fell silent.

"I need to go home."

"You're coming over tomorrow, right?"

"You know I will." Shaundra headed home full of doubt and fear.

The fall semester at the Felder Academy began a week earlier than the public schools. Their bus picked LaVern up at the end of her block. On that first morning, Freeman accompanied his daughter and stood with her. Neighborhood kids passed by and stared. She was dressed differently. She had on a dark green and gold plaid skirt with a solid gold collared blouse, and black knee-high socks. A uniform! Pretty soon word got around. She wasn't going to School 50 anymore. She was going to that rich White people's school. Freeman was way ahead of the troublemakers on this one. He knew what hood children would say and possibly do if his little girl had to stand out here by herself. So, there he stood, each and every morning, alongside his adolescent daughter ready to swat away any jealous, would-be Earl Jackson's.

He couldn't see much through the tinted windows except little heads bobbing up and down as the bus ambled toward him.

"Are you nervous Peaches?" he asked. "It's OK to be nervous. What did I always tell you to do when you get nervous?"

She kept her head down. "You always say to take a deep breath."

"That's right. Let me see you take one."

LaVern managed a very halted inhale followed by an even more uneven and nervous exhale. It wasn't a convincing display.

"It'll be alright Peaches. After a while it'll be like going to any other school. You'll see."

The bus came to a stop and the doors opened. He gave her a slight nudge to get her moving. Freeman stuck his head inside and looked toward the back of the bus. It wasn't full but the few children on board were Black. This gave him some relief knowing his little girl wouldn't be the sole Black child on her ride to and from school. LaVern took a seat by herself behind the driver. She looked so pitiful and alone. Freeman almost felt like taking her off the bus. Almost.

"Have fun LaVern, OK?"

She never lifted her head. She just weakly raised her right hand and wiggled her fingers. The door closed and the bus pulled off. Well, thought Freeman, it's done.

In time, Shaundra wanted to know all about LaVern's new school.

"Do you like it there?

"It's OK. It's different"

"Do you like the teachers?"

"There're a couple that I like."

Her eyes raked over her friend from head to toe. "Do you

like wearing that uniform all the time?"

"I hate it Shaundra. I only have one, and my mother makes me wash it every day."

"I bet they have a lotta new stuff though, don't they?"

"They have a lot more things to choose from." LaVern marveled about the school and all the activities that were available; the chess club, the student newspaper, debate teams, Future Leaders of America, the list went on and on.

"We don't have any of that stuff at 50. We just go to school and come home."

Shaundra felt a twinge of jealousy. Why did she have to be stuck in ol' run down 50? I can't compete with those new private school girls, she feared, the White girls and all their advantages. I'm going to lose my best friend.

One day Shaundra didn't come over after school. No big deal thought LaVern. She'll be over later, and they would do what they always did, study, eat dinner and then giggle and chat in her room. But Big Dog didn't show up. It was the same the next day and then the next. LaVern would go to the window to see if Shaundra was somewhere outside. No luck. She wouldn't dare go over to her house. Her parents might see her. She really missed her best friend. Desperate, she asked her mother what made Shaundra stop coming over? Jackie gave her young daughter her first lesson in relationships and human behavior.

"Sweetheart, this might be a little difficult for you to understand right now but I don't know any other way to explain it. Shaundra feels left out. She listens to all the great things you get to do at Felder and all the new friends you're making, and she feels like she is being left behind. Do you understand what I'm trying to say?"

"But Mommy, she's my best friend."

"It's nothing you did wrong baby. You were sharing things with her the way you always do. The only difference is, now you're sharing things that don't involve her."

LaVern was still a little perplexed. "I don't want to hurt her feelings, and I don't want to lose my best friend."

"I know you don't, Peaches. If you really don't want to lose Shaundra as a best friend, you should tell her."

"But she already knows she's my best friend."

"Well, here's the difficult part, Peaches, and even adults have trouble with this. Things in *your* life have changed but *her* life hasn't. It's not anyone's fault, that's just life. This won't be the last time this will happen to you. But, if somebody is really special to you and they're worth having in your life, let them know that, even though your life may be changing, they're still a valuable part of it. She needs reassurance." Jackie stared into her young daughter's eyes and tilted her head, looking for recognition. "Do you understand what I'm trying to say?"

"If I want to keep Shaundra as my best friend, I have to tell her."

Jackie was proud of how quickly her little girl grasped something so abstract.

"Nobody can tell you what to do, Peaches. You have to decide for yourself."

"Then I have to tell her Mommy. I only have one best friend."

Jackie gave her little girl a bear hug, looked into her eyes, and ran her hands over the thick braids that ran from front to back on her head. She thought to herself, *this is my baby's first dose of real-life issues. I hope I made her decision easier.*

"Mommy?"

"What is it baby?"

LaVern dropped her head and stared at the floor. "Is it alright if I go over to Shaundra's house to talk to her?"

"Of course, sweetheart, but just this one time, alright?"

LaVern lifted her head and grinned like it was her birthday.

"And then you come right back, OK?"

"I promise. I'll be right back."

Jackie and Freeman watched through the living room window as she paused, took a deep breath, and began her slow and pensive trek across the street.

"She looks like she's got the weight of the world on her shoulders," said Freeman.

Jackie just nodded and watched. As LaVern reached the other side of the street and stood in front of Shaundra's house, she looked up and noticed something startling. Peering out from behind torn curtains was Shaundra's tiny face. LaVern saw her little fingers tentatively waving at her. Both girls smiled and LaVern frantically waved for her friend to come out. The tiny face disappeared and the shabby curtains reunited behind her. The door opened and for the first time in several days, the best friends were face to face. LaVern gazed up at Shaundra and quickly lowered her head. She climbed the steps and quietly sat down. Shaundra took her place beside her. They sat in silence for a few seconds.

"I missed you, Shaundra."

"I missed you too, Peaches."

With her head still down, LaVern asked, "Why did you stop coming over?"

She stared at her feet, she looked down the street, she twisted her fingers then ran them through her long braids. "I'm really sorry, Peaches. I don't know why. All I know is I really missed you and I'm sorry."

LaVern's mind went back to what her mother told her about how people sometimes felt left out. She raised her head and looked Shaundra straight in the eye.

"You are my very, very best friend." Her eyes began to well up. "A new school won't change that."

Big Dog began to sob. She put her arm around her and laid her head on her shoulder. "I feel the same way Peaches. I don't have another friend like you."

"Make me a promise, Shaundra. Promise me we will always be best friends."

"I promise, Peaches."

LaVern stood up and said she had better head back. "Are you coming over tomorrow?"

"Hell yeah."

Both girls had a hardy laugh at that one.

As Freeman and Jackie watched their daughter recross the street, they noticed a more delighted and relieved child than the one who left a few minutes earlier.

The girls resumed their old routine of talking and gossiping in LaVern's bedroom. Shaundra asked more questions about her new school; how did she like going to school with White kids? Did she hang out with the other Black students? How was she treated? LaVern did her best to answer; No, she wasn't completely accepted by everyone, she wasn't friends with all the Black kids, she still felt very self-conscious being one of a few Black students in an all-White school, sometimes she felt very alone but she had made a few friends. "My daddy said it would take a little while, that I would get used to it. He said I would get a better education."

"Well, you're already smart Peaches. You'll be smart no matter what school you go to."

"Well, it is harder than 50, but I'm doing OK.

"I know you, Peaches. If you say you doing OK, I know you killin' it."

LaVern looked down at her feet. "Well, I'm doing alright."

But the Big Dog was right. She was killing it.

Setting The Stage
Chapter Two

At dinner during her ninth-grade year, LaVern muttered softly, "Mommy… Daddy… I think I want to be in a play."

Freeman and Jackie looked at one another, stunned. LaVern kept her face pointed directly into her plate of meatloaf, mashed potatoes and gravy and peas. Their shy, timid daughter wanted to get on stage in front of strangers?

"Ahh…" stammered Freeman, "you said you want to act… in a play?"

"Yes, Daddy."

"Well, that's great sweetheart," said a shocked Jackie. "What brought all this on? You've never mentioned this before."

"I was in the auditorium watching a rehearsal and my English teacher, Mr. Collins, who is also the drama coach, said he needed extras, was I interested. I want to try it. What do you think?"

LaVern still had not looked up to gauge her parents' reaction. Without hesitation both parents erupted with, "Absolutely."

LaVern finally raised her head and smiled a reassured smile. "Thanks, I will."

After dinner, when LaVern headed up to her bedroom, the Whitakers continued to talk.

"Wow, that came out of nowhere," stated Jackie.

"Yeah, that was a real shocker," said Freeman. "But it would do her a world of good if it helps her get over her shyness. It takes a lot of guts to get up on a stage, even as an extra."

"I still can't believe those words came out of our daughter's mouth," said Jackie.

There was a knock on the front door. When Jackie

answered, she just pointed toward the stairs.

"She's already up there."

Shaundra beelined right up the steps. The bedroom door was already open and LaVern was sitting on the floor doing her homework.

LaVern looked up from her books as Shaundra ran into her room. "I have something to tell you."

Sensing something juicy, Shaundra flopped down beside her. "What is it?"

"You have to promise you won't tell anybody, OK?"

"I promise, I promise. What is it?"

"I'm going to be in a play."

Shaundra was caught off guard. "A play? Like on a stage in front of people?"

"Yes, at school."

Shaundra thought for a moment. "Did one of your teachers make you do it?"

"No," replied LaVern. "I want to do it."

"Oh", said Shaundra, still mulling over the newness of it all. "Are you the star?"

"No, not even close. I'm just an extra and I go to my first rehearsal tomorrow."

"Well, I don't care who else is there, I still say you should be the star."

LaVern giggled, realizing only a best friend would say something like that. "Thanks, Shaundra. It just looks like fun, that's all."

The play was "Fiddler on the Roof" and the Whitakers were both nervous and delighted on opening night. LaVern appeared dressed as a villager, one of a gaggle of peasants who walked on stage, sang together, then hung around in the background and looked busy until the end of the scene. They watched her every move. For all they knew, this might be her last appearance on a stage.

In the car, the proud parents voiced measured praise.

"You did a good job, Peaches. We're proud of you."

"I'm surprised you could even tell which villager I was. We all looked the same... like boys."

Then came a surprise statement.

"I was watching those other kids, the ones with the speaking parts. I can do what they did. I'm going to ask Mr. Collins if I can have a bigger part in the next play."

This was a revelation. Neither Freeman nor Jackie ever heard their daughter speak with so much confidence and conviction. She was evolving right before their very eyes. Jackie urged a bit more caution.

"Peaches, there are other more experienced students there and they want those roles too."

"I know Mama, but I know I can do better than they can."

Jackie shot a sideways glance at Freeman. He returned the same side eye look. The car went graveyard quiet, but the thoughts careening around in the heads of all three Whitakers were clanging like church bells. There was something different about their daughter.

In the next play she did indeed get a bigger part. LaVern seemed to really enjoy being on stage. One day, while waiting to pick her up, Freeman spotted the drama coach, Marcus Collins, walking to his car. Freeman approached and introduced himself. They shared a little small talk then he got to the point.

"You know, Mr. Collins, I don't know if you're aware of it but all this desire to perform came as quite a surprise to me and my wife. LaVern was always the one who avoided being the center of attention, always content to be in the background. Then, out of the blue, came this urge to get up in front of people and perform. Have you ever seen anything like this?"

"Lots of shy, quiet kids find that by acting, they can become someone or some*thing* besides what they are in real life. They tend to love the *art* of performing. Having said that, Mr. Whitaker, your daughter has a knack."

Freeman's eyebrows raised in surprise.

"LaVern has the ability to become a character and assume their behavior and mannerisms and make it believable. I too was pleasantly surprised by her metamorphosis."

Metamorphosis, he sounds like an acting coach. "So, you didn't see this coming either?"

"No, but I recognized it when I saw it."

LaVern was approaching. It was time to end this

conversation. "It was a pleasure meeting you Mr. Collins. I learned a lot."

"Likewise, Mr. Whitaker, and I assume I can expect you at our next production?"

"Oh yes, without a doubt."

LaVern got into the car and buckled up. She noticed her father staring at her. She ignored his gaze at first, waiting for him to start the car. But he continued to stare.

"What is it, Daddy? Let's go home."

"I'm sorry sweetheart, I didn't mean to stare."

He started the engine and pulled off. He wanted to learn how she felt about this entire performing thing.

"Mr. Collins says you're pretty good, but how about you Peaches? Do you still like it as much now as you did in the beginning?"

"I love it even more, Daddy."

"Why do you love it?"

At this point LaVern shifted in her seat and turned to face her father. She looked directly into his eyes. "To be honest Daddy, I like the fact that I'm right in front of people but I'm someone else."

Marcus Collins hit the nail right on the head, thought Freeman. But he had to make an important point.

"He said you had a knack for making your roles believable. But just remember one important thing, Peaches, the *real* you is a good person to be too. Don't ever forget that."

LaVern glanced down at her feet. "I know Daddy. I just like to pretend sometimes."

At the dinner table Freeman told Jackie of his conversations with both Marcus Collins and LaVern. He also mentioned one important but subtle change in her behavior.

"Have you noticed how she makes more eye contact lately? While we were talking in the car, she turned to face me when she was explaining how much she loved acting. She never used to do that.

"I've noticed the same thing," replied Jackie. "Being on stage has done a lot for her confidence."

They heard muffled footsteps thumping down the stairs. LaVern and Shaundra entered the dining room and sat down at the table. LaVern didn't notice both her parents looking at her… silently… and in a different light.

By her junior year, LaVern's seriousness about acting was plainly evident. She sought out local theater groups. Freeman suggested the Bmore Players, a Black performing arts theater company. She was told to ask for Arthur Caldwell, the Artistic Director. Always eager, she arrived early. He was anxious to see what kind of acting chops this newbie had. She rehearsed a short scene with one of the resident actors. LaVern impressed in her reading and Arthur recognized the same nascent talent that Marcus Collins had. He took her under his wing. Over time, he took his new protege backstage at live performances around the city to witness firsthand the hustle and bustle and angst of a professional production. He introduced her to actors and directors and writers. Being surrounded by all the trappings of the acting profession only motivated her more. LaVern was brimming with confidence and gaining experience.

As a senior, LaVern was head and shoulders above any other cast member. No one was more delighted than Mr. Collins. He had a resident "star". He chose to put on Lorraine Hansberry's play "A Raisin in the Sun", with LaVern in the role of Ruth Younger. It seemed as if their daughter was a professional surrounded by amateurs. In the lobby afterwards, every parent went out of their way to praise the Whitakers and tell them how talented their daughter was. Freeman and Jackie were gracious, but they were just as shocked as they were. This performance was leaps and bounds beyond anything they had seen.

On the quiet ride home Shaundra was the first to bring up "the elephant in the room".

"Peaches, you were soooo good girl. That was amazing. You made everybody else on that stage look like losers." She held up her thumb and forefinger to form the letter "L".

Freeman chimed in. "I agree. Peaches, you dominated the stage. Every eye was on you the entire time."

"I'm so proud of you sweetheart," said Jackie. "You were

superb."

LaVern kept things in perspective. "Thanks everybody, I appreciate your compliments, but it was just fun. I was only having fun."

"I wish I could get a standing ovation for just having some fun," said Freeman.

"Peaches," said Shaundra, "you should have seen all those White folks coming up to your parents telling them how good you were. I know they were jealous as hell 'cause they sure couldn't say that about their own kids."

The Whitakers began seriously considering which College or University LaVern could attend. Her grades were superior, and she scored 1300 on her SAT's. She had already received acceptance letters from several out-of-state Universities but, as always, it boiled down to money. These were top notch schools, and the yearly tuition was $40,000.00 a year and up. Jackie began looking into grants, scholarships and fellowships. Experience taught her there's always some money available at these major institutions, money they try to hide initially, but if you pry and probe long and hard enough, they'll find something for an excellent student like their daughter. Or as Freeman said at one point, "These places halfway expect Black folk to need some kind of financial assistance."

Going away to school was attractive, but six years at Felder was expensive enough. A superior Fine Arts Department was LaVern's primary concern, and they decided to apply to in-state colleges. One evening, the Whitakers received a call from Marcus Collins. He wanted to see them, along with LaVern, in his office after school the following day. Freeman and Jackie asked LaVern if she knew what he could possibly want. She was completely in the dark. They would all find out together tomorrow.

LaVern led her parents down the shiny, marble floored hallway lined with display cases, bulletin boards, administrative offices, a health suite and the closed entrance to the auditorium. Mr. Collins' office was straight ahead at the end of the nearly deserted corridor. When they opened his door, he lifted his head, rose out of his squeaky, wheeled wooden chair and extended his hand to Freeman.

"Good afternoon Mr. Whitaker. How are you?"

Freeman grasped his hand firmly. "I'm doing fine Mr. Collins, nice to see you again."

The teacher turned his attention to Jackie. "Mrs. Whitaker, It's always a pleasure ma'am"

"Likewise, Mr. Collins."

"It's good to see you too, LaVern. I haven't seen much of you since the play closed."

"I've been mostly concentrating on my studies Mr. Collins."

"I understand," he said. "Please, everyone, have a seat."

Three cushioned office chairs were arranged side by side facing Marcus Collins' desk. The family took their seats as he settled in, leaned back in his chair, clasped his hands behind his head, and began the conversation.

"I know you're curious as to why I requested this meeting."

Jackie answered for everyone. "I must admit, I am very curious, Mr. Collins. We've never been asked to a conference concerning LaVern."

"I'll get right to it. Have you guys been successful in finding an institution of higher learning for LaVern?"

Every Whitaker eyebrow raised simultaneously. Jackie was quick to answer. "LaVern has been accepted at several Universities Mr. Collins, but we haven't settled on one yet."

Marcus Collins crunched his mouth and moved it from side to side. "Are you satisfied with your choices?"

Freeman spoke up. "Well, we still have some financial matters to work out, but those things always take time. Why do you ask?"

"Let me be direct." Marcus Collins leaned forward on his elbows. "I personally know the head of the Fine Arts Department at the New York College of the Performing Arts. On my recommendation, they are willing to offer LaVern a four-year scholarship. Are you interested?"

All three Whitaker jaws dropped in unison, as if on cue. They each stared unbelievingly at the bow tied man behind the desk.

"What!?" said Freeman, "What did you say?"

Marcus smiled broadly and repeated the offer. "Your daughter is extremely talented," he continued. "I've watched her evolve from the ninth grade 'till now and I have no reservations whatsoever in recommending her. If you accept, you'll receive a formal letter that will officially extend to you the scholarship, along with the application information."

Marcus Collins leaned back in his chair. LaVern's hands flew up to cover her mouth, her heels tapped the floor nervously. Jackie covered her face and lowered her head into her lap. Freeman was stumped for words. Marcus knew he had delivered a bomb.

"Do you have any questions?"

"I don't know what to say Mr. Collins," sputtered Freeman. "I'm still trying to process all this."

"I know it's a little overwhelming, but believe me, I can't think of a more deserving student."

Jackie finally found the words to speak. "Mr. Collins, I just don't know what to say, except thank you. I am profoundly grateful."

"If you have any questions, please don't hesitate to contact me."

Freeman stood and extended his hand. "Mr. Collins, I can't thank you enough. What you have done is life changing."

The two men exchanged another firm handshake. Jackie and LaVern rose from their seats. Jackie walked behind the desk.

"Mr. Collins, you deserve a hug, come here."

The two shared a long embrace. Jackie started to cry again. LaVern walked over. Her hands still covered her mouth. Only her wet eyes could be seen.

"Thank you so much Mr. Collins. I will never forget what you have done for me."

Marcus Collins stared resolutely into Lavern's eyes. "Young lady, it was an honor for me to do this for you."

The teacher and the student hugged, and the Whitakers exited the office.

In the middle of their row house living room, the Whitakers shared a very special family hug. After everybody slowly unraveled, LaVern sat on the sofa. She looked up at her parents, still in disbelief.

"Mom...Dad" she began, "I had no idea..." Her voice trailed off.

"No one knew Mr. Collins would do what he did," said Freeman. "There's a lesson to be learned here, Peaches. Always try to do the right thing. You never know who's watching that can make your bumpy road smooth."

There came a knock at the door. Freeman looked out. It was Shaundra. When he let her in she was taken aback that everyone was in the living room at the same time. Something was up.

"Where y'all been?" she asked, surveying everyone suspiciously. "I came over earlier and nobody was here."

"Believe it or not, you're right on time, Shaundra," declared Freeman.

"On time for what?"

"We were just about to go out to eat...to celebrate, and you're invited. Isn't that right, family?"

LaVern sprang up from the couch and answered with a resounding, "That's right!"

Shaundra's eyes lit up. Going out to eat was special, something the Jacksons never did.

LaVern asked, "Where should we go, Dad?"

Shaundra was quick to respond. "How about Burger World?"

All the Whitakers stopped and stared. Jackie, in her most motherly, nurturing voice explained they were going to a restaurant... with waiters... and menus. Shaundra's embarrassment registered on her face. LaVern came to the rescue.

"Let's go to DeNiro's Dad. You came with us last time, remember Shaundra?"

"Oh yeah, I remember," said a sheepish Shaundra.

"Good," replied Freeman, "DeNiro's it is."

Everyone headed out the door with Shaundra asking, "Hey, what are we celebrating?"

June was graduation time for both girls. Their respective ceremonies couldn't have been more of a contradiction. When the Whitakers went to Shaundra's graduation, her mother Traci made a brief appearance, made sure her daughter saw her, and left early. When Shaundra waved from the stage, she was waving to the Whitakers. Through her symbiotic relationship with LaVern, an unmotivated and lackluster fifth grader had transformed herself into a high school graduate in the top quarter of a class of 200. It was certainly something her brother Sweat, her currently incarcerated brother Ricky, and her other crime riddled sibling Earl would never do.

LaVern's ceremony, on the other hand, was a love affair. She was number 1 in her class of 50. She was Valedictorian, gave the commencement address and received that scholarship to NYCPA. Praise was heaped onto her by faculty and the student body alike. Jackie and Freeman beamed and applauded until their faces and hands ached.

LaVern spent the remainder of her summer soaking up knowledge with the B'More Players. Shaundra, with college not being in her plans, had begun working as a counter person at a local drug store chain. She was still a regular at dinnertime in the Whitaker household, but more and more LaVern wasn't there. Real life was beginning to intrude.

The morning of her departure for NYCPA was both solemn and joyful. Jackie was upstairs making sure LaVern packed everything, the whole time bravely fighting back her tears. Shaundra was there too. She was both depressed and excited. This would be the first time since the fifth grade they would go months without seeing one other. Freeman stayed downstairs in his favorite chair. His mind replayed years of happy, frightful, proud and inspiring episodes that culminated in this moment. They were right where they had planned to be all those many years ago. Nobody knew then exactly how they'd get here, yet here they were. Freeman's eyes began to well up. He heard footsteps and luggage bumping their way down the steps. Everyone gathered in the living room and an uneasy silence ensued. Finally, Jackie reached her arms out to hug her daughter.

"I'm going to miss you so much sweetheart. I'm so proud of you."

The tears began to flow.

"I'm going to miss you too, Mom."

"I miss you already, Peaches," cried Shaundra. "You better text me every day."

LaVern broke her tight hold on her mother and transferred it to Shaundra.

"I told you a long time ago that nothing will ever come between us. I meant it then and I mean it now." She clutched her best friend even tighter. Then it was Freeman's turn. He'd been holding off his goodbye intentionally. He wrapped his arms around his daughter and held on. He rested his chin on her head. LaVern was sobbing uncontrollably, but she didn't let go. He finally relaxed his grip and looked directly into LaVern's crying eyes.

"I want you to know you have made your mother and me so proud, Peaches." He wiped a tear from his daughter's face with his thumb. "You're ready for this. You've been preparing your whole life."

"Thank you, Daddy. I love you so much."

He released his daughter, picked up the luggage and, along with everyone else, headed outside. LaVern turned to take one last look. The realization that she wouldn't be back for months was just hitting her. *It's really happening,* she thought. *I'm actually leaving.* She closed and locked the door. The second part of her life was about to begin.

NYCPA
Chapter Three

Freshman Year

LaVern arrived on the NYCPA campus ready to take on the world. She was a 5'4" brown skinned beauty with dark brown eyes and shoulder length, curly black hair. Being on her own in the "Big Apple" was both invigorating and intimidating. As she looked around her new dorm home, she said to herself, *this is my new reality, a roughly 20x20 cubicle. There's no going back home now.* She ambled over to take in the view from her curtainless, 5th floor window.

"Hello," came a voice from behind her.

LaVern whirled around and saw a lone figure in the doorway.

"Sorry, I didn't mean to startle you."

"No, no, you're fine." Her gaze came to rest upon a well-dressed, petite, curly headed Black girl with light brown eyes.

LaVern approached. "Hi, my name is LaVern Whitaker."

"I'm Melissa Frazier."

"Hi Melissa, nice to meet you. Come on in and make yourself comfortable, even though there's not a lot of room."

Melissa entered and placed her gear down, then made a quick perusal. LaVern read her mind.

"I left some room for you in the closet."

"Thank you, I really appreciate that."

The new roommates sat on their respective beds and began the process of familiarization. Melissa was from Philadelphia and wanted to major in costume design. She wanted to turn her eye for style and fabric into a career in wardrobe on Broadway. LaVern talked about Baltimore and her love of the theater. Their conversation lasted about an hour while they unpacked. Her roomie was a tad shy but likable and LaVern had a good vibe about her.

LaVern made it her business to become a familiar face to the Neuman School of the Performing Arts staff and made contact with the head of the Drama Department as soon as she was settled. Abby Walters was in her office when LaVern walked in unannounced and introduced herself. Mrs. Walters said she and the staff eagerly anticipated her arrival.

"If you have the time now, I'd like to give you a brief tour of our building."

"I would love it."

She led LaVern to the lobby of the Landsman Auditorium. There she saw framed photos of all the famous alumni. It was an impressive assemblage of well-known performers. LaVern made a mental note, *my picture will be up there some day.* Abby Walters introduced her to another member of the Drama Department, acting coach, George Coombs.

"Nice to meet you, LaVern. I'm looking forward to seeing your work."

As LaVern and Abby Walters were walking down a narrow, cluttered passageway behind the stage, they encountered a trio of student actors.

"Jesse, Trent, Angie, I'd like you to meet one of our newest students. This is LaVern Whitaker."

Angie immediately reached out her hand. "Nice to meet you, LaVern. I'm new here too."

The two males took a few seconds to study the newest female addition to their cast. Their eyes suggested approval. Jesse spoke up first.

"Very nice to meet you, LaVern. I've heard good things about you."

"So have I," chimed in Trent. "Looking forward to working with you."

"Thanks everyone. I feel at home already."

LaVern met some of the other incoming freshmen on their tours of the facilities and she listened very carefully to see if anyone else was greeted with "heard a lot of good things about you" or "I hear you do good work". Not a single one was adorned with such a label of expectation.

LaVern and Melissa became close friends. They studied

together when possible, they explored the city and developed a mutual trust and respect. Even so, LaVern missed her BFF. Despite texting and messaging, she still very much needed to hear her voice. They talked just like old times. Shaundra brought her up on all the recent neighborhood happenings; her father made one of his drunken visits, she still spent lots of time in her parent's house, and work was going fine. LaVern brought Shaundra up to date on college life; she liked her new roommate, the work was rigorous, but she was handling it, and she got lots of chances to move around New York. Thanksgiving was fast approaching so they would see one another very soon.

LaVern traded one cityscape for another as the train pulled into Penn Station. She climbed the metal steps and entered the main concourse through the old, weather worn, wooden swinging doors. And there they were, The Pack, all smiles and outstretched arms. LaVern sprinted, mouth agape, arms straight out in front of her, screaming like a little girl. She ran smack into them without even slowing down. All three wrapped their arms around her. LaVern was barely visible. From her hidden location came her muffled cry.

"I missed everybody sooooo much. I really did."

"Ohhhhh, we missed you too, Peaches," cried Jackie.

"Sweetheart," said Freeman. "It's so good to see you."

Shaundra was the last to speak. She had her eyes closed, trying to relish the moment. "Girllllll, I missed you sooooooo much. I'm not lettin' you go."

There they remained, four people completely oblivious to the commotion all around them. After several more seconds, LaVern's muffled voice could be heard again. She said what everybody wanted to hear.

"Let's go home. I want to go home."

Jackie Whitaker prepared a splendid meal for her daughter's return. Everything she loved, turkey and stuffing, mashed potatoes, green beans, mac and cheese, sweetened tea and apple pie. They talked and laughed and thoroughly enjoyed their reunion. Freeman told the story of a new hire's first day on the job. He was on the forklift trying to restock a shelf and he raised the forks so high that he knocked out some fluorescent lights in the ceiling and was showered with the broken glass. Jackie told about when she wore new dress pants to school, and they started to come apart at the seams. She had to finish the day teaching draped in a size XXXL football jersey supplied by the coach. Shaundra told about her dislike of all the women who go grocery shopping in the same clothes they slept in.

"I mean, come on," she complained, "You can't take the time to even get out of your pajama bottoms and bedroom slippers?"

Finally, Freeman pushed himself away from the table.

"I'm full ladies. I need to find my recliner and remind it who's boss. Don't interrupt your conversation because of me." He headed toward the living room, the TV and football.

"Well," observed Jackie, "it *is* getting late, and I've got to take care of these dishes, But if you girls want to–"

LaVern interrupted. "No way, Mom. I'm not letting you do these dishes." She rose and began clearing the table.

"That's right Mrs. Whit," said Shaundra. "Why don't you go into the living room with Mr. Whit and relax. Peaches and I will take care of this."

Jackie sat there in mild shock… and appreciation. "Well, if you insist. Thank you, girls."

Later that evening in LaVern's room, they told stories that neither would dare share with Freeman or Jackie. Shaundra revealed that her oldest brother, Ricky, was still in prison, middle brother, Sweat, was in drug rehab, and Earl was rarely home now. She didn't know where he was sleeping but she seldom saw him. LaVern told Shaundra about a frat party she and Melissa attended.

"It was noisy and there was liquor and drunken boys everywhere. You know me Shaundra, I'm not a party person. We both got out of there in a hurry!"

The week LaVern spent at home was rejuvenating, both emotionally and physically, but soon it was time to return to school. There was the customary, emotional hug fest at Penn Station and with her batteries now recharged, she plopped down into her seat. As she watched a worn and deteriorating East Baltimore pass by, LaVern knew she was ready for any obstacle.

The second semester workshops took place on stage, in the empty Landsman Auditorium, and they were intense. George Coombs pushed to get the most out of each artist, and demanded that they, in turn, push themselves. Once the set was ready, everyone took their places. From an unseen perch came a familiar voice.

"Alright, on my command."

George had placed himself in the inky darkness of the last row.

"Action!"

On his direction, the scene began, and the drama coach listened and watched in silence. Occasionally, his baritone voice, in mid scene, boomed like Moses in The Ten Commandments; "project more!" or "where are you coming from?". At the conclusion, he slowly let the light reveal his arrival as he approached the stage. He assembled the cast and critiqued their performances, ("you missed your mark.") or relocated props ("move that lamp closer, it's too far away").

LaVern was in her element; on a stage, in an auditorium, honing her craft. She was doing something she knew she was good at and was only getting better. LaVern also decided to begin vocal training. The voice coach was pleasantly surprised with her raw ability, but she was still a project. The normal procedure at NYCPA meant that freshmen would not be cast in plays performed before the public. That was the domain of sophomores and above. LaVern was mildly disappointed but undeterred. She was determined she would be that much readier in the fall.

She returned home during Spring Break. This visit was more subdued than before. Everyone still met her at the train station, there were just as many hugs, and as much love as ever, but human nature dictated that there just couldn't be fireworks every time. She informed her parents that she eagerly anticipated the fall semester because it meant getting on stage again. And she still savored her bedroom exchanges with

Shaundra.

The remainder of her school year provided LaVern the chance to separate herself even more from her fellow freshmen and blossom as an artist. George Coombs became even more convinced of what a special talent she was. LaVern wasn't aware yet, but he began formulating special plans for her sophomore year.

Sophomore Year

LaVern had a new roommate her second year. Lori Burkhardt was an aspiring scriptwriter from Bridgeport, Connecticut. Her short blonde hair and blue-eyed perky cheerleader persona belied the deep seriousness she applied to her writing. She didn't need a coterie of noisy friends clogging up the room, and that suited LaVern just fine because she decided to hit the ground running this semester. The last thing either wanted was unnecessary stress and unwanted distractions. Midway through the semester, LaVern was instructed to report to George Coombs' office. When she arrived, he was brief.

"LaVern, the upperclassmen would like to offer you a pivotal role in their upcoming production."

LaVern's mouth flew open.

"You may not realize it, but this is a very unusual request. These upperclassmen have put in a lot of work and have proven their worth, and they don't relinquish these hard-earned roles very easily."

It felt like déjà vu, like when she was in Mr. Collins' office back at Felder Academy. She sat there motionless and wordless, just staring at her drama coach, not able to process all that information at once. George Coombs added another tidbit.

"Let me say, LaVern, this was strictly their decision, but I wholeheartedly agree with it." He waited for some kind of reaction. "Well, what do you say?"

"I'm so sorry, Mr. Coombs. All this has caught me by surprise." It amazed her that her cast mates thought that much of her abilities. She took another few klutzy seconds before she spoke again. "I consider it an honor. And I promise to work even harder to justify their trust in me. And your trust too."

"Good, good," he replied. "I expect no less of you." George Coombs leaned forward and placed his elbows on his cluttered desk. He peered over his rectangular glasses. His lowered voice seemed to reiterate that he was about to say something important. "You know, Miss Whitaker, if you continue to improve, and strengthen your techniques, you can make a life out of this. And I don't say these kinds of things haphazardly."

This man has trained stars, like those famous faces on display in the lobby. Maybe he said those things to them too. And he called me Miss Whitaker. Before today it was always LaVern. This is too much. My mind is in a fog. Take a deep breath, girl!

LaVern stood up and extended her hand. George Coombs stood up and reached for it.

"All anyone can ask is that you give it your best, and I have no doubt that you will, Miss Whitaker."

As she crossed the crowded campus, LaVern adjusted her coat and wool muffler to keep the afternoon chill at bay. She was warmed by the thought she would finally be back on stage. This time in Landsman Auditorium in front of an audience. Her parents would be so proud of her.

LaVern skipped Thanksgiving and went home for Christmas. It was a strictly grownup affair now, consisting of adult conversation. LaVern talked about how George Coombs' workshops were making her a much better actress and how she got to rub shoulders with veteran performers. Jackie Whitaker expressed dismay at the deterioration of the public school system.

"It seems like all they do is move all our little Black children along, like they're on some kind of conveyor belt. None of them are being educated."

Shaundra brought everybody up on all the gossip in the store, like the photo of LaVern posing with handsome movie idol, and NYCPA alumnus Andre Nixon.

"Girl, they just about died. I was loving it."

Freeman would watch football, and Jackie would join him with a book in her hands. LaVern and Shaundra would go upstairs to share their private stories. And so it went, with everyone thoroughly enjoying one another's company. This had become the accepted holiday ritual. Instead of two adults and two young girls, it had morphed into four adults, and nobody minded.

Prior to the beginning of rehearsal, George Coombs walked from behind the curtains and onto the stage. With him was a tall, handsome, clean shaven young Black student named Lamont Hughes who had just transferred in as a sophomore from a performing arts college in New England. He arrived too late to participate in any of this year's productions. All of the parts had already been assigned but, reasoned George Coombs, he could benefit from the workshops by sitting in and watching and learning from his best actors. Everyone welcomed him to NYCPA. But then, it was back to work. Lamont descended the stage steps and found a seat in the first row where he watched the rest of the rehearsal intently. When it was concluded, LaVern began gathering her things, her mind on returning to her dorm and commencing her studies.

"You must be LaVern Whitaker," came a voice from behind.

She turned to see that it was Lamont. LaVern took a quick second to assess this new actor. He was indeed handsome with a lean, athletic build. He looked to be well groomed and had an engaging smile.

"How did you know my name?"

"The way Mr. Coombs described you and watching you rehearse, well, it couldn't be anyone else. You're very talented."

"That's nice of you to say …Lamont."

They stood there in a graceless silence, each anticipating the other would carry on the conversation.

"Well," said LaVern finally, "It was nice meeting you, but I've got to get going." She continued to gather her things.

"Can I walk you to your dorm?"

LaVern tilted her head back to make eye contact with the 6' 2" Lamont Hughes. "That won't be necessary. But you'll be attending the workshops and rehearsals, am I right?"

"Oh, you better believe it. I'll be at every one."

"Well, I'll see you then." LaVern whirled around and walked toward the edge of the stage, descended the wooden steps and headed up the aisle between the rows of empty seats until she disappeared into the darkness. He heard the exit door squeak open, saw a widening blade of white light pierce the blackness and silhouette the fine form of LaVern Whitaker. The invading white light began to shrink as the door slowly closed then slammed shut. Lamont watched until he couldn't see her any longer.

As predicted, Lamont was present at every rehearsal. He was just as persistent at pursuing LaVern as well. Initially, their relationship consisted of numerous friendly chit chats during down time at rehearsal, then slowly evolved into cordial and amicable strolls from the Landsman to her dorm building. In time, she realized he was considerate and polite, a complete gentleman. Most importantly, he was not loud. Loud and obnoxious people didn't remain in Lavern's orbit of friends for very long.

After several weeks, they had their first date. They drove, in Lamont's used Toyota, to an off-campus restaurant and talked and chuckled and truly enjoyed one another's company. She began to feel comfortable with him. She mentioned Lamont to Shaundra, ("he better show some respect!"), but not her parents because she wasn't sure if their relationship would progress beyond what it was now; a serious friendship.

A month later, The Pack were on campus for LaVern's first stage appearance since the Felder Academy. This was her first chance to do some serious acting, and she couldn't wait to impress her parents. The Pack met in the lobby, and everyone took the opportunity to stroll through the portrait gallery, pointing out their favorite stars. When the call came, they all filtered into the auditorium and took their seats. The lights dimmed and the curtain rose.

LaVern's performance was riveting. Her character cried, screamed in anger, showed empathy and in one memorable scene, when she was alone on stage, emoted without words. Jackie and Freeman were flabbergasted as they glanced unbelievingly at one another. LaVern had evolved into a seriously talented actress right under their noses. It made Jackie's eyes water.

"She's sooo talented," she said to herself.

At the end of the play, The Pack reassembled in the crowded lobby, they couldn't stop talking about what a talented performer LaVern had become. The doors to the auditorium suddenly flung open and the subject of everybody's conversation emerged, accompanied by Lamont. LaVern took a moment to search for her Pack. They formed their now traditional four-person group hug. Lamont wasn't sure where or how to inject himself into this touching, family scene. He elected to just observe. After unfurling, LaVern formally introduced Lamont to her Pack and announced that he would drive everyone to the restaurant.

"I'll go get my car, Mr. Whitaker," he said. "Everybody wait right here."

"Thank you young man," said Freeman.

When he returned, everyone piled in and settled back for the ride. This would be their first chance to meet LaVern's "male friend". Lamont earned some brownie points by offering to drive The Pack around while they were in New York. The Whitakers found him to be gentlemanly and articulate, not shy but not overly talkative either.

Later that semester, Shaundra received a call from LaVern. "Hi girlfriend. How long before you come home?" Silence.

"Are you there, Peaches?"

"Yes. I'm here."

More silence.

"Peaches, you're acting weird. What's wrong?"

"Shaundra… we did it."

"Who did what?"

"Lamont and I…we did it!"

"Whaaaaat! No you didn't," said Shaundra in mock denial.

"We did. Last night at his apartment."

"Are you alright? You don't sound so good."

"I'm fine." LaVern paused again. "It was my first time, you know?"

"Well, I know that," said Shaundra. "But you're OK though, right?"

"I'm fine. I just wanted to tell somebody and you're the only one I can tell."

"I'd better be the only one you tell something like that to."

Another pause. "Was it good?" Shaundra asked in her sneaky, nosey tone.

LaVern chuckled. "Yes, it was good."

"Well, it was good and you're alright. Sounds like a win win to me."

"You are so crazy, Shaundra. Look, I have classes to go to. I just thought I should tell my best friend."

"Like I always say Peaches, I'm here for you."

"I know you are Shaundra, you mean everything to me."

"Now, go on and take your fast ass to class."

"Shaundra! You know I'm not like that!"

"I know. I'm just joking. I love you girl."

"OK, I'll talk to you later."

LaVern spent the summer at home where Jackie wrangled a position for her at a daycare center run by a fellow teacher. She really loved being around the children. Their innocence and wonderment at the world was a constant source of amazement to her. It also left her evenings free to renew friendships at The B'more Players.

LaVern was clearing the table and preparing to wash the dishes one evening after dinner when she started to sing softly to herself. Freeman was in his favorite recliner watching the news. Jackie was sitting nearby on the sofa reading Zora Neale Hurston's "Their Eyes were Watching God". A pleasant sound diverted his attention. It was subtle at first. He lowered the volume which alerted Jackie. They both listened intently. They rose from their chairs and stealthily worked their way closer to the dining room where they could hear more clearly. Jackie covered her mouth in astonishment. For several minutes LaVern serenaded herself, for her own pleasure. As she emerged from the kitchen she looked up to see her parents standing at the entrance to the dining room, staring at her. Jackie started toward her daughter and stopped. She turned, still with her hand over her mouth, and looked back at Freeman. She then returned her gaze to LaVern.

"Freeman, did you hear that? She can sing. Our baby can sing!" Jackie rushed over to LaVern and hugged her like she was a just freed hostage. LaVern finally understood the zombie-like stares.

"It's no big deal mom. Everybody at school can sing."

"But, you have such a lovely voice, Peaches. We didn't know, did we Freeman?"

"I had no idea," he said. "Why didn't you tell us you could sing so well? The last time your mother and I heard you was when you were still at Felder. You've come a long way since then."

"Yes," declared Jackie, "what I just heard was beautiful."

"Thanks Mom and Dad. I guess hard work pays off." She winked at her father.

"Oh my God!" Jackie exclaimed, "My baby can sing!"

Junior Year

As she took the elevator to her new fifth floor dorm, LaVern wondered who her roommate would be for her junior year. She hadn't requested anyone in particular, just hoped for the best. As she made the turn into her new quarters she was met with a pleasant surprise.

"Hi LaVern."

It was Lori.

"I hope you don't mind that I requested you. I felt comfortable last year, and I was pretty sure the feeling was mutual."

"If I had been thinking, I would have done the same thing," said LaVern as she headed over to her bed and started unpacking. "By the way, how was your summer?"

"It was very productive. I spent my whole vacation working on my play."

"Your what!? You wrote a play?"

"Sure did."

"What's it about?" LaVern noticed Lori's face light up at the prospect of describing it.

"It's about a high-powered female attorney who gets a call, after many years, from a childhood friend. The friend is in trouble of their own making. The attorney believes this to be a pain in the ass case not worth her time, but it ends up being the biggest career-defining case of her life."

"Wow, that sounds pretty exciting. Are you going to show it to Mr. Coombs?"

"Yes, and I hope he thinks it's good enough to perform. It was harder to write than I anticipated, but I was determined to finish it."

LaVern had never considered the script writing aspect of theater. The thought of having to write all that dialogue made her head spin and made her even more impressed by Lori's effort.

"I have a big favor to ask of you, LaVern."

"Sure Lori, anything."

"No one has seen it yet. I want you to be the first to read it. What I need from you is to be brutally honest. Tell me whether you like it or not and why. I truly value your opinion."

Ah, this is probably the reason she wanted to room with me this year. She had this planned all summer.

"In that case, I'd be honored, Lori."

She went into her backpack and withdrew a large, black, loose-leaf notebook. Safely tucked inside was her valuable, original work, each page hole punched with the three metal loops carefully fed through. On the cover, written with a magic marker, was the title, "Juris Doctor in the House". She walked over to LaVern and presented it to her with both hands, like a mournful mother turning over her precious child for someone else to raise. For the next hour LaVern read through the pages. Lori's anxiety was apparent. She went into the hallway, came right back in, sat down and thumbed nervously through her phone. She laid down, she sat up, then stood at the window. When LaVern was through, she put the notebook down and looked over at Lori, who looked wide-eyed right back at her.

"You should be proud of yourself, Lori. I think your play is great. I can see us doing this."

"Really! Are you being honest? I told you to be honest."

"I kid you not. I really like what I read."

Lori's nervousness was replaced by excited relief. "Thank you so much LaVern. I feel so much more confident now."

"You obviously poured your heart into this, you can walk into Mr. Coombs' office knowing you're going to show him some quality work."

The ex-cheerleader felt like doing a back flip.

LaVern hadn't seen Lamont since the end of the previous school year. Summer vacation turned out to be an insurmountable barrier to their relationship. Their busy summer schedules, with him in Boston and she in Baltimore, prohibited any attempt at a get together. They resigned themselves to phone calls and texts and the infrequent video chat. When classes resumed, LaVern and Lamont reunited, and their relationship picked up where it left off.

The initial workshop took place on the stage at the Landsman. Everyone was sitting in wooden folding chairs in a semicircle when George Coombs described his vision for the coming season. There would be two productions this year. Both had already been chosen. That was bad news for Lori, thought LaVern. A month would be set aside for rehearsals for each. More if needed. This would be in addition to the regular workshops.

Weeks later, LaVern entered her dorm room and saw Lori seated on her bed surrounded by open course books. She barely noticed her entrance. LaVern quietly headed to her desk, placed her backpack on the floor and eased her body into her chair. She crossed her legs, leaned back and turned to face Lori, who pretended to not notice LaVern's glare. After several uncomfortable minutes, she raised her head from her books and stared straight ahead at the bare wall. "Why are you staring at me?" she asked, a bit perturbed.

"You haven't shown your play to George Coombs, have you?"

With her head still pointed straight ahead, she cut her eyes to look at LaVern. "Oh… that."

"Yeah, that. What are you waiting for? You're going to run out of time if you keep procrastinating."

Lori finally made eye contact. "You told me he already chose his plays for the season. It's already too late."

"But you haven't shown him *your* play yet. You're not giving yourself a chance."

"To be honest," admitted Lori, "I get antsy every time I think about taking it to him. What if he trashes it? I would be devastated."

"Your other option is to never show it to anyone, anytime, anywhere because you're too afraid of rejection. What about all that hard work you put into it? Did you do all that just to leave it in a closet somewhere gathering dust?"

Lori disgustedly exhaled. Her cheeks billowed slightly. *LaVern was right,* she mused. *What was the point if no one saw it?*

"Okay LaVern. I promise to show it to Mr. Coombs."

"When?"

"I can't do it now, I'm studying."

LaVern continued to stare wordlessly.

"You're saying I should do it now?"

"It's a short walk over to the Landsman. Go over there, drop your play off and you're back here studying in no time."

She hesitated, then rose out of her chair and reached for her backpack. "I'll be right back."

LaVern watched a more confident Lori march out of their dorm room and right smack into uncertainty. Half an hour passed before she returned. She sat down in the same spot she left.

"Well!?"

"I did exactly as you said, LaVern."

"And?"

"He didn't outright reject it. He said he would give me the benefit of a preliminary read, and that he was extremely busy right now."

The dejection showed on Lori's face. Her body slumped. "He was polite, but I don't have a good vibe about this."

LaVern tried to be upbeat. "If Mr. Coombs said he would read it, I'm sure he will. That's all you really want, Lori, to have him read it."

"Yeah, I guess so." Lori returned to her books. "I've got

some studying to do."

As the semester wore on LaVern knew going home for the holidays would be out of the question. With studying and workshops and rehearsals, her free time was becoming more and more scarce. Rehearsals for the first play of the season began in November and opening night arrived a month later. On that night, The Pack, as expected, was there. Keeping them away from one of LaVern's performances was like trying to sneak the sun past a rooster, it simply can't be done. After the final curtain, as she entered the lobby, LaVern overheard her father talking to Lamont.

"This was my first chance to see you on stage, young man. You did a hell of a job. I was impressed."

"Yeah," interrupted Shaundra, "you were pretty good." She wasn't going to give Lamont the same props as LaVern, but she had to admit he deserved some "atta boys".

"It seems as though this school is full of extremely talented young people," observed Jackie. "I know why there's so many photos hanging on the walls. You have to be very gifted to be here."

"Well, I'd like to think so, Mrs. Whitaker," said Lamont. "We all have to work hard to get here and even harder to stay. It's always nice to know that someone other than your instructors appreciate what you do."

LaVern interrupted. "Is anybody hungry? I know I am."

"Say no more," said Lamont. "I'll be right back with the ride."

As Lamont exited through the glass doors, LaVern heard her father say to her mother, "Nice young man. I like him."

After completion of the initial play of the season, all attention in the drama department turned to the next production of the year. George Coombs had not given any indication of what he intended to bring before them. Until otherwise notified, the workshops continued.

One crisp January afternoon, when LaVern was in her room studying, Lori came through the door and gently closed it behind her, barely eliciting a glance from LaVern. She slid her backpack off and placed it on the bed. She walked over to her desk but didn't sit down. Instead, she looked out the window, lost in her own thoughts.

"He's going to do it," she uttered barely above a whisper.

Several seconds went by before she realized Lori had spoken. "I'm sorry Lori, did you say something?"

She switched her gaze from the window to LaVern. "George Coombs… he's going to do it."

LaVern's eyes lit up. "We're going to do your play?"

Lori's face told the whole story. Her blue eyes became as big as saucers. Her grin was so wide that none of her thirty-two well maintained teeth had a place to hide. Her cheeks rounded into little balls of muscle. Her head was rapidly nodding up and down like one of those bobbleheads.

"That's exactly what I'm saying. He's going to do my play!"

LaVern stood and both women hugged and did a little jumping in place thing.

"Lori, that's fantastic. I'm so happy for you."

"I still can't believe it," she said as they both resumed their seats. "It's a dream come true."

"What happened? What changed his mind?"

"I'm still not sure, but when I got to my writing class my professor handed me a note from George Coombs stating that he wanted to see me this afternoon."

"Ooooh, I like this," cooed LaVern. "It's unfolding like a mystery. So, you go to his office and then what?"

"When I walked in, I saw my play on his desk. All I could think about was how, the last time I was here, he didn't seem very interested. He asked me to sit down, and he began to talk."

"What did he say?"

"I can't remember everything, but he mentioned that he read my play, and he was surprised at how good it was. He talked with Miss Weintraub, my writing professor, and they decided my play was worth bringing to the stage. Can you believe it?"

"Actually, I'm not surprised in the least."

"One more thing, LaVern. You can't mention this to anybody. Mr. Coombs wants to make the announcement at rehearsal. Evidently, he and Miss Weintraub have other things up their sleeves."

"No problem roomie. Not a peep out of me."

One day, the cast was milling around on the stage and from behind the curtain came George Coombs, followed by Lori. No one, besides LaVern, knew who the stranger was.

"Okay everybody gather 'round. I have some exciting news for you. For our second production of the year, I've decided to do an original play. A play written by one of your fellow students. I would like to introduce you to the talented writer of our next production."

He beckoned Lori forward and she stood at his side. She was slightly chagrined by all the attention, but LaVern was beaming.

"This is Lori Burkhardt. She submitted her play to me a little while ago and I am pleased to say it is a wonderful piece of work. When you read it, I'm sure you'll agree, this is a play worthy of our efforts."

He turned to Lori. "Miss Burkhardt, would you like to say something?"

She cleared her throat and took a quick, nervous glimpse around. "Thank you, Mr. Coombs. I just want to say that I hope my play measures up to the high standards this talented group of performers has established. Thank you for giving my play a chance."

LaVern initiated applause for her roommate.

"Thank you, Miss Burkhardt. I'm sure everyone here will work hard to give your play the justice it deserves. I have scripts for everyone in my office. Take two days to read the play and we'll meet back here to begin work. There will be no assigned roles. I will hold open auditions."

The fact they were doing a play written by one of their own brought with it a heightened level of passion and urgency. Nobody wanted to be the weak link that would cause this play to fail. After the auditions, it was obvious that LaVern was the only actress up to the daunting challenge of lead in an original play.

"Boy, Lori," declared LaVern days later, "your play has unleashed this tsunami of collaboration and creativity from wardrobe to lighting, props and makeup. Every department is bending over backwards to bring your play to the stage."

"My play is doing all that? I didn't know I would cause all this commotion."

"Because it's original, everybody gets to be super creative. That got everyone pumped."

George Combs loved every imaginative and competitive minute. The play and the intense rehearsals and all the interdepartmental coordination that was required meant LaVern wouldn't return home for spring break either. It was the first time she'd missed an entire school year.

After completion of the initial play of the season and all through rehearsals for Lori's play, LaVern and Lamont continued dating. When they were together, there was almost constant physical contact; hand holding, arms around a waist or shoulder, leaning against one another. LaVern was content and so, she thought, was he. Her cell went off one evening. It was Shaundra.

"Hi girlfriend," LaVern said. "Haven't heard from you in a while. How are you?"

Shaundra ignored the question. "Peaches, have you ever Googled Lamont Hughes?"

"No, why?"

"I was just laying here watching TV and I decided to snoop."

"Okay," said a dubious LaVern.

"Do you know his family is crazy rich?"

"Really? I didn't know that."

"Peaches, I mean stupid, crazy, drug cartel rich."

"Well, he's never talked much about his family. From listening to him I figured his people might be well off. He does have his own apartment, but not money like you say, Shaundra."

"I'm looking at it right now. They live like movie stars, in a mansion with a shitload of cars."

"Let me get to my laptop."

After several seconds Shaundra heard an audible gasp.

"That's where Lamont lives? I had no idea."

"He never let on that his people were filthy rich?"

"Never. Like I said, he doesn't talk much about his home life."

"Well, now you know why. He's holding back for a reason, Peaches. Are you going to bring it up?"

"No, I'll leave that up to him. I liked him before I knew all this, so his family's money makes no difference to me."

"Well, it's your call. It just seems funny to me that after all this time, he would keep you in the dark. I'm just sayin'."

"I guess he'll share all that with me when he feels comfortable."

"Okay. I'm going to do some more snooping, then I'm going to crash. Talk to you later."

"Okay, later Shaundra."

I'm going to do some snooping of my own, decided LaVern. She swiped through page after page of the Hughes' extravagant lifestyle. No wonder he seemed much older than his twenty years, she realized. He has traveled all over the world and mingled with celebrities and politicians and captains of industry. But, I've never heard of any uber rich Hughes's. LaVern discovered that Lamont's father was a successful land developer. He had invested well and took great pains to stay well under the publicity radar. He donated millions each year to HBCUs nationwide. *That's why their name is unfamiliar. They wanted it that way. That may explain Lamont's reluctance to discuss his family life.*

A few days later, while they were taking a leisurely stroll across campus, Lamont received a call. When he answered, he turned his back to LaVern and talked in a hushed tone. Even so, she could still make out that he was talking to his father. She was not intent on eavesdropping, but she deciphered bits and pieces of the conversation; the mention of "spring break" and "both of you? That's fine". She drew the obvious conclusion they were visiting over the break. This would be a good time to finally meet them. After all, he'd met her parents twice.

After the call, Lamont didn't mention anything about the chat he just had. Spring break was only a few days away. What was he waiting for? As they walked hand and hand toward the campus eatery, LaVern asked about the call.

"I couldn't help but overhear part of your conversation, Lamont. It sounds like your parents are coming for a visit."

"Oh, you heard that?"

"Well, I couldn't help it."

"It's still undecided," he said, "but they might."

"If they do, I would be delighted to meet them."

Lamont was becoming visibly uneasy.

"They'll probably only be here for a day…or a couple of hours. Not enough time to really get to know them."

"That's okay, I just want to meet them. They're probably very nice people."

"Well, I can't make any promises, LaVern. I'll see what I can do."

She wondered why he was being so evasive. It sounded like he was coming up with a bunch of lame excuses. LaVern stopped their stroll. She released his hand.

"You seem to be making this much harder than necessary, Lamont. I'm not asking to occupy all their time, I just want to meet them."

"You're right, LaVern. It's not asking much, but… I'll have to let you know."

LaVern became indignant. Let me know? What the hell did that mean?

"Lamont, I don't understand why you can't tell me right here and now I can meet your parents. What is it? You don't *want* me to meet them? If you have a problem with me, let me know now."

LaVern's ire was rising quickly. It was a side of her personality that Lamont had never seen. It wasn't necessary before now. He became defensive.

"Now LaVern, there's no need to become angry. I don't have a problem with you meeting my parents."

He didn't sound convincing. He didn't *want* to do it. She walked straight up to Lamont and even though she only came up to his chest, she glared directly up into his eyes. She pointed her finger inches from his face.

"I don't believe you, Lamont. You have turned a simple mundane act into a major obstacle. Are you too embarrassed to have your parents meet me?"

"No, no Lavern" came a weak reply. "That's not it."

"That's not *it?* For there to be an *it* there has to be a *something* Lamont. What's my *it?*"

"Now you're overreacting, LaVern. You need to calm down."

She was now shouting and her eyes filled with rage. "I'll calm down when you can answer me!"

Lamont nervously scanned the passersby seeking to avoid an embarrassing public spectacle. But he didn't answer.

"Do your parents even know about me? Why haven't they been to any of your performances?"

Lamont had a look of resignation on his face. He was busted and he knew it. All he could do was stare into the distance with his lips pursed and his arms folded in front of him. When he didn't respond, LaVern had her answer. She backed away, knowing it was over. He couldn't even look her in the eye. She inhaled deeply, regained her poise and said, in a calm, clear voice, her last words to him.

"I'm done with you."

She turned and walked hurriedly back to her room.

She talked with Shaundra about the breakup. LaVern became emotional and even cried when she retold the entire sad episode.

"I didn't let him know, but he really hurt me, Shaundra."

"You handled him too classy, Peaches. He better be glad I wasn't there. I would have gone straight East Baltimore on his ass!"

LaVern chuckled through her tears.

"You just have to let it go. He wanted to get over for as long as he could."

That thought hadn't even occurred to LaVern. But Shaundra was right.

"Just forget about his trifflin' ass. Having money don't give you class. All his money won't even make a down payment on all the class you have." She heard LaVern's sobs. "Are you alright, Peaches?"

"I'm better now. You're always there for me when I need you most. I love you so much, Shaundra."

"Stop, before you have me bawlin' too. Even if we're miles apart, we're always in it together. Remember that."

"Thank you so much Shaundra. I miss you."

Lori's play was coming along nicely, and it took an Oscar-worthy effort to rehearse with Lamont in such close proximity. Thankfully they didn't have any scenes together. Due to the increased preparation and coordination required, it took longer than anticipated to ready the play. On opening night, once the audience was seated, George Coombs came from behind the curtain and stood mid stage, a lone figure lit by a single spotlight.

"Good evening ladies and gentlemen. My name is George Coombs, and I am the acting director here at NYCPA. Tonight, we have something special for you. You're about to see an original play, written by one of our own student writers. Her name is Lori Burkhardt."

A few yelps erupted from the quiet darkness, obviously members of her family.

"This is a first for us and gauging by the quality of this work, it will not be the last. I present, for your pleasure, "Juris Doctor in the House.""

George walked off, stage right, and the curtain pulled back.

When the final scene concluded and the curtain closed, the audience rose to their feet and gave the cast a rousing standing ovation. In the midst of their applause, George again appeared alone on stage.

"That was an excellent piece of work wasn't it? Now, permit me to introduce our cast for tonight's play." He brought each actor out one at a time and each got a standing ovation. "And finally, it is my honor to introduce to you, the creative mind behind tonight's entertainment, our own Lori Burkhardt."

Lori emerged from behind the curtain to enthusiastic applause. She bowed gracefully and blew kisses to everyone. She looked to her left and then to her right and in complete synchronicity, led the entire cast in a deep bow. After bathing in the adulation, the entire cast took one step back and the curtain closed.

LaVern entered a lobby more jammed packed than usual. Freeman got to her first and gave her his customary big hug and kiss on the forehead.

"Where's Lamont? I don't see him anywhere."

LaVern stole a quick peep at Shaundra. She stared back mutely. LaVern answered in a subdued and solemn voice.

"That's over daddy."

"Oh." Freeman heard the sadness and heartbreak in his daughter's tone. He didn't pry. He hugged her harder. Lamont would withdraw from NYCPA at semester's end.

As the surrounding chit chat continued to drone on, Lori came through the auditorium doors. She was immediately converged upon by family members and well-wishers. They were hugging and crying and gushing about how proud they were. As LaVern watched, she knew she had to say something.

"I'll be right back, family."

When Lori noticed LaVern coming toward her she squealed with joy and rushed over to hug her neck.

"Congratulations, madam playwright."

"Thank you, LaVern. This night would not have been possible without you. I'm so grateful."

"You did all the hard work, Lori. I just gave you a little nudge."

"Call it whatever you want, you're responsible for all this. I'll never forget what you've done for me."

The two roommates hugged and returned to their respective families.

Senior Year

LaVern didn't room with Lori her senior year. She registered very late, and the room assignments were already issued. LaVern was alone, reading, when her new roomie entered. She looked up to see a very fresh-faced young Black girl who brought way too much luggage. She was tall, dark skinned, and slim with large black plastic framed glasses and shoulder length, straight black hair. She was a freshman actress.

"You're LaVern Whitaker! I can't believe I'm going to be

your roommate. I saw you last semester in "Juris Doctor in the House" and you were great."

"And you are?"

"Oh, I'm sorry. My name is Janeesa Robinson." She reached out her hand and they shook.

"That's nice of you to say, Janeesa. I have to admit I'm a little shocked you've seen one of our productions. Normally it's mostly family and friends, not many members of the public."

"I've always wanted to act, and a friend suggested I check out NYCPA. My family and I came to the play, just to get a feel for the school, and I remember watching you and we were all impressed with your performance. You're so talented."

"You're too kind, but I appreciate the compliment."

Janeesa became like a little sister, so eager, always asking questions, probing LaVern's mind for all the why's and how's of performing. During rehearsals, she could feel Janeesa's eyes on her, examining and probing for any scrap of acting expertise.

George Coombs' first play of the year was a musical comedy, a first for LaVern. It was a rare opportunity for her to utilize her vocal skills. In her stage experience, LaVern heard all kinds of reactions and noises from an audience; groans, gasps, sneezes, even conversations. This was the first time she heard laughter. Little did she know this would be the last play of her NYCPA life.

George decided to throw a curveball for his final production of the year. Until now, all his offerings consisted of stage plays. This time he elected to shoot a film. This was in keeping with his desire to utilize as many theater departments as possible on a single project. This effort would not only include most of the departments that collaborated on Lori Burkhardt's original play, which reconnected LaVern with her freshman roommate, the costume designing Melissa Frazier, but it would now include the film making students. They normally did public service or documentary style films. Their work would now involve working with an ensemble and a script. The actors had to learn to work on location with plenty of distractions, and with cameras and camera angles. It was like going to a movie set. One day they would be in midtown, on a crowded street, the next, in Central Park or driving through the Holland Tunnel. It was a wonderful training ground and George knew it.

On the night of the viewing, the school added a few perks. There was a concession stand selling soda, popcorn, candy and bottled water and parents got a free copyrighted DVD of the movie. At the appropriate time, the actors escorted their families to their seats. For LaVern and her fellow actors, this was the first time any of them watched a performance from the soft, bright red cloth theater chairs. All their time in the Landsman had been spent on stage. LaVern noticed nearly every seat was taken. The lights dimmed, the hubbub subsided, and the screen slowly descended from the ceiling above the stage. The theater went dark and the movie began.

After an hour and a half, the lights came up and the crowd burst into applause. The entire audience rose to their feet to pay homage to the excellent work they had just witnessed. The tribute lasted for several minutes until the screen lifted, and the rotund figure of George Coombs appeared on the stage. The audience returned to their seats, and he began his address.

"That was excellent work, don't you agree?"

The audience responded with another enthusiastic ovation. Once the hand clapping ebbed, he began again.

"At this time, I would like to invite all the seniors who were involved in the making of this fantastic piece of cinema to join me on stage."

Male and female bodies began to rise out of their places, feet began to shuffle along the floor, backs were slapped, and hugs and kisses were shared all over the playhouse. Soon, a line of jubilant, air punching, fist raising young people filed down the aisles and threaded their way toward the stage. One after another they mounted the worn wooden steps and soon, fifty students stood facing their most ardent admirers. They were bathed in applause once again. George Coombs let the performers enjoy their well-deserved moment before he continued.

"Everyone here is aware this talented band of performers has worked hard for four years to earn the right to stand before you this evening. These will be among their final steps across this stage and what better departing legacy could one possibly ask for than the magnificent piece of film work presented for your viewing pleasure tonight?"

There was loud applause and shouts of approval. George turned his back to the audience and faced his soon to be former students.

"Seniors, please join me one last time."

He turned back around to the sea of faces. He led his group in one last deep bow. They straightened up, paused, and bowed again, all to a resounding ovation.

In the lobby, LaVern's group were watery eyed and emotional. They did their traditional group hug and all around the jam-packed lobby the same scene was repeated, families in small groups smiling and laughing and hugging.

"Oh, I have something for you Mom" said LaVern. She reached into her backpack and pulled out the DVD that was gifted to each family.

"Thank you so much, sweetheart." She immediately placed the collector's item in her purse.

Everyone went away happy on this memorable evening.

A month and a half later came graduation. LaVern completed her four years with a 3.9 GPA and a Bachelor of Fine Arts degree in theater. The degree was the most coveted prize as far as the Whitakers were concerned. It had always been, ever since they began reading to her while she was still in the crib. The ceremony took place in the Landsman Theater. When LaVern looked out from her seat on the stage, she viewed a mostly empty auditorium. There were only fifty students in the class, but The Pack was front and center. As she glanced down at her support group, she began to reminisce about her journey to this point.

Every person I love in the world is seated right there. My parents prioritized educational excellence, even when I protested having to learn my ABC's in Pre K. My mom never gave up on getting me into the Felder Academy. My father's guidance and wisdom was, and is, steady and dependable. And

Shaundra, Big Dog. Many years ago, she chose me to be her best friend. To this day I don't know why, but I've been reaping the benefits ever since. These people are my foundation. I owe them so much. Whatever I make of myself in this world won't be possible without them.

"LaVern Whitaker!"

The call shook LaVern out of her daydream. It was her turn to walk across the stage and receive her well-deserved degree. When she approached Department Head Abby Walters, LaVern noticed a smiling George Coombs standing among the other administrators. She mouthed the words "thank you" to her mentor. He simply placed one hand over his heart, then continued clapping. As she headed back to her place on the stage, with her new sheepskin held over her head in triumph, Jackie was covering her mouth and peeking out over her hands, Freeman was leaning forward in his seat with his elbows on his knees and his fingers nervously clasped and Shaundra was standing and shouting,

"Way to go Peaches. My girl!"

After everyone received their diplomas, the now ex-students milled around on the stage and exchanged hugs and best wishes. LaVern spied Lori Burkhardt. They hugged and thanked each other for all their hard work.

"You did something very special for me, LaVern. I'll never forget it."

"You improved me as a performer. I'll never forget *that.*"

The two former roomies hugged one last time, and waved goodbye. LaVern, for the last time, descended the few steps from the stage and walked into a trio of waiting arms. They did their ritual group hug and jumping thing and wiped tears from one another's eyes. Shaundra asked to see her diploma. LaVern was the only schoolmate she knew with a college degree. There, in bold fancy-schmancy script it read:

The New York College of the Performing Arts confers upon LaVern Renee Whitaker a Bachelor of Fine Arts Degree...

Shaundra stared at the object of four years of hard work, knowing she would never have one.

"Well, you did it, Peaches. How does it feel?" asked Freeman.

"To be honest Dad, except for this degree in my hand, I feel the same as I felt yesterday. I'm happy and relieved and proud, but I feel like the same person."

"That's understandable, sweetheart," said Jackie, who had her master's in education. "Even after that degree, life goes on. Try to enjoy it for a little while at least."

Everyone migrated up the aisle toward the swinging doors that led into the sunlit lobby, and through the heavy gauge glass doors that opened onto the sidewalk. The Whitakers huddled in the warm summer air as a cab pulled up. They gave their daughter one last hug, one more "I love you".

LaVern started to have misgivings about having everyone travel so far just to spend a couple hours on her behalf and then turn right around and go home. She had an audition scheduled for later that afternoon.

"I'm so sorry we don't have more time to spend together. I didn't want it to be this way."

"Peaches," said Shaundra, "you don't have to apologize. We all understand."

"Yes, baby," said Jackie. "Stop feeling guilty. It wouldn't matter how short our stay was, we wouldn't miss your graduation."

LaVern smiled and stepped back to watch her base pile into their ride. She stood there as her loved ones waved from behind partly lowered, tinted windows as the cab pulled off and melted into the afternoon New York traffic. She turned and looked at the Landsman Theater. Just like her old bedroom, this place had served its purpose. LaVern glanced down at her watch. It was time to take the first step down the road to becoming a working actor. She didn't want to be late for the first day of the rest of her life.

Lean Years
Chapter Four

The Mayfair Theater was in a hardscrabble part of Brooklyn. It was a brick building located mid-block, with two large black wooden windowless doors. A red, domed shaped awning rested on four skinny rusting metal poles. The poles bowed under the scant weight of the canvas. The flaking black doors were accented by a pair of large gold painted handles. There were two vertical, transparent, fiberglass enclosed cases attached to the brick wall on each side of the doors. Inside each was a poster advertising the current play, "She loves Me?" The neighborhood was seedy with a small complement of homeless people. The streets could use a more regular cleaning and to top off the neglected look, someone chained a bicycle to a no parking sign directly in front. LaVern and Angie Rosinski stood in front of their new place of employment, thanks to George Coombs' connections, mere hours after graduation. They assessed their situation; no more classes, no more Mr. Coombs, no NYCPA to cushion any fall. It was 2011 and they were on their own.

"This is where it begins huh, Angie?" said LaVern as she scanned her new work environs.

"I guess so."

LaVern opened the heavy, wooden door for the first of what would be many times. Just inside was an elevated booth where sat a goateed, afro-coiffed, middle-aged Black man they would come to know as "Boulder." His name was Clayton Watkins and his was a dual role. On performance nights he took vouchers from the attendees, and at night's end, he would stand vigil outside until all the cast members were safely off. During rehearsals, he minded the door. Boulder looked up from his phone as LaVern and Angie entered.

"How can I help you two ladies?" His voice was gravely,

like he had spent way too many nights in way too many smoke filled clubs.

"We're here to see Mark Jacobsen. My name is LaVern Whitaker, and this is Angie Rosinski."

"Oh yeah, he's expecting you two." He stood up and revealed his true size. He was humongous, like a building with legs. He stepped down from his perch and began walking toward a side door. He reached for the knob, which disappeared inside his meaty hand, and gave it a slight twist. "This way ladies. First door on the right."

As he held the door open, LaVern and Angie worked their way around his bigness and into the narrow hallway.

"Thank you, sir," said LaVern.

"Just call me Boulder, ladies. Everybody calls me Boulder."

"Well thank you very much… eh… Boulder," called out Angie.

This Boulder looks more like a mountain, marveled LaVern.

The first door on the right was already open. The room was empty. Boulder was still hovering around at the side door.

"Just go on in and make yourselves comfortable, he'll be right back."

"Thanks, Boulder," said LaVern.

The two ladies found themselves in an absurdly small, windowless and cluttered space. There was barely enough room for the two ratty chairs they had to sit in and the air was dank and musty. Papers and folders were sloppily spread on top of the metal desk, the folders barely clinging to their contents. A small, decrepit bookcase held a few old and dust-covered books, barely able to remain upright, while others were lying on their side, as if knocked unconscious. All this was engulfed by all manner of office supplies: reams of copy paper, staplers and boxes of staples, paper clips, markers, scotch tape, business envelopes, and plastic bins for holding more papers and folders. And, alone in one corner, an obviously well-used and out-of- date copier.

In walked a surprisingly young man, White, probably in his late thirties, surmised LaVern. To get to his desk he had to deftly step over the debris piled up on the floor. He sat down and took in the two young actresses seated in front of him.

"My name is Mark Jacobsen and I'm the director of "She Loves Me?" Which one of you is LaVern?"

"I'm LaVern Whitaker, Mr. Jacobsen."

"Nice to meet you. That means you must be Angie Rosinski."

"That's right Mr. Jacobsen, nice to meet you."

"Nice to meet you too, Angie."

Mark leaned forward in his chair and got right down to business.

"I'm glad you guys are punctual. You'll find that in this business, being on time and knowing your lines makes things much easier for everybody involved. We don't have a lot of time so let me get right to it. We're in the middle of rehearsals right now and both of you came highly recommended."

He selected two manila folders from the many strewn atop his desk. They appeared to be empty.

"These are your lines. What I need from both of you right now is to follow me into the auditorium and we'll rejoin the rehearsal."

Mark rose from his chair and headed for the door. LaVern and Angie were shocked by the rapidity of it all. It felt like trying to catch up to a transit bus that had just passed them by. They just grabbed their scripts and hastily followed their director. On the way, Mark went over what would be required of them today. They were to study their lines and be prepared to rehearse the scene when he was ready for them. LaVern would have extra work in that she would sing with a chorus in two different scenes, so she had to learn some song lyrics as well.

"Excuse me, everyone." He waited for the buzz to diminish. "I know each of you are working hard to prepare for opening night, but I would like to introduce you to our newest cast members." He extended an open palm toward LaVern.

"This is LaVern Whitaker. She'll be a member of our chorus as well as playing the role of the bar patron."

They gave her a hand and shouted out their welcomes.

"And this is Angie Rosinski. She will play the role of the

female passerby. Let's all welcome them."

The entire cast broke into applause and came over to greet their newest members. They all carried thick binders containing the entire play, not just the measly manila folders LaVern and Angie had.

"All right, we're going to do scene three again. Everybody on their marks and action on my cue."

At the end of the day, they were once again called into Mark's office. He expressed how pleased he was with them, gave them the date for opening night and, most importantly, he discussed their pay. True to their lack of business savvy, they had never thought of asking what their salary would be. Due to their bit roles, Angie would get $700.00 a week and, because LaVern would also be singing, she would get $750.00.

"Is that okay with you ladies?"

He knew newbies had no bargaining power. They would accept whatever was offered, but it sounded like a fortune to them.

"Yes sir, Mr. Jacobsen," replied LaVern.

"Yes sir, Mr. Jacobsen," said Angie.

"Mark…call me Mark. In that case, be here at 7AM tomorrow for rehearsal."

As the girls exited the office and entered the lobby, they encountered Boulder. He was there along with a smattering of other cast members. They were waiting for their rides. Some had family coming, some were waiting on cabs.

"You ladies need a ride?" he growled.

"Yes, we do Boulder," said LaVern. "Can you call a cab?"

"One for the both of you?"

"Yes," said Angie. "We're roommates."

"No problem." Boulder hesitated. "Just for your information ladies, most actors have the same driver each night. That way, it's safe all the way around, you know what I mean? I can arrange something for you, If you'd like."

"That would be perfect," said Angie.

"Of course, I'll be outside too…just to make sure."

"Thank you so much Boulder," said LaVern. "That's very nice of you."

A month previous to graduation, LaVern and Angie made the decision to search for a cheap apartment, if there was such a thing in New York City. The cheapest rent they could find was a third floor studio, that was $2000.00 a month. It was a tiny open space with a small kitchen and outdated appliances. The only private area was the bathroom. The walls were rice paper thin and cried out for a fresh coat of paint. Cheap area rugs covered aged and warped wooden floors. There were two narrow, curtain-less windows that served as their only air conditioning. There was a TV that required cable access, and just like the air conditioning dilemma, it would have to wait. The only live entertainment was the easily overheard arguments that seeped through the thin walls or whatever clatter rose from the busy sidewalks below.

Without a source of income, they did what most young people did when they struck out on their own for the first time. They hit their parents up. The Whitakers dipped into their meager savings and managed to gift LaVern $6,000.00, enough to cover rent for three months. Her rent was $1000.00 more a month than their mortgage. Angie's parents donated $8,000.00. So, the new roommates now had 6 months' rent in the bank. With their combined salaries, at least they could eat and pay for utilities, but not much else.

The previous occupants abandoned a sofa and a coffee table. LaVern decided to sleep on a newly purchased inflatable mattress while Angie elected to bed down in a sleeping bag her family used when camping. They threw a blanket over the sofa until they could afford to buy a new one. It was to this place LaVern and Angie returned after their first day as working actors.

When the cab pulled up to their apartment building, they rushed up the three narrow flights of stairs and immediately tore into their food in a manner that would put a pack of hyenas to shame. They talked about their day with their mouths crammed with Chinese takeout.

"What a day," observed Angie. "I'm starved."

"It was crazy, wasn't it?" said LaVern. "And kind of scary too."

"I know what you mean. Who goes directly from their graduation to work?"

LaVern shoved another forkful of pork yat gat mein into her jaws. "How about Mark Jacobsen? He got right down to it, didn't he?"

"Yes, he seems to be all business." Angie paused to swallow her shrimp lo mein. "I guess that's how it's going to be from now on, LaVern. Strictly business."

When the girls finally emptied their food containers, sleep and fatigue conspired to lower their eyelids and the two ex-classmates, now struggling actors, said their goodnights and drowsily wandered off to reap a well-earned night's sleep.

In short order, the girls fell into a twelve hour a day routine of rehearsal, home, then repeat. Each received updated playbills, and they anxiously thumbed their way through it looking for their names. LaVern was credited as the "bar patron" and Angie was the "female passerby". Despite such ambiguous descriptions, the girls were delighted to see their names in the playbill of a Broadway production. Mark also advised them that opening night would be on Wednesday, July 7. Plenty of time for LaVern to alert her clan and have them in the audience.

On opening night, The Pack got their first look at The Mayfair Theater. It was nighttime and the illuminated marquee and the procession of headlights pulling up to discharge their riders was thrilling. Shaundra stood on the sidewalk gawking at the entire scene. It was unbelievable to her that she was coming to a place like this to see her best friend perform. She watched as one party of theater goers after another passed through the massive, black doors and into the brightly lit lobby. The Whitakers were in awe themselves.

"Well, let's not stand around outside like a bunch of groupies," said Jackie. "Let's go inside and buy our tickets like everyone else."

Inside, they had their first encounter with Boulder. He was even more imposing in his XXXL tuxedo.

"Good evening, folks," he greeted in his rock grinding voice.

"We're the family of LaVern Whitaker," announced a proud Shaundra. With her hand, she gestured toward Freeman and Jackie.

"It's a pleasure to meet you folks. She's a very nice and classy young lady."

Boulder noticed none of them had a ticket in their hands. "If you need to buy your tickets, see Marybeth at the booth."

"Thank you young man," said Freeman.

The sight of cash and credit cards being flashed was a reminder their daughter was now a member of a money-making industry. This was show *business.*

"This is awesome," exclaimed Shaundra.

"It is something to behold," said Freeman.

"She also has playbills for sale," barked Boulder.

Of course, the playbill, thought Freeman. This is her first professional performance, verification of her membership in the industry. He purchased three tickets at $35.00 per and the playbills. Everyone immediately leafed through the program until they found it.

Bar patron...... LaVern Whitaker.

It didn't matter that LaVern's part was small. All that mattered was it was there, for all the world, and their relatives, to see. The three entered the main body of the theater through the ornately embroidered curtains that separated the lobby from the auditorium. The Mayfair's decor was black and oxblood red, which was replicated in the ceiling-to-floor curtains on stage, and the felt covered house seats. It was a small venue, with space for only 99 patrons. Their seats were five rows from the stage and on the aisle.

"This is good", said Shaundra, "just in case we have to beat the crowd out at the end of the play."

Shaundra needn't have worried. Despite all the activity and brouhaha outside, the auditorium was only half filled when the hall went dark and the curtain opened.

At the play's end, the emptiness of the hall swallowed and muted the smattering of applause by the audience. LaVern's brief appearances gave The Pack great joy. She sang a little and she had a few lines. It was a successful evening as far as they were concerned. As they waited, LaVern came into the lobby.

"Hi everybody. I tried not to keep you waiting too long."

"That's alright, baby," said Jackie. "You didn't keep us waiting at all."

"Sooooo," Lavern began, pausing to take a quick survey of faces, "how did you like the play?"

Shaundra erupted first. "I loved it, Peaches." She thought for a few seconds. "You know, there's a big difference between these actors and those at NYCPA. Everybody· here is much better."

LaVern chuckled. She realized this was Shaundra's first Broadway play. Of course, there's a difference. Then her mother spoke.

"I was so proud to see you up on that stage, in your first professional production."

"Well, I wasn't on stage for very long but–"

The pragmatic Freeman cut her off. "But you have to pay your dues, Peaches. You can't just walk in, fresh from NYCPA, and think you can leapfrog over all these grizzled, veteran actors. So, don't worry about the amount of stage time you got tonight. You're just starting out. In the meantime, I'm going to treasure this playbill that has my daughter's name in it." He stared at the cover and spoke with reverence and pride. "Your first Broadway play."

A group hug ensued as a cab pulled up outside. The cabbie leaned over from his driver's seat and locked eyes with Boulder through the lowered passenger side window. Boulder pointed a chubby forefinger skyward to signal the cabbie to wait. He stuck his head inside the heavy doors.

"Your cab is here Miss Whitaker."

"Thank you so much Boulder." She returned her attention to her family. "I'm sorry I can't spend time like we used to. It's opening night and–"

Again, Freeman intervened. "Peaches, no need to explain. There'll be other times."

LaVern turned to Boulder. "Would you please make sure my family gets a ride back to their hotel?"

"No problem, Miss Whitaker. I'll take good care of them."

After two months, the run for "She Loves Me?" sputtered to an end. Following a Saturday matinee, Mark Jacobsen called the cast together and everybody took a seat in the empty auditorium. The silence was deafening. The veterans knew this scene well, a scene all of them had parts in at one time or another. The signs were always there; the sparse attendance and the lukewarm reviews, death blows to any production. Only LaVern and Angie seemed to be blindsided. Mark got right to the point.

"It kills me to have to tell you this but, our final performance will be this coming Sunday. We've been struggling from the start. We had a good product, everybody worked their asses off, but, in this business, it's all about the bottom line. We just were not making money. I'm sorry. We all tried our best."

After the final performance, cast members headed to Mindy's, their regular after work night spot. The significance of this place was not lost on the veterans. It was where you met industry people, but more importantly, it was where industry people met you. LaVern and Angie watched as the veterans worked the room, flitting from table to drink covered table. This grownup crowd felt odd to them, like they were socializing with their parents' friends. Both girls sat, frozen. They had no contacts to flit to. A familiar figure sat down in the empty chair at their table. It was Aubrey Wright, a fellow cast member with a half full shot glass of Larceny bourbon.

"It was a real bummer with the play closing so fast, huh?"

"Yes, it was," said Angie. "We didn't see it coming."

"None of you newbies ever do. It was a shock to my system the first time too."

"Shock or no shock," said LaVern, "we need to find work. We only have four months of rent money left."

"Which brings me to why I sat down here." Aubrey took a final swig. He motioned to the barmaid to bring him another. "I've been where you two are heading. You need some kind of dependable income in order to continue looking for acting work, right?"

"Right," stated LaVern.

"And you need something now."

"Right again," said Angie.

"Well, I think I can help both of you. How good are either of you with kids?"

"I love them," said LaVern. "I worked with kids one summer."

"I know about a daycare center and I'm sure if I recommend someone, they'll pretty much get the job."

"Are they a bunch of unruly monsters?"

"No, on the contrary, these are pre-K kids. Mainly you're a babysitter. They play games, they eat, and they sleep."

LaVern was wary now. "You make it sound so easy and inviting. Why don't you take it?"

"I've got an opportunity in Chicago. Friends are telling me to come now. If you like kids and you're interested, I can give you the info and you'll start in a week."

Without waiting for an answer, Aubrey began writing down his information. As he wrote, he spoke to Angie.

"I have a lead on another job. This one is actually a surer shot than the daycare gig, but it may not be as fun."

"And what's that?"

"It's waiting tables. There's a restaurant that hires struggling actors. They don't mind accommodating our erratic schedules. A lot of actors who are looking for work wait tables there now. And they're always looking for waiters."

"I've never waited tables before, but it has to beat chasing around a bunch of screaming babies all day long."

"Great. I'll set it up for you."

The waitress came and placed Aubrey's drink down. He immediately took a sip. He traced a finger around the rim of his glass, deep in thought.

"Like I said before, I've been where you two are headed. You may find that you spend more time at some dead-end job than practicing your craft. That's just the price you pay to stay a working actor."

He was giving them good, real-world advice.

"You have to jump on this merry-go-round of casting call, audition, call back maybe, rejection, then repeat. I'm not trying to dissuade you from following your dreams. I just want you to go into this business with your eyes wide open. I hope I've helped you make a bridge from this play to the next. Good luck." Aubrey rose from his chair, grabbed his drink and rejoined the other cast members.

The future was scary sounding but, the next day, LaVern headed to the Little Angels Day Care Center. Aubrey had done just as he promised and gave notice to the Director, Janice Waltherson. The interview process and the background check went smoothly, and she started in a week. Angie, on the other hand, started work immediately. The "First Act" was a vibrant, bustling but charming neighborhood eatery and like Aubrey said, most of the waiters and waitresses were out of work actors. Her job was a gold mine of industry insider information and gossip. Everybody shared info on auditions, play closings, which heavyweights were in town, status of current plays, everything. In the interim, Angie's boyfriend would visit occasionally and spend a night or two. They were discreet enough to restrict their lovemaking to the early mornings, when LaVern was at the daycare center.

After a month, Angie's job paid off. Word was that open auditions would be held for an upcoming off, off Broadway production. When they entered the hotel lobby, they were greeted by a handwritten sign taped to the top of a metal post. It simply read "auditions" with an arrow pointing to the right. When they looked, the sight was instantly disheartening. They saw an unbroken line of chairs arranged in a rectangular pattern, close to one hundred in all, each chair occupied by an actor seeking work. Angie mouthed the words "oh my God." LaVern, as intrepid as ever, took a deep breath and, with Angie close behind, took their seats at the end of the queue. After fifteen minutes, an older, balding man emerged from behind the closed door and proceeded to where the audition sign was posted. He removed it and walked, crumpled sign in hand, back toward the office door. He looked at the first performer in the line and pointed.

"You're up."

The actor rose and disappeared inside, quickly followed by, who would turn out to be, the Director. After about ten minutes, the actor reemerged. LaVern and Angie tried to gauge by his facial expression or his body language how things went.

He was as blank as copy paper. The director stuck his head out again and called for the next in line. And on it went.

An hour and a half later it was LaVern's turn. She stood, took a deep breath and went through the door. Behind a desk sat four people, the Producer, the Director, and two members of the cast. They introduced themselves and conducted a small interview: What's your name? What other plays have you been in? What talents besides acting do you have? LaVern was handed a script, and she did a short scene with one of the actors. She was also asked to sing for them.

"Thank you, Miss Whitaker. We'll have callbacks in a week. Please leave your contact information on this card."

And that was it. All that anxiety and angst and it was over in fifteen minutes. The director opened the door and motioned for Angie. As they passed one another, she searched LaVern's face for some silent indication, but there was no time to say or do anything. LaVern took her seat and waited for her roommate.

After returning to their apartment, the girls collapsed onto their sofa as if they had just finished a marathon. LaVern went to their fridge, pulled out some cold pizza and stuck it in the microwave.

"That was sooo nerve wracking," exclaimed Angie. "I'm going to need the rest of the day to recuperate."

"I know what you mean."

"I almost died when I saw all those people. I felt so intimidated."

"I did too," said LaVern. "I'm glad we got the first one out of the way though."

A week passed and neither girl got a call back. Over the ensuing two months, they went to several auditions and neither LaVern nor Angie got a single callback. Their rent money was getting very short. They were two months away from being evicted. It occurred to LaVern that she and Angie had become just what Aubrey Wright had predicted months before. They were now regular passengers on the casting call "merry-go-round": audition, callback(maybe), rejection, repeat.

One evening Angie came back to the apartment with

devastating news. She was pregnant.

"What! You're kidding me, right?"

"I wish I was, LaVern. I just found out yesterday."

An awkward silence cloaked the apartment. A million consequences blitzed through LaVern's mind in milliseconds.

She'll have to go home. She can't audition when she's pregnant. Where will that leave me? I can't afford this place by myself. Her job has all the connections too. Awww damn!

"I'm so sorry, LaVern. My mother wants me to come home and have the baby there." Angie began to cry. She covered her eyes with her hands and leaned forward until her head was in her lap. LaVern still had not uttered a word. Her mind was still numb.

"I know what kind of predicament this leaves you in. I was so stupid to let this happen. Please don't hate me."

LaVern finally managed to corral her jumbled thoughts. "Well," she was stumbling through her words, "I guess going home is… best. You can't undo what's already done."

Angie was still crying into her hands. "We were going to become stars together and I've let you down. That will haunt me the most…that I let you down."

LaVern moved over to comfort her friend. She placed her arm around her shoulders and squeezed tightly. "It's okay, Angie," she lied. "Don't worry about me, I'll be alright. You have to take care of yourself and your baby."

LaVern had no idea if she'd be alright or not. She didn't know how to right this. After her last day at the "First Act", Angie told LaVern of an upcoming audition.

"I want to pass this on to you and hopefully, things will work out. You deserve it so much."

LaVern thanked her and they hugged.

Now, alone in her apartment with one month left before her rent money ran out, she went to the audition and got the now customary "callbacks in about a week" speech. LaVern needed someone to vent to, a confidant. She didn't want to burden her parents with more bad news about her shaky financial status. They had stretched themselves enough for her. She phoned Shaundra. She listened while LaVern cried, complained, fumed, and became practically inconsolable.

"It's too bad about Angie. What's wrong with her, she never heard of birth control?"

"It was very irresponsible, Shaundra, and she left me in a tough spot. But I can't control other people's lives."

"You're right Peaches, you just have to move on without her." Shaundra paused. "Well, rich or poor, you can't get rid of me. I'm in for the long haul."

Lavern's cell phone went off while she was at "Little Angels." She barely heard her custom ringtone over the screaming commotion of her kids on the playground. She casually searched through her purse until she felt it vibrating.

"Darius, stop running!" she yelled before she looked to see who had called. The number popped up, but no name. A sure sign of spam, so she let it go to voicemail. If it was important, they'd leave a message. Her phone beeped. Someone had indeed left a message.

"Hello," said the voice. "This is Richard Hoffman. You auditioned for me last week. I'm inviting you to a second audition scheduled for Saturday at 1PM at the Royal Theater."

LaVern couldn't believe her ears. She started to panic. I have to call him back immediately or he might call someone else, she feared. She brought up the last number received and called it.

"Hello?"

"Hello, Mr. Hoffman? This is LaVern Whitaker. I just heard your message."

"Oh, that's great, LaVern. Do you have an agent?"

She had never given any thought to hiring an agent.

"No, I don't, Mr. Hoffman. Not yet."

He didn't miss a beat. "I can count on seeing you Saturday, right?"

"Absolutely, Mr. Hoffman. I'll be there."

"Great and be prepared to sing."

"Oh, I will be Mr. Hoffman. I always—"

He hung up. *All these Broadway types were short on chit chat,* she said to herself. *They made their point and moved on.*

"LaVern."

It was Center Director Janice Waltherson.

"You can bring your children in now. Thank you."

"Right away, Mrs. Waltherson."

Even while rounding up her charges, LaVern's mind was still on her first call back. She had to tell somebody. She considered calling Shaundra. *But, what if I don't get the part? I'd get her hopes up then have to call her again with more bad news. I've done enough.* The same applied to her parents. *No, I'll keep this to myself until I know for sure.*

LaVern had never been inside the Royal Theater. From the outside, it seemed like a much grander venue than the Mayfair. She arrived fifteen minutes early, expecting to see the customary cattle call of actors. To her amazement, she was alone when she entered the lobby. There was a sign affixed to the door that led to the auditorium. It read "Closed Auditions". She had no idea this audition was closed. This was a first. Just then the door opened, and a young, pale, hairless face peered around the partially opened swinging door.

"May I help you?" he asked.

"Yes, my name is LaVern Whitaker and I'm here to audition."

The still partially hidden figure consulted a clipboard with several sheets of paper attached. Using his forefinger, he searched down his list.

"Oh yes, here you are." He opened the door fully and allowed LaVern to enter. "Just follow this aisle down to the stage. Richard Hoffman and the others are already here."

LaVern looked down the aisle and saw a small gaggle of people gathered near the center of the stage, the same people who were at her audition. Richard Hoffman noticed her approach.

"Over here, LaVern. Have a seat in the first row please."

LaVern quietly eased into the first available seat. She looked around and saw there were only ten other people seated nearby. The woman beside her introduced herself.

"Hi. I'm Carrie Norwood. Good luck today."

She stuck out her hand. LaVern reciprocated.

"I'm LaVern Whitaker, nice to meet you."

The two women exchanged some friendly chit chat as three men and one woman entered the auditorium. One of the men and the woman seated themselves near LaVern. The other two men went to a section of seats on the other side of the auditorium. That's when she noticed a small cadre of silent, suited, crossed legged male figures partially obscured in the shadows. They numbered about ten. *Who were they,* she wondered. *Why were they seated way over there?* Richard Hoffman went to center stage and all the idle chatter ceased.

"I want to thank all of you actors and your agents," he paused and extended his hand to where the suited figures were seated, "for being here today. From this group we will select the final cast members. We wish everyone luck. We'll begin in a moment."

Agents? Everybody here came with their agent. I bet I'm the only one to arrive alone. I feel so amateurish now. But how can I pay an agent when I'm close to losing my apartment?

Richard Hoffman reappeared at center stage and called out the first name on his list. The actor mounted the stage and huddled with him and the others. They handed him the script, and he wandered off as he read it through. In a few minutes he was ready to start his scene.

This is everybody? wondered LaVern. *Things sure narrowed down pretty fast.* When it was her turn, she took a deep breath, mounted the stage, studied her script and pronounced herself ready. After her scene, the producer asked her to read for a second role. She gave it everything and felt good about her performance. Near the conclusion, Mr. Hoffman asked her to sing one of the songs from the play. Then, it was over. When the other actors finished their auditions, their agents approached, and they held a brief confab. The agents then approached Richard Hoffman and did the same. LaVern had no one to speak for her and simply thanked everyone and walked out. She wasn't sure if not having an agent would work in her favor or prove fatal. Something would give in two days.

The next morning, Sunday, LaVern was relaxing on her sofa reading James McBride's "The Color of Water" when her phone went off. It was Richard Hoffman.

"Hello?"

"LaVern, I'm calling to say welcome to the cast of "The

Apple Tree."

LaVern was dumbstruck into silence. She couldn't respond.

"Hello, LaVern are you there?"

"I'm sorry Mr. Hoffman, I'm here."

"First of all, call me Richard. Secondly, rehearsal begins on Wednesday. Be at the theater at 7AM and we'll talk salary and your role with you and your agent."

LaVern, still in her dazed state, completely overlooked the "and your agent" part. She managed a weak reply. "Yes, Mr. Hoffman. I'll be there at 7. Thank you so much."

His reply was characteristically brief. "It's Richard, and don't be late." He then clicked off.

She was in. She didn't know her role, but she didn't care, she was working again. LaVern lay back on the sofa and let it sink in. A Mount Rushmore sized burden was lifted from her shoulders with a single phone call. She was finally going to be back on stage, and it felt good. She picked up her cell phone and called Shaundra.

"I knew it was just a matter of time, Peaches. You are too damn good. I'm proud of you, girlfriend."

Lavern called her parents with the good news, then she informed Janice Waltherson at "The Little Angels" that she would not be available starting Wednesday.

LaVern was early, as usual. Inside the vacant lobby, she encountered the imposing figure of Jamal Crutchfield, the "Boulder" of the Royal Theater. Or, as he so carefully explained to the cast upon meeting them for the first time, "Just call me J.C."

There must be a fraternity of big, Black doormen in this business, she assumed. LaVern made her way to Richard Hoffman's office and sat nervously in the only chair available.

"Good morning, LaVern. Where's your agent?"

"I don't have one sir…I mean Richard."

"Oh…Okay, that's fine." He got right down to business. "Let me bring you up to speed. The name of the play is "The Apple Tree". It revolves around the simple act of a child who eats an apple and throws the core away in the backyard. The core surprisingly takes root and starts to grow. The tree bears witness to the trials and tribulations of the Carter family over the next twenty years."

"Wow, I like that," said LaVern. "That sounds intriguing."

"Good, I'm glad you like it. Based on your audition, which was fantastic by the way, we're considering one of two parts that you read for. The part of Ella, the best friend of one of the Carter sisters, is the more generous role. Maddy, as you know, is the next-door neighbor. Hers is a lesser role. Despite your inexperience, we've decided to let you play "Ella.""

Her heart leaped. She surprised herself by how unaffected she seemed externally.

"Thank you, Mr., I mean Richard. I'll be ready."

"Good. Now… salary. I'm prepared to offer you $950.00 a week. We believe that's fair for someone at this stage of your career."

That was a raise in LaVern's book. A raise and getting back on stage. That was a no brainer.

"I think that's very fair, Richard." replied LaVern.

"Good." He reached into a nearby file cabinet and pulled out a thick, neatly bound notebook. "Here's the script, LaVern. Take this and head out to the stage. Most of the cast is already there. Get to know everyone and study your lines, rehearsal begins as soon as the entire cast arrives. Welcome."

LaVern stood and reached out her hand. "Thank you so much for this opportunity, Richard. I can't wait to get to work."

They shook hands just when another actor entered his office. LaVern excused her way past him and headed toward the auditorium. Just as he said, the cast was already on the stage. As LaVern approached, all heads turned to see their latest addition. As she climbed the short steps, the entire company warmly welcomed her. They explained they were going over their lines and invited her to grab a chair and join them. The part of "Ella" would be her most extensive role to date, and she wanted to demonstrate right out of the gate that she was serious and ready to work. She sought out those actors who would be in her scenes and rehearsed with them.

After a week of rehearsals, the cast was taking a lunch break when LaVern found herself in a conversation with one of the understudies. Freda Parks was from Los Angeles. She had dark, smooth skin, expressive brown eyes, a medium build and an easy smile. She was displeased with having to live in a hotel.

"You know, LaVern," she complained, "the show pays for my accommodations as long as I stay in the hotel. It's a really nice hotel but since I'm from out of town, I'm the only cast member there. I feel so apart from everybody and everything."

LaVern listened with interest.

"I plan on asking the cast and crew about apartments near here and, believe it or not, you're the first person I've approached."

"But, if you move out of the hotel, would you have to pay your own rent?" inquired LaVern.

"Yes, but that's fine by me. That hotel is so, what's a good word…sterile. It's driving me insane."

If LaVern had a tail, it would be moving faster than windshield wipers in a hurricane.

"Well, believe it or not, I'm looking for a roommate. It's not glamorous, it's on the third floor and there's no elevator, but you can take a look and see if you like it."

"When can I come over?"

"Is after rehearsal good for you?"

"Great. We can go together, right?"

"Absolutely," responded LaVern. "We can get something to eat on the way."

Freda wasn't bowled over after seeing LaVern's studio apartment. Yes, it was neat and clean, but it was just one big room, no privacy. This bothered Freda and LaVern sensed it.

"It's okay if you decide not to move in. I'm sure you're used to better."

She was, and unknown to LaVern, Freda decided to pass on moving in.

"Well, we have all this food and, I don't know about you but, I'm starving, so let's eat."

LaVern and Freda ate and talked and laughed and shared childhood memories. LaVern found out that Freda liked to cook. She wasn't a reader, but she liked to talk about the theater and the art of performing in front of an audience, the nuances that contributed to creating a great stage actor. Freda was 28 years old and had been in the business for eight years, including parts in TV and films. Work was scarce in L.A., so she took this understudy role for the money. LaVern told her how exceptionally talented she was, and she deserved to be more than an understudy. They talked until late in the evening and found they genuinely liked each other.

"Wow," said a surprised Freda, "it's midnight already."

"Really?" said LaVern. "I had no idea it was that late. I can call you a cab."

"Well, I've been here this long, I might as well stay the night…if that's alright with you. I really enjoyed our conversation."

"Oh, you're more than welcome. You can use my inflatable bed if you want to. I can't have you sleep on the couch."

"I'm fine with the couch. It wasn't in the plans for me to stay here tonight anyway. The couch is fine."

They left for rehearsal together the next morning. At the end of the day, Freda approached LaVern.

"How would you like a new roommate?"

"Really? I thought you would go back to your hotel room."

"I am going back to my hotel room."

LaVern was confused. "You're going back?"

"Yes, I'm going back. I'm going back until I can buy a new bed to put in that matchbox you call an apartment. I can't spend another minute on that nightmare of a sofa."

They stared at one another for a split second. Then, laughter erupted like water from a burst pipe.

With Freda sharing the rent, anxiety around being evicted disappeared. She proved to be truly beneficial in several ways. Her love of cooking kept food on the table and LaVern kept the kitchen clean, a deal that both women could live with. In the evenings, they would watch television or movies and then break down the performers' techniques. Now she had a mentor, and she took full advantage. Freda, the bottomless pitcher of water and LaVern, the ever-thirsty potted plant.

One day, during a break in rehearsal, a young, well-dressed Black man approached LaVern and introduced himself. She recognized him as being among the cadre of agents present at every rehearsal. He was of average height, stocky build with a short, neatly trimmed beard and mustache.

"You're LaVern Whitaker aren't you?" he asked.

"Yes, I am and who are you?"

"My name is Darien Cheek. I'm with the Galloway and Green Agency, I'm sure you have heard of us."

"Honestly, Mr. Cheek, I haven't. I've seen you and your partner at practically every one of our rehearsals though."

"That's good LaVern... may I call you LaVern?"

"No, you may not. Miss Whitaker will do fine."

"Then Miss Whitaker it will be." Darien didn't miss a beat. "I've never seen you before this play, are you new to Broadway?"

"Why do you ask?"

"I've been watching…ahh observing you."

"Oh really?" said a careful LaVern.

"Yes. From what I understand, you don't have representation, am I correct?"

"That's right, Mr. Cheek, I don't have an agent."

That was all Darien needed to hear. He started right in with his pitch. "In order to navigate your way around and avoid all the schemers and con artists that proliferate in this business, you will need trustworthy representation."

That sounds so rehearsed and phony. "I appreciate the offer Mr. Cheek, but right now I have my hands full preparing for this play. Maybe down the road somewhere."

"Miss Whitaker, inevitably, you will need a good agent like me to take care of all the distractions so that you *can* concentrate on just your preparation. We represent two of your castmates and they can tell you that an offer from an agency like G&G is not insignificant."

Darien thought this newcomer would jump at the chance to sign with G&G. He didn't realize LaVern didn't know his agency from any other. She had not been around long enough.

I don't have to make a commitment right now, she reasoned. *Afterall, I already have the job.* Even though the future was always uncertain, her talent would be there no matter when she changed her mind.

"Mr. Cheek, I'll think about it, but I'm not going to make a decision right now."

"Miss Whitaker, please take my card." He reached into the inside breast pocket of his three-piece suit coat and pulled out an expensive, leather bound card case. He withdrew an embossed G&G business card and handed it to LaVern. "You'll be seeing a lot of me around here. If you change your mind, I won't be hard to find."

LaVern watched intently as the disgruntled agent returned to where his associate, an older, gray haired, Black gentleman, was seated. She watched as they talked in whispers and intermittently, glanced in her direction.

"Welcome to the club," came a voice from behind her.

It startled LaVern, it was Freda.

"Huh? What do you mean?"

"I see the young cub finally made his pitch, huh?"

"Oh yeah, that. He said he was an agent. He came off a little too pushy for me, like he wanted me to make a rash decision right now. I'm always suspicious when people don't want to give you a chance to think things over."

"You should always trust your instincts, LaVern. He probably came off that way because he is inexperienced. He's just a guppy. Now, that older brother he's sitting next to, he's the real Whale."

LaVern squinted in the direction of the shadows.

"He represents a bunch of top-notch performers." Freda paused. "Have you ever watched those nature documentaries where the mother cheetah captures a baby gazelle but doesn't kill it?"

"Yes," answered LaVern, not sure where this was going.

"She doesn't kill it because she is trying to train her cubs to hunt. She lets the fawn go and her cubs learn to chase and capture. That's basically what the momma cheetah, seated up there, did for the young cub. You're not big enough prey for him so he let his cub practice on you."

"What?" gasped LaVern. "You mean he didn't really want to sign me? I was just practice?"

"No LaVern, he would sign you in a heartbeat. But he's got to get his first kill some time. None of these veteran actors want to risk signing with such a young inexperienced agent. They make too many mistakes. As far as I know, he still hasn't made his first kill."

LaVern was the recipient of yet another sip from the deep pitcher of wisdom belonging to Freda Parks.

"All right. Break time is over," boomed Richard Hoffman. "Back to work. Let's pick it up at Act I, scene three."

After two months of rehearsal, "The Apple Tree" was ready for the public. LaVern joyfully notified her parents that this time, "I get to act."

On opening night, The Pack were seated front and center, as usual. The theater was filled to capacity and scores had to be turned away. Freeman eagerly bought playbills for everyone and flipped through his until he saw it.

Ella…….LaVern Whitaker

Not the ambiguous "Bar Patron " like before. Freeman decided right then he would save every playbill from every play LaVern was in, as a tribute to his daughter's blossoming career.

After the final curtain, J.C. secured a taxi for LaVern's troupe, and they met Freda for dinner. No obligatory opening night festivities this time. LaVern could simply choose not to go, and she didn't. She told everyone how influential Freda had been since they became roommates and explained how her valuable insight and advice had provided her with an entirely different kind of education, a post NYCPA theatrical education. Freda and Shaundra became instant friends. Their personalities were polar opposites, but they talked like they had been friends for years. Everyone was thrilled that LaVern had such a quality influence like Freda in her life.

"The Apple Tree" received good reviews and LaVern even got a mention as a "breath of fresh air" on Broadway. The production ran six days and seven performances a week for over a year. She had a steady paycheck for the first time since leaving school, but she felt bad for Freda. In her role as understudy to the supporting actress, she never got a chance to get on stage. But their friendship deepened. In that years' time, LaVern became more seasoned as an actress and Darien Cheek continued to make his presence known. He would appear backstage at the occasional performance just as a reminder that she still needed an agent, and he was still available. She and Freda had a conversation one morning.

"I hear young Darien is keeping in contact."

"Yes, every so often. Why do you ask?"

She didn't answer right away. Freda, still in her pajamas and slippers, moseyed over to the small wooden table in their kitchen area and took a seat. She motioned LaVern to join her. Freda took a sip of her favorite drink, sprite and cranberry juice spritzer, then looked right at LaVern.

"I'm going to throw something out there and you can make up your own mind about what you want to do with it."

"Okay" replied LaVern, who started to feel apprehensive.

"You have been a regular working actor for a year. When you're part of a production that has run for this long, it's inevitable that directors and producers know your name. Plays don't last forever. If you don't want to subject yourself to those painful and depressing open casting calls, you will need an agent to pitch you for certain roles."

"I've been giving some thought to that lately. What about your agent?"

"Cherrie is strictly west coast. She's very successful out there and doesn't feel the need to come east."

"Oh."

"I was thinking more along the lines of Darien."

"Oh really. Why him?"

"True, he's short on experience, but a lot of agents in his situation make up for it with effort. They really stretch themselves for their clients because, until they make a name for themselves, effort is all they have going for them."

LaVern listened with more interest.

"If you think about it, you two are in similar situations. You're both trying to survive in this business, and each of you needs a break. Sharing in the struggle could develop into a longtime trusting business relationship."

Freda paused to take visual stock of the effectiveness of her talk. LaVern was deep in thought, mulling over everything said to her, and Freda was ready to give her all the time she needed.

Finally, her protege had a question.

"How well do you know him, Freda?"

"I have never even talked with him."

LaVern found this a little disconcerting, and her expression betrayed it.

"But, I am familiar with the G&G group. They don't hire slackers. They hire people who are highly motivated. The bottom line is, sooner or later you'll need an agent because they cut through all the red tape for you."

There was another long, silent, pensive pause.

"I place a lot of importance on knowing people on a personal level, Freda. And I don't know him well enough."

Freda came with a shocker. "Get to know him."

"What do you mean by that?"

"Simple, if you want to know Darien the person, ask him to dinner."

"What! I don't like that, Freda. I have never asked a man out to dinner."

"A business dinner, LaVern. It's done all the time in this industry. You ask him to a business dinner, and you pose all the questions you want. You can gauge his responses by his facial expression and his body language and go with what your gut tells you. In any case, you'll know him better than you do now, for better or worse."

It was sound advice, even if, on the surface, it seemed a little wonky. She rose from the table and meandered, spritzer in hand, over to the sofa to bask in the warm sunlight coming through the window. LaVern remained at the table, immersed in her thoughts. *How do I do this?* she wondered. *Just call a man up and ask him out? Just like that? I do need to know more about him, though. I simply can't trust a stranger.* LaVern cast a curious eye over to the relaxed and composed Freda. She was calmly sipping from her glass, seemingly oblivious to the emotional torment LaVern was going through only feet away.

Without looking up, Freda said, "It's just business, LaVern. Don't turn it into a major undertaking."

Agents of Change
Chapter Five

LaVern met Darien for lunch two days later. Lunch seemed less forward. The Villagio was a small, intimate neighborhood eatery and the owners, a Persian husband and wife team, knew her well. She arrived early and was seated at a table when Darien came through the glass doors. He paused for a second to find her. LaVern waved her hand and signaled him over.

"Nice to see you again, Miss Whitaker." He reached across the table and offered his hand. LaVern shook it and used her other hand to urge him to sit down.

"Nice to see you too, Mr. Cheek. I hope you're hungry, this place has a very nice lunch menu."

"That's good. I've been on the go all morning."

They settled into some small talk and placed their orders before getting down to the business at hand.

"I have lots of questions I need to ask you Mr. Cheek, but before I begin, I want you to know something."

Darien didn't verbally respond. He locked eyes with LaVern, clasped his hands in front of him on top of the table and nodded his head in anticipation of what was to come.

"What I insist on first and foremost, Mr. Cheek, is honesty. I'm going to ask you some questions and if I feel that you are being disingenuous, I promise you, I will get up and walk out."

"Understood, Miss Whitaker."

Just then, LaVern's Caesar Salad and Darien's Tah Dig arrived. LaVern waited for the waitress to depart.

"If I am to put my career in someone's hands, I need to be able to trust that person implicitly."

"I agree, Miss Whitaker. I wouldn't want it any other way."

"Good. Tell me about yourself."

Darien wasn't expecting that question. This was the first time a prospective client asked him to talk about himself. He explained he was married to his high school sweetheart, Erika, and they had two children, Darien, Jr. and Olivia. They've been married for six years. He's been with G&G for a year and was a graduate of Howard University with a degree in business. The older gentleman she saw him with during rehearsals was his mentor, Oscar, who was helping to break him into the business.

"I decided to try becoming a talent agent because I like being around creative people. Artists start with a bare slate, a sculptor begins with a slab of marble, a painter begins with a blank canvas, a writer begins with an idea. And by the time they've applied their artistry and ingenuity, they have, seemingly out of thin air, created this amazing work of art. You, Miss Whitaker, are an artist. You bring words on a page to life, just like that sculptor working with a slab of marble." Darien feared that he had gotten carried away. "I'm sorry, I talked too much. Ask me your questions."

No need to be sorry. That sounded pretty honest to me.

"As my agent, what will you do for me?"

He explained that agents negotiated salaries, pitched their clients for roles, scheduled auditions, followed up on any submissions and many other things.

"Can I ask you something personal, Miss Whitaker?"

"Go ahead."

"How much are they paying you for this role?"

LaVern hesitated, unsure if she wanted to disclose such personal information.

"It won't go beyond this table, trust me."

"I'm being paid $950 a week, why?"

"I could have gotten you $1,500 a week. You didn't realize how badly they wanted you for the part of "Ella".

An astonished LaVern hid her surprise.

"That's a major part of what I would do for you, make sure you get paid what you are worth."

"How many other clients do you have?"

At this point, Darien lowered his head, as if he were deep in thought. When his head lifted, he looked directly into LaVern's eyes. "You wanted honesty Miss Whitaker, and I will be honest. I have none...zero."

LaVern already knew that, thanks to Freda. This was a tactic learned from her father. To gauge someone's degree of honesty, ask questions you already know the answer to.

Darien continued.

"Nobody wants to take a chance on an unknown, untested agent. The agency hasn't put any pressure on me but it's common sense that sooner or later, I have to produce. Oscar is a patient guy, but like I said, I need to prove myself in this business."

"What would you do if they dropped you?"

"I would use my degree to start my own business, but I really love what I'm doing now, as frustrating as it is. That's the whole truth Miss Whitaker. I don't want you to feel sorry for me, I'm a survivor. I'll just be successful at something else rather than the thing I want the most. I won't leave this business before giving it everything I have." Darien paused to gather his thoughts. "I want you to know that I would be a tireless advocate for you, Miss Whitaker. I don't give up easily. That's not my nature. I have seen you perform, and I really believe in you and your talent. Whoever gets to represent you would be getting a future star."

Darien sat back in his chair, emotionally exhausted. He had never laid bare his feelings like this, and he was now at the mercy of whatever decision LaVern made. At the conclusion of lunch, LaVern thanked him for his time and started to reach into her purse.

"I'll take care of the check, Miss Whitaker. Whenever we meet, it's always business."

LaVern stood and thanked him for taking care of the tab. She didn't betray her ultimate decision. As she left the restaurant however, she was convinced that she now had an agent.

The run for "The Apple Tree" lasted fourteen months. After the last performance, Richard Hoffman convened the cast and thanked them for their hard work and declared the play a success. It was a financial success as far as LaVern was concerned too. The long run ballooned her savings, and she was sure more work was right around the corner.

New York wasn't working out for Freda. She was getting restless. One morning her agent called. LaVern had a feeling of foreboding, as it turned out, for good reason.

"That was Cherrie. I need to get back to L.A. quickly. I'm up for a part in an upcoming movie."

"When do you have to leave?"

"Tomorrow morning."

LaVern felt like crying. They had become so close in the past year and a half. Now she'll be gone by the morning. It was happening too fast.

"I'm sorry, LaVern. But this business is so crazy. You never know which door will be *the one*, you know? You have to open all of them when the time comes."

Tears were coming down LaVern's cheeks now, but she knew she was right.

"Freda. You would be a fool to blow this chance."

"I'm going to miss you so much, LaVern."

She reached her arms out and they hugged…and hugged…and hugged.

Freda pulled away and said, "Tell you what roomie, why don't I cook you a special dinner to remember me by."

With blurry eyes LaVern managed a weak nod.

That night, Freda prepared a spectacular stripped beef with red peppers and rice dish and the women reminisced about their time together. LaVern thanked her for all the valuable life lessons. Freda made her promise to keep working hard because she had what it took. They stayed up late, trying to make the most of their last moments together. By the next morning, she was gone and LaVern was once again the lone occupant of her apartment. Freda covered her portion of the rent for an additional three months. LaVern didn't find out until later that day when she was straightening up. Tucked under her pillow was a pink envelope with a smiley face drawn on it. It read,

"We will see each other again."

Several failed auditions followed. She and Darien were a team, she was LaVern now, not Miss Whitaker, so the disappointments were a blow for both. But he remained upbeat.

"That's okay, we'll move on to the next one," he said.

Four months later, he came through as promised. LaVern won a key role in another off, off-Broadway production. The play ran for ten months and LaVern's salary, thanks to Darien, increased to $1,700.00 a week. After that run came another play, another salary increase and a move to a better apartment. No more treks up three flights of stairs with groceries or shopping bags. Her new place actually had a separate bedroom. She was working regularly and had achieved a measure of notoriety in the industry but was growing dissatisfied. It had been four years since she left NYCPA and even though the steady money was life sustaining, she was eager for more challenges in the bigger venues.

Darien knows Broadway is my goal, but no matter how much I want it, those decisions are out of my hands. I can't worry about things I can't control. Just be glad you're working, girl.

LaVern's new frame of mind comforted her, she was at peace, and she began singing to herself around the apartment. Darien did what good agents do. For two years he kept LaVern working, albeit in off, off, Broadway productions until he eventually landed an audition for her in an off-Broadway play. Two years ago, this bit of news would have been cause for celebration, but this new, liberated LaVern Whitaker simply proceeded to knock their socks off with her singing and reading and when she was done, she thanked them and headed home. Three days later Darien notified her that she got the part.

"Really?" she said. "That's pretty cool."

Darien was mystified by her low-key reaction. "Pretty cool? Is that all you have to say LaVern, pretty cool? You've made it to off Broadway!"

"I apologize Darien, I didn't mean to sound so blasé."

He was right, she reasoned. *Why shouldn't I take the time to enjoy this moment? I earned it. And it is a kind of milestone in my career.* She marked her milestone event alone at home; by opening a bottle of wine someone had gifted her the previous Christmas.

Opening night was sold out for "The Revolt" and Darien, his wife Ericka and the Pack were in attendance. LaVern sang and danced, and her performance was magnificent.

Afterwards, Darien treated everyone to dinner at Ellen's Stardust Diner, home of the singing waitstaff. The reviews were overwhelmingly positive, and the producers were convinced the play was in for a long run. LaVern was, once again, singled out, this time in a supporting role. Terms like "refreshing" and a "star on the rise" were used to describe her. Through Darien, she began getting requests for print and television interviews. Instead of being able to leave anonymously after every performance as was her custom, she now had to stop and sign autographs. LaVern couldn't make sense of it all. It was just a month ago that nobody wanted her autograph, no one noticed her.

"The Revolt" ran for two years and LaVern gained an ever-widening reputation as an accomplished Broadway performer, respected and admired by her peers. Her name still wasn't well known to the public outside of New York, but she was definitely a Broadway insider.

She was between plays and relaxing in her apartment with a book of short stories by Black authors called "Black Noir" when her call waiting tone beeped. She let it go to voicemail.

"Hello LaVern, this is Lori Burkhardt. I know it's been a minute, and you're probably rocked to hear from me. I contacted your agent to get this number. When you get the chance, please call me. I'm looking forward to hearing from you."

Lori Burkhardt! After all these years. She returned the call immediately.

"LaVern, it's so good to hear your voice."

"Lori, I can't tell you how great it is to hear from you. What a pleasant surprise!"

"I know it must have been a major stunner. I was hoping you were sitting down."

"It was a shock, but a good one. I haven't seen you since graduation day."

"Who thought six years would go by that fast?"

"So, tell me roomie, what have you been up to since NYCPA?"

"I'm glad you asked, LaVern. I live in L.A. now and, believe it or not, I'm a screenwriter."

"Whaaaat! Really? That's so great!"

"I hear you're doing very well there in New York. I'm proud of you. You were always so talented."

"Thanks, but tell me Lori, are you married? Do you have any kids? Bring me up to date."

"I'd like to LaVern, but right now I'm in a room full of movie execs and they're all waiting for me to end this call."

"Oh, I'm sorry, I didn't know. I can always call you later."

"Don't you dare hang up. Your callback was perfect timing."

"O…kay…" she said haltingly.

"Let me get to the point of my call. You remember my school play 'Juris Doctor in the House', right?"

"Of course I do."

"I wrote a screen version, and I pitched it to Lion studios and they agreed to produce it."

LaVern remained silent, she didn't know where this conversation was headed.

"I had only one absolutely non-negotiable requirement. And that was that you play the lead."

There was still nothing coming from LaVern's end of the line.

"LaVern… are you still there?"

After her foggy mind cleared, she responded. "Let me get this straight, Lori. You are bringing 'Juris' to the screen, and you want me to play the lead?"

"That's it in a nutshell. What do you say?"

More silence from LaVern's end. "I'm sorry for all the long pauses, but… are you serious?"

"Absolutely. Right now, all I need is a verbal commitment, because this room is waiting to hear you say yes or no."

LaVern fought to get her thoughts straight. *What just happened? I was sitting here minding my business, I returned a call from an old friend and now a room full of movie executives are waiting for me to decide if I want to star in their film.*

"This is incredible, Lori. My answer is yes."

"You will not regret this, LaVern. I'll give you a call later this evening to share the details. Welcome to Hollywood my friend."

The follow-up call ironed out all the details; a private plane to L.A. for the next day, Darien included, a private audition for the studio, two rooms at The Hills, an A list hotel, and a rental.

LaVern called The Pack to share the good news. After getting over the initial shock, Freeman and Jackie told her how proud they were of her and made her promise to divulge all the details as soon as she could. Shaundra was more geeked than normal.

"Hollywood, Peaches! You're going to Hollywood? Oh. My. God! I can't believe this!"

LaVern heard crying and weeping, but no words. Shaundra's emotions took over.

"I'm sorry, Peaches. I just can't handle this. I'm a mess. I told you," she blubbered, "I told you that you would be a star!" She returned to uncontrolled, convulsive wailing.

"Well, pull yourself together long enough to hear this. I'm going out there and knock them right on their asses."

"Damn right Peaches, that's what's up!"

Chapter Six
The West Coast

Lion Studios was not a major player in the movie making industry. They were known for their independent films, but many had gone on to earn critical acclaim, millions of dollars and serve as a launchpad to fame for many unknown actors. Neither LaVern nor Darien could believe how fast things had changed. Yesterday, LaVern was waiting on her next Broadway gig, and today, they were flying toward what could be a career altering meeting 2,500 miles away.

"Tell me again how you know Lori Burkhardt."

"We were roommates back at NYCPA."

"And you haven't seen or talked to each other in six years?"

"That's right. We became very close, but we went our separate ways after graduation. Her call was totally out of the blue."

"She must hold you in pretty high regard to think of you for this part after all these years. This could change your life forever. You know that don't you?"

"Believe me Darien, I know what's at stake here."

Much of the rest of the flight was spent in contemplative silence. The enormity of what was ahead was without a doubt weighing heavily on both their minds. When they landed at LAX, their plane was taxied to Signature LAX, a terminal for private planes. Lori was there to greet them. As soon as their eyes met, they rushed toward one another and embraced like long lost relatives. Both ladies began to cry and rub the tears out of one another's eyes.

"LaVern, you don't know how happy I am to see you again. You're still so beautiful."

"Oh, stop it Lori. I'm so proud of *you*. I'm not surprised you've become such a success." LaVern realized Darien was just standing there, patiently observing.

"Oh…I'm sorry, Darien. Forgive me." LaVern guided him closer. "Lori, this is my agent Darien Cheek. Darien, this is Lori Burkhardt, the reason we're here in L.A."

"Glad to meet you, Lori." Darien extended his hand. "LaVern has told me so much about you."

Lori shook his hand firmly. "Glad to meet you too, Darien." She glanced around. "Come on folks, let's get away from this airport and get you to your rooms."

The trio walked through the terminal unnoticed. The paparazzi gave them a momentary glance, then resumed their search for the more recognizable and lucrative prey. They ducked into their waiting limo and talked while their luggage was being loaded.

"Your audition is scheduled for tomorrow at Lion Studios at 11AM. I'll have both of you picked up around 10:30." Lori paused. "There are no other actresses auditioning for this part, LaVern. It's yours. But you still have to earn it. These studio execs don't know you like I do. They have to be convinced."

"I'll be ready, Lori."

Lori smiled. She knew she would be.

After getting settled in their rooms, Darien suggested they get something to eat and do some serious talking about the next day. They went downstairs to the hotel restaurant.

"How do you feel, LaVern?"

"Like I'm going to another audition. I've done this a few times, you know."

Darien was surprised at how at ease she seemed. "You know this is not just another audition, right?"

"Darien, no one will be more disappointed than me if I don't get this role. All I can do is go in there and show them I'm the right actress for the part. Everything else is out of my hands."

Darien knew she was right, but the stars may never align like this again.

"I'm glad to see you're taking all this in stride."

"If it makes you feel better Darien, I am somewhat nervous. My father always said, 'It's okay to be nervous, just be prepared.' And I've been preparing for this moment all my life. Now, let's order."

The following morning Darien and LaVern were waiting in the lobby when their limo arrived. The twenty-minute ride to the studio was made mostly in silence. Darien uttered only one sentence.

"Bring your "A" game today, LaVern."

She did not respond. When the limo arrived at Lion Studios it turned out not to be a studio at all. Not in the classic "back lot" sense. They were taken to a glass and concrete encased, twelve story office building in downtown Los Angeles. Lori was already in the lobby.

"We're on the twelfth floor. That's where we'll hold your audition."

LaVern and Darien followed her through the sun-lit entryway and onto the elevator. Darien noticed on the panel that Lion Studios occupied the entire twelfth floor. As they emerged, there was a huge, circular, polished wooden desk with the Lions Studios logo, the snarling head of a male lion, front claws framing its face as if it were in mid pounce, staring at them. A secretary looked up from her work.

"Hello Cindy. Our 11am is here."

"Yes, Miss Burkhardt. They're waiting in conference room two."

"Thank you. Follow me guys."

They proceeded through an empty, marble floored lobby flooded with the sunlight from a giant picture window. Then, down a narrow, artificially lit hallway until they reached a closed, wooden door with a tiny viewing window. Lori paused and looked at LaVern.

"Knock them flat on their asses."

LaVern just smiled and took a deep breath. Then, they entered.

At a large rectangular, gleaming wooden table sat several nattily attired White men. The youngest looked to be in his mid-thirties and chubby. The sides of his head were shaved bare, exposing his white scalp, with long, black, wet looking hair combed straight back. The oldest looked sixty-ish, with bifocals, his short gray hair parted on the side and combed across the top. They all stood as Lori's group entered.

"Gentlemen, this is LaVern Whitaker. With her is her agent Darien Cheek. LaVern, Darien, this is the Lion Studios Executive Board."

Lori proceeded to work her way around the ample table, introducing each executive individually, ten in all, including the movie's director, and an actor with whom LaVern would do her scenes. Time was taken for a few pleasantries and some background information then it was down to work. They wanted her to perform a particularly vital and challenging scene. LaVern and her "co-star" studied their lines briefly, then LaVern made an unusual request.

"I'll need some room to do this properly."

The men moved the giant table off to one side of the room and even brought in the few needed props to help facilitate the performance. When the scene was done, there was absolutely no reaction. It was as though they had just watched dust settle on a shelf. They asked LaVern to do a second scene and, again, they watched impassively. They stood, thanked LaVern for her time and said they would be in touch. Lori escorted them out of the room and spoke with them as they waited for the elevator.

"You did great, LaVern. Don't let those stone faces scare you. I'll call you later."

LaVern felt good about her effort, but she and Darien left Lion Studios unsure of their fate.

"LaVern, you brought your A+ game today. I was proud to be the one representing you in there."

"Thanks Darien. I think I did my best too. We'll just have to wait and see if they feel the same way."

When they returned to their hotel, they decided to go to a nearby sidewalk café for lunch.

I know my audition was great. But what if I don't get it? Where should I go from here? I could stay out here. Lori could be a valuable contact. What would that do to Darien and me? He can't operate on both coasts. Should I return to Broadway, to safer, more familiar environs? At least everybody knows me there.

As Lavern's mind was overflowing with pros and cons, their lunch was coming to an end. It had been a little over an hour and a half since they left Lion Studios when her cell went off.

"It's Lori." She glanced momentarily at Darien. "Well, here goes. I'll put it on speaker because I want you to hear it firsthand, be it good or bad."

Darien's eyes became as big as pancakes, but he didn't say a word.

"Hello Lori, I didn't expect to hear from you so soon."

She got right to the point. "LaVern…you got the part. Girl, you bowled a strike!"

Darien leaped out of his chair with his fist raised in the air and screamed, "Yesss!" He punched the air several times and did a little victory dance right there on the sidewalk. LaVern had never seen him this excited.

"Is that Darien screaming in the background?"

"I'm afraid it is Lori. And I'm about to join him."

"Well, you two are going to have a lot to celebrate. They loved you, LaVern. They're certain this movie will be a big hit. They wanted to hold out for a more famous face, someone they considered more bankable but, after what you did in there today, they would have to be brain dead to not see your talent. I couldn't wait to tell you."

"Lori, I can't believe this is happening. I don't know how to thank you."

"You can thank me by showing up for dinner tomorrow night."

"What dinner?"

"Steph Boston and a few of the other execs want to have dinner with you and Darien tomorrow evening to go over the details and talk contract. Can you make it?"

Can I make it? Is a school bus yellow?

"We'll be there even if we have to crawl."

Lori laughed softly. "Fortunately, I'll have you picked up, so you won't have to. But, I won't be there. They don't need the screenwriter when they talk money but call me when it's over."

"I will Lori, I promise. Thank you so much."

"No…thank *you* LaVern. Don't forget to call…bye."

"You did it, LaVern. You did it. I'm so proud of you." Darien's bearded face froze between childlike giddiness and unabashed admiration. "I've got to contact the agency. They're waiting to hear from me like a bunch of expectant fathers. All their clients have been Broadway performers. You will be their first Hollywood connection."

"And I've got to call my parents."

LaVern got through first and she didn't waste words.

"Mom, I got the part. I'm going to make the movie."

"Oh baby… you did? You really got it? That's so wonderful."

LaVern heard her mother sobbing on the other end. She too began to sob. Then LaVern heard yelling.

"Freeman! Freeman! Our baby is going to be in the movies!"

Freeman's slippered feet thumped their way through the house to the phone. "Peaches, what's going on? Your mother is crying and shaking."

"Daddy, they loved my audition, and we're going to talk money and a contract tomorrow."

"Oh my God sweetheart, that's awesome news!"

"Daddy, I can't hang on too long. Darien and I have to go over some things before the meeting tomorrow."

"Of course, Peaches. We're so very proud of you!"

"Thank you, Daddy. I'll call you soon. Bye."

When his call ended, Darien's demeanor took on a more serious tone. "We should head to my room, LaVern. They'll call me back in a little while and then you and I will go over some things so we can go into this meeting prepared."

"Sounds good to me. I have to call Shaundra anyway."

As always, it was two rings and a pickup. "Peaches, I know this is about that audition. You got it didn't you?"

LaVern was taken aback by her calmness. "How did you know?

"I've known since high school you would be a star. You think I was saying that all these years just to hear myself talk?"

She was right. She *had* been saying that her whole life, but movies always seemed like some distant, misty vision. How can anyone grab a handful of mist?

"Well, you're right Shaundra. I got the part, and we talk contract tomorrow. I don't know how you can stay so together. Darien and my mother lost it."

"I guess it's like planting an acorn, Peaches. You don't know exactly when you'll get an oak tree, but when you do, you're not surprised. I saw you as an oak a long time ago."

Where did that come from? That was beautiful.

LaVern dabbed her moist eyes. "I have to go now, I'll call you soon. Thank you Shaundra."

"I'm so happy for you Peaches. Bye."

Darien spent over an hour on the phone with Galloway and Green. The entire time, he was jotting down notes, asking questions and winking at LaVern. She felt confident because Darien always believed in being prepared.

"OK LaVern, here's what we have. Despite this being new territory for us, we do have a couple of key leverage points." He explained that Galloway and Green made some calls and found that Lion Studios really wanted her for this role. And they were absolutely convinced they had a hit on their hands and may consider a two-movie deal."

"You're kidding!" LaVern was flabbergasted.

It benefited her that she had Lori on the inside, Darien said. If things bog down, she may be the grease that keeps the gears from grinding to a halt.

"If they offer a two-movie deal, we're going to turn it down."

LaVern was astonished. "Why!?"

"This is a bit of a gamble on our part. If this first movie is as big as expected, we can ask for more money next time rather than being locked into an agreed upon salary. Of course, I'll do whatever you want, but I think waiting is the better option. And another thing, the first offer is always their lowest. We're going to reject that right away."

Darien went on like this for quite some time. LaVern was impressed. As far as she was concerned, all was ready.

The next evening their limo showed up right on time. They went over some last-minute details on the ride over. Upon entering the La Brea restaurant, they were immediately escorted to a large, secluded table where five execs sat waiting, drinks in hand. Re-introductions were made, and appetizers were ordered. There was the obligatory small talk before the exec Lori identified as Steph Boston got things going.

"Lori fought uncharacteristically hard for you to get this role. We had several other better-known actresses in mind, but she was absolutely convinced you were the best candidate."

Darien was ready for this ploy, and he adroitly addressed it. "I'm sure, Mr. Boston, neither you nor your esteemed colleagues would settle for anything less than the best for any production your studio decided to undertake."

The negotiating games went back and forth all night. Their initial offer was $350,000.00. LaVern almost choked on a crouton. As they previously agreed, Darien rejected this. He eventually settled on an out-front salary of $750,000. There was much consternation and disagreement around this figure, but it was ultimately agreed to. The execs also brought up the possibility of a sequel and would they consider signing a two-picture deal? They were surprised when Darien turned them down.

"That's another guaranteed 750 grand even if the movie bombs!" they declared.

Darien offered a polite no. The group discussed LaVern's pre-release publicity obligations and, after two hours, a contract was agreed to. Darien informed them he had to forward a copy to the legal department at Galloway and Green before LaVern would sign it. LaVern and Darien were to be flown back to New York, and she would be notified when shooting would begin. The first installment of her salary would be in her bank account within a week after she signed. At the end of the evening, a toast was made to what was hoped to be a mutually beneficial relationship. On the limo ride back to the hotel, LaVern couldn't help but gush about how well Darien handled things.

"You were magnificent! I didn't have to open my mouth one time. You did exactly what you said you were going to do. I'm so lucky to have you representing me."

He sat quietly for a moment and stared out at the passing, night-time scenery. He knew how much depended on his performance. His mind replayed the events of the evening. "It means a lot to me to hear you say that."

LaVern leaned over and gave her agent a friendly, grateful peck on the cheek.

When she got back to her room, she changed into her nightclothes, turned on the TV and snuggled under the elegant, oversized, eucalyptus comforter.

What a day! It's actually going to happen. I'm going to make a movie. And they're giving me $750,000.00. All I have to do is sign a piece of paper. There was a time when I was glad to be making $750 a week.

LaVern knew she couldn't possibly get any sleep. Her system was still wound too tight. She called Lori.

"I was wondering when you were going to call. I've been waiting up all evening."

"I'm sorry, Lori. I didn't want to call this late, but I couldn't sleep."

"Are you kidding? It's only 11 pm. Remember, this is L.A."

"In that case, let me tell you how it went." She explained all the details, all the conversations, all the money, everything. She ended up by saying they agreed to a deal, pending approval of G&G's legal department.

"Are you satisfied with the money, LaVern?"

"Satisfied? Are you serious? That's more money than I ever dreamed of making."

"I'm glad to hear that. This business can be very predatory and unforgiving. You have to work your way through the minefield very carefully."

"Darien did a great job. I was proud of him."

"That's great. So, when can we get together and have a glass of wine and talk about good 'ol NYCPA? There's nobody out here I can talk to about those days."

"Whenever you like Lori. I am at your disposal."

"How about lunch at my place tomorrow? I'll come get you."

"Sounds like a date."

"I'll see you at one."

Lori had a spacious, modern home in Santa Monica, on a

quiet street lined with soaring palm trees. She parked her white BMW two-seater convertible on the pad outside of her garage. After LaVern emerged, she gazed at the impressive single-story structure. Her ex-roommate was obviously doing very well.

"Don't just stand there. Come inside where we can relax."

LaVern followed her into the house. It was splendid; ultra-modern, laminated wood floors, original artwork on pastel colored walls.

"This is a really nice house, Lori."

"Don't be too impressed. In my business, this is considered low-income housing. Head out onto the patio. Lunch is ready."

In short order, the two women were sitting in the shade on Lori's beautiful flagstone surfaced patio with a warm breeze wafting past them. Between bites of her Chef salad, LaVern was brought up to date on Lori's life; she's not married, she came out here right after graduation, she dated only periodically because she stayed too busy.

"In fact, I've already started work on my next screenplay."

LaVern shared stories about working in New York and what she was doing when she got Lori's phone call.

"I want you to know I heard about how hard you fought to get me this role. I really appreciate you going the extra mile for me. I'll never forget it."

Lori placed her fork down beside her plate and her demeanor visibly changed. She spoke in a solemn voice.

"You know, LaVern, there's something I've been waiting six years to say to you, and this is my first opportunity."

"What's that, Lori?"

She shifted nervously in her padded chair. "Remember back at NYCPA, that day in the dorm when I told you about my play?"

"Yes, I remember very well."

"If it wasn't for you encouraging me and insisting that I show it to Mr. Coombs, I would never have done it. You kept telling me how good it was." Lori was getting emotional now and she grabbed a napkin and dabbed one eye. "At the end of the year, when my play was performed, I told you I would never forget what you did. And I meant that. When the opportunity to bring my play to the screen arose, I decided right then, if they wanted my screenplay, it had to have you as the lead. My fighting for you now was my way of not forgetting what you did for me back then. Neither of us would be sitting here if it wasn't for you."

LaVern was shocked to hear that what in her mind was such an unremarkable thing, done years ago, had such powerful ramifications.

"Oh my God, Lori," exclaimed LaVern. "I didn't know—"

"I know you didn't. That's why I had to tell you. You're responsible for who I am and where I am today and where I will be in the future. Thank you so much, my friend."

LaVern covered her mouth with her hand in disbelief. *What am I supposed to say after something like that?* she thought. She stood and reached out and they collapsed into one another's arms, one big, sobbing mess. By the end of their lunch, LaVern and Lori had established a whole new level of love and trust and understanding.

When she pulled up to LaVern's hotel, both women shared one last hug.

"You're leaving the day after tomorrow and you're going to need this." Lori ducked into her car and came out with a thick, leather-bound text. The cover read "Juris Doctor in the House".

"This is your script. There's been some updating quite naturally, but it's essentially the same story." She handed it to LaVern.

"Thank you, Lori. Thank you for everything."

Lori made one last statement. "LaVern," she said, "this movie will make you a star."

LaVern smiled shyly but didn't answer. Lori placed her hands on her shoulders and looked straight into her eyes.

"No, no, listen to me, LaVern. This movie...will make you...a star!"

Back in New York, the G&G legal department OK'd the contract. After an initial deposit of $150,000.00, LaVern would have $75,000.00 deposited every two weeks. This was more money than she knew what to do with. She decided to leave New York and head to Baltimore because she now had a more compelling reason for returning home.

"Mom, Dad" announced LaVern, "I've decided to buy a house out in the county so I can be closer to you guys. The housing market here is so much cheaper."

"She's got a point, Freeman," added Jackie. "Besides, I like the idea of Peaches being closer to us."

"Just be careful when you deal with these real estate people," warned Freeman. "You don't want to use up every penny you have. Always keep your knot in the bank. You never know what's coming down the road."

Keeping a "knot" was something Freeman had preached to LaVern since she was a child. *"Always make your own money,"* he said. *"Never depend on anybody else to put food in your mouth, clothes on your back or a roof over your head."* She never forgot those words.

"I'm glad you brought that up, Daddy. That's the very reason I want both of you to help me look. I've never bought a house before and who better to keep me out of trouble than you two."

"I'll do what I can," said Freeman, "but even I don't know *all* the tricks these real estate folks can play."

LaVern reached out to Darien and G&G to find a local real estate agent and the following Sunday, The Pack began a house hunting expedition that lasted for several weekends. They began looking in areas where Freeman and Jackie couldn't even dream of searching. The houses began at $400,000.00 and Freeman began to worry that LaVern was needlessly overspending. When they entered one home, Freeman felt he had to slow things down.

"Peaches, do you really need this much room? It's a nice home, but it's just you living here. You're spending more than you need to."

"Yes," agreed Jackie, "this is a lot of house for just one person."

"But you and Daddy will be spending time here too. I want enough room for you guys and Shaundra too."

Shaundra remained uncharacteristically mute.

"We appreciate that, Peaches, but don't go overboard," warned Freeman.

"I'll keep that in mind. What do you think of it though?"

The Whitakers looked around and peeked into every room and pronounced it so-so.

"I have one other unit you may find more to your liking," chirped the female agent. "It's only a few minutes away."

"Good, let's go," said LaVern.

When they arrived at the next home Jackie couldn't help herself. "Oh, this is beautiful, Peaches."

As they walked inside, the two-story structure became even more appealing. The agent explained all the features and guided them through all the rooms. It had a wood burning fireplace, something Jackie had always wanted. It was constructed of brick and had plaster walls, something Freeman always valued. Along with a beautifully chandeliered dining room, there was an exquisitely appointed living room, four bedrooms, four bathrooms, a sunroom and a quiet den. There were polished, real wood floors and crown molding throughout, and a handsome finished basement, another asset Freeman valued. Then came the single feature that sold everybody. The kitchen. Jackie always talked about having a huge kitchen with an island, plenty of cabinet space and enough room for everyone to sit and eat. The open concept kitchen looked out onto a family room with enough space to relax and watch the big screen television. It had big, natural light providing windows and was, through sliding glass doors, accessible to a grand patio.

"I'll tell you one thing," said Freeman, "if I had the money, this is the place I would get."

"This is so nice, Peaches," said Jackie. "But what do *you* think?"

"I don't know, I'm not sure mom. This isn't exactly what I was looking for," she said sarcastically. "Do you guys really like this house?"

"It looks pretty solid," said Freeman as he knocked on one of the plaster walls. He turned his attention to the agent. "How much are you asking?"

"This goes for 550."

"$550,000.00!" squealed Freeman. "That's a little pricey, Peaches. I think you should find something cheaper.

"But you like it, huh?"

"It's beautiful," observed Jackie, "but I agree with Freeman. That's a lot of money."

LaVern nodded at the agent, and she reached into her logo embroidered coat pocket and drew out a set of keys and handed them to LaVern. She took the keys and reached her hand out to her parents.

"Then, it's yours."

Neither Freeman nor Jackie reacted. LaVern stood there with her arm extended.

"What are you talking about, Peaches?" asked Freeman.

"Mommy, Daddy, it's yours. This house is yours."

"You're too old to play games like that young lady," Freeman admonished.

LaVern shifted her weight from one leg to the other and continued standing there with her arm outstretched, keys dangling, not saying a thing. Her eyes started to fill with tears. The Whitakers fixed their gaze on their daughter. They glanced over to Shaundra, who had a hand covering her mouth and was teary eyed as well. Freeman and Jackie looked back at LaVern. She was nodding her head up and down and fighting back tears. When it finally hit them, Jackie covered her mouth, sat down in the nearest chair and put her head in her hands. Even the stoic Freeman was deeply affected. He placed his thumbs into the corners of his pants pockets, looked down at nothing in particular and began to weep.

"Is somebody going to take these keys," LaVern shouted. "My arm is getting tired."

Freeman finally looked up and with tears staining his face, reached out for the keys. He put LaVern in a bear hug and squeezed tightly.

"I don't know what to say," he sobbed. Freeman had always been the provider, the protector, the one on whom his family depended. Being the recipient left him speechless.

"You don't have to say anything Daddy, but I do." LaVern walked over to where her mother was still crying. She led her to her father and held both their hands. "Mom and Dad, this was always my plan ever since I watched you work and struggle to put me through the Felder Academy. I promised myself that the minute I made enough money, I would do this. I don't know if I'll ever be in this position again, but I want to make sure the two most important people in my life are taken care of. This house is yours, mortgage free."

Freeman, Jackie and LaVern collapsed into a bawling, whimpering mass. Freeman looked over to Shaundra.

"You knew about this, didn't you?"

Shaundra couldn't answer. She simply nodded her head.

"Get over here." Freeman ordered.

The wailing, weeping Pack was now complete. All that was left was to move in.

Moving day was a mixture of sadness and relief. On her final day, her final minutes in her childhood home, LaVern took one last nostalgic look at her bedroom.

My safe haven. It's so tiny. I looked out onto the big, bad, dangerous world from these windows. My "Peaches" is still on the wall. I remember when I showed it to Shaundra for the first time. I remember when Daddy painted this room, simply because I asked him to, and Mama checked on me to make sure I was doing my homework. So many memories.

Shaundra interrupted LaVern's wistful walk down memory lane. She peeked into the room and entered respectfully, being careful not to disturb the scene, as if something precious and fragile might be shattered. LaVern turned to look at her childhood friend. Shaundra spoke in a soft voice, the way people do at a wake.

"Everything is loaded, Peaches. We're all waiting for you."

LaVern took one more glance around the empty room. "OK. I'm ready."

When they exited the front door, Freeman and Jackie were standing amongst the small crowd on the street, going from one person to another, hugging and shaking hands. The Whitakers knew the majority of those gathered wouldn't get the opportunity their daughter had provided for them. They wouldn't get out. So, this was their way of saying goodbye to her too, even though her one and only true friend was standing right beside her.

As LaVern and Shaundra stood atop the stoop, LaVern's eyes met Earl Jackson's, Shaundra's criminal brother. He was across the street, sitting on his family's steps. She hadn't seen him since she left for NYCPA. She once feared looking him in the eye. As their eyes locked briefly, he still looked like the thug she remembered, only older and more worn. When she looked away, it wasn't out of fear, but pity. Street life had not been kind to Earl Jackson. As they descended the marble steps, Earl was silent. He just followed her with his eyes.

"We're proud of you, LaVern," someone shouted. "Don't forget where you came from."

LaVern was her usual uneffusive self. She thanked all those who wished her well and spoke personally to the few she could remember. Gorsuch Avenue, like Felder, like NYCPA, had served its purpose. It was a steppingstone to something better. When the cars pulled away, no one looked back. They followed the moving van toward a life that no one could have imagined just a year ago. The caravan took 83 north past the Beltway to Padonia Road, east to York Road, north through Timonium to Wyndgate Rd. Their new home was halfway down the block on the left.

"This is a long way from East Baltimore," muttered Shaundra as she eyed the manicured lawns and well-maintained homes on their tree-lined street. The procession stopped in front of the house.

"What's that?" exclaimed Freeman.

There were two cars parked in the driveway. Everybody got out and walked over.

"Wait," noticed Freeman. "These cars are brand new."

He and Jackie immediately swerved around to look at LaVern.

"Surprise!"

"Peaches, you've got to stop doing this," said Freeman. "Stop spending all your money on us."

"You and Mom need a new car." She looked at the vehicles they just got out of. "Yours are ten years old."

"Hey, my car runs fine."

"And so does mine, honey," said Jackie.

"I knew you would say that."

"I'm serious, Peaches," said Freeman. "You have to watch out for yourself. You're in a fickle business. You might need this money later."

"You're right Daddy and I will. But let me do this one last thing for you and Mommy, please?"

Freeman turned to look at Shaundra. "I guess you knew about this too, huh?"

"Yes, I did Mr. Whit. And I'm with Peaches, both of you deserve a new ride."

Freeman placed his thumbs in his front pockets in resignation. He looked over at his wife. "You heard what she said right, Jackie? This is the last time."

"Oh, I *heard* her, I don't know if I *believe* her."

"Y'all haven't even checked out the cars yet," urged Shaundra. "Take a look inside."

Freeman and Jackie spent the next several minutes oohing and aahing over their new rides. LaVern bought her father a forest green Range Rover SUV with a luggage rack. He liked that they sat high off the ground, the easier for his long frame to get in and out. Jackie was gifted a black, four door Volvo with tan seats, tinted windows and a sunroof. While they were preoccupied in the driveway, the movers began unloading. When Freeman and Jackie entered their new residence, they immediately realized they now had more house than furniture. The belongings from their modest east Baltimore row house were quickly swallowed up by their spacious new digs.

"We're going to have to fill out this place with some new furniture," Jackie said.

"It does look a little sparse," echoed Freeman.

They both stared at LaVern.

"I don't want you spending another dime on us or this house. You've done enough. I still work and I can still provide." Freeman's working-class pride was seeping out.

"Okay, Daddy. I promise. I'm done."

Jackie was already in love with the kitchen. On Gorsuch Avenue, pots and pans and mixing bowls had to remain out, hogging what precious little counter space there was because the small cabinets were already packed. Not anymore. Big, roomy, soft-close cabinets ringed the entire space. The house sat on a quarter acre lot and the ninth hole of a private golf course abutted the rear of their grounds. Jackie finally had a garden to spend her weekends tending and Freeman was actually looking forward to cutting grass and trimming hedges, even though most of his well-heeled neighbors hired contractors.

Over the next two months, the Whitakers got a feel for the vibe of their new neighborhood. In this upper middle-class environment, where all the residents were white and college educated, a suit was the required uniform instead of a collared shirt with your name on the pocket. Everyone worked out of an office, not a truck or a warehouse. And the silence. It was so quiet at night it was spooky and unnerving. It was like the entire neighborhood had a curfew. It would be an adjustment for all, especially the street educated Shaundra. The Whitakers offered her a room in their new house. How could they not? She was like family, living with them, more on than off, since elementary school.

"You need to get out of that neighborhood too," said Freeman. "But this is not a free ride. You're going to pay us rent, but I want you to think about your future, and put away as much money as you possibly can. If you do that, you can stay here as long as you like."

The rent request was ridiculously low and Shaundra grasped the significance of the gesture. It was his "knot" theory again.

"Thank you, Mr. Whit, I appreciate that."

Over time, the spacious kitchen became the main gathering place. It had all the essentials, good food, lively conversation, and the easily visible big screen television.

One morning, LaVern's cell phone played her familiar ringtone. It was the studio. It was time to go to work. The next day a limo picked her up and whisked her to the airport. A private jet flew her back to L.A. to begin rehearsals. LaVern felt immense pride in that she left her family better off than when she arrived.

Lion's Roar
Chapter Seven

Lion Studios arranged for LaVern to stay in The Hollywood Roosevelt Hotel, a five-star iconic hotel in Beverly Hills. It had been the residence of the Hollywood elite since the silent movie days. The cast rehearsed for two weeks and LaVern was excited and jittery to begin her first day shooting a movie. The set was a beautiful, modern house high in the hills above L.A. overlooking a smog-shrouded downtown skyline. She was amazed at the amount of crew needed. There were small groups everywhere discussing everything, tinkering with the lights or the camera angles or the acoustics or the audio, every minute aspect of shooting the scene came under their intense scrutiny. What was at first exciting and adventurous rapidly transformed into boredom and ennui. The director, Tony Rideout, being sensitive to LaVern's live performance background, recommended she wait in her trailer until it was time for her scene. LaVern spent her time alone, daydreaming and singing to herself. The actor in her scene stopped by and they read lines together. She even took a short nap. She didn't get a knock on her door until 1PM.

"Miss Whitaker," came the voice, "you're wanted on set."

What surprised her was the number of takes and retakes required, and the number of setups and resets. There were dialogue adjustments and close ups and long shots and reaction shots. It was pure drudgery with a few moments of excitement sprinkled in. Her day started at 7AM and the director didn't send everybody home until 7PM. In that time, LaVern only filmed one scene. Ninety percent of her time was spent waiting to go on set.

Is this how it's done? Everyday? On Broadway, once the curtain goes up, you go from start to finish and you're done. This movie making is so dull and monotonous.

After the day's shooting, LaVern returned to her hotel, ordered room service and collapsed on her bed. She had never been so tired after doing so little. The ensuing days offered more of the same. The studio allotted two months for shooting and LaVern wondered how she would make it through. Tomorrow, she decided, I'll bring a book.

Shooting for "Juris Doctor" wrapped a week early and postproduction took a couple of months. Then, the craziness began in earnest. Her publicity schedule was exhausting, Los Angeles, New York, Atlanta, Chicago and San Francisco. Then it would be released to the rest of the country and finally to the streaming services. There were newspaper and magazine interviews, late night talk shows, morning news shows and entertainment programs. Then there was the nonstop air travel, (the studio provided her with a private jet, and a three-person entourage; a makeup artist, a tour manager, and a wardrobe person), the elegant but redundant hotel rooms, never staying anywhere for more than a couple days, and the same mind-numbing interviewer's questions. Lion even added Miami, Houston and Las Vegas to the tour list.

By the time LaVern arrived in New York, the last stop on her promo tour, her name and face were in the public domain. The studio expressed delight with how the tour unfolded. There were already rumblings throughout the industry about this "jewel of a movie", and her exceptional acting debut in it. The national release was only days away and it seemed everyone was pleased. But LaVern needed to rest. She had been going virtually nonstop for a month, and her mental and physical batteries were drained. She returned to L.A., not to the swank Hollywood Roosevelt, but to the solitude and comfort of Lori's house.

"I have the space, and I would love the company," Lori had told her.

The move reminded LaVern of Freda Parks' desire to move into her tiny studio apartment rather than stay in a hotel room that was paid for. Both needed to live in a home.

"Besides," said Lori, "you'll need a refuge, the circus is just getting started."

The ticket sales for the opening weekend were disappointing. The following week sales rose slightly and the following week they jumped tenfold. Numbers kept rising every week until "Juris" racked up an unbelievable twenty million dollars. It only cost Lion Studios eight million to make. Lori, the studio and everybody associated with it were ecstatic. "Juris" was becoming a blockbuster.

LaVern's name was on everyone's lips. Every media outlet in the country wanted an interview. Galloway and Greene hurriedly sent Darien and an assistant out to L.A. to control and capitalize on the exploding media attention. LaVern was caught totally off guard by the suddenness of it all. One day she could go into her favorite supermarket and shop unbothered. The next day she would be shadowed around the very same market by strangers who would point and whisper. In the hair salon, where she was previously only known as LaVern, the stylists and the customers asked if she was LaVern Whitaker the actress. She admitted she was and soon all their attention was focused on her.

"I was sitting in the cineplex with my boyfriend last night," said one stylist as she washed her customer's hair, "and I said to him that that actress looks just like LaVern from the salon. And I was right."

"I loved 'Juris', Miss Whitaker," said a customer.

"Please, just call me LaVern."

"Can I get a selfie before you go?"

"I'd be happy to."

This unexpected attention made LaVern very uncomfortable and self-conscious. She tried carrying on with her life as she did before "Juris" but found it to be impossible. After a particularly harrowing day trying to run errands, LaVern returned to Lori's home exasperated.

"I'm not sure, but I think someone actually followed me back here."

What began as a modest little movie had become a privacy ruining behemoth. By the time "Juris" had run its course, it had grossed over 150 million dollars at the box office. It turned into one of the highest grossing movies of the year, and LaVern was in demand as an actress. Released from her Lion Studio obligations, Darien orchestrated promotional events that elevated LaVern's profile and exposure even more. She began reappearing on all the top-rated nighttime talk shows, she received endorsement deals, and she appeared on magazine covers and in print interviews.

Along with the bright lights came the dark and predatorial side of fame. Social media and the TV tabloids had a field day, giving life to all sorts of misinformation and innuendo. One supermarket rag even suggested she was a member of a cult. After an appearance on a late-night talk show, a handsome, slightly older, well known veteran actor asked her out. She was flattered and happily accepted. After only a few dates, the true reason for his attention became obvious. His career was stalled and LaVern was a publicity lightning rod. Their every move was carefully orchestrated for maximum media exposure. Worse, he was boring and self-centered. She wasted no more of her time and cut him loose. She next dated an actor closer to her age. His main aim was to get her in bed or in front of the paparazzi. He got neither. More attempts at dating were equally disappointing and LaVern quickly became disillusioned with the quality of men in Hollywood. Fame and money did not guarantee integrity or class. The only benefit derived from so many dead-end relationships was that she could now spot trouble a mile away.

While they were enjoying a perfect, Southern California summer day on the patio, Lori looked up from her lunchtime salad. "Well, how does it feel?"

"How does what feel?"

"Stardom. How does it feel to be a star?"

"Lori, I've only made one movie."

"Correction, you've made one *blockbuster* movie, my friend."

"I don't feel like a star. I feel like a specimen…under a microscope. I don't know how people can live like this for years on end."

"They adjust, LaVern. You have to realize that your life will never be the same. You will never be that 'normal' person you once were, no matter how badly you wish it." Lori fed another forkful of Caesar salad into her mouth. She dabbed her lips. "Your name and face are instantly recognizable. And from now on, they always will be." She paused. "This is just the beginning."

That was a sobering thought. It was like getting a life sentence…with perks. LaVern had another problem too. Her finances were dwindling. She hadn't had a check since the Lion Studios money was paid almost a year ago. As if on cue, Darien contacted her to say Lion wanted to talk about a sequel.

"Aren't you glad I didn't lock you in at the initial negotiations? I'm going to get you millions."

Exactly how glad soon became evident. The deal would pay LaVern 20 million dollars plus 3% of the profits. LaVern would get 1 million dollars a month for twenty months. If "Juris II" simply matched its original earnings, LaVern would garner an additional 4.5 million dollars. It was a mind boggling, life altering arrangement. Immediately after signing her contract, Darien made another insightful suggestion.

"LaVern, you're now dealing with sums of money that ordinary people have no idea about. For your own protection, I suggest we seek out a financial professional to look after your funds."

"I trust you Darien. Who do you recommend?"

"Let me meet with Mr. Galloway and I'll get back to you. Meanwhile…," Darien stared right into LaVern's eyes, "welcome to the big leagues. It took a while, but we made it. Congratulations."

"Thank you so much Darien. You told me a long time ago you would always have my back. You have never let me down."

The two longtime associates, now friends, shared a hug. *One of the best decisions I ever made was to give an opportunity to a struggling, untested agent who only wanted a chance. Darien is indispensable.*

The sequel to "Juris" required LaVern to travel to London. It would be her first trip out of the country. Before she left, she received another important phone call. It was from Freda

Parks.

"Oh my god. Freda, is this really you?"

"It's really me. I know it's been a while."

Freda had been so instrumental in her success, and she never got the chance to tell her because she had to leave so suddenly. Freda listened to her sobs on the other end.

"Are you okay, LaVern? I can call later."

"Where are you, Freda? Are you in L.A?

"Yes, I'm just leaving my agent's office."

"I must see you. If you have even a second, I've got to see you."

"Well, I'm heading home. You can meet me there."

Freda gave her the address and immediately LaVern jumped into her car and zoomed across town. Her heart was racing faster than her ride. As she walked up the curved pathway, the portal swung open and Freda stood in the open door. LaVern ran toward her, so happy to reunite with her mentor, and the two former roommates hugged.

"Come on inside, it's so good to see you."

The interior of Freda's two-story home spoke of an owner with taste, very well off, but not extravagant. An open foyer revealed a winding staircase, underneath which could be seen swinging, glass pane doors that accessed her large patio. On the right was a sunroom with exercise equipment. On the left, the living room was decorated with expensive, custom upholstered furniture, and original artwork by Black artists mounted on cream-colored walls. This is where they were sitting when LaVern began to sob.

"Is everything okay, LaVern? Are you alright?"

"I apologize for being so emotional, Freda, but you just don't know how much your friendship meant to me back in New York. I finally have the chance to tell you." LaVern talked about how important their daily heart to heart conversations were. "I was just starting out. You taught me about how a working actor approached their craft, the real nuts and bolts of this profession. I received a master's degree in the performing arts through you. Your true love for what you did for a living, I carry that with me today."

Freda handed her a tissue to dry her eyes. LaVern

continued.

"What you gave me was so much more valuable than material things. I owe you so much."

"You give me too much credit, LaVern. I was just doing for you what others did for me. It's really as simple as that." She changed the subject. "How's Shaundra doing?"

"Shaundra is still my best friend. I don't get to see her as much, now that I'm out here. I really miss her."

"Best friends like her are hard to come by. You should keep her close. By the way, I see you *have* been very busy lately. Congratulations. Actors can work a lifetime and never have a movie as big as yours."

"I'm so lucky. That was a play my ex-roommate wrote way back in college, and she held out for me to play the lead when they wanted to make a movie version.

"You sound almost apologetic, LaVern. Don't ever apologize for any success you have in this business. It's not a fair industry, and by the time you beat the odds, if you ever do, believe me, you've earned it."

LaVern reminded Freda that it was her suggestion to give Darien a chance. "It was the best career decision I've ever made. He negotiates all my contracts, and I trust him implicitly."

"I just made a suggestion. You had to make the decision."

LaVern also reminded her of the pink envelope she left under her pillow with three months' rent in it when she had to return to L.A.

"Well, you were kind enough to take me into your place, and I knew you could use the money."

LaVern saw through her deflections. "You can minimize everything all you want, Freda Parks, but the fact remains that no price can be put on what you did for me. I had to rush over to see you because I'm leaving for London in a few days, and I wanted to say these things to you before I left." LaVern began to get teary-eyed again. "I had to let you know what you meant to me."

Freda put her hand in LaVern's hand. "I'm sorry if I made you think what you've said to me wasn't meaningful. It warms my heart to know I've had such a significant effect on your life.

I am truly honored."

Both women sat in silence.

"There is a way that you can repay me, LaVern."

"Anything you want, Freda. But I know it won't be enough."

"The best way to repay me…is to do the same for someone else. That's all I ask."

What a woman, what a selfless person, thought LaVern. *My parents would love her.*

"I promise, Freda. As sure as I'm sitting here. I promise."

Their visit lasted for over an hour. As LaVern got up to leave, the two best friends hugged one last time and LaVern headed back down Freda's well-kept walkway. As she neared her car, something Freda said about Shaundra reverberated in her mind. Keep her close, she said. LaVern vowed to do something about that.

Here I am feeling so grateful for the opportunity to tell Freda how beholding I am for her impact on my life, and Lori was just as eager to do the same when she saw me. Freda and I were merely doing what we thought was right. It's funny how life works.

After four months on location in London, LaVern returned to L.A. When it was released, "Juris II" was a bigger hit than the first. It grossed over 500 million worldwide. With LaVern's negotiated 3%, it meant that she earned an extra 15 million dollars. The sequel shot LaVern to superstardom. Darien had scripts arriving daily, accompanied by salary offers that would choke an elephant. Lion Studios tried desperately to re-sign LaVern but, as Darien so aptly described it, it was time to "test the waters". Lion Execs didn't take the rejection well.

"After all," they said, "we gave you a chance when no one else did."

They were looking out for their own self-interest and G&G knew it. The decision was irreversible.

Even though LaVern's profile was in the stratosphere now, public recognition was still an intimidating factor. Even with wigs, dark sunglasses and frumpy clothing, her highly valued privacy was becoming harder to protect. Fans and paparazzi even discovered she was staying at Lori's house. They would hide behind bushes or inside windowless vans to get exclusive photos that would wind up on social media platforms worldwide. LaVern was fed up. The sustained effort required to maintain her sanity convinced her that moving would be beneficial in another way. Privacy! As she moaned to Lori one day, "Fame is exhausting."

With guidance from the recently hired Winnefree Financial Group, Lori and LaVern engaged a top real estate agent to help find the "appropriate housing". Lori kept pushing the purchase of a mansion.

"But it's only me, Lori. What do I want with all that space?"

"Think of it as an investment, LaVern. These places never lose money. By the time you decide to resell, maybe in a few years, the value will have increased exponentially. You're a star now, you can afford it."

Her statement, "you can afford it" resonated in a strange way. It was the factual nature of it. She actually *could* afford it. It seemed as unreal as walking on the moon. LaVern settled on one in the Hollywood Hills, for a measly 10 million. Best of all, this was a gated community. No more anxiety surrounding who might be hiding in the hedges or who might follow her home. She may have too much house, but it was better than having too little peace of mind. It was time to share this with The Pack.

LaVern would have loved to have seen her Pack's faces when a car and driver pulled up to the house, or when they were escorted to their private jet at BWI airport. Freeman would have balked at the expense, Jackie would have cried at the wonderment of it all and Shaundra would have loved every decadent minute. In L.A., LaVern knew her presence, despite any attempts at disguising herself, would cause a scene at the guarded, private airport entrance. The paparazzi was a permanent fixture there, on constant lookout for celebrities, so she elected like in Baltimore, to send a car and driver.

As they traveled up a winding road to her residence, the driver stopped at an ornately designed iron gate. Everybody in the car gasped in astonishment. Through the bars they spied an ultra-modern mansion. The gate creaked slowly open. The car drove up to the entrance where the entourage emerged and stood frozen before a magnificent, multi-story, stucco and wood structure. The large oaken door opened and a smiling LaVern came into view. Everyone was speechless, except Shaundra.

"Peaches," she screamed, "you live here!?"

"Surprise?" was all LaVern could mutter.

A wide-eyed Jackie said, "You actually live here? My daughter lives in this mansion?"

"Afraid so, Mom."

Freeman, as down to earth as ever, went in another direction.

"Sweetheart, this is an impressive place. But why do you need so much house? It's just you living here, right?"

"First, give me my hugs, then everybody come inside, we'll eat, and I'll tell you everything you want to know."

The Pack embraced for the first time since LaVern left to film "Juris I". When the party entered the marble floored foyer, there were two massive skylights in the sixteen-foot ceiling that coated everyone in sunlight. They were greeted by a smiling, aproned middle-aged female.

"Everyone, this is Alma, my housekeeper. Alma, this is my family. As you know, they'll be staying here for a while."

"Si, claro Senorita Whitaker. Mucho gusto everyone. Your lunch is ready."

LaVern escorted the awestruck Pack through the indoor/outdoor dining area, past a screening room, and into a fabulously equipped, open concept kitchen. While they ate at the granite counter island, Alma reported that the luggage had arrived.

"Gracias, Alma, we'll get it later."

"Si, senorita Whitaker." She walked off to resume her household duties.

"Wow, Peaches," said Shaundra, "private jets, a mansion, maids, this is a long way from Gorsuch Avenue."

"Everything I have, all of you have too. I mean that. As soon as we're done eating, I'll give you a tour."

As they walked, LaVern explained why she bought such a large, pretentious home. Not only was it for the investment value, but it also provided her with the precious privacy she craved. They passed an office, an entertainment area and her immaculate bedroom with a huge walk-in closet. A marble staircase led them to five second floor bedrooms and bathrooms and above that, a rooftop pool area. Sliding glass doors and massive picture windows provided spectacular views of the Hollywood Hills. She told them they were welcome to visit whenever they wished and stay as long as they desired, even when she wasn't here. She would fly them in the same way they flew in today. She disclosed the incredible amounts of money she earned and the movies she was being offered.

"Mom…Dad," she said in a very subdued and somber voice, "I can buy anything I want. I can buy you guys anything you want." She said it like she was embarrassed.

"This is crazy, Peaches," said Shaundra. "Do you realize how crazy this is? You can buy ANYTHING you want?"

Freeman interrupted and stated he was glad his daughter was aligned with a financial institution as sound as The Winnefree Group. "Just because you *can* doesn't mean you *should.* That's the mistake lots of Black folks make when they get their hands on a substantial amount of money. It's not always spend, spend, spend."

As the week went on, Freeman and Jackie got a firsthand look at how turbulent and nuts their daughter's life had become. They were amazed at the amount of preparation required to simply leave the house. In addition to an endless array of disguises, stores provided access after regular hours for her to shop in peace. When she wanted her hair and nails done, they came to her. Alma did her food shopping. Her credit card company assigned her a personal assistant. Once, when they were dining, LaVern's card was declined. *How could someone with millions have their credit card turned down?* everyone thought. She placed a direct call to her account assistant.

"Oh, was that you Miss Whitaker? I thought it was fraudulent. I'll put it right through. I apologize for the inconvenience."

It was yet another window into how life was different for their daughter, now counted among the privileged few.

"That's why I'm glad you guys are here. I need my family around me."

As time dwindled down to their final day, LaVern was saddened by her Pack's imminent departure. Their time together was the best she had spent since she came to California, and she was not eager to be alone again. At breakfast, LaVern probed Shaundra about her future plans.

"What are you going to do when you get back to Baltimore?"

"What do you mean what am I going to do, Peaches? I'm going back to work. Just because I took a vacation doesn't mean the bill collector did."

Everybody laughed except LaVern.

"But you better believe everybody in the store will know about your big mansion because I'm going to show them every single picture I have on my phone…whether they like it or not."

"What if you didn't have to go back?"

Shaundra stopped midway before putting a forkful of homemade blueberry pancakes in her mouth. "What do you mean 'If I didn't have to go back'?"

"Shaundra, how would you like to stay here with me… permanently?"

"What!?" Shaundra dropped her fork onto her plate, creating that high pitched, tinging tone only expensive China can make.

"I want you to stay here with me after my parents leave. When you guys go, I'll be here all by myself again. I have few real friends here, and you've already seen how crazy it gets." LaVern reached across the table and grasped her hand. "I need my best friend."

Shaundra was in shock. As intuitive as she was, she didn't see this coming.

"What about my job?"

"What about it?" countered LaVern as she released her hand.

"I can't just leave."

"Why not?"

"But what am I going to do out here?"

"Anything you want."

"What about my things?"

"We'll get new things."

Shaundra was struggling for rebuttal material, and LaVern went in for the kill.

"Shaundra, we've been apart for most of the past eight years. I want that to end, starting now."

Shaundra peeked over at the Whitakers. "You knew about this didn't you?"

LaVern answered for them. "We've already discussed this and we're in full agreement."

Jackie Whitaker opted in, "We can't speak for you, Shaundra, it's your decision. But we would consider it a huge favor, and we'd feel a lot less apprehensive if you were out here with her. She needs you."

Shaundra stared into her half-eaten plate. She lifted her head and glanced around at the palatial accommodations. Her mind went back to her dysfunctional childhood home on Gorsuch Avenue. "In this place?" she muttered quietly.

"With me. It's not like I don't have the room."

There was nervous laughter from everyone except Shaundra.

"I can't believe this." She shook her head in disbelief.

"It's done then. When the driver drops my parents off at the airport today, you're staying here with me. It'll be like old times again." LaVern glanced around her home. "Well sort of."

Freda said best friends should be kept close. I couldn't agree more.

LaVern and Shaundra began their new lives together on a high note. They went to a car dealership and LaVern bought her a new, sea moss green BMW convertible with a cream-colored interior. They went to LaVern's favorite clothing designer on Rodeo Drive, after store hours of course, and had her fitted for every dress, skirt, and blouse she desired, with matching accessories. Shaundra picked out which bedroom she wanted. She chose the one right next to LaVern with a balcony that overlooked the spacious backyard patio. Then, they went shopping for new bedroom furniture.

LaVern introduced her to all the major players; Darien, Lori, Freda (again), her manager Amy Pennington and her publicist, Melanie Brown. Shaundra was now a part of her team and accompanied her to all her shoots, both in the United States and abroad. And just like on Gorsuch Avenue, Big Dog had no qualms about getting people straight when it came to protecting Peaches. LaVern was right, it was like old times again.

Louiston
Chapter Eight

LaVern had worked nonstop and made five films in four years when Shaundra first noticed it: weariness, a marked decline in energy. *Maybe she was working so much she didn't realize it*, she thought. One evening at home, Shaundra mentioned it to her.

"How are you feeling, Peaches? You been acting like I need to plug you into that USB port over there."

"I feel a little worn down. But I've been tired before. I'll be alright."

"You been going through stop signs ever since I first got here. It's not against the law to take some time off, you know."

"Really? I didn't even realize it had been that long. Maybe I should cut back."

"Yeah, go somewhere off the beaten path where you can relax and enjoy yourself, where you won't be hassled."

"And where exactly would that be?"

"Let me research it, Peaches. It's out there somewhere."

Shaundra's search centered on something specific. *All the "Apple Valleys" and "Sandy Shores" sounded attractive*, she mused, *but why not find a nice, quiet, pleasant-sounding spot with people that look like us? I guarantee no paparazzi hang out there.*

A week later, Shaundra bull rushed into the bedroom like a dog was chasing her, eyes as big as silver dollars, laptop in her hand. She paused momentarily to gather herself, taking deep breaths, like a sprinter at the finish line. She straightened up and made her way slowly over to LaVern sitting on the bed.

"Girrrrl, I found it. I have found IT."

"You found what?"

"That getaway place. It was harder than Chinese arithmetic, but I found it."

"You have? Let me see."

Shaundra sat beside her. On her laptop was a map of the state of South Carolina. Shaundra clicked on the magnifying glass icon and enlarged the image until a small town came into clear view.

"Louiston?" asked a surprised LaVern. "Louiston, South Carolina? I've never heard of it."

"Neither have I, but I did some digging. It was founded by freed slaves in 1870 and it was named after one of the original settlers, Armistead Louis."

LaVern wrinkled her nose. "Who in their right mind would name their child Armistead?"

"Never mind that. It's been an incorporated town since 1900, and relatives of the original freed slaves still live there. It has a population of around 10,000 and it's right on the coast."

LaVern marveled at her research and dedication.

"There's a beach, some farms, a hotel–"

"Whoa, wait," LaVern interrupted, "a hotel…as in just one?"

"Yes, Peaches, there's just one hotel, but there are several BnBs and, according to this information, most vacationers seem to prefer those."

LaVern was not too excited. "What else is there?"

"Well, Miss Persnickety," mocked Shaundra, "it's quiet and peaceful and out of the way just like you want. You'd be hard to find there because it's not a vacation hot spot. You can fish, there's a small marina where you can rent boats, a golf course, local shops and restaurants–"

"Shaundra, neither of us fish or golf, and besides, it sounds too small."

"I think it's worth checking out, Peaches."

LaVern stood up and walked to her bedroom balcony. She looked out onto the Hollywood Hills, and her sizable outdoor barbecuing area with grills and ovens that neither she nor Shaundra knew how to operate. But LaVern didn't see any of this now. She was lost in her thoughts.

I've been going at an exhausting pace. L.A. will drain you dry if you let it. I really do need a break, from this town, from my work. I need to feel normal again.

"OK, Shaundra, let's do it." LaVern walked away from the windows and perched herself onto one of her imported and elaborately embroidered bedroom chairs. She leaned back and propped her manicured feet onto one of the equally expensive companion ottomans. "I'll have to make some calls."

The first call was to her publicist, Melanie.

"It looks like we can't leave for at least another month. Mel's got me booked with interviews, photo shoots and I have to go over some scripts Darien just received. There was more but my mind went blank even though Mel kept talking."

"That's exactly why you need to get away, Peaches. Don't let this business run you into the ground."

A month and a half later, a private jet took off from LAX and after a four-hour non-stop flight, landed at Charleston International Airport. Its only two occupants emerged and descended the air stairs. Other than a few airport baggage handlers pushing empty carts, there were no other people around. A short walk took them to a private reception area. There, a freshly detailed, black Lexus SUV sat gleaming in the late afternoon sun. They thanked the rental company employees, placed their luggage in the back and took possession of their chariot. Shaundra started the engine, engaged the car's GPS, put it in gear and off they went, headed to Louiston.

On this sunny, warm day, the trip took them through fertile farmland, along coastal plains and down two-lane country back roads. They remarked at how beautiful the countryside was.

"It's so green and pretty, and it goes on forever," said Shaundra.

After an hour-long ride, during which they firmed up their fake biographies, they saw the "skyline" of Louiston. The highway deposited them right onto Main Street.

"Ain't it funny," observed Shaundra, "no matter where you go, there's always a Main Street."

It wasn't as small as they had envisioned. There were several office buildings, City Hall, the Police Department, the Armistead Hotel, the municipal bank, and the post office. They rode through the business district which included restaurants,

The Mount Zion Baptist Church, a drug store, the farmers market, a variety of locally owned shops, and who knew what else along the many side streets. The two women swiveled their heads from side to side as they rode, taking in as much as possible. Shaundra listened carefully to the GPS voice as it guided them through the tangle of unfamiliar, residential streets until, finally, they heard it.

"Your destination is on the right."

Ahead they saw a white, two-story clapboard house with a wraparound porch, and a decorative, wooden railing. Twin baby blue shuttered bay windows bookended the front. Flowering plants of every color bordered the length of the porch. The hand painted sign in the front yard read, "The Home Away from Home." As the car pulled up, LaVern noticed what would turn out to be some of their fellow guests lounging in the porch swings and in the many cushioned wicker, fan backed chairs. She turned to Shaundra.

"Well, we're here."

Before they could even exit the car, a nimble youngster burst through the screen door and bound down the steps, his toothy grin leading the way. He bent over and peered into LaVern's window.

"Good afternoon, ladies. We've been expecting you. I'll take your luggage up to your room."

Without another word, he headed for the rear of the vehicle.

"Thank you young man," LaVern yelled through her open window, "that's very nice of you."

Shaundra and LaVern opened their doors and stood looking up at their new home for the next week. As he passed by with a few bags, LaVern reached into her purse and withdrew a ten-dollar bill.

"Here you go young man."

Shaundra did the same.

His face lit up like somebody plugged him into a socket.

"Thank you. I'll have your things in your room in no time."

The teenager raced up the wooden steps and through the screen door. He passed a slim, middle-aged, brown-skinned woman in a white apron, wiping her hands with a red and white striped hand towel. She took her first look at her new arrivals.

She saw two young Black women, both in floppy straw hats with dark sunglasses. They wore decorative muumuus, sandals and carried colorful, canvas beach bags.

"Good evening, ladies. My name is Mary Scales, and I am the proprietress of The Home Away From Home. And you must be Miss James and Miss Davis."

The impromptu rehearsal during the ride from the airport was about to pay its first dividends. They climbed the steps and LaVern reached her hand out.

"Nice to meet you Mrs. Scales. I'm Vicki James."

Shaundra was next. "It's a pleasure to finally meet you Mrs. Scales. I'm Barbara Davis, we spoke on the phone."

Shaundra had chosen the name Barbara Davis because the initials were B.D., as in Big Dog. LaVern used the name of one of her movie characters.

"Nice to meet both of you young ladies. Welcome to Louiston and welcome to The Home Away From Home."

Just then, the teenager came bursting through the screen door, whizzing by both his mother and her two newly arrived guests.

"Slow down Andre! Those bags ain't going nowhere!" Mary Scales looked at Shaundra and LaVern. "Sometimes, fourteen-year-olds have more energy than brains."

LaVern and Shaundra chuckled. Within seconds, Andre made the return trip with the last of the luggage. Mary then introduced LaVern and Shaundra to her other guests, who were scattered all over her spacious porch.

"Come inside ladies and Andre will show you to your rooms. I'll have dinner ready in about an hour."

When they entered the lobby, LaVern and Shaundra were pleasantly surprised. They took off their sunglasses to truly appreciate it. The room was enormous. It occupied almost the entire first level. There were antique Tiffany style lamps and matching polished, mahogany tables, snug and beautifully upholstered sofas and wide back chairs, lovely, expensive area rugs and even a piano in one corner. There was a wood burning, brick fireplace with an exquisitely carved wood mantel, on top of which rested numerous small artifacts symbolic of the local environment; artsy pieces hand carved from driftwood, irregularly shaped glass vessels filled with multicolored sand, and preserved starfish and sand dollars harvested from the ocean bottom. The entire space screamed comfort and home. Andre was coming down the steps when his mother stopped him.

"Andre, can you please show Miss James and Miss Davis to their rooms? Thank you." She didn't wait for a response. Mary Scales turned and headed to her kitchen to put the finishing touches on her homemade wonderments.

"Come this way ladies."

They both watched him as he scampered up the steps, taking two at a time.

"Having that much energy is just plain scary," said Shaundra.

They followed Andre up the wooden stairs, down a short hallway to a closed door.

"This is your room, Miss Davis. And next door is your room, Miss James. They're connected just like my momma told you. These are the most expensive rooms in the house," he proudly proclaimed. "I put everything in here, I hope that's OK."

"Thank you very much, Andre," said LaVern. "You've been very helpful."

Andre walked down the hallway then stopped suddenly and turned around. "Remember, dinner in one hour." He disappeared noisily down the steps.

When Shaundra opened her door, she and LaVern were astonished. The walls were a gentle, eye pleasing color LaVern recognized as sage. The space was roomy and neat and tastefully appointed. There was a gorgeous, canopied bed against one wall with a beautiful, white satin bedspread decorating it. Resting on the floor was a splendid, mosaic oriental rug which in turn lay atop a gleaming, shiny wood floor. There was an antique bureau with a matching side table and lamp. The two windows overlooked the front of the inn and were adorned with delicately laced white curtains which allowed glorious amounts of the summer sun to fill the room. She also had her own bathroom and closet. On the wall opposite the bed was a large flat screen television, and the room smelled heavenly. Mrs. Scales chose a light, airy, pine scent that was a delight for the senses. The women stood motionless and silent for a moment.

"I didn't expect this," said an utterly impressed Shaundra. "What about your room, Peaches? I'm dying to see that."

They used the connecting door to pass into LaVern's quarters. The color scheme was different, the walls were a soothing, blush pink color, the furnishing similar and just as stunning. They looked at one another and smiled an approving smile.

"So far so good," said LaVern.

As she unpacked, LaVern stood in front of the full-length mirror. She removed her floppy hat to reveal her new short, curly-haired, light brown wig. No more straight, shoulder length black hair for a while. The light brown hair matched her new tinted contact lenses. She stared long and hard at the new her. She wasn't particularly pleased, but circumstances demanded change. Shaundra's alterations were more simplistic. She simply wore a straight, long haired black wig that came down to the middle of her back.

"I've always wanted long hair," she crowed.

Dinner was served on the screened-in veranda on the back patio. It was a lovely space. There was Mary Scales' prize flower garden in full bloom just feet away, the expansive, well-manicured lawn, two large shade providing oak trees, and the pleasant tweeting and chirping of the native birds. There was a string of lights inside the enclosure for anyone who wished to stay outside after sunset.

While dining on the deliciousness prepared by Mary Scales, the guests took the opportunity to get acquainted with their newest lodgers. LaVern and Shaundra stuck carefully to their fake backgrounds. They were from Baltimore and were childhood friends. LaVern owned a hair salon and Shaundra managed a retail outlet. The rest of the group was composed of a dentist, a home builder and a married couple from Norfolk, Virginia. After more conversation and homemade lemon meringue pie, the guests slowly drifted away from the table until just LaVern and Shaundra were left. The evening light was waning and a calm wind persisted and threatened to make an enchanting first day even more so. Just before the sun dipped below the horizon, Shaundra and LaVern decided to turn in. When they entered the lobby, Mary Scales was there straightening up.

"I want to compliment you on that magnificent meal, Mrs. Scales. It reminded me of home," said LaVern.

"That's so right," said Shaundra. "Do you make meals like that every night?"

"I sure do. I offer breakfast at 7:30 and lunch at noon. I don't have all my guests here all the time, good food is everywhere in this town."

"Yeah", added Shaundra, "we'll be trying some other places too. But, trust me, we won't be staying away from your kitchen for too long."

As Shaundra and Mary were talking, LaVern took a closer look at the décor of the lobby. She was intrigued.

"You have a lot of nice things in here, Mrs. Scales. They have a time-honored vibe to them. In fact, this whole house has that same traditional feel."

"That's very observant of you, Miss James. All the items in my lobby have a cultural and historical significance to this community."

"Really? Tell me about it."

Mary walked over to a large, ornately framed photograph on the far wall. It was obviously a vintage portrait taken some time in the late 19th century. "This is the only known photograph of the founder of Louiston. His name is Armistead Louis."

"I recognize that picture," said Shaundra. "I read about him."

Mary wandered over to a piece of furniture against the wall. "This buffet belonged to the Green's here in town. It was in their family for over 70 years and recently sat unused and in storage. It was water stained, and time had withered it badly when I asked the family for permission to get it refurbished. Now look at it."

"Oh, my Goodness. It's a beautiful piece of furniture." LaVern went over to examine it more closely. She ran her fingertips slowly over the smooth, finished wood surface.

"You can't tell it was damaged at all."

"I keep my tablecloths, linen and stationery in there now."

She went throughout the lobby, from end tables to lamps to an antique China closet, to other photos, all with the same history of major local significance. Even the piano in the corner was donated by a local family, the Walkers.

"This house and that fireplace over there were all built by Blacks. The buffet that needed refinishing, that work was done by Black craftsmen in and around Louiston. "And," added Mary with a sly smile, "in the midst of all this history and tradition, I have cable, Wi-Fi and central air." She couldn't hide her amusement at the paradoxical nature of it all. Then, she became serious. "I realize that an old house like this is not for everybody, but it's a source of pride and joy for our community."

They were spellbound by Mary's tales of ancestral ingenuity and artistry.

"What you have, Mrs. Scales, are precious heirlooms, a museum," said LaVern. "This lobby is a living record of Louiston's history from the beginning right up until today. I had no idea what a true gem of a place this was."

"I second that," said Shaundra. "I read about Louiston, but I wasn't ready for all this. You and this place are very special."

"Awww, you two are so nice. You make an old…er middle aged woman feel good."

LaVern and Shaundra snickered, bid her goodnight and headed to their rooms.

On their first full day in Louiston, LaVern woke up at 10 o'clock. She heard Shaundra stirring in her adjoining room and entered to see her friend awake but still covered up to her neck in one of Mary Scales' comfy, needlework bedspreads. It was a beautiful, sunny morning.

"Damn," Shaundra exclaimed, "I can't believe how comfortable this bed is. I love this canopy. I want one of these when I grow up."

"It's already 10 o'clock. Let's get going because I really want to explore this town. Besides, aren't you hungry?"

Shaundra flipped back those snuggly soft blankets and sat on the side of the bed. "Give me twenty minutes and I'll be ready."

When they finally descended the staircase, they were in full disguise. LaVern, with her short wig now pulled down like bangs to cover her forehead and Shaundra with her long hair now in a bun. They maintained the dark sunglasses, which were perched on top of their floppy straw hats. Armistead Louis was staring down at a hushed and vacant lobby. They walked through the screen doors and onto the porch.

"Well, good morning."

It was Mary, serenely rocking in one of the porch chairs, reading a magazine with her eyeglasses pushed down on her nose. She peered over the top as she spoke.

"I was wondering when you two would get up. Everybody else is gone already."

"Morning Mrs. Scales" said Shaundra. "Sorry we missed breakfast. That bed of yours is better than a sleeping pill."

"I'm glad you enjoyed it."

"Where can we get a good breakfast?" inquired LaVern.

She rose from her chair and walked to the edge of the porch. "This is Herkimer Street. Just follow it down to the end of the block and go right. Halfway down is Grady Johnson's place. He's still serving breakfast."

"Thank you," said LaVern. "We're going to eat something and then walk around a little."

"There's a lot to appreciate if you pay attention."

"Thanks Mrs. Scales," said Shaundra, "we will."

From Grady Johnson's eatery, the girls began their walking exploration of Louiston. Along the same street was Duhon's drug store, Smitty's shoe repair shop, a dry cleaner and a grassy plaza where both women sat on a park bench and watched the citizens go about their daily business.

"You know," observed LaVern, "the pace of life in the south is so slow and unhurried." A black and yellow butterfly lazily zigzagged its way past. "Even the butterflies seem to take their time."

They returned to the BnB and continued their exploration by car. They parked on an uncluttered Main Street. During their downtown stroll, they discovered all the quaint shops. There was the intimate candle shop where the owner pridefully described her age-old candle making process. Across the street was a charming hat shop where the merchandise was woven out of many of the local, marshy, phragmite grasses, again, a process passed down through the generations. In the next block was an old-fashioned hardware store with creaky, aged wood floors and next door, a florist shop. They sauntered past the Mt. Zion Baptist Church where screaming, playful children were just let out of vacation bible school. Then, there was Cora's Beauty Palace whose slogan was, "We curl up and dye for you." As they moved around, Louiston looked more and more attractive.

"Have you noticed that almost every business in town is Black owned," asked LaVern.

"How could I not?" replied Shaundra. "I love it."

"This is a Black owned and operated municipality that is thriving!" exclaimed LaVern. "How could we not have known about this place?"

After dinner that night, they probed Mary Scales further about the character of Louiston. She was the Niagara Falls of information.

"People here know what a special place this is. We're not trying to hide, but it's OK if we stay off everybody's radar. There's been plenty of interest in the past from a few shady land developers, but nobody here is interested in selling off the land that's been in their family for over a hundred years. We're proud we can take care of ourselves. We own our own businesses, and we run all of our government offices. We have a Black mayor, a Black Police Chief, a Black Fire Chief and a Black City Council President. We have a sprinkling of White folks, and everybody gets along. But it's no question that this is, and always has been, a Black incorporated town. The notion is to be content with being able to provide and live comfortably. No one feels the need to chase money for money's sake. When I got the idea to turn this house into a BnB, I went right down to Cyrus at the Metropolitan Bank, and he gave me the money to get started. I doubt if any other bank would have done that for me."

By the time Mary Scales was through, they knew and appreciated Louiston much more.

During the following week, they availed themselves of all of Louiston's amenities. They went to Carr's Beach and strolled along the boardwalk, where they gave high marks to the native and vacationing male population. They even went sailing and fishing, where they received an education in harvesting lobster, shrimp and oysters from the leather faced, sun beaten, water men. They ventured out into the farmlands where Mary Scales said relatives of the original settlers still proudly worked their land after all these generations. Their calloused hands grew sweet potatoes, rice, cucumbers and raised cattle. Many of these landowners still maintained family cemeteries on their property. They found out that Louiston was located on what was known as Black Island, and that it was a low-lying coastal plain susceptible to storms, hurricanes and floods. They learned there was such a thing as heirs' property, which is land passed down in the family through the years without benefit of a will. Not being golfers, they didn't go near the golf course.

LaVern recounted, *everywhere I go and every person I meet turns into another history lesson.*

After a week, Shaundra and LaVern, regretfully, had to return to L.A. Their time in Louiston was far more enjoyable and satisfying than either envisioned. They were especially proud of the fact that LaVern went unrecognized and there was no sign of the paparazzi. The only reminder of her Hollywood celebrity was the occasional call from Darien or Melanie, annoying her with the fact that the real world awaited her return. Their hardest task was saying goodbye to Mary Scales. She had become more than just a proprietress. She was a confidant and a friend. The three women stood on the front porch and shared one last emotional moment.

"I can't express in words how grateful I am to you for all that you did to make our vacation so memorable," began LaVern. "It was a privilege to stay here."

"Same here Mrs. Scales," said Shaundra. "You made us feel like family."

"You ladies are the type of guests I went into this business for. I really appreciate both of you."

"We plan on coming back next year," stated LaVern. "Can we get the same accommodations?"

"If you make reservations early enough."

"How about right now?"

"For next year?"

"Yes, if it's alright."

"I've never had anybody reserve a room this far ahead of time. It's a long time away, but, if you're sure…"

"Oh, we're sure," blurted out Shaundra. "We'll be back, and we want the same rooms."

"In that case, it's yours. But I'll have to have everything paid for at least by the first of the year. Not that I don't trust you ladies–"

LaVern interrupted. "Give me a second." She took out her phone. There was some hushed conversation. "You have an account at the Metropolitan Bank, right?"

Mary had a confused look on her face. "Yes… why?"

"If you check, you will find our payment in your account."

"What!?" She pulled out her phone. Much to her surprise, there it was, not a week, but a full month's payment. "My Lord," she exclaimed, "that's incredible!"

She stared at both LaVern and Shaundra and absentmindedly scratched her head as if she were trying to solve a riddle. "I really thank you ladies because most vacationers like to stay in places like this and these rooms go fast."

"We won't make that mistake," said Shaundra. "We can't wait to come back."

"Good. Now give me a hug."

They shared an embrace and LaVern and Shaundra got into their SUV, waved at Mary Scales and they were off. *This place is a paradise*, thought LaVern. *I think I've found my home away from home too.* An hour later they were comfortably belted into their private jet, headed back to reality.

Louiston Rerun
Chapter Nine

In the following year, LaVern read through several movie scripts before she decided on one that required her to, once again, fly to England. This time her Pack accompanied her. Their first time out of the country proved to be an eye-opening experience, especially for the street hardened Shaundra. Being the least well-read of the group, she was prone to making the most outrageous misstatements.

While roaming through Piccadilly Circus she said, "Everybody speaks so proper. Don't anybody ever say ain't?" or, "I like the Queen. I'd vote for her every time."

After England, The Pack traveled to France, Italy and Spain. Experiencing new cultures made her worldly shortcomings embarrassingly evident. She realized she was moving in a distinctly more sophisticated crowd of well-traveled and well-read people who could care less that she knew how to survive the perilous sidewalks of Baltimore. Could she intelligently discuss great writers or ancient civilizations or world events?

One evening, Shaundra was lazing in the family room *not* watching what was on the giant flat screen. Her mind was occupied by much weightier thoughts.

"Hey Shaundra," said LaVern after arriving home. She kicked her shoes off, pulled off her bra without removing her blouse, and tossed it to the side. "I'm going to the kitchen for some leftovers. Do you want anything?"

"No thanks, I'm good."

She returned with a plate of baked salmon, diced potatoes, and a salad, and took a comfy place in front of the giant screen. "What are we watching tonight?"

There was no response. LaVern glanced over. Shaundra was looking at the television, but she seemed distant, disconnected.

"Can you hand me the remote, Shaundra? I want to find a good documentary."

Watching a documentary would ordinarily elicit a barrage of protestations. This time, there was just a worrisome silence.

"Shaundra, you're not yourself tonight. You know I'm here if you want to talk."

In a subdued voice, she replied. "It's not you, Peaches, it's me."

"What do you mean?"

Shaundra shifted in her seat to face LaVern. She took a deep breath. "I want you to know that I've always loved you Peaches and after I say what I have to say, I'll still love you."

LaVern swelled with angst. *Oh my God! I'm scared.*

"You know nothing could ever come between us," said LaVern. "We've been through too much. Just say it."

Shaundra cleared her throat. "Peaches, our friendship is way out of whack. Please, don't misunderstand. I deeply appreciate everything you've done for me. I was ready to stay in Baltimore and be the best friend of a movie star. I never thought you would want me to live out here with you. Because of you, I've visited foreign countries, I live in this big mansion and travel by private jet, I've met lots of famous people. I could never have done that on my own. But..."

Oh no, here it comes.

Shaundra stood up and extended her arms straight out from her sides. "I look around and none of this belongs to me. I'm not responsible for any of this."

She dropped her arms in resignation. "I have no expenses because you take care of everything. I'm completely dependent on you Peaches and I don't want to be." Shaundra sat down and took another deep breath. "I've always been a survivor, but among all *this*, I'm merely... here." She went silent and resumed staring at the screen. Without looking at LaVern, she ended in a hushed tone. "It was fun at first, but..."

"First of all, Shaundra, you're in many ways responsible for all *this*. I wouldn't be here without you. I wouldn't enjoy any of this if I couldn't share it with you." LaVern gathered her thoughts. "But I understand. I didn't realize how stunted you felt."

That's a good word, thought Shaundra. *Stunted.* LaVern rose from her recliner and slowly walked over to her best friend.

"You told me years ago; we're in this together. Just tell me how I can help, you know I'll do it."

Shaundra finally took her gaze off the TV. "I just want to know more things Peaches. All the traveling we've done reminded me of how much I *don't* know. I just want to learn as much as I can."

Shaundra needed personal and emotional growth, realized LaVern, and she hadn't even noticed. This was Shaundra's epiphany, taking place in real time.

"Peaches, you're always reading, that's why you're so smart. Can I look through your collection and pick out a book?"

"Of course you can, Shaundra. What kind of question is that?"

Shaundra had never shown the slightest inclination to read…until now. She selected a book about someone she had never heard of. It was the autobiography of Madame C.J. Walker. Her vintage photograph was on the cover, and she had a distinguished air about her.

"Did you know," stated LaVern, "that she was the first millionaire businesswoman in the history of this country?"

"Whaaat? The first…and she was a millionaire… and she was Black?"

"Yes, yes and yes" grinned LaVern.

That was all it took. Shaundra was off and running. She decided to read about strong Black women. Both past and present. LaVern suggested she start frequenting bookstores and keep every book she bought.

"Pretty soon, you'll have your own collection."

Having her own books would be the first step toward satisfying her need to "have something here that belongs to me".

When the time came, they again began making preparations to flee to their secret South Carolina hideaway. This year, LaVern sported a more natural, shorter Afro wig with a multicolored, Afrocentric head band. Shaundra rid herself of her waist length ponytail and chose shoulder length curls, dyed light brown at the ends. And, for the first time ever, she packed a couple of books. They both maintained their floppy straw hats and big sunglasses and were as giddy as schoolgirls at the prospect of pulling off another vacation escape.

Shaundra called ahead during the ride from Charleston and when they pulled up to The Home Away From Home, Mary Scales was waiting on the porch. It looked like the same well-maintained, neat and inviting place they left a year ago. And, just like then, Mary was clad in her apron with a dish towel in her hands.

"Well, here's my two favorite guests."

She came down the wooden steps and made the short trek to the car. Shaundra was the first to get out.

"Mrs. Scales, it's so good to see you again."

"It's good to see you, too young lady. Give me a hug."

They embraced like mother and daughter. LaVern hastily made her way around the front of the car.

"Mrs. Scales, I've been looking forward to this day since we left last summer. I want a hug too."

"That ain't no problem darlin', I got one for you. I'm so glad to see both of you." She stepped back. Her eyes surveyed them from head to toe. "And y'all still look good."

"Thanks Mrs. Scales," said Shaundra.

"Come on in here and let's get you situated. I got your same two rooms ready."

The trio had started up the steps when a young man came through the screen door. LaVern recognized him first.

"Are you Andre?"

"Yes ma'am, it's me."

"Oh my God!" shouted Shaundra. "You look like you grew a whole foot since last year."

"I'll be sixteen next month."

"His voice is deeper too," said LaVern. "Oh dear Mrs. Scales, I think you have a lady killer on your hands."

That brought a wide toothy smile to young Andre's face.

"Hmmmmp!" uttered an unimpressed Mary, "right now the 'lady killer' had better get your bags up to your room."

"I know Ma. I'm going."

LaVern reached into her purse and fished out a twenty. "Thank you, Andre."

"Here Andre," said Shaundra, "If you have a girlfriend, take her out to lunch…on me."

Thank you, Miss Davis…Miss James. I can use the extra cash."

The girls followed Mary Scales through the squeaking screen door and into the lobby. LaVern immediately noticed some new items.

"Oh," replied the matron, "we'll have plenty of time to talk about my new stuff. Right now, you two need to go to your room and wind down before dinner. I'm sure you need some rest after that flight from Baltimore."

LaVern and Shaundra looked at one another and smiled. Their ruse was still intact. They proceeded up the stairs and into their rooms. It was immaculate. It was like returning home.

Their month's stay only made them more enamored of Louiston. They continued to be amazed at the knowledge and wisdom that seemed as omnipresent as the acorns that were scattered everywhere. On their boat excursion they hired the same old salty boat captain whose conversation was infused with common sense and down-to-earth insights on life. When Shaundra asked him why, at seventy, he didn't retire, his response was brief and profound.

"Work is what life's all about, ain't it?" said Augustus "Gus" Gordon. "Just because you're old ain't no reason to let the barnacles grow!"

They revisited the hat shop where the owner remembered them immediately because, "I've never had nobody buy five hats apiece like that." The shop owner, Mamie Johns, regaled them with her views on life as the girls marveled at the craftsmanship of her wares.

"Sometimes, these young people think the White man's ice is colder. But, when they get out there, they realize Louiston is just as good as anyplace else."

When they exited the store, Shaundra turned to LaVern.

"Did you hear that, Peaches? She said, 'young people think

the White man's ice is colder'."

"I know, Shaundra, these people say so much without saying a lot. I love that."

Through Mary Scales they learned Louiston had three elementary schools, two middle schools and two high schools. One high school was a Blue Ribbon School, considered one of the best in the state. Ninety percent of the graduates went on to college. The other school was a Vocational-Technical school.

"Everybody is not college material," said Mary. "Those that ain't, need to learn a skill. That's how we've always done it here."

Again, thought LaVern, present day remedies based on tried-and-true lessons learned in the past. That was so Louiston.

As the girls relaxed in the oh-so-comfortable porch chairs one cloudy, breezy morning, a utility truck pulled up and a tall, well-built Black man got out and walked up the steps.

"Good morning, ladies."

"Morning," they replied in unison. He disappeared into the lobby with Mary Scales. After an hour, the utility man and Mrs. Scales came through the screen door together.

"Thank you so much Willy, I'm glad it was a quick fix this time."

"Just some minor maintenance issues Mrs. Scales, no big deal."

Mary spied LaVern and Shaundra and did the polite thing. "Oh, by the way ladies, this is Wilson Davenport. He's our HVAC guy. He keeps everybody cool in the summer and warm in the winter. Willie, these are Barbara Davis and Vicki James. They're vacationing here from Baltimore."

Wilson Davenport was 6'2" with an athletic build. He sported a close cropped, neatly trimmed beard and short fade haircut. As he talked, he rose ever so slightly onto the balls of his feet.

"Pleasure to make your acquaintance, ladies."

"Likewise, Mr. Davenport, nice to meet you," said LaVern.

Wilson returned his attention to Mary Scales. "Now, if anything else crops up you better call me, OK?"

"You know I will. You say hello to your mother for me,

alright?"

"Sure will."

Wilson skipped lightly down the steps, got back into his utility vehicle and was gone.

"He looked pretty good in those shorts, didn't he Barbara?" said LaVern.

"Yes, he did", she replied.

Days later, LaVern and Shaundra were idling their time away in beach chairs, beneath a huge floral umbrella that was planted in the sand on an angle to block out the morning sun on Carr's beach. Shaundra pulled out her book as LaVern took in the activity around them. There were people standing on the nearby pier with their lines in the water, motorboats, with the sun glinting off their shiny hulls making rooster tails in the distance, a few sailboats negotiating their way over the calm waves, some young people boogie boarding and body surfing, and families simply taking advantage of a perfect day to spend time with each other.

In her bathing suit and wide brim hat with sunglasses, LaVern said, "This place is a gold mine. I don't have to look around every corner or behind every bush to see if somebody's following me or trying to snap my picture." She gripped the top of her straw hat to keep the stiff wind from blowing it away.

"It's just so relaxing, Peaches. What makes this work is that no one would expect to run into you in a place like this. Not a single person has even looked at you twice yet." Shaundra noticed someone familiar approaching. "Look," she whispered, "isn't that the maintenance guy we saw at Mrs. Scales place a few days ago?"

LaVern squinted from behind her shades. "I think it is Shaundra. He's got a little girl with him."

Wilson Davenport was approaching hand in hand with his three-year-old daughter. She had two thick, expertly executed braids that ran front to back along both sides of her head and cascaded down onto her shoulders, where the ends were accented with bright, carefully knotted yellow ribbons. She wore yellow shorts that covered her yellow bathing suit, matching yellow plastic crocs and kid's sunglasses. They were laughing and chatting like they were the only ones on the beach.

"Look at her, Shaundra. She looks so cute."

"Yeah, she's a cutie pie, but if we don't say anything, he'll probably walk right on by us."

"It wouldn't hurt to be polite. We should say something."

As the father and child passed directly in front of them, neither noticed the two women eyeing them.

"Hello there," shouted LaVern.

Wilson stopped and both he and his daughter stared at the umbrella where the voice came from. LaVern stood up and approached.

"Remember me? I'm Vicki James. We met a few days ago at Mrs. Scales place."

"Oh yeah," said Wilson. He peered back toward the umbrella. "And that must be your friend under there. How are you?"

"My name is Barbara and I'm doing fine, thank you."

"Nice to see you two ladies again. I hope you're enjoying our wonderful town and beach."

"Oh, this is our second time here and we love Louiston."

LaVern removed her shades and looked down at the little girl.

"Oh, pardon me. This is my daughter Brittany. Brittany, this is Miss James."

"Hello Miss James. It's nice to meet you."

"It's a pleasure to meet you too, Brittany. You look so cute in your bathing suit and crocs."

"Thank you."

There was an awkward moment of silence before Brittany spoke up.

"Daddy, can we get my ice cream cone?"

"Oh, I'm sorry," said a slightly chagrined LaVern, "don't let me interfere. I just wanted to say hello."

"That's alright Miss James. No need to apologize." Wilson looked down at his restless daughter. "I think I should be on my way though. It was a pleasure meeting both of you again."

"Likewise."

From underneath the umbrella came a final salutation. "It was nice meeting you again too."

Wilson and Brittany resumed their journey to the ice cream stand. LaVern returned to her shaded chair and replaced her sunglasses. She turned and looked at Shaundra.

"See, that didn't hurt, did it? I removed my shades and he still didn't recognize me."

"Like I said before," reminded Shaundra, "nobody would expect to find a movie star in a place like this."

That's exactly why LaVern, again, reserved her space a year in advance. Louiston was part of them now. As indispensable and as life-giving as a pulse. And Mary Scales was a member of their family.

Horace
Chapter Ten

The trip to Louiston was old hat by now. LaVern was scheduled to be on the set of her new movie in Mexico City when her vacation ended so they went into relax mode immediately. While having lunch on the veranda one balmy afternoon, Mrs. Scales arrived with Wilson Davenport in tow.

"Please excuse us ladies, it's that time of year again. I don't know if you remember, but this is Willie Davenport, our HVAC repairman. He won't be here long, so you can stay put."

"We remember Mr. Davenport," said Shaundra. "How are you sir?"

He still looked good in those shorts.

"Good afternoon, ladies. I see you're back again."

"We wouldn't go anywhere else," replied LaVern. "We're practically permanent residents."

"I'm glad you enjoy our small town. If you'll excuse me, I'll get to work."

"And I'll get back to work too," said Mary. "See me before you leave, Willie."

"Sure will."

For the next several days, the local news was rife with the forecast of a major hurricane. South Carolina, and Louiston in particular, were in the landing zone. LaVern and Shaundra were only mildly concerned but Mary Scales had seen her share of hurricanes and took the advisories seriously. She warned her guests that in case of an emergency, there were plans in place to keep everyone safe. Meanwhile, she monitored the forecasts and kept her guests informed.

Two days later the weather turned ominous. The morning skies darkened, and the wind began gusting dangerously. The proprietress informed every guest that an evacuation was imminent and to assemble in the lobby.

"I want to thank all of you for responding so quickly. I have arranged transportation to take everybody to the evacuation site, the gym at Ralph Bunche High School. It's only a short ten-minute ride. Until then, I want all of you to stay put right here in the lobby."

Mary Scales headed toward the front door. When she opened it, the wind snatched the screen door out of her hand and slammed it against the house. She poked her head out enough to see down the street. The wind tousled her short, graying hair in every direction. She stepped onto the porch and the forceful gale whipped her long dress and wrapped it tightly around her body. She clutched her sweater close to her as she gazed down the street, then ducked back inside.

"OK everybody, Andre is here with the van. Time to roll out!"

As her guests exited, Mary handed each a wool blanket wrapped in protective plastic. "You'll need these when you get to the gym."

The entire group filed calmly and orderly out onto the porch and into the elements. It was the first time any of them actually felt the storm. The commanding winds spawned airborne projectiles, trash, leaves, branches, and face stinging dirt.

"That's it, nice and orderly folks" shouted Mary over the howling wind. "It's just a little gust, that's all. We get this all the time."

Once everyone was settled, she gave Andre the order to move out. He tuned the radio to the weather station, adjusted the rear view and side view mirrors, turned on the headlights and pulled off.

"Welcome aboard folks," he announced. "No reason to be concerned. It's only ten minutes to the school and the real storm is about two hours away. Just sit back and relax."

LaVern and Shaundra took one last fretful glance at The Home Away From Home and hoped that it would be there when they got back. The van was deathly quiet. The only sounds were the rushing wind, the twigs and small branches pelting the van and the updates blaring on the radio. LaVern peered out of the window. Trees bent with the wind, the streets were mostly deserted, businesses were closed and boarded up, electricity was off, and traffic lights swayed violently on their power lines. *Louiston knew how to shut down*, she thought.

Just then, big, sloppy, wet sounding plops of rain, propelled sideways by the ceaseless wind, started to impact the van. Andre got the windshield wipers going at top speed and then shouted over the noise.

"They're calling this one Horace. Won't be long now folks. Another two miles."

As the van neared the school, Mary's guests began to see other vehicles arriving. There were pick-up trucks, school buses, cars, people on foot and even a few on bicycles. People were getting to the gym any way they could. Andre stopped near the open doors.

"Alright everybody," shouted Mary, "take your time, walk into the gym, and find an open spot on the floor. If you're lucky, there's still some cots left." She turned to her son. "Andre, you park the van. Everybody else, I'll see you inside."

As soon as they exited the van, everybody made a mad dash for the doors. By the time LaVern and Shaundra reached the entrance, they were drenched. They stood inside and looked at one another.

"How can we get so wet so fast?" said LaVern. "We were only in the rain for a few seconds."

She realized they were still carrying Mary Scales' blankets. "Thank you, Mrs. Scales," LaVern said to no one in particular. They tore off the plastic in seconds.

Now cocooned and cozy, the ladies stared in amazement at the constant flow of refuge seekers. The gym was filling up fast.

"We'd better find a spot quick Peaches, before we end up having to sit near some cryin' assed babies."

"I see a place right over there," said LaVern. "Let's go."

The girls weaved their way through the throng, their blankets gently dusting the wooden floor as they went.

"Here," said LaVern. "We can rest our backs against this wall."

The girls took their place on the floor, underneath a basketball hoop, and kept their eyes wide open as they took everything in. The gym was mostly dark, despite it being only

11am, and almost full. The bleachers were pushed back against the walls. There was no electricity. The only light streamed from the rectangular, roof level windows that rimmed the gym. The cots were taken up mostly by families, another one of those unwritten courtesies practiced in Louiston. Everyone seemed calm but alert, as if this was business as usual. People brought flashlights, games for the children, blankets, snacks, rain gear, laptops and most importantly, radios. The ladies settled back and snuggled up inside their wool blankets. After an hour, Shaundra nudged LaVern.

"Look, over there, on that cot. Ain't that the repairman?"

LaVern straightened up and strained to see in the dim light. "Yes, the one Mrs. Scales introduced us to."

He was with an older lady and his daughter, whom she recognized from the encounter at the beach the summer before. The older lady and the little girl shared the cot while Wilson sat on the wood floor. *At least he's considerate*, she thought. The family brought along some sandwiches, and juices and, not surprisingly, blankets. The little girl reached into her knapsack and pulled out several books. Wilson and the older woman continued to talk while she read silently. After a few minutes, the child slid off the cot and sat between her father's crossed legs to continue reading. LaVern smiled. She looked so comfortable and at home and loved. Every now and then the howling wind and battering rain made it sound like the building was under attack. This caused the girl to cringe in fear and seek safety in her father's arms. He would whisper in her ear and hug her closer and say reassuring things to make her feel protected. It was beautiful to see. She had to go over there.

Shaundra was dead asleep when LaVern zig-zagged her way towards the Davenports. As she neared, Wilson spotted her.

"Well, hello Miss James."

"Mr. Davenport… nice to see you again."

Wilson looked past her. "Where's your partner?"

"Barbara is over there near that wall. That girl can sleep even through a hurricane."

Wilson patted the empty space on the cot. "We have a spot; would you like to join us?"

She unleashed her best Hollywood smile. "Why thank you. Don't mind if I do."

LaVern took her place beside Gloria Davenport.

"Ma, this is Miss Vicki James. She's on vacation and we met at the Scales place when I had to do a little maintenance over there. Miss James, this is my mother, Gloria."

His mother, thought LaVern. *Of course.* "It's a pleasure to meet you, Mrs. Davenport, even under these trying circumstances."

The grandmother eyed the stranger warily. If, like her son said, she was a vacationer, why'd she pick her family to cozy up to?

"It's nice to meet you too, young lady. Where are you from?"

LaVern went right to default mode. "I'm from Baltimore. I'm a hairdresser, Mrs. Davenport and I have my own shop."

"Oh, that's so nice. A businesswoman, I like that."

Ever the actress, LaVern ran her fingers through her wet locks, shook the fake curls to and fro and stated boldly, "You see this mess up here? I'll have this together in no time, once I get back to my room."

Gloria took a moment to scan LaVern from head to toe. She seemed well groomed. Smooth, brown skin, no heavy makeup, fingers and toes painted and well maintained, dressed casually but with touches of class. The bracelets on her wrists looked expensive, but they couldn't possibly be the real thing, and she wore a beautiful set of gold, teardrop earrings.

"How long do you plan on staying?"

"Barbara and I plan to return to Baltimore at the end of the month. We've vacationed here for three straight years, and we love it."

"Oh really," stated a surprised Gloria, "you like it here *that* much?" Louiston is not on most folks' list of vacation hot spots."

Just then, the smallest Davenport made her presence known. She was leafing through her book.

"These are my favorite, daddy, they're so pretty."

"Where are my manners? Miss James, you may not remember but this is my intelligent and precocious daughter,

Brittany. Britt, this is Miss James."

"Hello Brittany," said LaVern as she reached out her hand. "I remember that cute yellow outfit you wore. It's a pleasure to meet you, again."

"Hello," the girl replied, as she shook hands.

"What are you reading?" asked LaVern.

"This book is about seashells. We have lots of them on our beach."

"I see you brought along a few other books."

"I like insects too."

"You must really like to read."

"Yes ma'am I do. I have lots more books at home. I have my own library."

LaVern was truly impressed, a four-year-old who expressed herself so clearly and intelligently.

"Wow, your own library. That's pretty special."

"Do you like to read, Miss Vicki?"

"I certainly do. I had my own library when I was a little girl too."

A familiar voice broke into the conversation.

"Well, there you are," blared Shaundra, "a girl can't go to sleep for more than a few minutes before you go wandering off?"

LaVern did the honors. "Everyone, this is my best friend, Barbara Davis."

"Good seeing you again, Miss Davis. This is my mother Gloria and here in my lap is my daughter Brittany."

"It's a real honor to meet all of you folks."

"Nice to make your acquaintance, young lady," said Gloria.

"Hi," added Brittany.

"I'm sorry we can't offer you a seat Miss Davis, as you can see, space is pretty limited," said Wilson.

"Sit here Barbara," said LaVern, "I don't mind sitting on the floor."

Wilson interjected, "Sit on this blanket then, Miss James. This gym floor is too dirty."

"Thank you so much."

Shaundra and Gloria, now sitting side by side, exchanged nervous smiles and the obligatory nod. Shaundra addressed

LaVern.

"How long was I out?"

"About a half hour."

"Yeah," added Wilson, "this hurricane didn't seem to bother you one bit."

"I've always been a heavy sleeper, Mr. Davenport."

"Willie is good enough. Mr. Davenport sounds too formal."

"In that case, call me Barbara."

"OK Barbara, you've met my family, what about you? What do you do back in Baltimore?"

Shaundra hesitated just long enough to get her alibi straight. "I'm a manager of a retail store and I volunteer at my neighborhood day care center and spoil my dog, Jelli."

Oh my God, thought LaVern. *She sounded like one of those Miss America contestants. The only thing she left out was "Peace for all mankind".*

Wilson began to speak. "Miss James said–"

"Please, call me Vicki."

"OK…Vicki said you've been coming here for three years. What attracted you to Louiston?"

"We were looking for an out of the way vacation spot and I found this place. It was only later that we realized that Louiston is steeped in Black history."

That was impressive, thought LaVern. They exchanged knowing glances.

Just then, a nearby radio crackled to life with updates. The winds were around 120 miles per hour. Everyone was required to continue to shelter in place until the National Guard gave the OK to leave. LaVern looked up to the narrow windows along the top of the gym. There was still lots of light pouring in and she could see debris like tree limbs, litter, and roofing tiles fly by. The wind was howling like a wounded animal, but the building seemed to be remarkably unaffected, even though she could hear airborne objects flung against the sides and the doors. No one seemed the least bit worried. Life simply carried on. Wilson's voice brought her back to the group.

"You're right, Barbara, there's plenty of Black History here in Louiston. For instance, did you know that the slaves introduced rice to America and to South Carolina?"

"No, I didn't know that," said Shaundra.

"The White farmers tried raising tobacco, cotton, sugar cane, silk and ginger but all those attempts failed. The Africans who were raised in West Africa taught Whites how to plant and harvest rice in these low, swampy regions of the state."

Wilson now had a rapt audience. The women absorbed his every word.

"After that, White labor was never seriously considered. The historical record says that over 50,000 Africans were imported between 1740 and the Revolutionary War. Those original Africans became known as "Gullah" people."

LaVern's eyes widened in surprise. "Gullah people. I've seen documentaries and interviews about them. Are you a Gullah Mr. Davenport? I'm sorry, I mean…Willie."

"Afraid not, Vicki. I've been here for twenty years though, and I feel like I'm one of them. If you look around this place, many of the faces you see are descendants of those original Africans. That's how intact and stable this community has always been."

For the first time Shaundra noticed Brittany's reading material. "Oh, I see you brought along a book."

"I have books and board games too," said a proud Brittany.

"Really? I'm impressed. You and Miss James have a lot in common. I've known her since we were children, and she always liked books."

Brittany peeked across to where LaVern was sitting. "I know. She said she had a library when she was little."

"You're so right. She had books all over her house."

Now it was Gloria's turn to be impressed. As a retired college professor, having books indicated curiosity, a lifelong learner. A lack of the same meant a lack of intellectual growth. LaVern, unbeknownst to her, had passed her first test. Young Brittany tilted her head back to look up into her father's face.

"Daddy, can I read my book to Miss James?"

Wilson looked at LaVern. "Sure, if it's alright with Miss James."

"Absolutely. I'd be honored."

To everyone's surprise, the child rose from her safe place in her father's lap, walked over to LaVern, sat between her crossed legs, and opened her book. The Davenports looked on in utter astonishment. LaVern was both surprised and flattered. Gloria's mouth flew open, but she didn't speak a word. Brittany proceeded to read "Run, Bug, Run" flawlessly. When she finished, Gloria was the first to speak.

"Good job baby. I'm proud of you."

"Thanks, Meemaw," said Brittany, with a smile that revealed all her baby teeth.

This was the first time his daughter read to a stranger, and Wilson beamed with pride. "Brittany, that was beautiful."

LaVern had to ask. "How did you learn to read so well?"

"My Meemaw taught me."

LaVern looked at Gloria. Before she could ask, Gloria said, "Young lady, education comes first in this family. No excuses, get the work done."

For the next several hours the group passed the time with conversation and, at Brittany's insistence, board games. Shaundra and LaVern enjoyed the easy flowing dialogue mixed with fits of laughter. A nearby radio crackled to life again and announced that the hurricane had passed. Everyone was free to return home.

"How long has it been?" asked a startled LaVern.

Wilson looked down at his watch. "We've been here for about five hours or so. That's about average. Now we get to go back and see what kind of damage Horace did."

LaVern and Shaundra stared at one another. They were having such a good time, they'd forgotten about the hurricane and its dangerous consequences. What if Wilson's house was destroyed? What about The Home Away From Home? Will it still be standing? They looked around the gym and wondered, which of these nice families will return to ruined homes and businesses? Wilson got to his feet.

"It was a real pleasure spending time with you ladies. Me and my family really appreciate that." He briefly, slightly went up on his toes.

"Believe me Wilson, said Lavern, it was our honor and privilege to have been in your family's company."

"Absolutely," chimed in Shaundra. "You folks are quality people."

As Gloria Davenport struggled to her feet, Wilson rushed over to help. "It was a real pleasure ladies," she said, "I really enjoyed our conversation."

LaVern and Shaundra approached, and Gloria gave them both a hug.

LaVern stooped down to Brittany. "And you, you little angel, I REALLY enjoyed meeting you. You are so special."

Brittany shyly replied, "Thank you."

"Yeah girl," said Shaundra. "I have grown brothers that ain't as smart as you."

More laughter. The two ladies then turned to Wilson.

"Mr. Dav..., I mean Willie, you have a beautiful family. Meeting all of you has been the best part of my vacation."

LaVern reached out her hand and they shook. Shaundra also exchanged a firm handshake.

"Willie, it's been a pleasure. I'm going to tell everybody at the store about the nice family we met here."

Just as everyone was about to go their own way, a tiny voice spoke up.

"Daddy, can Miss Vicki come by my house and see my library?"

LaVern was unsure as to how she should react. She looked down at Brittany, she glanced over to Wilson and finally over to Gloria. Wilson and Gloria peeked at one another. Gloria broke the impasse.

"Sweetheart, Miss James is here on vacation and with the hurricane and everything I don't think she'll have enough time."

"I promise, I won't keep her long," pleaded Brittany. "Please, Daddy."

LaVern's heart was melting. "Brittany, if it's alright with your father and grandmother, I would be glad to come by and see your library."

Wilson gave in too. "Since Miss James says it won't be an inconvenience to her, I guess it's alright."

"Yaaay!" shouted the excited Brittany.

"I'll have to see what Horace did to the house first. Why don't I give you ladies a call at the Scales' place tomorrow?"

Gloria gave a knowing nod of approval. No sense inviting

visitors over if there's no house to invite them to.

"OK" said Lavern. "I'll wait to hear from you."

The two ladies turned and headed back to their spot under the basketball hoop, against the wall. All the families were preparing for the return trip, not knowing what was awaiting them. The whole scene seemed so organized, so ritualized, the gathering of personal property, the folding up of blankets, the counting of heads. They were doing something they had done who knows how many times before.

When they arrived back at their starting point, a familiar voice rang out.

"Alright ladies, time to start heading out. Andre went to get the van. I want everybody at the door when he pulls up."

"Yes Ma'am," both ladies replied.

Mary scurried off to round up her other guests. The ladies picked up their blankets and began to work their way toward the now open doors. There were still plenty of families inside, but the intention was clear. It was time to go.

The group rode mostly in silence. Only the radio, blasting its non-stop weather updates, and the slowly decreasing winds managed to cut through the quiet. As the van meandered its way through town, the extent of the devastation became clear. Houses were blown off their foundations, debris littered the streets and roofs lay beside the homes they once protected. The overhead power lines swung like strands of spaghetti. Andre announced he would have to take an alternate route because trash and rubble clogged the streets. Shaundra's eyes were wide with disbelief.

"Can you believe this, Peaches? Is this even the same place?"

LaVern couldn't answer. What she saw beyond the windows of the van left her dumbstruck. Some buildings were totally obliterated while others were left untouched. Horace left his calling card everywhere. Mary leaned over and whispered something to Andre. He answered in a barely audible tone, and they continued this under their breath exchange for several minutes.

The van turned the corner and straight ahead was The Home Away from Home… still standing. Spontaneous shouts of

"Alright!" erupted inside the van. The guests had been thinking the same as LaVern. They came to a stop and Mary Scales was the first to disembark. She stood there for several seconds, Horace's residual winds whipped her hair and clothing. She wordlessly pored over the exterior of her pride and joy. There seemed to be only minor damage, but the matron bowed her head, her chin rested on her chest.

"She doesn't look too happy," Shaundra whispered under her breath.

Just as quickly, her chin popped up and Mary marched up her steps, onto her porch and into the house. No one tried to exit the van. After a few minutes she reemerged, came gingerly down the steps and poked her head into the open window.

"OK everybody, just head into the lobby and wait for me there."

All the guests unbuckled their seat belts and began the fearful trek out of the van, up the creaky steps and onto the porch of what was their home for the past week. Now the true extent of the damage revealed itself. The angry looking sky was visible through the holes in the roof over the porch. The wind that rushed through the openings created a haunting, whistling sound, as if Horace sought to mock Mary with one final tortuous reminder of his visit. The shutters that were once such a beautiful, homey accent to the bay windows were gone. All but one, and that one was hanging on for dear life by a single hinge, still banging against the house. Much of the window glass was missing, leaving only jagged, shark tooth shaped remnants as its replacement. Through these craggy openings, her prized, handmade curtains fluttered with their now frayed edges on full display. The scene stopped everyone dead in their tracks. Mary Scales was still back at the van giving instructions to Andre, when he pulled away and she turned to see all her guests standing in one big silent pod, their backs to her, taking in the devastation that was once her comfy, cozy front porch.

"Everybody please, continue inside into the lobby and wait for me there… please."

Despite her determined and stoic facade, her voice betrayed an internal doubt and uncertainty. The first of the guests opened the creaky door, its screen torn and ragged, and led the group into the dimly lit lobby. Everyone paused. They were amazed to see that the lobby had survived surprisingly well. Louis Armistead was lying on his side against the wall, lamps were broken and tables overturned, but the structure was solid. Everyone heaved a sigh of relief. Mary entered the lobby.

"OK folks, I'm going to give it to you straight. I've been through the house and unfortunately there's more damage, and it wouldn't be fair to ruin your vacation further by having you stay here. There are rooms at the Armistead, therefore, I'll make arrangements for everyone to go there."

There was dead silence. Only the nervous shuffling of feet on the oriental rug as she continued.

"I have no electricity, and in one room, that would be yours, Mr. Blackston, there's a hole in the roof. Not a gaping one, but nonetheless..." Her voice trailed off, her disappointment evident. LaVern and Shaundra, realizing they were only in the first week of their month-long vacation, didn't protest.

"I'm sorry this had to happen, Mrs. Scales," said LaVern. "You've always been a caring and gracious hostess. I feel like I'm abandoning you in your hour of need."

Shaundra joined in. "I feel the same way. I hate to leave you just because things got tough."

The other guests echoed the same sentiments; Mary Scales didn't deserve this. But all her guests reluctantly agreed to relocate.

"If you need him, Andre will transport you, and your things to the Armistead."

LaVern and Shaundra loaded their belongings into their slightly dinged SUV and motored over to the Armistead Hotel where they shared a room. When LaVern entered, she flopped face down on the bed and let her sandals slide off her tired feet, relieved to put today's traumatic episodes out of her mind; the evacuation, the waiting out of Horace and now having to move out of The Home Away From Home. This was a full day for anybody. After resting, they ate the snacks that were provided and then slept.

The following morning was bright and sunny. The sky bore no trace of yesterday's carnage. LaVern woke up first. She sleepily threw her clenched fists upward, yawned mightily and peeked over at Shaundra. Her head lifted off the pillow and in her semi-conscious state, she searched the room with her eyes. Her gaze fell on her best friend.

"What… what time is it?"

"It's time to get up, sleeping beauty."

LaVern ambled over to the third-floor window and parted the curtains. She peered out onto the street and was immediately reminded of yesterday's events. It was eight o'clock and Louiston's inhabitants were already busying themselves with the task of rebuilding. People were sweeping and piling up debris, pumping out water from their businesses and clearing the streets of obstacles.

"How does it look out there, girlfriend?"

"You have got to see this." LaVern stared silently for a few seconds. "This scene reminds me of a nature documentary I saw about how ant colonies begin immediately repairing and rebuilding their damaged nest. These people are like ants."

Shaundra rose and walked over to see for herself. She shook her head. "They are so determined. They seem to take it all in stride." Shaundra's cell phone went off. It was Mary Scales.

"Morning Miss Davis. I hope you and Miss James rested well."

"Nothing beats your place, Mrs. Scales, but we got our sleep on."

"That's good. I got a call from Willie this morning. He said, if y'all still want to come by, you're more than welcome."

This seemed like a strange request, especially right after a hurricane.

"Thank you, Mrs. Scales. Can I get his number?"

"You sure can darlin'." She recited his digits. "Have y'all made any travel arrangements yet?"

"Not yet, we just woke up."

"It's a shame that Horace fouled up everybody's vacation. Unfortunately, it's just a part of life around here."

Shaundra was still looking out of the window. "The people here are amazing. We hate to have to leave."

"Well, you two get home safe, OK?"

"We will, bye Mrs. Scales."

LaVern snapped her fingers. "That reminds me, I've got to call Amy and make new travel arrangements." She strode quickly to the nightstand, sat on the bedside and phoned her business manager. "Hello, Amy. Yes, it got a little hairy for a minute, but Shaundra and I are fine. Listen, I have to change travel plans. I want you to arrange for the jet to meet us at the airport later today because I need to cut my vacation short. No, I'm not sure when yet but get things started, OK? I'll know more later. Thank you so much and I'll see you soon, bye."

LaVern decided on her plan of action; visit Brittany and then head straight for the airport. They would fly home for the remaining three weeks of their vacation, then head to her shoot in Mexico.

"I'm glad I get to keep my promise to Brittany. I would've really disappointed her if I didn't give her the chance to show me her library."

"Yeah, she really wanted you to see it." said Shaundra.

Shaundra phoned Wilson to inform him they would be over shortly. But before they headed there, they drove to The Home Away From Home to say a proper goodbye to Mary Scales. There was no one on the porch, but the main door was open. They quietly entered through the damaged screen door and there she was, broom in hand, sweeping up broken glass.

"Hello ladies. I didn't expect to see you two this morning."

LaVern got right to the point.

"We're leaving, Mrs. Scales, and we couldn't go without seeing you."

"That's so nice of you darlin'."

"Mrs. Scales, can I ask you something? I'm not trying to be nosy and get into your personal business…"

"Ask me anything you want."

The two were now facing one another.

"Do you plan to be here next year? I know it might be costly to rebuild and who knows what other obstacles might prevent you from reopening."

"Sweetheart don't worry yourself about that even a little bit. Like those ol' cowboys always say, 'this ain't my first rodeo'. People in this town are used to starting over. It ain't always easy, but there's a reason I've lived here for thirty years. So, unless YOU change your mind, I expect to see you here next year."

Wilson was right about this town and its inhabitants, thought LaVern. *They are a prideful and stubborn bunch.*

"I'm so glad to hear that, Mrs. Scales. The money will be in your account before the day is out."

"Call me Mary. You've been coming here long enough to drop the formalities."

"Well, you can call me Vicki, but I'll still call you Mrs. Scales. I have much too much respect for you to call you anything else."

"I'm so sorry things turned out this way Mrs. Scales," said Shaundra. "But you made everything so exceptional anyway. You're a very special woman."

"Thank you so much, Miss Davis. I'll see you next year, right?"

"If you call me Barbara you will. I'm going to miss you."

"I'll miss you too, darlin'."

Everybody hugged and the pair exited.

The route the GPS chose through town only magnified the damage. There was serious flooding, streets were still choked with debris and there was no electricity or gas.

Simultaneously, citizens were dutifully cleaning up what they could, and government FEMA personnel were already on the ground. The duo drove slowly and made a left turn down a secluded road with a gentle incline. These houses emerged largely unscathed. They pulled up to a brick rancher with a huge shady oak tree stationed in the yard. There was debris; paper, clothes, and cardboard boxes entwined in the branches.

"Daddy, they're here!" It was an excited Brittany looking and smiling at the car through the screen door. Wilson swung it open, and Brittany rushed out. LaVern stooped down to receive the hug she knew was coming.

"How's the smartest little girl in the world?"

Brittany tee hee'ed. "I'm fine, Miss Vicki."

"Hey, don't I get a hug too?" asked Shaundra as she stooped down.

"Yes ma'am."

They too embraced.

"Don't keep our guests out here Britt." Wilson opened the door and extended his arm toward the inside of the house. "Please ladies, come in."

Brittany grabbed LaVern by the hand and practically dragged her into the house. The living room was small and tidy. Against one wall there was a large, brown, felt-covered sofa with white, knitted arm covers. At each arm were matching wood end tables with lamps, which sat atop white, lacy doilies that, like the arm covers, were handmade. Furthest from the door was Wilson's well-used black leather recliner. One patchwork area rug covered the middle of the hardwood floor. On the opposite side of the room, beneath a large, flat screen TV, was an upholstered recliner. Next to it, on a third end table, sat a wicker basket overflowing with knitting materials with two knitting needles standing at attention. No mystery whose space that was. With the screen above and behind her head, Gloria Davenport was certainly no fan of television. There were two large east-facing windows that allowed the morning sun to coat everything in its light. It was simple but homey. LaVern noticed that there were magazines, but no books.

"The sofa is the best place to sit, Miss Vicki," exclaimed Brittany.

"In that case, that's right where I'll sit."

Brittany flopped down right beside her. LaVern smiled and gave the little girl another hug.

"I'm sorry my daughter's hospitality seems so one-sided, Barbara," said Wilson. "Please, have a seat."

"Thank you."

She sat on the sofa with Brittany between her and LaVern. "By the way, you have a lovely house."

"Yes, it is," added LaVern. "I already feel at home."

"Well, any credit for that should go to my mama. She keeps everything running smoothly around here."

As if on cue, Gloria Davenport appeared from the kitchen.

"Well, hello ladies, it's nice to see you again."

"Hello Mrs. Davenport," said LaVern. "I was just telling Wilson what a lovely house you have."

"Yes," added Shaundra, "it's so comfy and homey."

"First things first, stop calling me Mrs. Davenport. Gloria will do fine. Secondly, I'm almost done in the kitchen, then we can all sit down and have breakfast."

LaVern wondered what she prepared without gas or electricity.

"You didn't have to go through all that trouble for us," said LaVern.

"Yeah," said Shaundra, "but we won't turn it down."

Everybody got a hearty laugh at that. Lavern decided she didn't feel comfortable calling Gloria Davenport by her first name. Just like Mary Scales, a Black woman of her age deserved more respect than that, even if they requested otherwise.

"Good, y'all make yourselves comfortable for a few minutes and I'll be back with the food. The table is already set." Gloria disappeared into the kitchen.

"Daddy, can I show Miss Vicki my library?"

"Now Britt, they just got here, give them a chance to rest and relax."

"Oh, it's alright Willie," said LaVern. "I'd love to see her library."

"Yaaaay" squealed the little girl. She grabbed LaVern by the hand and excitedly led her out of the living room and down a short hallway. Wilson and Shaundra followed them with their eyes until they made a left and disappeared into her bedroom. They found themselves alone in the living room.

"She's usually not that excited around strangers. I'm surprised she's taken to Vicki so quickly."

"Oh, Vicki is really good with children. She loves them and I guess kids pick up on that."

Gloria soon re-emerged from the kitchen with breakfast; a charcuterie platter loaded with bread, strawberry jam, cheese, crackers and assorted meats, and placed it on the table. "OK. everybody, time to eat."

Wilson and Shaundra rose and headed for the dining room. Brittany exited her bedroom and once again had LaVern by the hand, tugging her toward the table.

"Baby", Gloria said, "you need to stop dragging Miss Vicki around like that. She's a grown woman; she can walk on her own."

"Sorry Meemaw. I'm sorry, Miss Vicki."

"That's quite alright, Brittany. I'm ready to enjoy this food. It looks delicious."

"Yes, it does," agreed Shaundra.

Gloria returned to the kitchen for orange juice and tea. Not bad, observed LaVern looking at the spread. Kudos to Mrs. Davenport for creativity and resourcefulness without utilities.

Everyone ate and shared wonderful conversations. The discussions revealed several things that intrigued LaVern. Both Gloria and Wilson were readers. Wilson was deeply immersed in Black History, and he had an extensive library. He collected autobiographies, non-fiction, science and American History. LaVern found that Gloria Davenport retired as a Professor of Sociology from Elizabeth City State University. Her reading material, fiction and mysteries, was on shelves in her bedroom. LaVern was especially fascinated that Wilson volunteered at Brittany's pre-school, and he sat on the City Council. This was an impressive family.

LaVern's cell phone went off. It was Amy. "Excuse me everyone. I've got to take this call." She rose from the table, headed through the living room, and onto the front porch.

"If everybody's through, you can head out back to the patio and relax while I take care of these dishes. There're some downed tree limbs out there, so watch your step."

Wilson, Shaundra and Brittany wandered onto the patio. They heard and felt the crunch of twigs and leaves beneath their shoes, reminders of yesterday's calamity. Each found a cushy chair to lounge in. The cheap plastic cushions had been wiped dry. Brittany glanced back through the house, toward the front door, searching for the first sight of an approaching Miss Vicki. After ten minutes, she jumped to her feet.

"Here she comes." She slid open the patio door and invited LaVern to share a chair with her. "Sit with me Miss Vicki, pleeease."

"Of course I will."

Wilson eyed the scene with surprise. "I was telling Barbara that Brittany normally doesn't take to strangers this quickly. This is totally out of character for her."

"Well, I'm honored. Really, I am. I think you and your mother should be commended for the job you're doing raising such an incredible young lady."

Brittany put both arms around her waist.

"Thank you, Vicki, we're extremely proud of her too."

"Who was that on the phone?" Shaundra asked, knowing full well it was Amy with their travel arrangements. LaVern directed her answer to Wilson.

"We have to leave in a half hour for the airport. We were lucky enough to get our flight changed."

"Great," said Wilson. "You ladies can hang out here until then."

"Thank you so much," said LaVern. "You and your family have been such gracious hosts. I can't wait to tell my family about what quality people you guys are. I mean that."

Shaundra joined in. "Yeah, we've really enjoyed ourselves."

Shaundra looked out over the expanse of property and what she saw was truly amazing. A lush green carpet of mowed grass with trees and bushes trimming the entire landscape, acting as a natural privacy fence. There were some downed limbs, and a few uprooted trees scattered around. Bordering the patio was Gloria's passion: her well-tended garden. It was an explosion of color with pale blue hydrangea, pink gladiolas, purple and yellow irises, and red and white roses, and not a weed among them. A weed wouldn't dare reveal its ugly self in Gloria Davenport's floral sanctuary. All had managed to avoid Horace's wrath. There was a shade producing oak tree on one side, and on the other, the traditional giant patio umbrellas. She asked Wilson how much land he owned. He raised his arm and pointed straight ahead and moved it left to right.

"I own everything you see to that tree line out there. All in all, about an acre and a half thanks to my daddy."

LaVern and Shaundra took in the astounding beauty.

"Would you like a tour, Vicki? I'd be glad to show it to you. I promise I won't make you late."

LaVern called upon her best glamour magazine smile. "I'd be happy to, Willie. Just lead the way."

Shaundra and LaVern exchanged a quick glance. The couple began walking away. Gloria, having finished her chores in the kitchen, arrived at the patio.

"Where are those two going?"

Brittany answered first. "Daddy and Miss Vicki are going for a walk Meemaw."

"Oh… OK."

Gloria plopped down and, like everybody else, didn't take her eyes off the pair as they slowly receded in the distance. What they saw was a man and a woman enjoying each other's company. Wilson would point and LaVern would look. He explained that the brunt of Horace, the right quadrant, had missed the town and, despite appearances, the damage wasn't as extensive as it could have been. There was laughter and heads nodded in agreement and lots of eye contact. No one on the patio spoke a word, but everyone was thinking the same thing. What's going on here? When the strolling couple finally stepped back onto the patio, Gloria and Shaundra stared unblinkingly for several seconds. Wilson and LaVern noticed the unexpected attention and uttered "What!" simultaneously. This caused them to look at each other with surprise, which caused them to burst into laughter. Gloria and Shaundra exchanged befuddled looks before they returned their gaze to the giggling couple. LaVern's timer went off.

"Aw shoot," she cried out, "we have to go."

Brittany looked at LaVern. "You're leaving Miss Vicki?"

"I'm afraid so, angel."

Gloria broke out of her trance and said, "Britt, Miss James has a home and a job to get back to. Remember, she's just vacationing here."

The little girl stared gloomily down at her feet. "OK."

LaVern placed her arm around her shoulder, and they began a sorrowful walk back through the house. On the front porch, a dejected Brittany said, "I'm going to miss you Miss Vicki."

LaVern stooped down to eye level. "Ohhh, I'm going to miss you even more sweetheart. I really am."

"When am I going to see you again?"

"Well, I vacation here every year, so I'll see you again next summer."

"Next summer?" She was now sobbing. "But that's a long time."

Wilson interjected. "Britt, we've explained to you why Miss James must leave. She can't just come and go like that."

"I know Daddy, but she'll forget about me."

It was LaVern's time to sob now. She hugged her tightly and promised to stay in touch until they saw each other again. She stood, looked at Gloria and said, "Thank you for everything Mrs. Davenport, Thank you for sharing your beautiful family with me."

"The pleasure has been all mine, Vicki. You and Barbara have been wonderful." Then, they hugged.

Shaundra stooped down to give Brittany a hug too. "You're such a special little girl. I can't wait to see you again."

The whole departure was more than Brittany could handle. She ran crying into the house.

Gloria said, "She'll be alright. She's just four."

"I know," said Shaundra. "It just breaks my heart, though."

The two ladies hugged, then Wilson, Shaundra and LaVern started down the walk. Gloria stayed behind on the porch. As they neared the car, Wilson turned to LaVern.

"There's something you need to know about Brittany. You have to understand what kind of child she is."

LaVern looked puzzled.

"If you promise her you'll stay in contact, she'll hold you to that. As I said before, she doesn't take to strangers very easily, and the way she attached herself to you, I can't explain it. My mother can't explain it either, but I don't want my little girl's feelings hurt. If you don't feel like you can keep your end of the bargain, let me know now. I won't be upset, just leave it to me to explain it to her. But don't have her waiting for something that's not going to happen."

LaVern's eyes began to swell with tears. She placed her hand in Wilson's and looked right at him. "I meant every word I said to Brittany. Don't you worry about me hurting her feelings, I would never do that." She gave his hand a tight, reassuring squeeze.

Wilson looked down into LaVern's eyes and smiled. "Thank you, Vicki."

"No, thank YOU Wilson Davenport."

She gave him a tight hug, and he hugged her back. He held it a teeny bit longer than he should have.

Shaundra gave him a tearful but wordless hug, and the two friends ducked into the car. As they were pulling off, LaVern looked back one last time. In the window of Brittany's room, she could see a little face peering out through the curtains watching the car drive away. LaVern broke down in tears.

The Gem
Chapter Eleven

LaVern kept her promise to Brittany. A week after their departure, she called.

"Hello Willie, this is Vicki. How are you?"

"This is a pleasant surprise. How're things in Baltimore?"

LaVern never broke character. "Oh, things here don't change much. It's back to work as always."

"I'm glad you called because Brittany was worrying me and her meemaw to death with 'why hasn't she called'? I told her it's only been a week, but you know how children are when they are expecting something, a week seems like a year."

"Awww, bless her heart. I thought she might get a little anxious."

"She's in her room now, let me go get her, hold on."

LaVern heard the faint babble of the evening news in the background. She heard excited screams.

"It's Miss Vicki!"

Those cries were immediately followed by the thumping, muffled sound of running four-year-old feet. LaVern heard Gloria admonish her to "slow down girl. Stop running."

"Hello, Miss Vicki, is this you?"

"Yes, it is Brittany. How are you?"

And so began the first of many conversations that autumn with the effervescent, inquisitive and energetic Brittany Davenport. After each call, Wilson expressed his gratitude to LaVern for taking the time to not disappoint his little girl. Soon, the conversations between LaVern and Brittany became shorter and those with Wilson became longer.

"You sure are spending a lot of time talking to that Wilson Davenport," commented Shaundra one day. "You're not starting to like him, are you?"

"He's a very intriguing guy, Shaundra. You haven't gotten

to know him the way I have."

"You didn't answer my question. Do you like him?"

"At this point, he's at least worth getting to know."

"So, you do like him."

"Well, I like what I know so far. Stop being so nosy."

"As your best friend, it's my job to be nosy."

"I guess it's way too late to change that," acknowledged LaVern.

"Remember, he still doesn't know who you really are. And depending on how far you take this, you'll eventually have to tell him before some snoopy-assed tabloid does it for you."

LaVern adopted a very pensive look and Shaundra breathed a deep sigh.

"I just want you to be careful, Peaches. This thing could go left pretty fast, and it'll be messy."

"Don't worry, I'll be careful. The last thing I want is to get people hurt."

Wilson and LaVern were talking one evening when LaVern hinted that she may want to visit over the winter, and if he had any objections.

"But it's the winter time," Wilson said, "you saw what Horace did, the city is still recovering and I'm very busy with calls for heat."

"You're right, Wilson, it's a bad time. I don't know what I was thinking."

There was a long silence on Wilson's end.

"Could you come after the first of the year? Brittany will be out of school then."

"Oh, that's perfect. I'm really looking forward to seeing everybody."

As her flight date approached, Shaundra had one more warning for her friend. "Go slow and remember one other thing. Even though you two have been doing a lot of talking on the phone, you've been calling him. He hasn't called you once."

Good point. I hadn't even realized that. Maybe I'm more interested than he is.

When LaVern left Los Angeles, it was 75 degrees and sunny. When her jet landed in Charleston, the nighttime temperature was 45 degrees, and the sky was overcast. Shaundra stayed behind because, as she correctly surmised, this was not a trip for two. Besides, the real estate classes she was enrolled in demanded all her time. LaVern rented a car and drove herself from the airport to the Armistead. A phone call to Mary Scales, before she left, revealed that The Home Away From Home wasn't ready for guests.

Wilson picked her up the following morning and gave her a quick tour of a still recovering Louiston. It had been seven months since Horace's visit. LaVern stayed silent and watched as they rode slowly, as if in a one car funeral procession, through the now cleared streets. Utilities had been restored, as evidenced by the working traffic lights. The business district was still mostly boarded up, this included LaVern's favorite store, Mamie Johns' hat shop. Many homes were still nowhere near inhabitable. The miniature golf course was unidentifiable. But the town showed signs of recovery; the beach was cleared and the sounds of power tools and hammering could be heard everywhere. The ant colony was hard at work. Wilson was very optimistic about Louiston's resurgence. As he said, "we've been through worse."

They finally pulled up to the Davenport house and Brittany came running down the pathway in her cute winter coat and boots with matching gloves, screaming all the way.

"Miss Vicki! Miss Vicki!"

LaVern opened her door and barely got to her feet before Brittany grabbed her around the waist. She stooped down and wrapped her arms around her little frame and held on for dear life. "I've missed you so much," she whispered.

"I missed you too, Miss Vicki. Guess what?"

"What?"

"I have some new books. Can I read to you?"

"Well, you had better," Lavern replied, "I didn't come all this way for nothing."

"Let's get inside and out of this cold," said Wilson. "Meemaw has a good breakfast ready for everybody."

Wilson followed as the two walked hand in hand to the

house, still dumbfounded at the sight of his normally reticent daughter showing no inhibitions around Vicki James. As they entered the house, Gloria was standing in the living room.

"Well, it's good to see you again Vicki. I thought I'd next see you in the summer."

"So did I Mrs. Davenport, but I really wanted to see what Louiston was like in the wintertime, despite ol' Horace. And besides," she looked down at Brittany, "I couldn't wait to see this face again." LaVern shot a quick glance over to Wilson as if to silently convey that he too, was included in her reason for being here.

"Well, have a seat. I'll have some breakfast on the table in a few minutes."

"Sit over here, Miss Vicki," said Brittany, indicating a space right beside her on the sofa.

"Now Britt," said Wilson, "she doesn't always have to sit next to you. Give her a choice."

"Then, I choose to sit right here." She took a seat next to Brittany.

After a few minutes of small talk, Gloria called everyone to the table. They caught up on one another's activities since the hurricane; Brittany's pre-school was undamaged, Wilson was overwhelmed and had to hire three techs to handle the increased workload, Gloria's precious garden, having survived Horace, was in its winter slumber, LaVern stated that her hair salon was doing well. After breakfast, everyone migrated to the living room.

"You're a wonder, Mrs. Davenport. The morning after Horace you performed a miracle by feeding everyone despite having no electricity or gas. This morning's breakfast proves you are a true superstar."

"Thank you so much, Vicki. I'm glad you enjoyed it."

Brittany grew bored with all the adult conversation. "Can I read my new book to Miss Vicki now Daddy?"

"Well, if she doesn't mind, it's alright with me."

"I don't mind one bit," LaVern said.

Gloria Davenport interrupted on LaVern's behalf. "You can read just one book, Britt. After that, I want you to read on your own, OK?"

"OK Meemaw." Brittany rushed into her room and quickly returned. She stood in the middle of the living room and read "One bug, two bugs in the Rug," flawlessly. When she was finished, everyone gave her enthusiastic applause.

"That was exceptional Brittany," gushed LaVern. "You're amazing. I love to listen to you read."

"Thanks, Miss Vicki." Brittany closed her book and marched off. When she shut her bedroom door, Gloria whispered to LaVern.

"As much as you adore Britt, I know you want to do more than listen to her read."

LaVern just smiled because she was right.

She spent the week in Louiston enjoying the simple things. She, Brittany and Wilson took chilly, breezy walks on empty Carr's beach, she visited Mary Scales and was happy to know her BnB would be ready for the summer season. Everyone watched movies and laughed and joked in the intimacy of the cozy living room. It brought back fond memories of her parents' Gorsuch Avenue row home. *This is what I miss*, she concluded. *This is what I can't get in L.A., anonymity and true friendship.*

She was truly amazed when Wilson showed off his personal library, a built-on addition that doubled as an office. Wooden bookshelves lined every wall. The floor was a finished, dark wood laminate. His mahogany work desk sat in the middle, atop a woven, expensive looking, handmade area rug. In one corner was a black leather La-Z-Boy recliner. It had shiny, brass studs that followed the curve of its rounded armrests and continued down the front of each leg, which gave it that wealthy, aristocratic air. Nothing like its weary cousin in the living room. It was accented by a silver arc lamp. Sliding glass doors provided access to the adjacent patio. Wilson sat down in the hand assembled, ergonomic office chair behind his desk, leaned back and stretched his long arms out.

"Welcome to my world," he proudly exclaimed.

LaVern was still standing in the doorway, spellbound.

"Willie, this is magnificent. I had no idea."

"Most people don't get to see this."

LaVern walked around slowly, wordlessly, pulling out

books here and there and reading just the spines on others. There were autobiographies, fiction, historical and contemporary non-fiction, sports, and music. There were encyclopedias, atlases, reference books, science, world history, nature and more.

"Have you read all these books, Willie?"

"Yes I have. I don't put them up until I've read them."

Just like Brittany, thought LaVern. She pulled out a book and began thumbing through it.

"That's a good one Vicki. That's about the diaspora of Black people from the Jim Crow south to the cities in the north. The author said when Black's first made the move north in numbers, starting around 1915, it was the first time we, as a group of people, made a decision we didn't first ask White folks for permission. That's a powerful statement and I've never forgotten it."

Wilson was able to recall facts from every single book she showed interest in. He was becoming more amazing by the minute. Right then and there LaVern felt that the moniker "Willie" didn't seem to fit. She decided she'd call him Wilson.

One evening after he returned from a city council meeting, Gloria had a serious discussion with her son. She was having trouble discerning LaVern's true motivations. The fact that she came back in the dead of winter caught everybody by surprise.

"She seems to be a nice young lady. But please be careful Willie. You've worked hard for many years, and you have a thriving business. You never know what people's true intentions are."

"Momma, you're worrying for nothing. I like Vicki too, but nothing and nobody will jeopardize my business. She seems more interested in the simple things."

"You may be right Willie, but just take it real slow with her until you're sure."

"Alright Momma. I'll take it slow."

Shaundra and Gloria Davenport had the same worries, but for different reasons.

As her week in Louiston was nearing its end, LaVern's cell phone started to blow up. Shaundra called. Darien called.

Melanie called. Everyone was reminding her that she had to get back. On their final evening, Wilson and LaVern planned to take a last walk on the beach. LaVern was waiting in the living room as Wilson went into his office. Gloria took this opportunity to ask LaVern directly about her son.

"Miss James, I need to ask something, and I hope you don't take offense, but I have to know before you leave."

LaVern thought she and Gloria were getting along great. Now she was alarmed.

"Yes ma'am," she replied. "What do you want to ask me?"

"Miss James, do you have deep feelings for my son?" She followed her question with a very scrutinizing stare. A more scrutinizing look than she ever used before.

"To be honest, Mrs. Davenport, I wasn't sure before I got here. I knew I wanted to get to know him better, but now, after this past week, I'm certain, I have deep feelings for Wilson."

Gloria held her gaze and nodded her head. Wilson appeared and sensed he had missed something.

"What are you two talking about?"

"Just some girl talk, Willie. You go on and enjoy that walk on the beach."

Wilson and LaVern, both dressed for the brisk ocean wind, headed out the front door. As they strolled hand in hand on the hardened sand, in the vanishing sunlight, they talked about their week together. Yes, she enjoyed her time with him and his family and yes, she would be back in the summer. They shared a hug and kiss before Wilson drove LaVern back to the Armistead. As she closed his passenger door and Wilson came around to her side, Shaundra's comment came back to her, "remember, he's never called you".

"You know Wilson, we've been staying in contact only because I've been calling you. You can call me sometimes too, you know."

She placed his hands in hers and craned her neck up to look straight into the eyes on his six-foot two-inch frame.

"Wilson Davenport, I like you. I like you a lot and I know you like me. I don't regret a minute of the time I've spent with you and your family. But, after I leave here tomorrow, I will wait to hear from you first. If you don't call me, I'll know how you truly feel." She released his hands, turned and walked into the Hotel.

When LaVern returned to L.A., Shaundra, quite naturally, wanted to know all the details. And LaVern told her everything, including the part about waiting to see if he would call first.

"What if he doesn't call, Peaches? I hope he does, but what if he doesn't?"

She pursed her lips and exhaled through her nose. "Shaundra, I'll just have to move on."

LaVern made that statement with absolutely no conviction. She would be devastated if Wilson didn't reciprocate her feelings. For her best friend's sake, Shaundra hoped it wouldn't come to that. LaVern hadn't put her heart out there for a very long time. And she didn't do it very easily. She busied herself that day by going over scripts. Shaundra gave the thumbs up to some, held her nose on others. LaVern laughed and, at least momentarily, forgot about that dreaded phone call. As the afternoon wore on, every time her phone went off, she rushed to see who was on the other end. Afternoon turned into evening and still no call. LaVern was becoming despondent. At 7PM, her ringtone sounded again. She glanced over and gasped.

"It's Wilson." LaVern took a second to gather herself. She didn't want her voice to betray any of the angst she endured that day. "Hello Wilson, I'm glad you called."

"Hi Vicki. Are you still up? I didn't want to wake you. I didn't know what time you went to bed."

Bed? What's he talking about? It's only seven. Oh... wait. He thinks I'm in Baltimore, and it is ten in the evening there.

"I would have called earlier but an emergency council meeting put me way behind. Things got pretty heated in there. I don't make it a habit to call people this late, but I wanted to talk with you the first chance I got." He paused. "I owe you an apology."

"Oh?" responded LaVern.

"Yes. I apologize for making you feel unwanted and unworthy of something as simple as a phone call. You were right, I do like you a lot and I promise to never make you feel like that again."

LaVern was moved beyond words. It was so raw and honest…so Wilson. She felt like a schoolgirl, giggly and upbeat and obviously relieved. They talked for another hour before Wilson said he had to get some rest. Shaundra was still unsure where this would lead or how it would turn out. For right now, she was content that her BFF would not get her heart broken.

By mid-July, Shaundra and LaVern were back in Louiston. On the drive in, Shaundra, not having seen the city since the hurricane a year previous, was astonished at so much residual carnage. LaVern expressed delight and assured her that much had been done since her last visit. When they pulled up to Mary Scales' place, she was there to greet them, with her customary apron tied around her waist as she wiped her hands with a dish towel. The Home Away From Home had rebounded from Horace's visit quicker than many other businesses. Andre came swiftly down the steps, prepared to perform his normal unloading duties. Shaundra stopped him.

"Andre, the last time I was here we left so suddenly that I never thanked you for all you did during the hurricane. Here, I want you to have this." She handed him a fifty-dollar bill.

LaVern reached into her purse and handed him another fifty.

"Wow. I never got a tip this big."

"We just want to acknowledge how much we valued your service last year." announced Shaundra.

"Thank you, Miss James, Miss Davis."

"Come on up girls," shouted Mary, "let me introduce you around."

On the porch they were greeted with the sight of some of Mrs. Scales' other guests. All were new to her BnB.

"Evening everyone," began Mary, "these are two of my regulars. This is Vicki and Barbara. They've been coming here for four years."

"Hi Vicki, Hi Barbara," came the unified response.

"Hello everyone," LaVern replied.

"Hi everybody," added Shaundra. "Nice to meet you all."

"Come on inside ladies," said Mary. "I know you want to rest up"

When they entered the lobby, LaVern and Shaundra were relieved to see the space restored to its previous splendor; Armistead Louis was back on his exalted perch on the wall, the oriental rugs and mahogany tables had been saved and returned to their rightful places, and the piano was intact and still commanding attention in the corner. Some items were different; there were replica Tiffany table lamps now and stylish new floor lamps. The fireplace mantel had new water themed artifacts.

"Dinner will be ready at six. Are you eating here tonight?"

"You know it," said Shaundra. "And we won't be late."

That evening, as the sun sought refuge below the western horizon, Mary and LaVern were sitting and chatting alone on the porch.

"I hear you and Willie are getting pretty tight, huh?"

"Yes, Mrs. Scales, Wilson and I are dating. We like each other a lot."

"That's good to hear, he's a good man."

They stared briefly at the vanishing sun. A dog wailed in the distance.

"Willie is one of the most honorable men I've had the pleasure of knowing. I've watched him grow up." She paused. "You know, Brittany's mother was his high school sweetheart. She left because Louiston was too small for her. He refused to relocate. She broke his heart."

I've never asked about Brittany's mother, thought LaVern, *because I assumed he would tell me in his own time.*

"His father died when he was in high school and Gloria retired early to be home and help raise Brittany." Mary paused again. "He's a characterful man, and he always tries to do the right thing, even if it's not the easy thing."

LaVern didn't say a word. This was unsolicited testimony, a time for listening.

"He's a dedicated family man and he doesn't let people in very easily. I guess, since you two are so close now, you already know all this."

Some, but not all.

Mary stopped talking and, for the first time in several minutes, made eye contact with LaVern, as if she suddenly feared she was giving away too much information.

"Let me shut up," she said. Another pause. Then, "I'll finish by saying this. Willie deserves a good woman. He really does."

Mary Scales is giving me a subtle warning. If my intentions aren't honorable, back off. It was her way of protecting him. She need not worry. I've found the man I want to marry.

One evening after dinner, LaVern made a request of Shaundra.

"Wilson is on his way over. Can you leave us alone for a little while?"

Shaundra raised her eyebrows. "Oh, it's *that* time? I'll give you all the room you need. I have lots of reading material."

When Wilson arrived, he was in a harried state. Shaundra was sitting alone in the lobby reading a book.

"What's wrong?" he asked. "She sounded stressed."

"She's fine. She's upstairs."

Wilson bounded up the stairs two at a time. He knocked on the door.

"Come in Wilson, it's not locked."

He entered expecting to see a frazzled and distressed Vicki. She was instead sitting quietly on the side of the bed fully dressed. She was looking at him and smiling brightly. He glanced around the room and couldn't detect signs of an emergency.

"Is everything alright Vicki? Are you okay?"

LaVern rose from the bed and walked over to him. "Everything is fine, Wilson." She reached up and placed both arms around his neck and kissed him passionately. She held it for several seconds, then pulled back and looked into his eyes.

"Oh," he said, and wrapped his strong arms around her back. She kissed him again, long and hard. He picked her up and carried her over to her bed. LaVern and Wilson made love that night. Afterward, they cuddled and enjoyed one another's closeness. Both felt wanted and safe and secure. As they spooned, LaVern spoke.

"Wilson, I know you have to work tomorrow. It's okay if you go."

"I don't want to Vicki. I love holding you like this."

They snuggled against each other more. LaVern held his arms tightly against her body.

"I don't want you to go either, but if you have to, it's OK." LaVern turned to face him and tenderly traced her fingertips over his mouth, nose and eyes. "We'll see each other tomorrow."

He kissed her and ran his fingers through her hair. "I'm staying. I won't be able to sleep at home because I'll be thinking about you."

"Good," she replied, "that's the way it's supposed to be."

LaVern and Shaundra became a regular presence in the Davenport household. They dined together, they watched TV together and enjoyed the city together. Wilson even showed Shaundra his library. Her newfound appreciation of the written word made this revelation even more impressive to her. LaVern was past being impressed. This handsome, unpretentious, intelligent man was a gem. Her gem.

One evening, Gloria had everyone watching one of those rumor spreading celebrity investigative shows that Wilson detested. LaVern and Shaundra were worried that something about LaVern would pop up.

"I don't understand why famous people need to put their personal business out there for everybody to know," he said. "Keep your personal business to yourself."

Amen, thought LaVern.

"There're so many movie stars and athletes and businesspeople in this country who have more money than they can spend in ten lifetimes," he ranted. "They have everything they ever wanted and have traveled everywhere they want to go. Why don't they spend some of that wealth on causes that help ordinary people?" He was so much like her father. She couldn't give any man a greater compliment than that.

By the time she left Louiston, LaVern was convinced that Wilson Davenport was the man of her dreams. But, like Shaundra warned a while back, she now had one monumental problem. She wasn't who he thought *she* was. How would he react to her deception? Would he be angry? Would she lose him? Suddenly, LaVern was scared.

"It Ain't Easy, But it Ain't Complicated"
Chapter Twelve

LaVern may have felt she had time to resolve the "Wilson" issue before she left for Louiston, but she was out of time now. If her relationship was to continue to flourish, she would have to make some difficult decisions. During the ride to Charleston, even though Shaundra maintained a steady stream of conversation, LaVern's mind drifted back to Wilson.

I have to tell him who I really am, but how? He places a great deal of importance on honesty and candidness. As much as I love him, I'm ashamed to say, I haven't been either. I can't leave with this unresolved. The pressure would grind me into dust. My father would say. "You owe it to this guy to be honest, Peaches. Tell him the truth and accept the consequences. It ain't easy, but it ain't complicated."

But first. LaVern had to be sure of one thing. She pulled out her phone.

"Who are you calling, Peaches?" asked Shaundra, her head pivoting from the road to LaVern and back.

LaVern held her forefinger over her lips.

"Hello Vicki," Wilson answered, "I didn't expect to hear from you so soon."

LaVern got right to the point. "Wilson, I have to ask you something and please…please answer me truthfully."

This call was like a boxer's stiff left jab. It definitely got his attention.

"Ahhh…OK Vicki."

"Wilson, do you love me?"

This felt like a left hook, he was knocked back on his heels.

"The honest answer is yes, Vicki. I love you. I've felt that way for quite a while. I should have let you know by now–"

LaVern cut him off. "The only thing that matters Wilson, is that you love me. Because I love you too."

"Well, I'm glad we got that straightened out. You had me worried. Are you OK?

LaVern hesitated, she dreaded all that was to follow. "The honest answer, Wilson, is no, I'm not OK."

A blind side punch. Wilson needed a standing eight count.

"If there's anything you need to talk about Vicki, you know you can talk to me."

"I do need to talk to you, Wilson, but I'll have to come back to Louiston."

"Come back? You just left."

"I can't do this over the phone. I have to see you... now."

Wilson was officially worried. Did she have a fatal illness? Is she in the witness protection program? Am I going to regret falling in love with this woman?

"If it's that important, then come on back."

"I'll be there in forty-five minutes. Please remember Wilson, I really do love you."

That last statement did little to quell any fears he had. He was not looking forward to her return.

"What's this all about, Peaches?" asked Shaundra.

"It's about you being right a long time ago. Now, I have to deal with it."

When they pulled up to the Davenport house it was dusk. LaVern felt her stomach knot up as she stepped out of the car. She wondered if this would be the last time she would be welcomed here. Shaundra gave her some words of encouragement.

"Peaches, I know how much you want this to work out. But, even if it doesn't, just remember, we have each other, like always."

True, but LaVern knew losing Wilson would be a totally different type of loss. Her mother's wise words came flooding back to her. "It's very difficult to find someone that's *right* for you."

If this was one of her movies, there would be a happy ending. But this was real life, with a potential for real heartache. Right at that moment, the front door opened, and Wilson stood in the doorway. LaVern headed up the brick path with Shaundra following close behind. He swung open the screen door and watched LaVern, trying to discern any tell-tale signs of what could possibly explain all this secrecy. They mounted the porch.

"Hi sweetheart," he said as he wrapped his arms around her.

She squeezed him with all she had and held on. LaVern placed her head on Wilson's chest and rested it there, never once relaxing the death grip she had around his waist. She did all this without saying a word. Wilson was perplexed. What could possibly cause Vicki to behave this strangely?

"I think we should get inside," he whispered into her ear.

She finally released him, and they entered the living room. Gloria rose from her chair and greeted LaVern and Shaundra warmly.

"I didn't expect to see you ladies again so soon."

"Thank you so much Mrs. Davenport" offered Shaundra. "I apologize if we have inconvenienced you and your family in any way."

"Oh no...no, no. Don't worry about that. Please make yourselves comfortable."

"Thank you," stated LaVern.

Gloria returned to her chair and looked at LaVern. She was alarmed at what she saw. "Vicki, you look weighed down and worried. It's all over your face and body. Unburden yourself. We're all family here."

"Is Brittany here?" asked LaVern.

"Britt is at the Tomlin's house," said Wilson. "We didn't know what this was all about, and we thought it would be better if she wasn't here."

LaVern was relieved to hear that. What was about to be discussed was not for the ears of a five-year-old. She visibly steeled herself, took a deep breath, and dove right into the deep end.

"Wilson, Mrs. Davenport...I am not who you think I am."

The Davenports looked confused.

"What do you mean?" asked Wilson.

"I mean my name is not Vicki James."

Both Davenports stared with open mouths.

"Why did you misrepresent yourself to me and my family?"

demanded Gloria.

"I needed to hide my true identity."

"Hide your true identity? What does that mean?" asked Wilson. "Are you wanted by the Feds or something?"

"Oh no, nothing like that."

Gloria's eyes narrowed menacingly. She sensed that her family was endangered, and she went into protection mode.

"Well, Miss whomever you are, what's your real name?"

"My name is LaVern Whitaker."

"Why did you feel you had to keep that from us?" asked Gloria.

The name didn't register like LaVern and Shaundra thought it would. She would have to expound.

"I'm LaVern Whitaker, the actress."

Now, the Davenports were really at a loss. Wilson, like Gloria, shifted into protection mode.

"Let me get this straight," he said in an increasingly adversarial tone, "you're not Vicki James, the businesswoman, but LaVern Whitaker, the famous actress? Is that what you expect me and my mother to believe?"

"Please believe me Wilson, it's the honest truth."

Wilson rose to his feet. He rolled up on his toes and back as he spoke. "Well, I don't believe you, whoever you are. At this point, I don't know, or care, what your real name is."

The irony was inescapable. LaVern came to Louiston to hide her celebrity, and now she had to prove she was one. She reached into her purse and pulled out her driver's license.

"Wilson, look at this please."

She handed it to Gloria, who briefly perused it, then handed it to Wilson.

"This doesn't prove anything," he exclaimed. "People with bad intentions always cover their asses. This could be a fake."

She turned to glance at Shaundra. Her eyes were pleading for help.

"Wilson," Shaundra said, "google her name and you'll see she's telling you the truth."

"Don't make me waste my time," was his angry response as he towered over them. "Britt asked me if you were going to be her new mother. I told her I hoped so. She was so thrilled.

What do I tell her now?"

Wilson was fuming. He couldn't believe that, of all the families in the entire United States, this total stranger would choose to bring her brand of misery to *his* family. He raised his hand with his thumb and forefinger approximately an inch apart.

"I'm this close to throwing both of you out of my house!"

LaVern panicked as she looked up at him. She felt everything she held near and dear slipping away. "Please don't do that Wilson. I'm sorry for all the deceptions. I know I seem like this utterly despicable person. I really am LaVern Whitaker, the actress, and I'm in love with you."

Shaundra made one last attempt to sway him. "Wilson, she's telling you the truth. Peaches, take your wig off."

This was news to Wilson. He never suspected Vicki wore a wig, or anything else false. LaVern hastily removed her brown, curly, short haired wig to reveal her natural, shoulder length, straight black hair. She took out her light-colored contact lenses and Wilson saw her naturally dark brown eyes for the first time.

"Now, google her," said Shaundra.

He pulled out his phone and was amazed. His eyes went back and forth from his phone to the woman sitting on his couch. They looked eerily alike. He sat back down.

"You have a resemblance to her but that doesn't prove anything either."

He wanted to kick both out of his and his family's life forever, but he wanted to make sure he was right. He asked her questions even the most prepared person would have difficulty answering if they were lying. Name the associate producers in your first three movies. He googled it and she was right. LaVern Whitaker can sing, sing for me. She did. Name the director of your first professional play. She was right again. When Wilson completed his mini cross examination, he was still unsure. It didn't make any sense. *If she was who she claimed to be,* he asked himself, *why did she come to Louiston?*

LaVern explained the plot from beginning to end. Falling in love with him was an accident, falling in love with Louiston was an accident, all the friends she had made was an accident.

But they were accidents she did not regret. She walked over to where the Davenports were sitting and poured her heart out.

"I'm a woman just like any other woman. I just happen to be in a business that pays well and keeps me in the public eye. Mrs. Davenport…Wilson, I'm so sorry I put you through this pain." Her eyes began to swell with tears. "Please believe me when I say this," she made eye contact with Gloria, "I love your son with all my heart, and I wish like hell I didn't have to show it to you this way. I love you both and I love this house, and I love Brittany. It would kill me if I couldn't stay a part of your wonderful family."

The Davenports sat in stunned silence. Shaundra stood and hugged and consoled her best friend.

"What about you?" Gloria asked Shaundra. "Is your name really Barbara Davis?"

"No ma'am, my name is Shaundra Jackson. Peaches and I have been best friends since elementary school. It was my idea to come to Louiston in the first place. So, in a way, all this is my fault. If you want to be mad at someone, be mad at me."

LaVern walked over to where Wilson was still seated in his recliner and spoke directly to him. "Just in case you still have doubts about who I am and my feelings for you Wilson Davenport, I want you to do one more thing for me. Wednesday night I'm going to appear on Dave Franklin's Late-Night Show to talk about a project I'm involved in. I want you to watch because during the interview, I'm going to bring my hands together in front of my face and I will bow my head. That will be for you, and right after the show I'm going to call to make sure you watched."

LaVern bent over and placed her hands on both sides of his thinly bearded face.

"I love you Wilson Davenport so much that it hurts. You're the best man I have ever met in my life. Please don't shut me out." She kissed him hard on the lips.

"I think we should get going," interrupted Shaundra, who had one last parting shot. "In case you still don't get it Wilson, think about this. Peaches could have any man on this planet if she wanted to, but she wants you. She chose you. Come Wednesday night, you'll find out she was telling the truth."

Neither Gloria nor Wilson knew what to think now. It was inconceivable that anyone would put themselves through such anguish to sustain a lie. A lie whose only reward was the love of another. Before they departed, everyone embraced cautiously, one last time. Wilson accompanied them to their rental where he and LaVern shared a friendly kiss. He watched as their taillights disappeared into the pitch-black distance.

LaVern kept her word. On Wednesday night, just before the show went to commercial, as the camera came in for a closeup, LaVern brought her hands together just below her chin and bowed her head to the camera. Wilson and Gloria were flabbergasted. The woman who swore her love to Wilson Davenport of Louiston, South Carolina, son of Gloria and father to Brittany, was a bona fide movie star. Mother and son stared at one another, still not comprehending the why of it all.

"Momma, I don't know what to say. I fell in love with Vicki James, and she turned out to be LaVern Whitaker. This cannot be happening."

"Willie, I don't know what to say either. But you can't fake what we just saw."

They sank back into their respective chairs in silence. Neither could conceive of such a scenario even in their wildest dreams. Then, his phone rang. It said "Vicki".

"Hi Vi…I mean LaVern. I saw the show."

LaVern caught the faux pas. "I guess you'll have to get used to calling me LaVern, Wilson. I want you to know I told you the truth and my feelings for you are genuine."

"I believe you, but it's all so overwhelming. My mother and I are sitting here in a daze. It's almost too much to handle."

"I'm not going to stop seeing you Wilson, and the first thing I need to ask is that you don't tell anyone outside of your family about us. Believe me, I speak from experience when I say this. We don't want any outside intrusions. It won't be pretty."

This was the first indication that his life was about to change. Normal people don't have to worry about such things.

"OK… LaVern. Anything else I should know?"

"Yes, there is. I would like your family to meet mine."

"I would love that," declared Wilson. "You've told me so much about them. I like meeting good people."

"Good. Let me know when you can free yourself and I'll get Amy to take care of everything else."

"Amy? Who's Amy?"

"Amy Pennington is my business manager. She handles all my travel arrangements."

She had someone to handle travel arrangements, he thought. Things were moving fast.

"I'll give her your number and when she calls, just let her know when you can travel, OK?"

"Alright LaVern. I've never been to Baltimore. I'm looking forward to it."

"Baltimore?" exclaimed LaVern, "no Wilson, you're coming to California."

Of course, thought Wilson. *Where else would LaVern Whitaker live?* This was becoming more confusing by the second.

"My mistake, LaVern. I'm trying to keep things straight, but it's a lot at one time."

"I'm sorry for bringing all this disorder into your life Wilson. It's one of the things I really agonized over before I came back to Louiston. But things will settle down, trust me. Then we can go back to the way it was."

Wilson couldn't see how that could possibly happen. Things were already careening out of his control.

"I have to go now," said LaVern. "I can't wait to see you again. Please come as soon as you can, OK?

"I will, I promise."

"I love you, Wilson. Give my love to Gloria and Brittany."

"I will. I love you too."

Wilson disconnected and looked at his mother, whose eyes were fixed on him. "Well?" she inquired.

"The first thing I've gotta do is change LaVern's name in my phone."

"Is that all?"

"No Momma, it looks like we're going to California."

Revelations
Chapter Thirteen

Just as LaVern had promised, Amy Pennington contacted the Davenports and arranged for their transportation. Gloria and Wilson were thunderstruck by the level of privilege accorded them. Not only were they being flown on a private jet, a first for both, but a car would pick them up at their home and take them to Charleston, where LaVern's parents would greet them. More concerns centered on Brittany. This would be her first plane ride. Will she think everybody has a car to pick them up and take them to a private jet? The potential for significant changes in their lifestyle was becoming tangible. Wilson wasn't sure if that was good or bad. His ringtone soon sounded. It was their ride, right on time.

"Alright, it's time to go, everybody." Wilson shouted. He flung the front door open, grabbed Gloria's baggage, and headed onto the porch and down the steps. The driver quickly approached.

"I'll take those for you, sir."

"That's OK," Wilson said. "I do this all the time."

The driver ignored him and reached for the luggage. "I must insist, sir. I'll take care of these for you."

Wilson was surprised by the driver's insistence. *Oh,* he thought, *this must be a part of the service the privileged get. This will take some getting used to.* He brought the rest of the baggage onto the porch and the driver hustled them down to the car. When Wilson looked at their vehicle, he was once again astounded. It was a brand-new gun metal gray Porsche Cayenne Turbo SUV, a car he could never, even in two lifetimes, afford. Gloria came out of the house and stared at a car she had only seen in the movies. Brittany rushed by, totally oblivious as to whether it was a Porsche or a Hyundai. The driver opened the door, and she jumped into the back seat.

"Come on Daddy, Meemaw. Let's go."

As they took their seats, Wilson and Gloria marveled at all the swanky features surrounding them, the buttery soft leather upholstery, the giant computerized touch screen on the dashboard, the video screens behind the front seat headrests, and the temperature controls for the rear seats. This ride to Charleston would be unlike any they'd ever taken.

When they arrived at the airport, the car went directly to a section that Wilson did not even know existed. They pulled up to a small nondescript building where their baggage was unloaded for them. They were escorted into a brightly lit, private reception area where there were cushioned chairs and stylish tables with live flowers on them. They were offered drinks and food and other niceties not available to the commercial traveler. The Davenports were alone and not sure what to do next, so they stood, unmoving, amid all this extravagance. A young woman came out of a side office and introduced herself.

"Hello, my name is Wendy, and you must be Mr. Davenport."

"Yes, I am, and this is my mother, Gloria and my daughter Brittany."

"Hello," chirped an excited Brittany. "This is my first plane ride."

"Oh, that's wonderful!"

She turned her attention back to Wilson. "According to my ledger, you and your family are the only passengers boarding from here."

"That's what I was told."

"Your plane is almost ready. Is there anything I can get for you while you wait?"

"No thank you Wendy," responded Gloria. "Everything is wonderful."

"If you need anything, I'll be behind the counter, please don't hesitate to ask."

Wendy returned to her duties and the Davenports returned to gawking at their surroundings. Brittany noticed the big picture window and raced over.

"Is that our plane Daddy? It looks smaller than the airplanes

I see on TV."

The Davenports walked over to the window and sure enough, on the tarmac, far away from the larger passenger jets, sat a small, gleaming, white, Gulfstream G650 midsize jet, with the baggage crew loading their luggage.

"Yes sweetheart," said Wilson, "that's our plane. It's smaller than the regular planes because they're only meant to hold a few passengers."

"Oh," answered a disappointed Brittany. She was looking forward to riding in one of the giant airplanes. From behind came Wendy's voice.

"Please follow me and I'll escort you to your plane."

She opened the door and immediately the noise of the airport that was mutated while they were inside blurted out at them. There was a gush of hot wind followed by the sounds and pungent odor of refueling aircraft saturating the air. The summer heat bounced off the tarmac as The Davenports followed Wendy to the foot of the retractable stairs. There she bid them farewell.

"I hope you have a pleasant flight." She whirled around and quickly headed back inside.

"Who's that Daddy?"

Brittany was looking up at the top of the stairs and pointing. There was a smiling face in a uniform shirt with epaulets and cap beckoning them on board. Gloria went first, followed by Brittany. As each reached the entry door, there was a quick conversation with the smiling face, a handshake, and then they entered. When Wilson approached, the smiling face introduced himself.

"Hello Mr. Davenport, I'm Captain Thompson, I'll be your pilot for this flight. Welcome aboard. Please head into the cabin and Janey will take care of you."

Everybody knows my name, thought Wilson. *More privilege.*

"Thank you, Captain."

Wilson turned to enter the cabin and saw his family introducing themselves to the Whitakers. He looked at the father, Freeman. He was a tall man, much like himself, with a goatee sprinkled with gray and a close-cropped Afro. He looked comfortable in his jeans, (his thumbs tucked into the front pockets) polo shirt, and Skechers casual dress shoes. Everyone exchanged hugs and the Whitakers offered them a seat. Freeman remained standing as Wilson approached.

"Wilson Davenport," he exclaimed. "At last, we meet."

The two men shook firmly.

"Likewise, sir," Wilson stated, "it's a pleasure to meet you."

"Dispense with the sirs Wilson, my name is Freeman, and my wife is Jackie. Have a seat."

Unwittingly, the two families seated themselves on opposite sides of the aisle. Just as everyone was getting comfortable, the stewardess emerged from the rear of the plane.

"Hello, my name is Janey Trafton, and I'll be your hostess for this flight. We'll be serving dinner a little later. I have some sandwiches and snacks if anyone wants something right now."

"Daddy, can I have some juice please?"

Before he could say anything the hostess responded, "Of course you can sweetheart. Can I get anything for anyone else?"

"Coffee for me please," said Gloria.

"Sweet tea for me," said Wilson.

Just as everyone was getting settled in, Jackie's phone went off.

"It's Peaches." she said.

Everyone remained silent as Jackie and LaVern talked briefly.

"Yes, Peaches, everybody's on board. We should be taking off any minute. OK … OK, I love you too. I can't wait to see you either. Bye bye."

Jackie looked at the Davenports. "She's always so worried about us."

"You two have raised a good daughter," said Gloria. "We've gotten to know her very well."

"You call her Peaches? I didn't know that," said Wilson.

"Yes," said Jackie. "She's been Peaches since she was born."

Wilson's phone went off.

"We all know who that is," mocked Freeman.

"Hi LaVern. Yes, everything is very nice. Yes, everything went smoothly."

Her conversation concluded with "I love you, Wilson."

He hesitated.

"It's OK to say it, they know I love you."

He regretted having been prodded. "I love you too, LaVern."

Over the intercom, Captain Thompson announced that everyone must buckle up and prepare for takeoff. Within minutes, the jet was accelerating down the runway, fuselage vibrating, pushing everyone back into their pillowy seats. Brittany's initial excitement fused into fear. She had never been inside of something that moved so fast or bumped so much. The ground outside became a blur. Soon, the vibration stopped, and the families were airborne. As the jet gained altitude, Wilson took time to assess the classy interior. It could hold up to eighteen people, he surmised. The double seats were soft, plush, off-white leather and reclined fully. The floor was carpeted and there was wood paneling throughout the cabin. Along one side was a long, luxurious, leather sofa. There were polished wood tables adorned with fine white linen and several flat screen TV's. throughout. Wilson thought, *so this is how the other half lives.*

Janey returned with the refreshments and the conversations started. The Whitakers asked Wilson about life in Louiston and his HVAC business. The Davenport's asked about how LaVern came into acting. In time, the families melded. The women found common ground in their educational backgrounds and wound up sitting side by side. They swapped tales about classroom antics, from the ridiculous to the inspiring. The men found a commonality in their views of Black pride, belief in family, and being providers. They shared a table. Brittany, having overcome her initial apprehension, became as energetic and curious as ever. She explored every inch of the jet from the pilot's cabin to the rear galley, peeking into every nook and cranny and bombarding Janey and Captain Thompson with endless questions.

The families shared a table at dinner and swapped fun, as

well as tragic family events. Brittany endeared herself to the Whitakers when she, without being coerced, went into her backpack for a book. She talked about her library and her desire to add to it when she got to California. Halfway into the flight, with bellies filled, fatigue took over. During the next few hours, a sleepy silence enveloped the cabin. By the end of the flight, The Whitakers and the Davenports had become great friends.

The previous summer, LaVern decided to relocate to Southern California. Los Angeles and the mansion had become little more than gaudy symbols of decadence. As Lori predicted, her investment sold at a profit. It was late afternoon when their jet landed at San Diego International Airport. After they taxied to a stop, everyone rose and started toward the front, where Captain Thompson and Janey were waiting. They thanked the pilot and the attendant for their professionalism. A blacked-out Lexus, with the engine running, was waiting for them and the driver hastily opened the doors. Wilson wondered aloud about their luggage.

"Oh, they'll bring those to the house later," said Freeman. He noticed the look of surprise on Wilson's face.

The driver jumped onto interstate five north and thirty minutes later, the car began winding its way through the streets of Solana Beach, a small, tight knit seaside community. The mostly White inhabitants strolled the sidewalks in tee shirts, tank tops, shorts, flip flops and sunglasses. The car pulled up to a set of elaborately designed iron gates.

"Who lives here Daddy?" asked Brittany.

"This is where Miss Vicki lives, baby," said Gloria.

Freeman punched in a code on his cell phone and the metal gates slowly pulled apart. As they drove up to the house, Wilson was pleasantly surprised at LaVern's choice of residence. It wasn't one of those typical Hollywood mega mansions. For a star of her magnitude, Wilson reasoned, she was living way beneath her means. As they pulled up to the front, there were two smiling female figures standing side by side, waiting and waving. As the families emerged, LaVern ran straight to Wilson and jumped into his arms and wrapped her legs around his waist. She kissed him and whispered,

"I've missed you so much."

As LaVern and Wilson clung to one another, Shaundra was left to greet everyone.

"Hi Mr. and Mrs. Whit. Good to see you again."

"Good to see you too, Shaundra," said Jackie. "Give me a hug."

Freeman waited patiently. "Shaundra, it's worth it to fly all this way just to see that beautiful smile of yours. Where's my hug?"

"The same place it always is, right here."

LaVern finally released Wilson and replanted her feet on the ground. She turned her attention to Brittany.

"How's the smartest little girl in the world? I'm glad you finally get the chance to visit me at my house."

"I'm glad too, Miss Vicki. I really miss you when you're not around."

LaVern bent over, took Brittany into her arms and held her tightly. "I miss you too, sweetheart."

Shaundra moved on with her greetings. "Mrs. Davenport, Wilson, welcome to California. I hope your flight was enjoyable."

"How could it not be? " said Gloria. "I've never been on a private jet before. It was wonderful."

The two women embraced warmly.

"Like my mother said, it was fantastic. So much special treatment. I'm not used to that."

Shaundra gave Wilson a hug too. LaVern approached Gloria.

"It's so good to see you again, Mrs. Davenport. Welcome to California."

"Thank you, LaVern, for everything."

"Oh, it was my pleasure."

It was Freeman and Jackie's turn now and LaVern hugged each long and hard with her eyes closed. With all the obligatory greetings out of the way, LaVern urged everyone to enter the house.

"Let's not stand around outside like a bunch of strangers. Everybody…go inside."

Standing just inside was a short, wide woman with a round face, dark eyes and dark hair tied in a bun. LaVern introduced her housekeeper.

"Everyone, this is Marta. She graciously agreed to stay late to prepare a lovely dinner for us. Muchas gracias, Marta."

"Oh, de nada Senorita," she said. "It was nothing."

Everyone thanked her for her hard work, and she retreated into the interior of the house.

Gloria gasped out loud, "Oh my goodness. You have a beautiful home."

"I want you and Wilson and Brittany to feel like this is your home too."

Right at that moment, "Lucy", the home security system, started to flash. LaVern went to her laptop and engaged the security camera.

"It's our luggage."

She dialed the code, and the gates separated. The driver drove up to the front steps and LaVern, via her security system intercom, told him to leave the bags at the door. Wilson was again impressed by the seemingly unending array of extravagances at LaVern's disposal.

After unpacking, everyone meandered back into the kitchen where they enjoyed Marta's delicious dinner of carne asada con frijoles. Afterwards, LaVern took the Davenports on a tour of her home.

Her beach house, unlike the L.A. mansion, was elegantly understated. It was a two-story residence with five bedrooms and five baths. There was an enormous kitchen with an island and all the modern conveniences, adjacent to a family area where everyone could congregate to eat and talk and watch the giant, 88-inch flat screen. Through the sliding glass doors was the enormous outdoor patio, perched high atop a cliff overlooking the Pacific Ocean. On the same floor was a stylishly furnished living room with original artwork mounted on the walls, a traditional, formal dining room and a finely appointed den. Outside was an automated two-car garage. Upstairs were four of the five bedrooms, a common area, and all but one of the bathrooms. LaVern's home bespoke money, not pretentiousness. There were precious few reminders of the glamorous business she was in. All the adults had their own room. Brittany and Gloria would share one. Wilson requested this arrangement out of old fashion deference. He wanted Brittany to see only married couples sleeping together.

"My goodness LaVern," exclaimed Gloria, "you have exquisite taste."

"Thank you so much Mrs. Davenport. I just try to keep things simple."

"It's so big, Miss Vicki," blurted Brittany.

Once again, the reference to LaVern as Miss Vicki brought into focus one of the primary reasons for this trip. It was time to have "the talk". All parties assembled in the family area and LaVern asked Brittany to sit beside her.

"Are we going to watch movies now, Miss Vicki?"

"Maybe later. First, we have to talk, Britt."

"OK."

LaVern nervously scanned the room. Wilson nodded his silent approval. She took a deep breath.

"Britt, I know you know me as Miss Vicki but that's not my real name."

The six-year-old looked confused. Her eyebrows furrowed and she looked down at her sandal-clad feet, which were hanging off the edge of the long, sectional lounger.

"Your name is not Miss Vicki?"

"No, it's not."

More staring at her feet, which were now twitching nervously.

"What's your name?"

"My name is LaVern...LaVern Whitaker."

"Can I call you Miss LaVern?"

"Of course you can, sweetheart."

Brittany looked up at her and smiled. Seeing those gaps where baby teeth had fallen out was the most beautiful smile she had ever seen. But the job wasn't complete. Wilson leaned forward in his chair.

"Britt, do you know why Miss LaVern changed her name?"

The little girl looked at her father, then at her meemaw, then back down at her feet.

"No Daddy."

"She did it because she's famous."

She looked up into LaVern's face. Her eyes seemed to be searching for something. LaVern nodded her head and smiled. Brittany looked back at her father.

"Like in the movies?"

"Yes, just like in the movies."

She looked back to LaVern. "How come I've never heard of you?"

Shaundra let out a howl, then quickly covered her mouth, trying, in vain, to stifle a laugh. LaVern ignored her.

"I haven't made any movies for children. You wouldn't be able to see them."

"Oh."

Wilson continued. "Famous people are recognized everywhere they go. They never have any privacy. So, when Miss LaVern came to Louiston, she used a different name to ensure her privacy."

"Oh."

"Miss LaVern wants you to know her real name now because she loves our family, and she loves you very much."

Brittany once again looked up at LaVern and smiled. LaVern gave her a tight hug and kissed her on the forehead.

"If you're famous Miss LaVern, do you know The Rat Tails?"

Now, it was LaVern's turn to look confused. Gloria came to her rescue.

"You wouldn't know them, LaVern. They're puppets in a video she saw that came with one of her books."

"Sorry Britt, I don't know them."

"Oh." Brittany sounded so disappointed. *How can she be famous if she didn't even know the Rat Tails?* she wondered.

"I can show you some clips from some of my movies if you want to see them."

"OK."

She retrieved some of her DVD's and they sat together, with LaVern's arm draped around Brittany's shoulder, and watched select scenes, ones where she looked more like the woman sitting next to her. *She has seen me in disguise long enough*, LaVern said to herself. She didn't like watching herself work so as soon as Brittany seemed convinced that Miss LaVern was a real movie star, she looked for a distraction.

"Hey everybody," she shouted, "the sun is going down."

Every head turned to look through the sliding glass doors.

"Oh, it's beautiful," sighed Gloria.

"This is my favorite thing about this house. I get to watch the sunset every evening. Let's go out onto the patio."

Brittany leaped from the couch, dashed ahead of everyone and stood on the bottom rail of the balcony. Gloria followed right behind. Everyone else remained inside. LaVern went over and put her arm around Wilson and breathed a sigh of relief.

"Boy," she said, "that wasn't as traumatizing as I thought it would be."

"Children are so amenable," observed Jackie. "So unpredictable."

"Yeah," said Freeman. "We were worried about the whole false name thing and her only concerns were 'how come I never heard of you' and 'do you know the Rat Tails?'"

Everyone got a laugh out of that. They joined Brittany and Gloria on the balcony and watched and held hands in silence as the sun retreated below the Pacific horizon.

The following morning, after breakfast, Shaundra urged LaVern, "Tell everybody what you have planned for today."

"Oh yeah… I came up with what I hope will be a fun thing to do. Has anyone been up in a hot air balloon?"

There was a unanimous no.

"Good," said LaVern, "Everybody go get ready." She disappeared into her bedroom and reemerged in her now familiar floppy straw hat, dark sunglasses, shorts and flat sandals. "I'll get the car."

After forty-five-minutes, they arrived at a mammoth open field in Temecula, California. LaVern brought the vehicle to a stop, and everybody gawked. Enormous balloons were scattered all over the spacious grounds. The huge bags were an artist's palette of reds, blues, yellows, greens and pinks. Some were already fully inflated, still tethered to the earth, their inflated bulk straining skyward. Others were resting lazily on their sides, only partially inflated, as if napping. Still others were already airborne, doting the sky both near and far, like upside-down floating, colorful Hershey's kisses.

"Look at how big they are!" exclaimed Brittany from her open window.

"Boy," remarked Wilson, "they're huge."

LaVern and Shaundra were the first out. The others followed tentatively. As the group approached, one of the pilots came to greet them.

"You must be LaVern Whitaker," he said.

"Yes, I am, and this is my family."

"Nice to meet all you folks. I'm Phil and I'll be your operator today. Follow me and I'll get us started."

The group followed the pilot as he headed toward one of the giant, fully inflated bladders.

"Because there are seven of you, you'll need two balloons. Our limit is four per basket plus the pilot."

"OK" said Freeman, "Peaches, Wilson, Gloria and Brittany stay here. The rest of us will go to another balloon." He pointed his forefinger skyward. "We'll meet you up there."

That's when Wilson noticed Brittany. Normally rambunctious and curious, she looked terrified.

"I don't want to go Daddy."

"Why not Britt? Meemaw and I are going."

"I'm scared."

"There's no reason to be afraid sweetheart," said Gloria. "We'll be with you."

Brittany looked up at the balloon, then looked at her father, and then down at the ground. LaVern tried to help by climbing inside.

"See Brittany, It's safe."

Even Gloria swallowed her apprehensions and went over to the gondola. It wasn't a graceful sight, but, with Phil's help, she made it into the basket.

"See Britt" said Wilson, "Even Meemaw knows there's nothing to be afraid of."

Brittany wrapped her little arms around her father's neck, and he climbed in with her. She was trembling. When she finally released her chokehold, she immediately slumped to the floor of the basket, knees against her chest, arms wrapped around her legs, chin buried into her knees, afraid to stand.

"Poor thing," sighed Gloria. "I didn't think she would be this scared."

LaVern sat beside her and held her.

"If everybody's ready," called out Phil, "I'm taking this puppy up."

He released the tether, fired the thrusters, and the basket began to lift. As they gained altitude, Wilson became fascinated.

"This is great. Look at the view."

He gazed at the hazy horizon in the distance and at the surrounding mountains. He looked down at the maze of roads and the sparsely populated landscape.

"And look," cried out Gloria, "there's lots of balloons already up here. This is not so bad. It's so quiet…so peaceful."

After a few minutes, the airship reached its maximum altitude and floated noiselessly through the mid-morning sky. The only sound was the occasional thrusting of the blue and yellow fire breathing burners. It couldn't be any quieter if you had ear plugs.

"Which balloon are the others in?" asked Wilson, as he leaned casually against the side.

"Let me call Shaundra," said LaVern.

A minute later Wilson saw arms waving from a nearby balloon. "There they are," he shouted. "They're all waving."

On the floor, LaVern was talking to Brittany. "Don't you want to wave at the others?"

"I'm too scared."

"Why are you scared?"

"I don't know, I'm just scared."

LaVern got to her knees and straightened up. "Try this." She raised her head high enough that just her eyes were above the side of the basket. "Just peek over the side like this. You don't even have to stand up if you don't want to."

Brittany cautiously pivoted onto her knees, eased her hands along the inside of the basket until she could wrap them around the rail. She straightened up and peeked out, her eyes barely above the top. She quickly resumed her place on the floor.

"We're up so high."

"You still haven't seen the others waving," said LaVern. "Don't you want to see them?"

Brittany raised herself again and peered over the side. "I see them waving," she said excitedly. Just as quickly, she ducked back to the floor.

"See?" said LaVern. "That wasn't so bad, was it?" She gave Brittany a big hug. "That was so brave of you."

Brittany, for the first time since she left the safety of the car, smiled brightly. Even though she never left the floor again, LaVern considered this a victory. She helped Brittany confront a fear.

Despite assurances that her presence would be kept quiet, word spread that LaVern Whitaker was at the field. The commotion began after their balloon landed. A woman approached.

"You're LaVern Whitaker aren't you?"

LaVern didn't have time to even reply.

"Would you please sign this for me? My friends won't believe me when I tell them I ran into you at a hot air balloon park."

As always, LaVern was accommodating. "Of course."

One fan turned into a trickle and before long she was surrounded. LaVern was signing everything from slips of paper to hats to tee shirts. There were many requests for selfies and others were taking videos with their phones. Wilson was unsure of what he should do, if anything. Freeman passed along some sage advice to the uninitiated Wilson.

"If you're serious about my daughter, you need to stand at her side at times like this and call an end when she sees fit." He paused. "And get used to it."

Wilson looked at the swelling horde. LaVern seemed to be getting overwhelmed by the sheer numbers. He knew she was too polite to say no, so he waded through the mass of autograph seekers until he was standing at her side. He whispered in her ear. "Have you had enough?"

"I'm worn out, to be honest."

That was all he needed to hear. Wilson raised his arms and

announced to the crowd. "Sorry folks, that's all for now. Miss Whitaker has to leave." He put his arm around her shoulders and led her away from her fans. Even when they reached the car some of them continued to beg for pictures and autographs from outside the closed, tinted windows. He started it up and pulled off.

"Can somebody please tell me where I'm going."

"I'm sorry sweetheart," said LaVern. "Just make this left and we'll be on the highway."

As they put distance between them and the fans, the Davenport's first experience with the day-to-day reality surrounding LaVern's celebrity was unnerving for them. Freeman had to put things into focus.

"You know Wilson…and Gloria, what happened back there is pretty much business as usual when you're out in public with my daughter. Even her hat and sunglasses didn't keep her from being recognized. And things can quickly get out of hand."

The Davenports listened intently.

"What you did, Wilson, will become, unfortunately, a regular chore. It's an unattractive part of the life of a celebrity."

"What did she do before I came along?"

Even though his question was directed at Freeman, Shaundra answered.

"I had to go East Baltimore on'em Wilson, you know, get'em straight. Some of these fools don't care about boundaries. They walk right up on you and shove a camera or a piece of paper in your face. I had to tell a lot of them off. But you handled it like a man. At least there was no paparazzi. They're the worst."

LaVern looked across at Wilson and gently squeezed his hand. "I'm glad *you* were there today, sweetheart."

He squeezed her hand in response.

A fatigued LaVern said, "I think we all need to take the rest of the day off."

The San Diego Zoo was the highlight of the trip for Brittany. She was a nonstop bundle of energy, in stark contrast to the frightened and sullen child at the balloon park the previous day. She flitted around, like a butterfly in a field of flowers, from one animal exhibit to another. After trekking for a half hour, the older adults gave in to their tired feet and found a bench to rest on.

"You guys go ahead," yelled Freeman. "We'll be right here if you want to find us."

It was a typical hot, sunny, Southern California afternoon and Wilson, LaVern, and Brittany stopped for ice cream. LaVern removed her sunglasses to dab her sweaty forehead. A visitor standing beside her glanced in her direction. LaVern saw the look of recognition. The visitor nudged his wife, and she looked also. She calmly replaced her shades and turned to walk away.

"You're LaVern Whitaker aren't you?"

"Please," she said, "keep your voice down and I'll sign whatever you have. I don't want to draw a crowd."

"Oh, thank you so much Miss Whitaker. I love your movies."

LaVern discreetly signed for both and quickly urged Wilson and Brittany to move on.

"Let's head back," she said quietly.

Wilson, by this point, knew what to expect. He grabbed Brittany with one hand and LaVern with the other and they headed to rejoin their group. After a short distance, LaVern looked back. The two for whom she signed were showing their autographs to others and pointing at her. She pulled out her phone and called ahead to Shaundra and told her to get everyone ready to move. Wilson looked back and noticed a small group following, but at a respectable distance. Then, a few of the followers broke from the pack and rushed forward. Wilson kept his arm around LaVern's shoulders to urge her to keep moving. The migrating crowd drew curious glances from those nearby.

"That's LaVern Whitaker!" someone shouted, and the size increased. They became so encircled they were barely moving. Freeman saw them coming.

"You ladies stay here while I give Wilson a hand. Then, we can move together toward the car."

Gloria was particularly horrified. She couldn't even see Brittany in all the confusion.

"I'm not staying here," she declared. "I'm going to save my grandbaby from being trampled!" She darted off in search of Brittany with Freeman right behind her. Shaundra turned to Jackie.

"When they get here, we can work our way to the exit, and we'll lose most of this crowd. They won't want to pay to reenter."

"Good thinking." replied Jackie.

Freeman and Wilson ran interference and kept the family moving. Gloria had Brittany by the hand, LaVern, still hidden behind her straw hat and sunglasses, signed what she could as they continued toward the exit. When they crossed under the famous San Diego Zoo sign, the crowd fell off dramatically and the party scampered to the car. As they drove, an exhausted and flustered Gloria called out.

"LaVern, how can you live like this? I've been here two days, and I'm worn out."

"When I want to leave this insanity, I go to Louiston, that's how."

Back at the house, they were greeted by Marta.

"Welcome back everyone. Dinner is almost ready."

They thanked her on their way to finding a comfortable spot to flop down. The Davenports were especially worn out. This was an entirely new ordeal for them. Shaundra rose from her cozy spot and walked over to "Lucy" on the kitchen island. She touched it.

"Lucy, lock all the exterior doors."

There was a red light followed by a beep. "All exterior doors are locked," came the robotic reply.

"Is that all it takes?" inquired Wilson.

"Yep," replied Shaundra as she wandered back to her nest.

"And all the doors are locked?"

"Every one of them."

She sat down and kicked her shoes off. The family room looked like a spa, with everyone, except the perpetually bubbly Brittany, flat on their backs with their shoes off, their feet up and their eyes closed. Brittany sat crossed legged on the floor, eyes glued to the flat screen. Just as everybody was about to doze off, Marta called them to eat.

"Do you want to eat in the dining room or aqui in the kitchen?"

It was unanimous for eating in the much more informal kitchen. Everybody could still chat and move around and glance over at the monstrous flat screen without missing a single mouthful of Marta's scrumptious, Ropas Viejas, a shredded beef dish. Afterward, both families retreated to command central, the spacious family area. A Disney movie was on but only Brittany was watching. The remainder of the clan were in various stages of recuperation.

During their week-long stay, the Davenports explored Solana Beach, with all its niche markets, trendy stores and neighborhood eateries. They went to San Diego Harbor where the men saw modern aircraft carriers, and toured the Midway, a WWII era warship. They took Brittany to the bookstore where she browsed slowly and carefully before finding three books to her liking, one being "The Hungry Caterpillar".

The sights and smells of the San Diego Zoo Safari Park were a big hit. It was as close to an African savanna as one could get without going to Africa. There were free roaming giraffes, rhinos, gazelles, wildebeests, and even a troop of gorillas led by an imposing, muscular silverback. All viewed from their open tram. Acacia and baobab trees dotted the entire plain. And everybody loved the cheetah race.

The time enjoyed by most was the family time at the end of every day. After all the hustle and bustle of going from here to there, it was the time together in the family area, command central, where everyone went barefoot and lounged in pajamas, where the conversation was jovial and relaxed, and snacks and the TV were just a few steps away, this is where the Whitaker and Davenport familial bonds were cemented. The scene filled LaVern with pride.

This group is my rock.

During one of the last days of their stay, Wilson emerged from the bathroom and LaVern was sitting by herself on the patio. Everyone else was in command central watching a movie. She motioned Wilson to join her.

"I'll never get used to having a flat screen in the bathroom," he said as he sat beside her. She cozied up to him and rested her head on his shoulder.

"I'm so glad our families got this chance to spend time together," LaVern said dreamily. "You have no idea how insanely happy I've been this entire week."

"I have to admit this week has been nothing short of a revelation. Your life is so crazy. I don't know if I can handle it."

LaVern straightened up and stared at Wilson. "What do you mean by that?"

"I have to be honest, LaVern. All this is nice but I'm not leaving Louiston and I'm not giving up my business. It has too much of my sweat in it. It may not be much compared to what you have, but it's mine. I fell in love with you before I knew who you were, and I can't imagine my life without you. But I have a business to run and I look forward to getting back to that. Out here, I feel like my life is out of control, like I'm on foot, trying to keep up with a speeding car. I'm used to things being more settled, more predictable." His voice lowered. "My family and I don't need a whole lot because we already have plenty. I hope you can understand that."

Wilson sounds just like Shaundra when she said, "none of this belongs to me". I forget how my lifestyle can smother people. I'm fortunate to have the people I love most in the world not give a damn about the material things I can provide. Wilson is a prideful man, just like my daddy. I love that about him. I have to let him know that my celebrity is not a threat to him... or us.

"NO, no, no sweetheart," LaVern replied. "You don't understand."

She locked eyes with him and held his head in her hands. "I'm ecstatic you're not taken in by all this glitz. It's just a necessary evil. I fell in love with you and Louiston for a reason, and that reason hasn't changed." She put her face inches from his. "Wilson Davenport is who I love. When you say your family has plenty, I hope you're including me."

With his head still firmly in her grasp, Wilson managed a reply. "I'm so relieved you feel that way. I really didn't want to lose you."

They kissed passionately and for a long time.

"Wilson, I'm not going anywhere."

Suddenly, Brittany pushed open the patio doors. "Miss LaVern, they're showing one of your commercials on TV Come on!" She rushed back inside.

LaVern kissed him one more time. They walked hand in hand into the family area.

Three Become One
Chapter Fourteen

The following spring, Wilson made an unusual request of LaVern. He asked her to come visit for a few days and, despite the irregularity of it, she eagerly accepted. Wilson phoned her at The Home Away From Home and said he'd be over after work. Good, she said to herself, that's something both of us will enjoy. When Mary Scales heard a knock on her door, she parked her tired feet inside of her woolen slippers and slowly trudged her way through the darkened lobby. At the door, she parted her lace curtains to see the Davenports standing there. She was used to Wilson stopping by to see LaVern, for obvious reasons, but not the whole family. She opened the door.

"Well, this is a pleasant surprise. Come on in y'all, get out of the evening chill."

"Thank you, Mrs. Scales," said Wilson.

"Good to see you again, Mary," said Gloria. She glanced around the lobby. "It's been a while since I've been over here. It's looking nice, as usual."

"Thanks Gloria. You're looking well yourself."

Mary looked down at Brittany. "Look how you've grown. You're going to be taller than your grandma pretty soon."

Brittany smiled broadly. "Thank you, Mrs. Scales."

Wilson looked toward the stairs. Mary took notice.

"You can go up. She's the only one here."

He walked to the steps, climbed them with ease and disappeared down the hall. He knocked on LaVern's door and heard a very sexy voice.

"Come on in handsome, I've been waiting for you."

Wilson opened the door and saw LaVern lying provocatively on her bed in a "barely there" negligee. He admired the sight briefly, but that was not what he was there for.

"Not tonight, LaVern. It's not the right time."

She was shocked and sat straight up. "I certainly have never heard that out of you before."

"It's not what you think. Can you please put on some clothes?"

"And I certainly never thought I'd ever hear *that* out of you either."

Wilson exhaled in exasperation. "I can't propose to you in that outfit."

"Whaat!?"

He reached into his pocket and withdrew a black, velvet covered box. Wilson started down on one knee. LaVern's hands shot up to cover her mouth. They were shaking wildly.

"Oh my God!" she exclaimed and started to cry.

"Miss LaVern Renee Whitaker, since you have come into my life, I have known nothing but happiness. Not only are you beautiful, you're intelligent, loving and unselfish. You've accepted my family and thereby enriched us beyond measure. I didn't know where or when or if I would find the right woman. I know one thing for sure… my search is over."

LaVern's sobbing and wailing became louder. Downstairs, Mary Scales heard all the commotion.

"Is everything alright up there?"

"Believe me Mary" assured Gloria, "everything is just fine."

"LaVern, I love you and I don't want a life without you. Would you please give me the honor and privilege of becoming my wife."

LaVern was as weak as Jello. Her body convulsed involuntarily. Her face was tear streaked as she stared down at the man she had loved for so long.

"Yes, Wilson" she replied in a shaky, barely audible voice. "Yes, I will be your wife." Still weeping, LaVern reached out and placed her arms around Wilson's neck. With her mouth next to his ear, she whispered again. "Yes, I will be your wife."

Wilson straightened up. LaVern's feet were now dangling a foot off the floor. They kissed and hugged and cried together. When their lips finally parted, Wilson lowered his fiancée.

"You haven't even looked at the ring," he said.

She wiped away her tears and took a deep breath. "You're right, Wilson. Forgive me."

He handed the box to her, and she slowly pulled it open. She gazed lovingly at her engagement ring as it rested in its black, velvety surroundings. Its brilliance was dazzling. LaVern carefully removed it, and Wilson gingerly placed it on her finger. She held it up to admire it even more.

"Wilson, it's soooo beautiful."

"I know it's not as expensive as you're used to but–"

"Oh, shut up you big…loving…perfect example of a real man. It's beautiful because it's from you."

"We should go downstairs," Wilson said. "Everybody's waiting."

"You didn't tell me people were waiting," said LaVern, still barely covered by her flimsy negligee. "Give me five minutes."

Wilson sat on the bedside and waited. "What do you think about having the ceremony here, in The Home Away from Home?"

"I think it's perfect. I wouldn't want to have it anywhere else."

As they descended the staircase, Gloria stood up immediately and looked for a sign. The glow on LaVern's face told her all she needed to know. Mary sensed something was in the air. All the silent communication was not lost on her.

"What's going on?" she asked. "Everybody's in on something except me."

"Mrs. Scales, I guess it's only fitting you should be the first to know," said Wilson.

LaVern couldn't contain herself. She was bursting at her emotional seams. "Wilson asked me to marry him, and I accepted," she blurted out, then proceeded to hold up her hand and show off her new ring.

"Congratulations," said Mary. "I'm not surprised though, you two are closer than bark on a tree."

"I'm sorry I couldn't tell you Mary" uttered Gloria. "The news had to come from them."

"That's OK. Gloria, I understand."

"But," said Wilson, "we do have a couple of requests of you."

"Sure Willie, anything you need."

"My fiancée and I request the honor of having our wedding here, in your house."

"Why, of course you can. I insist."

"And there's one other thing that's very important to us."

"Anything, just ask."

"We would like for you to keep our wedding a secret."

Mary was dumbfounded. "A secret! Why, for heaven's sake?"

"I'll get right to the point Mrs. Scales," began Wilson. "First of all, Vicki James is not LaVern's real name."

"Who's LaVern?"

"Here we go," moaned Gloria.

"Wilson, if it's alright with you, maybe I should explain everything to Mrs. Scales," said LaVern.

He breathed a sigh of relief. "By all means, go ahead."

"Let me begin, Mrs. Scales, by saying my real name is not Vicki James. It's LaVern Whitaker. I make movies and I am marrying Wilson right here in your BnB. And the reason we need you to keep this a secret is because, if it became public knowledge, Louiston would be inundated with reporters and paparazzi, and it would ruin everything I love about this place. So, please, don't mention this to anyone, not just yet."

The room went silent. Mary went from face to face. She looked at Gloria, who nodded in the affirmative. She looked at Wilson and he did the same. Brittany leaned against the arm of LaVern's chair, yawned and stared at the floor.

"I know this is a lot to handle," said Gloria. "You've known me for twenty years and you know I'm not given to playing games. Everything LaVern said is true. We ask that you keep it to yourself for the time being. That's very important to us. Please."

"OK," she said hesitantly. She stared at LaVern. Mary's mind replayed the events of the past few years. "Wait, I introduced you two!"

"You certainly did," said Wilson.

"I didn't know I was introducing you to a movie star."

"I didn't know you were introducing me to my future husband either," said LaVern.

Gloria brought everyone back on point. "Mary, we'd like to stay and chat, but it's well past Britt's bedtime. I know we can trust you with this."

"You certainly can." responded Mary. "I won't breathe a word."

When the Davenports exited through the front door, Mary remained in the middle of her dimly lit lobby, as LaVern reclimbed the stairs to her room. She was staring at her new jewelry. Mary's mind reeled.

"I've got a movie star staying in my place."

The next day, after a blanket twisting, sleepless night, LaVern began calling all her loved ones with the good news. She had to answer the same questions: no, we don't have a date yet, yes it will be here in Louiston, yes it would happen quickly because the BnB would start to fill with seasonal guests in a couple of months. Then, there was the privacy issue. How long could they realistically expect their marriage to remain a secret in tiny Louiston?

LaVern returned to California and intensified her preparations for relocating to Louiston. She informed her small coterie of business associates of her decision: Darien was in favor of anything that made her happy, Melanie and Amy were elated that she found happiness. Her most difficult conversation would be with Shaundra. Her lifelong crutch, her confidant, the person who had been through everything with her since elementary school. How could she tell her they couldn't be like they used to be? Life had interfered and altered her priorities.

I'll have a husband and a family now. I'll live in a different part of the country. I didn't plan it this way. My mother told me years ago that the only predictable thing in life is change. Boy, was she right.

One afternoon, as they were lounging in the shade on the patio, Shaundra was chatting it up, as usual, but LaVern seemed preoccupied and distant. After being inseparable for over twenty years, Shaundra could read her like braille.

"What's on your mind Peaches? And don't say 'nothing' because I know you better than that."

LaVern inhaled deeply. Shaundra knew what that meant.

"I have something very difficult to say and I don't know if I can do it." She wasn't looking at Shaundra. She was staring out over the calm Pacific. A tear tumbled from under one eye from behind her sunglasses. Shaundra was alarmed and sat up and turned to face her friend.

"Talk to me, Peaches."

She still couldn't look at her. "I'm relocating to Louiston."

Shaundra sat back in her chaise lounge. "I figured you would, Peaches. I'm not surprised."

"That means we won't be around one another like we used to be."

"I know," she said sadly. "I've thought about this too. It breaks my heart, but this was bound to happen. You don't need me hanging around all the time anymore, you have Wilson, and that's the way it should be."

"Thank you for understanding Shaundra."

She looked at LaVern. "Don't worry about me. I really like this real estate thing. It's something I'm good at and I enjoy it. I want to stay here and develop that." Shaundra reached over to grasp her hand. "Don't tear yourself up over this Peaches. I know you're worrying about me, but I'll be alright."

LaVern gripped her hand firmly. "You can live here for as long as you want Shaundra. I'll take care of everything." She hesitated before she continued. "Besides, I'll need someplace to stay when I come to visit."

The women giggled, then went silent.

"I want you to know that no matter how my life goes, no matter how far apart we may be, no matter how long we go without seeing each other, you will always be my very best friend. I love you Shaundra Jackson."

The best friends hugged and realized that life had indeed interfered and there was nothing either could do about it. LaVern felt unburdened enough to share all the details of her trip to Louiston. She talked about how Wilson proposed, with her in a nightie and everyone waiting downstairs, revealing her true identity to Mary Scales, and her plans to build a new house. LaVern also found time to reunite with Freda Parks. She and Shaundra motored up the picturesque I-5 to Los Angeles to lunch at her home. They dined on her veranda and Freda's meal didn't disappoint.

"Freda, girrrl," crowed Shaundra, "this meal was Gucci. If I was a man, I'd marry you."

Everyone laughed hysterically. They ate and gossiped for the rest of the afternoon then, LaVern confided that she was getting married.

"Really? I haven't heard anything. Is it anybody in the business?"

"No way, and please keep it to yourself for now."

LaVern also shared that she was relocating to Louiston. She extolled the virtues of life there; it's seclusion and tranquility and quality of people.

"You make it sound so wonderful, LaVern. I've been searching for a place like that for years."

"It's an unbelievable town," said Shaundra.

"You really should go, Freda," added LaVern "There's a fantastic BnB there and I know the owner personally."

"Well, I'm working now but I'll have some time later this summer."

"Let me know when you're free and we can get together."

They regretted having to depart because, as Shaundra said, "I love chopping it up with Freda."

The idea that those two were close gave LaVern great solace. In the beginning, it was LaVern who needed someone she could trust. Now, it was Shaundra who needed a confidant. *Thank you once again Freda Parks.*

The invitation list was short. Freeman and Jackie, Shaundra, Darien and his family, Mary Scales, Gloria and Brittany. Only the necessary few, and everyone stayed at the Home Away From Home. The Whitakers came in a week early and LaVern showed them around and shared all the reasons she fell in love with the town, from its founding, to its ideal location, to the precious objects in Mary Scales' lobby. Freeman appreciated Louiston's historical and cultural significance. And, despite being greeted by a multitude of citizens, the Whitakers were amazed that she circulated unrecognized.

"They don't know who I am, and they don't care," LaVern was proud to say.

On her wedding day, Jackie, Gloria, Shaundra, Brittany, Erika Cheek and her six-year-old daughter Olivia were gathered in LaVern's room. She was surrounded by all the women whom she valued most. But, more importantly, these women valued her. And she needed each and every one of them to help reign in her frazzled nerves. LaVern wore a white, beaded, floor length gown by Ramon, one of the top designers in the country, a floral headdress and veil. Her manager, Amy, had it shipped overnight. The women agonized about every little detail. Does it fall properly? Should she wear the veil? Which pair of shoes go best with the dress? Is her makeup perfect?

Meanwhile, at the Davenport household, the men were having a less stressful time. Wilson's custom-tailored tux was also shipped in, thanks to Amy. They talked sports or politics and lazed about for most of the morning. Five-year-old Darien Jr. was flat on the floor, in his suit, more interested in his Legos than an impending wedding. They didn't even start to get dressed until an hour before they were to leave. It was then that Wilson started to exhibit telltale signs of anxiety. He grew restless and started to pace more. He asked more than a few times if Freeman was sure he had the ring.

"Relax son," counseled Freeman as he put a reassuring arm around his shoulder. "Take a deep breath. Everything is fine."

They walked into Mary Scales' lobby and were immediately awestruck. It had been transformed into a flower laden, candlelit, incense scented paradise. Mary was standing amid all this splendor.

"Oh my God," exclaimed Wilson, "this *room* is awesome."

"I agree," said Freeman. "This is magnificent."

"I'm speechless," said Darien. "What a transformation."

"Well, I'm glad you like it, gentlemen. Nothing is too good for my Willie and his bride." She gestured toward some overstuffed chairs. "Have a seat and I'll let the bride know y'all are here."

The men took their seats as Mary headed up the steps. Simultaneously, there was a knock at the front door. Wilson turned in his chair and recognized the male figure through the curtains.

"That's Reverend Prentis."

Wilson hurried over to let him in. Reverend Marshall Prentis was the serious and studious Pastor of the Mt. Zion Baptist Church.

"Well," he stated, as he entered, suited, bible in hand, "you look like a man who's ready to take care of business today, Willie."

"I'm more than ready Reverend. I can't wait to marry this woman."

"That's what I like to hear, young man, that's what I like to hear."

Wilson escorted Reverend Prentis over to the others. All the men stood, including little Darien, when he made the introductions. They resumed their seats and chatted among themselves. Darien had the energetic and curious Darien Jr. securely on his lap.

After a few minutes, Mary Scales came down the steps, sat at the piano and started playing the wedding march. All the women, save for Shaundra and LaVern, appeared on the upstairs landing. The men watched in silence as the maids of honor descended single file, bouquets in hand, down the stairs, little Olivia in the lead. It was a beautiful and graceful procession. They joined their respective families. Then, Shaundra appeared on the landing.

"Gentlemen!" she cried out, "please rise."

Everyone stood. Reverend Prentis and Wilson strode forward and took their places at the floral altar. As Mary played, LaVern appeared on the landing with Shaundra holding her train. She was radiant as she stood there gazing down at her wedding party, smiling and weeping at the same time. Wilson had never seen her look more beautiful. LaVern seemingly floated down the stairs. At the bottom, Freeman reached for her hand. He whispered to her how beautiful she looked and led her over to Wilson. They stared into one another's eyes as if nothing and nobody else existed. Reverend

Prentis began the vows but before he pronounced the betrothed man and wife, LaVern requested that she be allowed to recite her own written vows. Her final words were most moving.

"Wilson Davenport, you are not only the best man I have ever met, but you are also the best person I have ever met. I am so grateful you have allowed me to share your life with you."

Wilson had tears in his eyes. Finally, the Reverend said, "You may kiss the bride," and Wilson raised the veil and gazed upon his *wife's* face for the first time. They kissed for what seemed like minutes.

"OK," Shaundra shouted, "you two can stop now. There're children here."

Everyone laughed and threw rice and clapped and hugged the newlyweds. As LaVern hugged Gloria she called her Mrs. Davenport.

"Please stop that. Call me Gloria. You're my daughter- in-law now for heaven's sake."

Everybody posed for photos, and this was the first time that Wilson, LaVern and Brittany posed together as mother, father and daughter. Three had become one.

In the evening, the festivities wound down and the wedding party began to say their goodbyes. Everybody had to resume their lives. There were four private jets waiting at Charleston airport to whisk people to their separate destinations. Wilson and LaVern were heading on their honeymoon, a European tour from London to Paris and then Madrid. Darien and his family were heading to New York. Freeman and Jackie were on their way to Baltimore and Shaundra was flying back to San Diego. Gloria and Brittany were driving across town.

After the guests left and the cleanup crew had completed their chores, after weariness invaded every pore in her body, Mary Scales decided to retire. It was prayer room quiet now. When she pulled back her bedspread, she spied a thick, pink envelope with a smiley face.

"What in the world...?"

She picked it up and looked inside. Cash. And a lot of it. There was a note.

Dear Mrs. Scales,

Regretfully, this will be the last time I will stay at your home. From the beginning, you have treated me like family, even though you had no idea who I was. I will always treasure those times. I will still be around though. As you know, I love this town. Please accept this token of my love and respect for all that you have done for me. I'll see you when we get back.

Love,
Mrs. LaVern Davenport

There was 10,000 dollars in cash inside the envelope. LaVern did for Mary Scales exactly what Freda Parks had done for her years ago.

During the two weeks the Davenports were away on their honeymoon, the rumor mill was working overtime in Louiston. Where was he? Was Wilson married? Why was he keeping it a secret? Gloria and Mary bravely refuted the noise, but, by the time of their clandestine midnight return, the issue had become untenable. The following morning, Gloria assembled the newlyweds in the living room.

"Everywhere I go people are asking me if it's true. They're nice about it, but it's relentless. We need to do something."

"OK," declared Wilson. "We've got to end all this foolishness right now." He turned to LaVern. "Sweetheart, we have to tell people the truth."

"I agree, but how?"

"I think the best way is to tell everybody at once."

"How are you going to do that?" asked the doubtful Gloria.

"I can call an emergency meeting of the council, invite the public, and reveal the truth about our marriage. We'll answer all their questions."

"The news will get out," said LaVern, "and there'll be media from everywhere converging on Louiston like locusts."

"She's right, Willie," agreed Gloria. "It would be just a matter of time."

"Unfortunately, this matter won't die. I'm betting on the goodwill of our friends and neighbors to respect our request for privacy. It's a gamble, but it's the lesser of two evils."

LaVern spoke up. "There's one more caveat."

"What's that?" asked Wilson.

"I must be in L.A. the day after tomorrow. Can you bring all this together by then? I'd feel guilty if I left you guys here to face this without me."

"Let me make a few quick calls."

In minutes it was done. The four other council members agreed to meet the following evening at City Hall.

That night after dinner, Wilson went into his office to read, LaVern and Brittany watched TV on the sofa, and Gloria fell asleep in her favorite chair with her slippered feet propped up on an ottoman.

"Hey Britt", whispered LaVern, "I have a joke that's for just you and me. You can't tell anybody else, okay?"

She looked up and smiled. "Just for us? I like that."

"OK here it is. What did one strawberry say to the other strawberry?"

She thought for a moment. "I don't know."

"If it wasn't for you being so fresh, we wouldn't be in this jam."

LaVern waited for a reaction. Oh oh, she thought, she didn't get it. This was going to bomb.

"Oh, I get it," she giggled. Fresh strawberries… in a jam. That was a good one Momma. That was funny."

She said momma! This is the first time Brittany has called me Momma. I feel like I'm going to burst into confetti!

"That's our joke, OK? It's just between us."

"Okay Momma. It's our secret."

LaVern gave her a tight hug and rose from the sofa. "I'll be right back, I have to speak to your father." She headed to Wilson's office and slipped in as quietly as a snake. She walked over and sat on his lap.

"Hey babe, was up?" he asked.

LaVern was physically shuddering. She moved her face closer to his ear. "Wilson, she called me momma. I didn't prompt her. She just came out with it."

This was significant, and he knew it. They had talked about it, but agreed to leave it up to Brittany, in her own time.

"Congratulations sweetheart. You deserve it." He gave her a kiss on the cheek.

LaVern stood up and exited without a word. She returned to her place beside her daughter, and they continued watching TV.

Louiston City Council meetings were usually dull, robotic affairs held in a drab, linoleum tiled, artificially lit snoozer of a space with an American flag standing at attention in one corner. It was uncommon to see more than a few citizens in attendance and meetings rarely lasted more than one hour.

This evening proved to be an exception. The rumor mill went into overdrive when word spread that Wilson had requested this emergency meeting. When the Davenports entered the chambers, much to their surprise, the room was already packed. Every rusty, uncomfortable metal folding chair was occupied.

The council members were already seated behind the old, heavily scarred but sacred wooden desk. The Davenports sat together at one end.

Present was Harvey Wallace, the Council President, and the owner of the Armistead Hotel. Always impeccably dressed and in his mid-forties, he was short and squat and had an embarrassingly high, squeaky voice. He was very demonstrative, flailing his hands and arms about, like someone falling uncontrollably through midair.

There was Bertram "Bert" Willoughby, a local farmer and lifelong resident. He was long and lanky and was never seen out of his overalls, work boots, and sweat stained baseball cap. His labor hardened hands bore testament to a lifetime of working the soil. In his mid-fifties, he was more of a listener and a thinker, blessed with down-to-earth common sense.

Then, there was Stanley Payne, the owner of the golf course, one of the wealthiest landowners in the county. Average height and in his mid-forties, he was a little overweight with a thick, black beard. He was his own worst enemy due to his almost constant, unrestrained oral impulses. He often had to be reined in during meetings, like a bucking bronco, once he launched into one of his vocal tirades.

And there was the pharmacist, Velma Duhon, a transplant from Brooklyn, New York. The sole female member of the council, she was a descendant of one the original settlers and, having grown weary of the big city grind, decided to return to her roots. She was tall for a woman, in her late thirties with short twisties for hair. She was soft spoken but could hold her own in this room full of men.

Lastly, the secretary, Ruth Van Meter, the owner of the candle shop, and the only White person at the table. She was an administrative assistant in her working days and, now retired, volunteered her time to record the council's minutes.

The Davenports looked intently at the faces of their fellow citizens. Most were friends and acquaintances, some were strangers. There were men and women, families and singles, old and young, Black and White. Council President Wallace stood and brought his mallet down hard on the desk.

"This emergency meeting of the Louiston City Council will now come to order." His shrill voice elicited snickers from some in the gallery. "I'm sure you all know that this meeting was requested by one of our members, Mr. Willie Davenport. He's here with his family." Harvey glanced over to where the Davenports were seated. "Willie, you've got the floor."

The room got deafeningly quiet. You could almost hear heartbeats. Wilson stood and walked to the center of the room. With his back to the council desk, he began by raising up on slightly his toes and back down again.

"I want to thank my fellow council members," he turned to acknowledge them with a nod, "for this opportunity to address not only them, but you, my friends and neighbors. I'll be brief." He took a quick look at his family to his right and breathed deeply. "I want to lay to rest all the rumors and innuendo swirling around me and my family for the last month or so. First of all, yes, I am married. And this is my lovely wife."

"I knew it," whispered one grandmother to another. "I ain't never wrong 'bout such things."

"My family has gone through this a few times already and if it wasn't absolutely essential, we wouldn't be going through this again. LaVern, will you come up here, please?"

No one caught the LaVern slip-up.

"Please introduce yourself to the citizens of Louiston."

She hugged and kissed Wilson. "Thank you, sweetheart," she turned to face her audience, "and thank you all for coming out. I, too, plan to be brief. All of you have come to know me as Vicki James. My real name is LaVern Whitaker, the one you have probably seen in movies."

All the air seemed to have been sucked out of the room when everyone gasped simultaneously. The council members' heads swiveled left and right in disbelief. This same gesture was repeated throughout the gallery.

"You're LaVern Whitaker, the movie star?" someone shouted.

"Yes Leo, I am."

LaVern acknowledged the bakery shop owner from whom she always bought fresh rolls and pastries. The council room din started to rise. There were lots of mumbled, mouth-covered mutterings. Harvey Wallace had to gavel them to order a second time.

"Alright everybody, calm down. Let her finish."

"I would like to apologize to everyone for my deception, but it was necessary at the time. In the years I've been vacationing here, I have come to treasure this city. I love its people, its culture and its place in Black history." She looked adoringly at Wilson. "And I have come to love one of your native sons. I chose this place, and I chose this man, and his family has chosen me. It's because of that, and all of you, that I want to continue to live here. You've accepted me without even knowing who I was. That was very important to me."

Wilson put an arm around his wife and signaled for Gloria and Brittany to join them.

He stated, "Now that you know what's going on, me and my family have a request. We realize it will be almost impossible to keep this from getting out. LaVern, as you now know, is a well-known figure. We're asking that you respect our privacy and keep this as much a private, hometown thing as possible. I've known most of you all my life and you've known my mother longer than that. We want to maintain all the friendships we already have, but things have changed for us. I'm just asking that you consider the feelings of the people you see standing here. All we can do is ask."

Wilson gathered his troupe and headed for the chamber doors. The crowd condensed around them and politely asked for selfies and autographs, and LaVern obliged, a simple act, a small down payment on their pleas for secrecy.

LaVern now considered Louiston her base of operations. Darien forwarded all projects; movie scripts, Broadway offers, endorsements etc., there. Conversations concerning huge deals and enormous dollar figures became commonplace in the tidy little household. Her career path was now determined by what was in the best interest of her family. She was also pleasantly surprised at how the locals reacted to their privacy requests. When vacationers asked probing questions about the rumors, they were greeted with shoulder shrugs, feigned ignorance, or outright denials. The overriding mindset among Louistonians was, yes, she was LaVern Whitaker, the star, but more importantly, she was Mrs. Wilson Davenport.

Then, there was the issue of the new house. The family hired a major Black architectural firm, Ambrose and Sons, to design and build their home. It would be a much bigger, ranch style abode, the biggest, by far, in Louiston, and every family member would contribute ideas for the design.

For the first time in her life, Gloria worked with interior designers on the look and layout of her kitchen. She would finally get a spacious cooking area with modern appliances. Brittany would get a larger room, in her favorite yellow color, with more closet space, dressers, and bookcases for her ever-expanding library. Wilson would get a new home office and new computer equipment along with a separate space for his library. The look and design of the rest of the house was left to LaVern. The Davenports also had one other stipulation for Ambrose and Sons. They must hire as many local craftsmen as possible. Every available bricklayer, electrician, plumber, painter, roofer, every skilled or unskilled worker must be offered jobs first.

"That's how communities stay strong," said Wilson, "by keeping people working."

After a couple of months, LaVern received a disturbing call from Shaundra.

"This is just a heads up. The rumors about you being married are everywhere, and they're getting worse. Freda told me the paparazzi are looking for you in L.A."

"You're kidding me," said LaVern.

"Peaches, they're like bloodhounds with a scent and they're determined to hunt you down."

LaVern appreciated the warning, but she felt safe in Louiston. Her choice of this off the grid locale was paying big dividends now. *I'm just the hot story of the moment*, she realized. *Somebody or something will come along to replace me. This will pass.*

Wilson returned from a city council meeting one evening to some unexpected news. He didn't see anyone when he entered the house.

"Where is everybody?" he yelled.

"We're in here," LaVern replied.

"I've been telling him since he was a boy, no yelling in the house," said Gloria.

Wilson headed straight for his office where the women were resting on the sofa. He plopped himself down behind his desk and began to talk.

"Velma Duhon had a great idea to highlight our local Black history."

There was no response.

"Her plan is to seek funding for our own museum. She said we need to get all those artifacts out of Mary Scales' lobby, and all the other hidden places in the area, and into its own space. She suggested area tours, an information center and symposiums. I think it's a great idea and so does the rest of the council. What do you think?"

The two women just stared back with a slightly bemused look. Both were seated precariously on the edge of the sofa. They appeared anxious.

"What's going on? You two are up to something."

Gloria looked at LaVern and nervously patted her on the knee. "Tell him. Tell him before I bust."

Bust? he wondered. *What does that mean?*

"Wilson, as you know I had my doctor's appointment today."

He was suddenly worried. "Are you alright?"

"I'm fine," she said. "I'm also pregnant."

The news hit Wilson like a clap of thunder and sent a palpable shudder through his body. Both Gloria and LaVern were wearing smiles that even 'ol hurricane Horace couldn't erase. Wilson's face lit up. He rose to his feet and walked to his wife, who stood also. They hugged and kissed, and he went down on his knees and gently caressed LaVern's flat stomach. And he kissed it.

"Wilson," sobbed LaVern as she looked down and rubbed his head, "we're going to have a baby and I'm so happy. I hope you are too."

"Happy? Sweetheart, you've made me the proudest man on earth. Now, both our kids will have a real mother, a loving mother." He glanced back in the direction of Brittany's room. "Does Britt know?"

"I haven't told her yet," said LaVern. "I wanted to tell you first."

He looked at Gloria. "Momma, are you ready for another grandchild?"

"Ready? I'm going to spoil this one more than the first."

"I don't know if that's even possible," said Wilson.

They all chuckled and started toward Brittany's bedroom.

For several weeks LaVern's thoughts were consumed by an issue that just wouldn't go away. She couldn't talk to Wilson about it, so she went to her traditional sources of sound, sensible advice. She called her parents. It was on speaker phone.

"Mom, Dad, I really need to ask you something."

"You know you can talk to us sweetheart," said Jackie. "What is it?"

"First, let me say I am deliriously happy. I've found a man I love with all my heart, and he loves me the same. I have a career that gives me financial independence. I have the sweetest little girl and Wilson and I are about to have our own.

I have everything I have ever wanted." LaVern went mute. "What do you do when you've spent your entire life working and sacrificing toward a goal, hoping to reach the place where I am now, and once you get there, you're disappointed because something is still missing. Something intangible."

Freeman was quick to answer. "Peaches, when you have every material and emotional thing you could ever want, what's left is to give back. You help people."

"But I have, Daddy. I've helped you guys, I've helped Shaundra, I've helped Mrs. Scales…I've helped all the people I love in this world."

"What your father means Peaches, is you help people you don't know. You help strangers. Maybe that's the missing piece."

They're right. Just the notion of helping strangers gives me joy. My parents are so wise. The richest man on the planet doesn't have enough money to buy what I can get for free.

Spring morphed into summer and Louiston sprang back, as if a pair of giant defibrillators had shocked the sleepy town to life. Vacationers were everywhere, patronizing all the local businesses. The Armistead was almost at capacity, Mary Scales, literally, had a full house, and the beaches and marina were beehives of activity. Stanley Payne's championship golf course was the destination of choice for most of the male tourists. Construction on the new house continued unabated. The front, just like the original, faced east, and the rear faced west. Wilson liked the idea of catching the first and last light of the day. This house would also have plenty of garden space, given Gloria's green thumb.

LaVern received a call from Freda Parks. She finally had the time to treat herself to a vacation and she wanted to visit Louiston.

"That's fantastic Freda. You'll love it here. Let me talk to Mrs. Scales and I'll get back to you." Due to a last-minute cancellation, Mary would have a vacancy in a week.

LaVern picked her up at the airport and during the drive back from Charleston, she reveled in retelling the first time she and Shaundra came along this same road; being astounded by the bucolic landscape, the pastoral scenes of farmers working their own land, and the history of Louiston and how culturally important the town was. Freda was intrigued.

"If this place has all that, why haven't I heard of it?"

"These people don't seek attention, Freda. They're proud of the fact they are land and business owners and have been for generations. They don't need nor seek any outsider's attention or approval."

As they entered the city, LaVern pointed out all the local businesses where she not only shopped but knew all the owners personally. She pointed to a small breakfast place. "That's Grady Johnson's eatery, he only serves breakfast and lunch. And that's Velma Duhon's drug store, she's also on the city council."

It went on like this for blocks, the dry cleaners, the hat shop, the hardware store, the shoe repair shop, Mt Zion Baptist Church and the miniature golf course. Then, they headed to The Home Away From Home.

"Mrs. Scales is one of the finest people I have ever met in my life. I would be doing you a disservice if I didn't introduce you to her."

"That's mighty high praise. I can't wait to meet her."

As they entered the lobby, the mild groaning of the screen door gave away their presence. Mary was vacuuming her precious area rugs when she looked up. She smiled and turned off her vacuum.

"Well, what brings you by this afternoon, LaVern? Give me my hug."

As the two embraced, Mary looked over LaVern's shoulder.

"Who's your friend?"

"Mrs. Scales," said LaVern as they separated, "this is Freda Parks."

"Oh, I've been expecting you."

Freda approached and reached out her hand. "It's so nice to meet you Mrs. Scales. I've heard nothing but good things about you and your place."

"Thank you, Miss Parks."

"Please, call me Freda."

Mary didn't answer immediately because she was scrutinizing the face in front of her.

"You look familiar. Are you one of LaVern's Hollywood friends?"

"Yes ma'am" she responded. "I'm an actress."

"Don't worry," she said as she lowered her voice, "your secret is safe with me. I'll call my son Andre, and he'll take your things to your room."

"Thank you so much."

Freda started to slyly scan the lobby. LaVern took this opportunity to acquaint her with the true significance of what she was surrounded by.

"You see this fireplace, Freda? It was designed and constructed by local Black craftsmen. And that piano over there was in Amos Livingston's house for generations before he donated it to Mrs. Scales for safekeeping.

Mary was astounded as she listened to her describe, in detail, each artifact in her lobby. She had no idea LaVern had committed all this history to memory. LaVern wanted Freda to feel the same profound sense of pride and dignity she did when Mary first described the same items to her.

"This is a treasure trove Mrs. Scales," stated Freda. "I'm impressed."

"Well," said LaVern, "I hope you'll continue to be impressed when you come to my house for dinner tonight. I want you to meet my family."

"I'm looking forward to it."

"Good. I'll be back at five."

During the short trip to the Davenports, LaVern mentioned, "The best way to get a real sense of the city and the people is to explore on your own. Then, you'll get the true flavor of Louiston."

Good idea, thought Freda, *I will.* As they pulled up to the house, Freda was shocked.

"Is this your place LaVern?"

She couldn't disguise the disappointment in her voice. The house she was looking at would come as a jolt to anyone expecting to see the home of a movie star, even in Louiston.

"This is Wilson's home, we're living here temporarily. It really is quite warm and cozy. But we're building a new house right behind this one."

"Oh, that's good." Freda sounded relieved.

As they walked up the path to the screened-in porch, the front door swung open and Wilson, Gloria and Brittany stood together, smiling and beckoning. For the first time in her relationship, LaVern was about to present her family to someone from the outside. As they reached the porch, she gave each family member a hug and a kiss and waved Freda closer.

"Freda, I am very proud to introduce you to my family. This handsome hunk is my husband, Wilson Davenport. Wilson, this is my very good friend Freda Parks."

Wilson stepped forward and reached out his hand. "Nice to meet you, Freda. LaVern has told us a lot about you."

"Likewise, Wilson. It's a pleasure."

"And this is my mother-in-law, Gloria. Gloria… Freda Parks."

"My pleasure Freda," she said. "I hear you're a wiz in the kitchen."

"Why, thank you Mrs. Davenport. I understand you're no slouch yourself. I'm sure I can learn a lot from you."

LaVern placed a loving arm around the shoulders of the littlest Davenport. "And this intelligent ball of energy is my daughter Brittany."

LaVern deliberately did not say stepdaughter. There was no such thing in her world.

"Brittany, this is Miss Parks."

"Hi Miss Parks," she said as she extended her hand. She was practically glued to LaVern's hip. "It's nice to meet you."

"Oh, aren't you sweet? It's nice to meet you too, Brittany."

"Well," interrupted Gloria, "now that we've got all that out of the way, let's get off this porch and come on inside so Freda can relax. It was a long flight from L.A."

Once they were comfortably seated in the living room, LaVern explained to Wilson how she and Freda met; that she was just learning her craft when Freda came east and wound up impacting her life.

"You know," said Wilson, "you do look very familiar. I've

seen you on television."

"I've been in this business a long time, Wilson. I've done movies, TV and Broadway. I just like to stay busy."

The aroma of Gloria's dinner wafted in from the kitchen.

"Ooooh, it *smells* like I came to the right place," said Freda.

"Dinner will be ready in five minutes," came Gloria's voice from the kitchen.

Wilson rubbed his palms together as he rose from his chair. "You're in for a treat Freda. My mother ain't no joke." He headed down the hallway to wash his hands and told Brittany to get ready for dinner.

After refueling on Gloria's exquisite meal, Wilson and LaVern offered to take Freda to the construction site where the roof, the outside walls, and the interior weight bearing studs were in place. Also, the rooms were framed out. LaVern explained where the kitchen would be, along with Wilson's den and the dining room and so on.

"Oh, this is going to be gorgeous." She scanned the property. "And it's such a lovely location."

When Wilson was walking slightly ahead of them, Freda leaned closer to LaVern and whispered,

"Well done Mrs. Davenport."

Mrs. Davenport. That's the first time anyone has referred to me that way. I like the sound of that.

During the week, Freda went on her walking tours. She started at the marina, where she indulged in one of her passions, boating. She engaged the services of Augustus "Gus" Gordon, the craggy, gray bearded coast guard veteran. It was a brief trip out into the calm, inlet waters, but Freda relished the summer breeze and midday sun massaging her face.

She visited every shop and enjoyed every open space. She worked her way to the outskirts of town, to the farms and ranches. She wanted to absorb every nuance Louiston had to offer. Freda attracted a few curious stares and a couple of double takes, but even when LaVern accompanied her, she was amazed that a star of her magnitude was able to meander with complete freedom. She promptly made two decisions; to extend her stay, even though it meant moving into the

Armistead Hotel, and to reserve a space at the Scales place for the following summer.

Freda and LaVern were relaxing on the back patio after another of Gloria's impeccable meals, when LaVern revealed her secret.

"Only my family knows so you have to keep this to yourself." LaVern became excited and started to bounce slightly up and down in her lounger.

"I'm pregnant Freda. I'm going to have a baby."

Freda's mouth dropped open, and her hands flew up and framed her face, with her fingers spread wide and straight. "Oh, my goodness. I'm so happy for you, LaVern. How far along are you?" She peeked down at her still unaffected mid-section.

"Only about two months."

Wilson came through the front door. He had just left a city council meeting. "Hey!" he called out, "where is everybody?"

"We're out here baby."

Brittany yelled out from her bedroom. "I'm in here reading, Daddy."

Gloria emerged from the kitchen slightly miffed. "I know all of you had better stop yelling like a bunch of coyotes. You have more home training than that."

Wilson walked straight through the house and onto the patio. He flopped down dejectedly.

"What's the matter sweetheart? You look upset."

"At the meeting tonight, a land development company started getting really pushy about buying up private property."

LaVern tried to allay her husband's fears. "Oh, it'll be okay Wilson. They'll give up just like all the others."

"I hope so," he said, "I really hope so."

Storm Clouds
Chapter Fifteen

Velma Duhon decided to push her idea to capitalize on the potentially lucrative Black history of Louiston. At the next council meeting, she unzipped a leather portfolio and withdrew four folders crowded with information and photos. She walked around the aged table and handed one to each member. "What you have in front of you gentlemen, are the details pertaining to the what, how, where and so on of what I am proposing." Her ideas included area tours, a boat ride, a museum, and symposiums. "All these are untapped sources of revenue."

"I like that boat ride idea Velma," said Wilson. "The story can be told of the slaves who were so desperate for freedom that they elected to jump overboard while still in chains rather than be forced into bondage. Being on a boat makes that more impactful."

"That's exactly the kind of thing I'm talking about, Wilson," she exclaimed. "Louiston has so much to offer."

"How are we going to pay for all this?" inquired Bert Willoughby, as he pulled off his sweaty and battered baseball cap and scratched his balding head.

Velma spoke right up. "The State of South Carolina has budgeted funds especially for endeavors like ours. Unfortunately, most of that money has gone for projects glorifying the Confederacy. I plan on submitting a request for funding this month."

"I love it," declared Stanley Payne, his impulsive nature clearly on display. "This is just what this town needs. I move that this body accepts Velma's proposal."

"Can I get a second?" asked Council President Wallace, in his high-pitched delivery.

"Second," said Wilson.

"It has been moved and seconded that the Louiston City

Council approve the aforementioned proposal. All in favor, say aye."

It was unanimous.

"The next item on the agenda is this pesky land developer issue. As everyone is aware of, the Hughes Development Corporation has expressed interest in attending a meeting to discuss their plans for bringing 'economic empowerment' to our city."

Harvey's short thick arms flew up over his head. His squeaky voice rose even higher. "We all know what that's code for."

"You told them we're not interested, right Harvey?" asked Wilson.

"I've made it crystal clear, in writing, that the land and business owners of Louiston aren't interested in selling. But they're persistent."

The reactionary Stanley Payne rose to speak. He leaned forward on the desk, his weight solidly resting on his meaty, balled up fists. As he spoke, his head pivoted from left to right, making eye contact with every council member.

"These imbeciles can't seem to take no for an answer. If a written rejection won't do it, maybe we *should* invite them to a meeting. That way we can say no to their faces."

"I agree with Stanley," said Velma, "but it doesn't have to be confrontational. It doesn't hurt to hear what they have to say. Maybe, after they've had their chance, they'll realize their time and efforts are being wasted."

"Let's put it to a vote," said Harvey. "All those in favor of granting an audience to the Hughes Corporation, say aye."

Again, it was unanimous.

"As directed by this body, I will grant an audience with the Hughes Corporation for next month's meeting."

The phone conversation LaVern had with her parents never completely left her mind. Help strangers, they advised. Give back, they said. She discussed it with Wilson and with his blessings, and a baggy, button down blouse and leggings, she flew to New York, to the Winifree Group offices, to establish a Charitable Foundation. The meeting lasted for two hours and after LaVern asked all the pertinent questions, she signed papers knowing that motivated people everywhere could chase their dreams because of her foundation's generosity. She also decided to make an unplanned stop, one that was way overdue.

"Driver, please take me to The New York College for the Performing Arts, the Landsman Auditorium."

When the car pulled up, she said she wouldn't be long.

"Take your time, Miss Whitaker."

Up to this point the driver never let on that he recognized his famous passenger.

She approached the auditorium for the first time in over fifteen years. She pulled on the tinted glass door. Yep, still as heavy as she remembered. In the lobby, she gazed up at its single most dominant feature, the wall of fame, still located over the dual entrances to the auditorium. Years ago, she received notice that she was added to their gallery of distinguished alumni, and there it was, a photo taken during her performance in Lori's play. LaVern went to the second floor where the classrooms were. The door to the first room was open. She cautiously peeked in, only her head was visible, and there he was, seated behind his metal desk completely absorbed by whatever was inside that manila folder in his hands. Still a rotund man, now with a balding head of short gray hair, his spectacles were resting on his creased forehead. She stepped into the doorway and waited wordlessly. George Coombs' head turned slowly. LaVern flashed her brightest smile. He stared for several seconds before his eyes widened in recognition. He swiveled in his chair and beamed like a new father.

"LaVern Whitaker!"

"Hello Mr. Coombs."

He attempted to rise out of his chair, but he was having great difficulty. He was using mostly his arms. LaVern quickly moved into the classroom, trying to shorten the distance he would have to traverse to greet her. As she got near, he stretched out one arm to signal her to come no closer. He carefully negotiated his way to his feet and proudly stood up straight. Only then did he stretch out both arms.

"Mr. Coombs, it's so good to see you."

George Coombs was stoic by nature, not given to spontaneous displays of emotion. But, when LaVern hugged him, she could feel his aging body involuntarily shuddering with joy.

"I'm so proud of you young lady. I knew you had what it took to make it in this business."

LaVern maintained her grasp as she spoke into his shirt.

"Mr. Coombs, I'm here today to do something I should have done years ago." She loosened her grip and looked up into his face. "I need to tell you how much I treasure and value all that you did for me."

George was greatly affected by her words even though it wasn't readily apparent.

"Well, I know you're a very busy person, Miss Whitaker, so let's make the most of the time we have."

The former student took a seat in front of his desk and watched as George gingerly maneuvered his way back into his chair. The effort wasn't as mighty as the struggle to stand up, but it was nonetheless difficult to watch.

He went through all that to stand, just for me. And he still calls me Miss Whitaker.

He leaned back in his chair and clasped his hands on top of his ample stomach, just like she remembered.

"Miss Whitaker, ever since we produced Lori Burkhardt's play, we've put on an original production every year. It has developed into very intense competition among our script writing students. It's a tradition now and I have you and Lori to thank for that."

"More Lori than me Mr. Coombs."

LaVern shared with him how much he affected her career.

"Even though you didn't mention it at the time, I found out you were responsible for Angie Rosinki and I getting our first acting jobs right after graduation."

"I don't deserve any praise for that. I do what I can for any of my students."

George mentioned he was particularly proud that Lori and she collaborated on bringing "Juris Doctor in the House" to the screen. The DVD the school sold that night was one of his most prized possessions. He also related this would be his last year at NYCPA.

After an hour and a half, it was time to go. As LaVern rose to leave, George tried doing the same.

"Please Mr. Coombs, you don't have to get up. You earned my respect years ago and you will never lose it."

He flopped heavily back into his chair. LaVern walked around the desk to give him one last hug. That's when she saw his cane clinging to the edge of the desk.

"I'm glad I got the chance to tell you in person how much you mean to me."

As LaVern was about to exit the room, she glanced back at the figure in the chair. The impassive and unflappable George Coombs was dabbing away tears from the corner of his eye.

LaVern was anxious to tell Wilson about the outcome of the meeting with The Winifree Group. As the family sat around after dinner, she pulled out all the legal papers and explained the inner workings of the foundation; why a family foundation would work best, the tax advantages, and the function of the Board of Directors.

"They strongly suggested that I name the foundation right there and then."

"What name did you choose?" asked Wilson.

LaVern placed her hands over her mouth and stared teary eyed at her husband.

"The Wilson and LaVern Davenport Charitable Foundation."

Wilson and Gloria were taken completely by surprise.

"Oh, my Lord," exclaimed Gloria. She placed her face in her hands and mumbled to herself under her breath. "I can't believe this is happening."

"You put the Davenport name on the foundation?" said Wilson. He kissed her and hugged her tightly.

"I love my family. But there's more good news. The Board of Directors."

"Oh yeah, the Board," said Wilson. "Who are they?"

LaVern displayed her best movie star grin and spread her arms wide. "You're looking at them."

"Us?" came the simultaneous reply from Gloria and

Wilson.

"Yes, you..." she swept her arm back and forth between the two, "...are both members of the Board of Directors of the Wilson and LaVern Davenport Foundation."

The pride in her voice was as evident as a rainbow after a thunderstorm.

"I've never been a board member," said Gloria.

"Neither have I," said Wilson.

"Well, you won't be alone. I'd like to add both my parents and Shaundra."

"Absolutely, you *should* add them," said Wilson. "We're all family."

"Can I be on the board too Momma?" asked Brittany.

Everyone smiled at the innocence of her question.

"Sorry sweetheart," said Wilson, "it's only for us adults."

"What do we do as Board Members?" inquired Gloria.

"The Board decides how, when, how much, and to whom we distribute our funds. I already made the initial donation."

"I'm afraid to ask," said the leery Wilson, "but how much was it?"

"One million dollars." She threw that number out so casually that an eavesdropper would have felt bludgeoned into insensibility at hearing it. Even the Davenports, who were by now accustomed to hearing such huge amounts tossed around, raised their eyebrows.

"So, as of this moment, we're open for business."

It took two months for the Hughes Corporation to meet with the City Council. In the interim, Ruth Van Meter, the council secretary and candle shop owner, foresaw problems. Her research revealed that their modus operandi was to buy or force out local property owners and build lavish ocean side communities. They had a profit above all mentality, were largely successful despite intense local opposition, and were known to resort to dubious and unethical business practices. They were among the top 10 wealthiest Black-owned corporations in the country and had powerful business and political connections. This was so alarming, she felt compelled to report her findings to the council.

Velma Duhon was having problems with her efforts to procure funding for the city museum. She unloaded her troubles on Harvey Wallace when he came into her pharmacy.

"Harvey, I submitted the proposal for funding to the state back in the spring. For some reason, the reviewing process has been stalled. Every time I call, I'm told it's on some bureaucrat's desk waiting for approval. And it's been there for two months. I don't get it."

Harvey looked perplexed. He scratched his graying head with a thick forefinger.

"Let me make some phone calls, Velma and I'll get back to you. It sounds like an easy fix though."

Harvey had his answer in a few days. He met Velma in his office at the Armistead.

"You were right," he began.

As always, he was dressed immaculately, this time in his three-piece, black pin- striped suit and vest with red suspenders. Seated in his plush leather chair, he leaned forward with his elbows on his desk.

"I talked with Bert's son, Jason, he works in the Capitol Building in Columbia. He can get information on all the filings and petitions and court actions that go through the state. Anyway, he looked into our issue, and he confirmed that your paperwork is sitting up there on the desk of some mid-level civil servant."

"I don't understand why everything came to a stop at *his* desk," said Velma. "Why is *he* holding everything up?"

"It's not him, it's the Hughes Corporation." Harvey sat back in his chair, folded his stubby hands onto his bloated midsection and waited for her reaction.

"The Hughes Corporation?" Velma was incredulous. "What does some pencil pusher have to do with them?"

"Seems as though he's caving in to pressure by the Hughes people to delay our funding.

Both went silent and Harvey watched Velma's face grapple with the connection between her project and the Hughes Corporation.

"Is this tied in with their development plans?" she asked.

"Is that what this is all about?"

Harvey threw his short arms into the air. His embarrassingly high voice rose embarrassingly higher. "Hell yeah it is. That's the *only* thing it's about. If you hadn't become suspicious, this delay would have gone on for who knows how long. That's a pretty sneaky and deceitful thing to do to this town." He turned his palms upward. "What did we ever do to them? Because we won't sell? Now I know why they requested a meeting. They probably think they can offer to cut through the red tape and make it seem like they did us a big favor, and they were the hold up all along."

"Do you think they'd stoop that low? I mean, that shows such a complete lack of integrity."

"I know I trust Jason more than I do them," stormed Harvey. "Major corporations don't get to be major corporations by playing nice."

"What do you want to do?"

"I'll give the council our information. Then, we'll come up with a strategy. They need to know what kind of businesspeople we're dealing with."

The night of the meeting, Harvey filled the council members in on what the Hughes people were up to. That, coupled with the ominous report by Ruth Van Meter, turned a once conciliatory and respectful attitude into outrage and mistrust. In the relative quiet of the council chamber, they heard the courthouse doors creak open, followed by the echoing sounds of footsteps moving rapidly through the marble floored hallway. When the footsteps reached the chamber doors, in marched two forty-ish looking, stylishly attired Black men, one taller than the other, with briefcases. They strode confidently and unsmilingly toward the council table. Both glanced around the empty room, placed their briefcases on the floor, then approached the council table.

"I hope we didn't keep you waiting too long. It took us an extra few minutes to find the courthouse."

Harvey Wallace spoke in response. "No problem gentlemen, you're right on time."

"Good, in that case, let me introduce myself. My name is

Maurice Conyers, I am the CEO of the Hughes Development Corporation."

Mr. Conyers had a shaved head, a full beard with just a hint of gray, and Cazal semi-rimless bifocals. He turned to his associate.

"And my name is Javon Wilkes, I am the Chief Operating Officer of the Hughes Corporation." Mr. Wilkes was taller and thinner with a goatee and black, Versace plastic frames.

Both men were dressed for business; dark, three-piece Armani cashmere suits, expensive tie clips with matching cuff links, and pricey, Santoni leather shoes. No one on the council offered a greeting, so Harvey diffused the tense situation.

"Nice to meet both of you gentlemen. Please, take a seat."

"Thank you," said Mr. Wilkes. They sat on metal folding chairs.

As the reps waited patiently, their body language and demeanor left no doubt they were battle tested. Their eyes scanned the row of council members seated in front of them, coldly calculating and appraising their opposition, looking for a chink in the collective armor. The council was doing likewise. Each member equated their very presence to predators, uncompromising heartless villains. Everyone felt the tension in the air. Harvey Wallace stood and addressed them.

"Gentlemen, you have the floor."

"Thank you, Mr. President," began Maurice Conyers. He rose and launched into why they had a continued interest in the property in and around Louiston. He touched on some of their development plans and Javon Wilkes went to his briefcase and withdrew five finely grained, black, leather-bound, zippered portfolios. Each was embossed, not stamped, with the Hughes Corporation logo. He distributed one to each council member. Maurice Conyers continued.

"Our Board of Directors wondered what it would take to convince Louistonians to part with their property. If you take a look inside, you will see what we think are substantial offers."

Each member unzipped their expensive portfolio's and unfolded it onto the desk.

"As you can see," said Javon, "we've offered to make major improvements which would increase the quality of public services for all your citizens." He paused to let them familiarize themselves with the new information. "We noticed that Louiston doesn't have a hospital."

He was right. Everybody, emergency or no, had to go to Roper Hospital in Beaufort, a half hour drive, if they required more than what the town's two doctors or the fire department EMTs could provide.

"Even *we* can't build a new hospital, but what we propose is the construction of an emergency ward and ambulance service to make medical treatment less of an inconvenience for all." He proposed an offer to upgrade the post office and the firehouse.

The fiery Stanley Payne had heard enough. He rose and confronted the Hughes execs.

"We told you no before because we like our town just like it is." Stanley was fuming. His mouth, as usual, was barely visible, being almost completely engulfed by his thick beard. Spittle was clinging to the hairs like dew. He narrowed his eyes and pointed a finger at the two objects of his ire. "If you get your way, everybody here will lose their land and their homes. Louiston has survived this long because of the very fact we've always been land and business owners."

Harvey stood and placed his hands on the irate Stanley's shoulders, trying to reign him in. "OK. Stanley," he said calmly.

"Yeah Stanley," came Bert's voice from the end of the desk, "let'em speak. You can't learn much by listening to yourself talk."

Stanley reluctantly sat down but he was still seething. The two Hughes reps were remarkably unfazed. They weathered Stanley's explosion with not even the slightest facial reaction.

"Thank you, Mr. President," said Javon. He calmly picked up where he left off. "If you'd please proceed to the last page of our proposal, you'll see where we took the liberty of ascertaining the market values of all of your respective businesses and properties."

That revelation caught every council member off guard.

"For instance, Mr. Wallace, we see that your hotel has been assessed at 3.5 million dollars. We're prepared to offer you 4 million."

Javon went on like this for every single member of the council. He knew everyone's exact worth and tendered more than market value for their assets. Their arrogance was off-putting, and this maneuver contributed to an already negative and untrusting perception of them. Maurice asked if they had any questions. As Wilson stood up, he placed a firm hand on Stanley's shoulder to keep him in place. It was his turn to speak.

"Yes, Mr. Conyers, I have a very important question for you and your associate. One of our council members, Velma Duhon, submitted applications for funding for establishing a Black Museum here in town. She was vigilant in monitoring the progress on those requests and everything was moving along unimpeded until a few months ago when, unexpectedly, those requests hit a bureaucratic roadblock. I have good reason to believe that your corporation is behind that holdup. What do you have to say about that?"

As was his habit, Wilson rolled up on his toes after posing his question. They raised their eyebrows but otherwise retained their composure.

"I don't know where you heard that Mr. Davenport," lied Javon. "I can assure you and your fellow council members that any delay in any paperwork had nothing to do with The Hughes Corporation."

"Let me get this straight," said the visibly annoyed Velma, "my applications were moving through the system unhindered until we rejected your offer to buy us out. You want us to believe it was just a coincidence?"

The two execs remained as impassive and unaffected as redwoods in a gale.

"First, let me say I will resist the urge to take offense at your unproven insinuation Miss Duhon. Other than that, I know our corporation wouldn't be involved in such trivial matters."

Trivial matters! thought Velma. Now she was truly offended, as was everyone else.

"But, if there's some way our corporation *could* intervene

on Louiston's behalf and ensure that your paperwork goes through, we would be delighted to look into it… if you wish. In the meantime, please consider our offers. And feel free to keep those binders as a token of our good faith in you."

Maurice Conyers and Javon Wilkes turned to collect their briefcases. That did it, thought Harvey. After a blatant lie and a slew of condescending statements, he had heard enough.

"Please, don't rush out gentlemen. We're about to vote on your proposal right now. All those in favor of the Hughes Corporation proposal say aye."

You could hear a feather fall to the floor.

"All those opposed."

Five loud and unmistakable ayes rang out loud and clear. The execs stood as stone faced as ever. Stanley picked up his portfolio and threw it in the center of the table.

"We won't be needing these handouts either."

Every council member followed suit and threw their expensive Hughes Corporation tokens in a pile on the desk. As expected, Maurice and Javon didn't betray any emotion. They simply turned and quietly headed out of the council chambers, briefcases in hand. They left their portfolio's behind.

New Neighbor, Old Enemy
Chapter Sixteen

There was joy and jubilation in the Davenport household. Their new home was finally ready for occupation. Items like clothes, linens, books, dishes and family mementos, had been transported by hand over the short grassy distance between houses. Gloria even dug up all her precious blooms and replanted them in her new, roomier garden. As a housewarming gift, Mary Scales utilized her considerable sewing skills to create a set of gorgeous handmade and embroidered window curtains for the kitchen. The Compound, as they came to call it, was full of all new furniture and appliances, and the latest in-home security technology; a video surveillance system, voice-activated lights and door locks, all accessible from a cell phone or laptop. It had real wood floors, "not that laminate stuff" as Wilson derisively called it, and plaster walls. LaVern's tasteful decorating eye provided the final, elegant touches. After everything was in its place, the Davenports stood in their new family room and marveled at what transpired over the past several months. No one had ever lived in a house that was built from the ground up, just for them, with everything in it brand new.

"I want to thank everyone," said Gloria, "and the good Lord above too. I'm grateful to have this family and I love you all very much."

They shared their first group hug.

Freda would be the first outsider to see it. Weeks later, she drove up and LaVern was waiting outside. She gasped as she exited the car and glanced down at LaVern's enormous mid-section.

"The house is not the only new thing around here. How are you doing, LaVern?"

"I'm eight months now and it's been, how can I put it, an

adjustment. I have a lot more empathy for mothers everywhere now."

Freda then scanned the property. "This is absolutely gorgeous. The last time I was here, you weren't showing, and you had to tell me where the rooms would be."

"Freda, this is my dream house."

"It's so quiet and secluded back here too. I'm jealous."

"Come on inside, let me show you around."

As they approached the front entrance, the custom designed wooden door opened to reveal the smiling visages of Gloria and Brittany.

"Hi Miss Freda," screeched Brittany as she rushed out to greet her.

She stooped down to place a long-awaited bear hug on the seven-year-old.

"Thank you, sweetheart. Your hugs are the best part of my visit."

"My meemaw is on the porch and she wants her hug too."

"I bet she does."

"How you doing Freda?" shouted Gloria. "It's good to see you again."

She approached Gloria with arms outstretched. "It's good to see you again too, Gloria."

"You know, you're the first outsider to see our new home."

"Well, in that case, I'm honored."

"Let's all go inside," said LaVern, "and I'll give you the grand tour."

A curious Brittany tagged along as she went room by room and proudly described the charming particulars in each, the living room, the den, the dining room, the family room, the sun room and Wilson's office. The tour ended in the kitchen where Gloria was already seated at the island sipping coffee.

"This house is so beautiful," Freda exclaimed. "I know everyone must be extremely proud."

"We're forever grateful to have this space," said LaVern. "We get to invite our family and friends to stay with us."

"And," stated Gloria, "one of these days I'll be able to use all these modern gadgets to cook a meal."

"You're not using your new kitchen?" asked Freda.

"It may take a while before I get the hang of all this. I still use my old kitchen for the most part."

"I can help you with that," said Freda. "Someone with your skills shouldn't be handicapped by a few modern updates."

"Oh my goodness, you're a Godsend."

"Can I join in too?" asked LaVern. "I need a tutorial worse than Gloria does."

"I'm an equal opportunity instructor," said Freda.

The women spent the next two hours listening and learning from Freda about all the touch features concerning the stove, the oven, the dishwasher and the refrigerator. They gossiped and laughed and ate all morning. Their tight bond became even tighter.

The next day, over breakfast, Freda mentioned to LaVern her desire to relocate to Louiston and asked if she could help. LaVern knew this tight-knit community was a tough nut to crack, even for her. She placed a call to Wilson.

"Have you talked to Bert Willoughby about this?" he asked.

"No, do you know something?"

"I was out there the other day checking his furnace, and he said that working his farm was starting to take a toll on him. He never mentioned a desire to sell any land, but you never know. It wouldn't hurt to ask."

LaVern immediately phoned Bert and asked if he had time to discuss some business. The following day, LaVern and Freda made the twenty-mile drive through the beautiful, agrarian, South Carolina landscape. Bert and his family lived in a comfortable, two-story brick house at the end of a gravel road that extended out to the main highway. As LaVern made the left onto his property, his house looked like a toy resting atop the distant horizon. As she drove, her tires kicked up stone pebbles that banged noisily against her car's undercarriage. The rattle alerted the Willoughby's that company was coming. Freda looked around in wonderment at the expanse of land whizzing by. They had to speak loudly due to the pebbles pounding beneath the car.

"How much land does he own LaVern?"

"I'm not sure, I just know it's a lot. Remember, he's not a

conversationalist, he's very direct and sometimes not very tactful, but don't take it personally, it's just his way."

As they got closer to the house, Bert and his family could be seen gathered on the porch. Freda ran her moist palms along the length of her jean clad thighs.

"I feel like I did when I went to my first audition."

"Girl, stop worrying, they'll love you. I wouldn't bring you here if there was any doubt."

As the car came to a stop, the noise from the undercarriage ceased and Bert stepped down off their porch. LaVern managed to work her belly past the steering wheel and plant both swollen feet in the loose gravel. By the time she walked around to the passenger side, Freda was standing there facing the Willoughby's. Four pairs of eyes silently scrutinized their visitor.

"This must be pretty important for you to come all the way out here in your condition." Bert reached out his hand to help LaVern up the few steps to his porch.

"Bert… Loretta, I would like you to meet one of my very best friends, Freda Parks. Freda, these are the Willoughby's."

She stepped forward and offered her hand to Bert. "Very nice to meet you Mr. Willoughby."

Bert placed his large, calloused hand in her small, soft, expertly manicured one. *They don't have hands like these in Hollywood*, she thought.

"Nice to meet you, Miss Parks. This is my wife, Loretta."
Loretta reached out and shook Freda's hand.

"Nice to meet you too Mrs. Willoughby."

"Loretta, everybody calls me Loretta."

"Then please call me Freda."

"And," continued Bert, "these are our kids, my son BJ, and my daughter Maddy.

I have one older son–"

Before he could finish, fifteen-year-old Maddy blurted out, "I've seen you on TV"

"Yeah," added thirteen-year-old Bert Jr., "I have too."

Loretta was also trying to resolve in her mind where she had seen Freda, but it was a struggle. Bert didn't have a clue who she was except that she was LaVern's friend.

"It's nice of you to remember me," said Freda.

"Oooh my," said Loretta as she glanced down at LaVern's midsection. "It won't be long, will it?"

LaVern placed both hands on her belly and proudly proclaimed, "I'm eight months."

"Do you know what it is yet?"

"No, Wilson and I want to be surprised."

"Oh, good for you. Just as long as it's healthy, right?"

"That's right, if it's healthy, we'll take it from there," she joked.

"Well," said Bert, "now that all that's done, let's go inside and get this business out the way. I have fields and workers to tend to."

As they brought up the rear, LaVern looked over to Freda and mouthed, "I told you."

"Have a seat, ladies, let's talk."

LaVern slyly glanced around, no frills, austere but functional, and comfy. *Not a whole lot of Loretta in this place*, she thought. She waddled her way over to the dining room table and managed to carefully wedge herself into one of the wooden armed chairs. Bert sat at the table, crossed his legs, removed his grimy cap, and placed it where he always did, on his knee. Freda sat beside LaVern.

"I'll be right back," said Loretta and disappeared into the kitchen.

"You kids get outta here." Bert ordered. "This is between us grown folks."

"Can we get Miss Parks' autograph first Daddy?"

"You can get it when we're done."

End of discussion. They wordlessly whirled around and headed out the front door. *How refreshing*, thought Freda, *kids who are actually obedient. Something else you don't see much of in L.A.*

LaVern explained about Freda's desire to relocate to Louiston. She wanted to buy a plot of land and build on it.

"What makes you think I have land to sell?"

"Honestly, I don't know if you do or not Bert," said LaVern. "Wilson happened to mention you may be getting weary of farming so much land."

"I did say that when he was over here," he admitted.

Freda spoke up. "Mr. Willoughby, I love this area, and I love the people. I want to become a part of this community."

"Everybody calls me Bert. Why do you want *my* land?"

"Mr., I mean Bert, I don't care who I buy the land from. I just want a little something in the country where it's nice and quiet and not too far from town."

"How much land you lookin' for?"

"A half-acre to an acre if I can get it."

Boy, thought Freda, *LaVern was right. That Bert Willoughby doesn't mince words. He looks you straight in the eye and doesn't even blink.* She decided to turn the tables, if only for a moment.

"Just out of curiosity Bert, how much land do you own?"

"I have 200 acres. I grow soybeans and corn and raise a few cattle," he said with pride.

"That's a lot of land," said Freda.

"'Bout average for these parts."

"Do you farm all that land by yourself?"

"I hire migrants. They come through here every year at harvest time. They get work from all the farms around here. Been doin' that for years."

Loretta reentered with a round glass tray and four tall glasses of fresh squeezed, sweetened lemonade, pulp, seeds and all. She served one glass to each before taking a seat.

"The Waiting Game!" she shouted. Her non sequitur caused every head to turn in her direction.

"What're you talkin' 'bout?" asked Bert.

"The Waiting Game. That's the movie I remember, Freda. You played the apartment building owner who had a bunch of crazy tenants."

"Well, I'm flattered you remember, Loretta."

Pouncing on an opportunity to soften Bert's inquisition, LaVern mentioned that Freda liked to cook.

"Loretta, you would not believe how good Freda is in the kitchen. I've had her food and … all I can say is you two need to talk."

Loretta was definitely intrigued now. "What's your best dish Freda?"

The two women were off to the races. The conversation switched from land purchasing to cooking. Bert wondered how his business talk became lost in this food dialogue. The taciturn farmer interjected and brought it back to business.

"If you ladies don't mind, I'd like to show Freda some of my property and maybe have her pick out a plot of land."

Freda immediately lost all interest in food and cooking and stood up abruptly. "I would be delighted to see your land, Bert."

He rose and straightened out his overall clad body, and replaced his sweat encrusted cap. "Let's take a walk."

The group followed Bert as he walked and talked and guided them through his still maturing soybean field, when he suddenly stopped.

"What do you think of this spot, Freda?"

She scanned the landscape. The land gently sloped down to Highway 17, barely visible in front of her. Behind was a distant cornfield. On one side was the Willoughby house, far enough away to not be intrusive, and on the other side was more of Bert's land. *If I buy this acre*, Freda pondered, *I can build my house right in the middle and have a boundary on every side. If I bought more land that would mean even more of a buffer.*

"I love this spot, Bert. This would be perfect. Would you consider selling me two acres?"

He hadn't anticipated this. "Two? I don't know."

Loretta spoke up. "Oh, sell her two Bert. That's one less acre you have to farm. You know you been talkin' about how you need to slow down some, how you're not as young as you used to be."

Everyone was holding their breath while Bert mulled over this latest offer. He stared at the dirt. Two fingers scratched his wrinkled head without removing his cap, tilting it to the side.

"OK. Freda, you got yo'self a deal."

The three women screamed and shouted and jumped around like they had hit the lottery. In true Bert fashion though, he brought things back to business.

"You know, land 'round here goes for about four thousand an acre."

"That's fine," Freda exclaimed. "If you get the documents

together, I'll have my lawyer look at them. After the papers are signed, I'll wire the money to your account the very next day."

Maybe the women *had* hit the lottery, the metaphorical lottery. Loretta was getting a new cooking friend as a neighbor, LaVern was getting an industry confidant who would be twenty minutes away, and Freda would finally be getting her place of solitude, her sanctuary. Bert was the only one getting paid.

When Freda departed, the time was right to bring both families together in the new house. Shaundra was the first to arrive and, having only seen her in cell phone videos, was wide eyed at LaVern's swollen stomach.

"Oh my God Peaches, look at you. It's so amazing to actually see you like this."

"It's pretty amazing to me too."

They hugged for the first time in almost a year.

"I missed you so much, Shaundra."

"I missed you too, Peaches. Video's just ain't the same."

"Let me show you the rest of the house."

Brittany came rushing out of her bedroom, eyes bright, with a smile that revealed teeth that filled in the baby gaps.

"Hi Auntie Shaundra," she said, and gave her a tight hug.

Shaundra stood back and assessed the changed little girl in front of her.

"Oh my goodness. Look how tall you are. The last time I was here, you were a child. I come back, and you're a young lady. And look at how long your hair is."

"Thank you Auntie Shaundra. I missed you."

"Awww sweetheart, I missed you too."

"I'm just showing eh…Auntie Shaundra the house, Britt–"

"Can I do it Momma?"

"Of course you can honey."

"I'll be right back." Brittany pivoted and hurried into her room.

In a hushed tone, Shaundra asked, "When did Brittany start calling me Auntie Shaundra?"

"That's a new one on me. I guess she came up with that on her own. I hope you don't mind."

"Absolutely not. I like the sound of it."

Brittany returned and immediately took over, having watched and learned from LaVern's tour with Freda. "OK, Auntie Shaundra, right down here is my daddy's den…"

During the tour, Shaundra revealed that Freda enlisted her as her real estate agent to sell her house.

That Freda is so relentlessly benevolent, recalled LaVern. *She's like a Black Tinkerbell who flits around touching things with her magic wand. And everything she touches means something good will happen to someone.*

The following day the Whitakers arrived, and Jackie came through the door first.

"Ohhh, look at my baby!" cooed Jackie. Her eyes went from her belly to her face and back again. She reached out for her hug. LaVern had to turn sideways to get her arms around her mother's neck.

"Yeah," observed Freeman, "she's really out there." He bent over from the waist.

"Mom and Dad, welcome to our new home."

LaVern then shuffled over to the nearest foyer armchair and slowly sat down.

"How are you feeling, Peaches? How's the baby coming along?"

"I'm feeling fine Mom. But I'm finding out that everything you warned me about is true. My back hurts, I can't sleep comfortably, I tire easily, and I eat like a runaway slave."

Just then, Brittany and Shaundra entered the foyer.

"Hi Mr. Whit, Mrs. Whit. It's been a while. Good to see y'all again."

They embraced warmly. Freeman spied Brittany.

"You get your hug too young lady."

She smiled and rushed over. "Thank you, Pop Pop." She looked at Jackie. "Grammaw, I missed you too."

"Come get your hug, sweetheart."

Jackie noticed someone was missing. Wilson was still at work. "Where's Gloria?"

"My meemaw is in the kitchen," said Brittany. "We'll see her at the end of the tour."

"The tour?"

"Yes Mom," said Lavern from her chair. "After I show you to your room, Brittany will take you on a tour of the house."

"Oh really?"

"Oh yeah, Mrs. Whit," said Shaundra. "I got the tour yesterday and she did a great job."

Brittany beamed proudly.

"I'm certainly looking forward to that."

Well, let's go then." LaVern struggled to raise herself out of her chair and Freeman rushed over to help.

"Thank you, Daddy. Now follow me."

That evening, Gloria prepared a meal that left everyone stuffed and happy. After Freda's tutorial, she was truly enjoying her new cooking space. It was now, as was her old kitchen, her domain.

"Everybody, go into the family room and relax," said Gloria. "Especially you, LaVern. I'll clean up in here."

When she joined the others, LaVern knew it was the perfect time to make her big reveal. After ponderously getting to her feet, she walked, her protruding belly leading the way, to center stage in the room. She gestured to Wilson to join her.

"Mom…Dad…Shaundra, I've been holding this news in for months and I can't tell you how delighted I am to finally share it with you."

LaVern looked right at her father. He stared at her belly. *Is she about to tell us she's having triplets or something?*

"Dad, do you remember I told you I was feeling unfulfilled, and I didn't know why, and you told me to do things for other people?"

"Yes, I remember."

"Well, that's just what I did." LaVern wrapped her arm around Wilson's waist. "I am proud to announce I have established The Wilson and LaVern Davenport Charitable Foundation."

Everyone's eyebrows rose in surprise and uncertainty. They weren't sure what that meant.

"Through the foundation, we can pick and choose causes we deem worthy enough to donate funds to and help them to accomplish their mission."

"Wow Peaches," said Shaundra, "that's awesome."

"Peaches, that's beautiful," said Jackie. "I'm so proud of you."

She put into practice what Freeman had preached for years. People with means should reach out to those less fortunate. He quietly rose to his feet, approached his daughter and hugged her long and hard.

"I'm so proud of you sweetheart. I know you'll do good things with the foundation."

"Tell them the rest please, Wilson," LaVern urged, as she dabbed her eyes dry.

"Well, as you all know, every foundation has a Board of Directors."

"That's right," declared the now seated Freeman, "you must be very careful who you allow on your board."

"I couldn't agree with you more." Wilson paused for dramatic effect. "That's why everyone here is a Board member of the Wilson and LaVern Davenport Charitable Foundation. Welcome."

Wilson, LaVern and Gloria initiated the applause for a still stunned, newly constituted Board of Directors.

"All of us?" asked a shocked Shaundra.

"Yes," responded LaVern.

"Just us, nobody else?" asked the pragmatic Freeman.

"Yes Daddy. This is the entire Board."

"Wow, I've never been on a Board before," said Shaundra.
And neither had anyone else.

"What do we do now?"

"I'm glad you asked Shaundra," said Wilson.

He reached into a nearby desk drawer and pulled out three leather-bound business portfolios containing the papers that legally established their foundation, including the list of its Board members. Quite naturally, everyone searched the list for their own name and were appropriately pleased when they saw it. Wilson proceeded to explain the intricacies of the Foundation; that it was a private one, its mission statement, the tax advantages, how and where funds are generated and distributed, and so on.

"Now, these papers are for your personal records. Keep

them safe, they are legal documents. Treat them as such."

Everyone was still staring at the papers, still adjusting to the fact that they were bona fide Foundation Board members.

"I included everyone I love and trust in the world on this board," said the proud LaVern. "I hope you're as honored as I am."

In the two months since the last contentious and calamitous meeting with the Hughes Corporation, many land and business owners had been approached independently with inflated offers to sell. Because of the amounts of money being thrown around, the council feared the weaker-willed citizens would submit to temptation. It was decided to invite the community to the next meeting to share all the information they had accumulated and warn about the corporation's dismal, community destroying business practices.

Until this point, the mayor was not an active participant in councilmanic matters, but it was agreed he should now be directly involved. Cornelius Greenlee could be a liability or an asset. In his forties and of average height and build, he was one of only two attorneys in town. His head was shaved clean, but he sported a bushy, caterpillar-like mustache and a matching pair of bristling eyebrows. Being the only true "politician" in Louiston, he always seemed to be campaigning; auditioning for the day when the political connections cultivated in Columbia would take him far beyond Louiston. While engaged in conversation, there was always some kind of physical contact other than shaking your hand; a touch to the forearm, if you were a woman, one on the shoulder or bicep if you were a man. His statements often led one to believe that something profound would follow. "Now listen to me very carefully..." he would begin.

On the evening of the meeting, and for the first time since the Davenports bared their souls, the chamber was overflowing, some had to stand and lean against the walls. Amidst this confusion, Mayor Greenlee made his appearance. Unsurprisingly, he waited for the most opportune moment to maximize his arrival. He entered the packed chambers and worked the room like it was a campaign stop. He slowly meandered his way through the crowd, making an effort to engage every person in a confidential, one-on-one conversation; touching arms and shoulders and hands and maintaining eye contact. He worked his way up to and along the council members' table where, at last, he took a seat in the first row. Harvey Wallace gaveled the crowd into silence.

"I'm pleased to see so many friends and neighbors here tonight." His high-pitched voice signaled more urgency than usual. "No doubt you've heard about the dire circumstances we, as a community, find ourselves in regarding the plans of a certain real estate corporation."

The room fell as silent as a tomb.

"The council is here tonight to share with you the facts as we know them."

Harvey asked Ruth Van Meter to stand and report on the research she had uncovered regarding the Hughes Corporation. She shared that they are extremely powerful and connected, they have a history of ravaging coastal communities nationwide, and they are not afraid to use their political clout to get what they want. Wilson stood, rocked back and forth on the balls of his feet, and updated the aggregation on Hughes' latest attempts at swaying property and business owners with above market offers, that the council had rejected them on two different occasions, they were now looking into eminent domain procedures, and Velma Duhon's efforts to establish a local historical museum was being derailed by them.

"And they lied about it," shouted firebrand Stanley Payne.

The verbally economic Bert Willoughby rose to contribute his usual no nonsense wisdom.

"I've been here all my life and y'all know I'm straight and honest."

Every head in the gallery nodded in silent agreement.

"I've always taught my children the value of hard work. When I look 'round this room, 'round this town, at all the farms and businesses in every direction, on every single day, I see the benefits of hard work. HARD WORK WORKS!! Always did, always will. I ain't selling."

Spontaneous applause erupted as he sat down. The nodding heads became more emphatic. Amid all the clapping, Harvey stood and extended his short arms, the gavel still embedded in his right hand, to quell the noise.

"The intent of this meeting is to let everybody know exactly who and what we're dealing with. They want you to think their plans for our city are in your best interest. They're not. We've seen their plans. What will we do when we don't have our land or businesses? Where will we go? If we stay united as a community, we'll defeat this. But we must remain united."

Harvey noticed Mayor Greenlee itching to make a statement.

"Our mayor has a few words to say."

Cornelius Greenlee rose and addressed his constituents. "I would like to say I am proud of what I witnessed tonight. I plan to do all I can to deter the efforts of the Hughes Corporation. I am with you, my fellow citizens, you can count on me."

As the council suspected, it was pure political puffery, and the people had heard what they came to hear. The gallery rose in noisy unison, the legs of the metal folding chairs scraped against the linoleum floor, the buzz of private conversations broke out and the once quiet chambers became a cauldron of commotion. As the people filed out, they mumbled their worries.

Harvey moved on to the final item on the agenda, which involved another request from the Hughes Corporation for a meeting.

"Again?" shouted the impulsive Stanley. "How many times do we have to tell them no? I say the hell with'em."

The wise and willowy Bert Willoughby stood and spoke. "Obviously, we've been talkin' to the wrong people. Or maybe the wrong person."

"What do you mean Bert?" asked Velma.

"I learned a long time ago that when you deal with large companies like these Hughes people, you're wasting your time talkin' with folks whose decisions can be overruled. We need to speak with the one individual whose decisions can't be reversed."

Ruth recalled her research. "That would be the president, the son who took over for his father, the founder."

"Then, that's who we need to meet with," said Bert. "At

least we know his decision, like it or not, can't be overruled."

"I don't think it's going to make a damn bit of difference Bert," blurted out Stanley. "Look at what they're already doing up in Columbia."

"Maybe it will do some good, maybe not. My point is, we ain't made our appeal directly to *him*. You'd be surprised how much common ground you can find once you meet a fella face to face."

"Besides," added Velma, "it's an option we should not squander."

Harvey put it to a vote. The council would meet again with the Hughes Corporation on the stipulation that their president be in attendance. It was unanimous in the affirmative. Mayor Greenlee then shared his legal expertise.

"This Hughes Corporation is indeed very powerful, but we're on strong legal ground. First of all, eminent domain cannot be instituted without compelling reasons. Building condos and luxury apartments don't fit the bill. Secondly, the city of Louiston owns our beaches, it's public property and can only be taken for public use, like roads and bridges. The Hughes people are trying to scare us into selling."

"Those sons of bitches!" shouted Stanley.

"I suggest we concentrate our legal efforts under the Historic Preservation Laws. Our land and beaches could be declared historically significant and thereby prevent development altogether. This could explain the true reason why Velma's museum plans are being held up. Their approval would bolster our claim that we are a culturally and historically vital community."

Velma's mouth flew open. It all made sense now. The developers were more diabolical than anyone thought. The lawyer/politician proved to be more lawyer this time.

After they got wind of Bert Willoughby's land sale, the Hughes Corporation lawyers intensified their efforts at eminent domain in the capital. They were trying to avoid the state courts where they had less clout. Their appeal shifted from what was best for Louiston, to what was best for the State of South Carolina; how the increased taxes would swell the state's coffers, how their project would generate publicity and increase tourism. All the while, they were persisting in their attempts to buy out individual business and landowners. And Velma's application was still languishing in the file cabinet of some mid-level bureaucrat.

"It seems like these boys want to play hardball," stormed Stanley Payne. "We need to stop playing defense and go on the offense. We've got to make a move."

"I have an idea," said Velma. "Why don't we send Mayor Greenlee to Charleston to challenge their illegal bullying tactics."

Harvey pointed a stubby, ringed finger at her. "That's an excellent idea, Velma. How 'bout it Mayor? Are you on board?"

The astute attorney reverted to verbose politician.

"I would be honored to represent our esteemed city in our state capitol on this crucial matter."

There were no dissenting votes. The Louiston City Council had made its first preemptive strike.

On a breezy August morning, LaVern and Wilson returned from a routine checkup at Dr. Grubbs to an extended family noisily socializing in the kitchen and family room. Gloria and Jackie conversed idly about the arrival of their new grandchild, Shaundra and Brittany had just finished breakfast, and Freeman was watching the news. As the expectant parents entered the room, every head swung in their direction. Wilson's arm was around LaVern's shoulder and LaVern was smiling but looking tired.

"What did Dr. Grubb say?" asked Gloria.

"He said I am dilated enough to start for the hospital. But it's not urgent, there's plenty of time."

Jackie was the first to react. "Ohh, my baby is going to have her baby!"

"OK then," said Wilson, "let's get everything together and get on the road."

The pre-packed bags were retrieved, and Freeman and Wilson loaded the luggage into two cars and they were on the way to Bon Secours St. Francis Hospital in Charleston.

LaVern phoned Darien to alert him that she was on her way.

He called ahead and notified the staff of the previously discussed precautions that needed to be observed when a person of LaVern's celebrity was admitted; a private room, her arrival, stay, and departure times would remain confidential, and her name was definitely not to be made public. Darien suggested a fictitious name. LaVern chose Jacqueline Carter, her mother's maiden name. Any details surrounding the identities of her family were also to remain undisclosed.

As the caravan headed up highway seventeen, they passed Freda's unfinished house. The brick exterior was up, and the roof was on. Wilson filled in the gaps.

"Yeah, the interior walls and the floor aren't done yet but it's ahead of schedule."

LaVern looked behind her at Shaundra. "By the way, Freda told me you did a great job selling her house."

"Thanks Peaches. I really like the real estate business, and, thanks to Freda, I'm getting all kinds of referrals now."

"I'm proud of you, Shaundra."

The day after LaVern arrived at the hospital, Gloria received a call from Wilson that she was being wheeled into the delivery room. Both families rushed from their five-star hotel accommodations to Bon Secours. They were ushered into a private waiting room with a flat screen on one wall, an inviting sofa, a couple of pillowy armchairs and a solid, expensive looking, wooden table with fresh fruit and live flowers on it. A nurse reminded them to notify her if there was anything they needed. Everyone settled in. Wilson was in the delivery room.

After an hour, he emerged clad in a wrinkly blue nylon top and matching, formless pants, blue stretch nylon netting on his head, and blue shoe coverings, along with a smiley, teary quality etched on his face. Everybody looked but remained mute.

"It's a boy! I held him!"

Freeman was the first to approach. "Congratulations my boy."

They hugged and Freeman reached into his shirt pocket and handed him a cigar that said, "It's a boy!" Then, the women crowded around, and the group hugged and kissed him.

"You're going to make a great father Wilson," cried Shaundra.

Gloria wrapped both arms around her son's waist and squeezed tightly. She looked up into his eyes. "I know how important it was for you to be there for this one. I'm glad you got the chance, son."

"It was beautiful, Ma," he said through watery eyes. "I watched him come into this world. I watched him take his first breath. It was amazing."

"I love you, Wilson," said Jackie. "I couldn't ask for a better son-in-law."

"Thank you, Jackie. If I'm half the parent you and Freeman were, I'll be happy."

Fifteen minutes later, a nurse burst through the swinging doors. "You can see her now."

When the group entered the room, LaVern was in her bed holding her baby boy against her breast.

"Hi everybody. I did it. Come meet the newest Davenport."

They formed a circle around her bed.

"Oh my God," said Shaundra, "Peaches, you're a mother. My Peaches is a mother."

"I'd better be, after all that labor."

"It's a boy Momma," said Brittany. "You did good."

Laughter erupted in the room.

"What's his name?" Freeman asked.

"We decided long ago that, if I had a boy, we'd name him after his father. Family, I present to you, Wilson Freeman Davenport II."

Freeman's eyebrows raised in surprise. Both men stared at one another and their eyes watered. Spontaneous applause erupted in the room

"Can I hold him?" asked Jackie.

"Of course you can Mom. All of you can."

LaVern whispered to her new son. "Wilson Freeman Davenport II, meet your family."

With that statement, young Wilson came up close and familiar with his new support group. He was passed from one set of hands to the other. The Whitakers, being first-time grandparents, were overjoyed. Brittany was amazed at the new life she held in her arms, her little brother. Shaundra held the tiny bundle close and kissed his head. Gloria gently enclosed the infant in her experienced arms and closed her eyes. He didn't cry once. By the time young Wilson made his way back to his mother, he was imprinted with the love and adoration of his village.

The Write Thing
Chapter Seventeen

On her return trip in October, Freda was accompanied by her mate and fellow actor Clancy Morgan. She extolled the virtues of living in Louiston so much he had to see it for himself. Clancy was 5'10" with a medium build, a pencil thin mustache and an easy-going personality. As usual, Mary Scales greeted her guests on the porch with her apron around her waist and a dish towel in her hand. It was as if arrivals were always interrupting her housework.

"It's so nice to see you again, Freda," said Mary. "Give me a hug young lady."

Freda spoke before they finished their embrace. "Mrs. Scales, you don't know how much I've missed this place. I'm looking forward to making Louiston my home."

They finally pulled apart.

"Well, we're glad to have you. I assume you're here to check on the progress of your house."

"That's partly true. I'm so in love with this city I'll use any excuse to come back."

Mary turned around to face her screen door. Andre Scales, having graduated from Ralph Bunche High, was now away at college, and had been replaced by a neighbor's young son.

"Antwan!"

There was no answer.

"Antwan!!" she yelled, with more force.

The energetic thirteen-year-old bolted through the door.

"I'm sorry Mrs. Scales. I was in the bathroom."

"Would you please take my guests' things up to their room?"

"Yes ma'am."

Freda motioned to her partner. "Mrs. Scales, I would like you to meet my dear friend Clancy Morgan. Clancy, this is

Mary Scales."

"It's a pleasure to meet you Mrs. Scales. I feel as though I'm meeting a legend. Freda speaks so highly of you."

"Well, Freda is good people." She looked closely at Clancy. "You're one of her movie friends."

"Yes, I do movies and television too."

"I thought so," said Mary. "Louiston ain't never had so many famous people here."

"From what I hear about this city," replied Clancy, "I should be the one to feel privileged to be here."

"Well, that's nice of you to say Mr. Morgan. Let's go inside and I'll show you to your room."

"Please, call me Clancy."

"And you can call me Mary. I tell Freda to do the same, but she don't listen."

"That's right," countered Freda, "and that's my choice."

As everyone headed toward the lobby, young Antwan raced past with the luggage.

"Slow down young man!" shouted Clancy. He reached into his wallet and withdrew a twenty-dollar bill. "This is for your trouble."

Freda did likewise and handed him another twenty.

"Wow, forty dollars. Thank you very much Mr. Clancy…Miss Freda."

The next thing anyone heard was the screen door creaking open and the thumping of tennis shoes and luggage across the wooden floor.

"I like that kid already," said Clancy.

Early the following morning, Freda and Clancy drove to the building site. The house was only halfway up but the peaceful, picturesque isolation filled him with envy. The sounds of the ongoing construction were the only interruptions to this tranquil setting.

"Freda, this is perfection," he said as he scanned the lush green scenery. "You hit the jackpot."

They then made the twenty-minute drive to the Davenport compound. As she worked her way through the small-town streets, Freda proudly pointed out the many places of business whose owners she had come to know. *Nice friendly looking places,* observed Clancy, *exactly the kind I would expect to find in a town like Louiston.* As Freda turned onto a secluded, shady street, she pulled into the driveway of a house sitting atop a rise.

"Who lives here?" Clancy asked.

"You'll see."

They continued past the house and around to the rear. Clancy was astounded to see a huge, stately, all brick ranch style residence. Not the kind one would expect to find in Louiston. At the front door, a female figure emerged, smiling and waving and holding a baby. *She seems vaguely familiar.* They got out and Freda rushed over to hug her.

"Hello Clancy," came the words in a voice he immediately recognized.

At this first sighting of LaVern, Clancy's jaw dropped.

"You're living here… and you have a baby? Oh my God, I had no idea."

"Sorry to shock you like this," LaVern said. "I've been a little busy since we last saw each other."

"So I see. And you've managed to keep this a secret."

"Yes, so far."

Clancy glanced over at Freda. "You didn't tell me any of this."

LaVern answered for her. "That was at my request. But I trust you or you wouldn't be here right now."

"I understand," said Clancy. "If the press got a hold of this, they would camp right on your doorstep."

"Exactly. Now, let's go inside. I want to introduce you to my family."

In the family room, Clancy was granted formal entrée into LaVern's inner circle. He met Gloria and Brittany. They talked about her first trip to Louiston; how she and Wilson met, why she relocated here, how Wilson wanted nothing to do with Hollywood, all the details that had been shielded from the public. Clancy was fascinated by Wilson.

"And he still runs his own business?" he asked disbelievingly.

"He wouldn't have it any other way," replied LaVern.

"This guy sounds too good to be true. I can't wait to meet him."

"You will," said Freda.

One evening, while relaxing in the soft light of the antique lamps in her lobby, Freda asked Mary to talk about the significance of the items she had elegantly arrayed around them. She joyfully did so. Clancy was enthralled and immediately reached for his cell phone.

"I can't pull you up on the BnB Finder."

Mary's answer said it all. "The what?"

"The BnB Finder," said Clancy. He was astounded she didn't know what it was. "It's an online site that lists all the BnB's worldwide. It makes it very convenient for anyone to find you and make reservations."

"I don't have a problem with reservations. I stay booked."

"But," added Freda, "you can post photos and have guest reviews or share your menus…anything."

"Let me show you the site." Clancy darted off to his room like a kid on an errand. He returned with his laptop, pulled up a chair next to Mary and began his tutorial. He showed her how other BnB's showcased their establishments.

"What do you think? Do you want this place on BnB Finder?"

"It all sounds real good, but I don't know a thing about setting up all this online stuff."

Freda and Clancy looked at one another and smiled. Before the evening was over, The Home Away From Home was online. It had beautiful interior shots and a nice photo of Mary. It still needed to be tweaked; some exterior shots, a posting of her menu, the history surrounding its artifacts and other things that would separate her establishment from others. They assured Mary it was very easy to maintain. Even thirteen-year-old Antwan could do that if she needed help once they left.

The time spent in Louiston was eye opening for Clancy. He was able to meet Wilson. "He's a stand-up guy, LaVern. I can see why you fell in love with him."

He played golf and went swimming and boating. By the time his visit came to an end, Clancy was convinced he must tell his friends about Louiston. It was a mecca, a truly underappreciated and unrecognized prize to be treasured.

By spring, gossip about the appearance of the President of the Hughes Corporation was all over town and preparations began a week early. It was decided that the meeting would be live streamed for those who can't make it to the courthouse, something being attempted for the first time. Fire Chief, Albert Coates, and Police Chief, Arthur "Art" Ransom, along with four of his officers, would be on hand, not because they expected any serious trouble, but city occupancy and egress laws had to be enforced. Their presence had never been required at any council meeting…ever! Such was the magnitude of this event.

On the evening of the March meeting, the public began trickling in a full hour before the five o'clock start, another first. By the time the council members began to arrive, the room was jam packed, and the excess was directed to the two nearby overflow rooms, which also filled quickly. Wilson and LaVern parted ways just inside the council room doors. LaVern chose a seat in the far corner, in the last row, from where she could see everybody and everything. Wilson took his place at the council table where everyone, except for Henry Wallace, was already seated. Mayor Greenlee arrived, as was his custom, strategically late. Once again, he unashamedly worked the crowded chamber, to much enthusiasm, until he found his usual spot in the first row, on the aisle. From the hallway came Fire Chief Albert Coates' commanding voice.

"Sorry, but we're at capacity. No one else is allowed in. Keep this door closed, Art!"

Police Chief Art Ransom's booming delivery came crashing into the chambers.

"Sorry Earle. Doors close right now. Back it up."

There came the dull thudding of the courthouse doors. Chief Ransom posted two officers at the door and two at the entrance to the meeting room. He headed for a position inside the council chambers. Henry Wallace strode into the room. His roly-poly body headed straight for his customary position, dead center of the council table.

Once seated, he whispered, "They just pulled up. I saw them from the bathroom window. You should see the crowd out there. You'd think this was some kind of Hollywood premiere."

The courthouse door creaked open.

"Back up Rudy," said the officer. "Let these gentlemen pass."

There was the thud of shutting doors again, followed by the rapid footsteps of several people reverberating off the marble floor. First to appear was a tall, clean shaven, expensive suit-wearing Black man in his early thirties. Heads snapped in that direction, wanting to get a gander at the object of their mistrust.

Lamont Hughes was one those rare Black men who was born and raised in the comforting embrace of wealth and privilege. He and his sister went to the best schools and socialized with society's elite. The struggle for survival most Black's faced daily was little more than a rumor to him, a mirage in the desert. Lamont was uncomfortable in the spotlight. The philanthropic Hughes family was content with being behind the scenes, the wizard manipulating the levers behind the curtains in the emerald city, but he was comfortable wielding power. That air of authority and superiority was an advantage in business, but a calamitous failure when dealing with the public, like the citizens of Louiston.

After his momentary pause, Lamont lifted his chin and adjusted his silk tie. He used both hands to pull his custom-tailored jacket together and proceeded resolutely toward the front of the room. On his heels, four more expensive suits filed silently in. Henry Wallace stood and extended his open hand.

"Right here in front gentlemen."

Council members recognized Maurice Conyers and Javon Wilkes from their previous appearance. The other two were unknown. They all exuded confidence tainted with arrogance. LaVern couldn't see their faces, but she could read the crowd. If stares were rocks, this group would have been stoned to death on sight.

Henry Wallace gaveled the council to order. The Hughes Corporation issue was last on the agenda, so the executives sat quietly as the council went about its business. There were periodic verbal exchanges as they glanced around trying to get a sense of their surroundings. Once all other agenda items were addressed, Henry Wallace stood and gazed out into the packed room.

"We have now reached the point in our meeting where we will attempt to seek a resolution to the issue that brought us all together tonight. Mr. Lamont Hughes, President of the Hughes Corporation, you have the floor sir."

Lamont Hughes. I haven't heard that name in about fifteen years. Ugh! But, it can't be him.

He rose and turned to face the citizens of Louiston. LaVern recognized him immediately.

Oh my God! It is him! I can't believe it. So, he's the mover behind all this buyout, takeover mayhem. Even when you think the most vile and wretched among us are already resting on the lowest possible rung reserved for the most repulsive of human beings, someone comes along to remind you that even their lowest is still not low enough.

Lamont Hughes thanked Henry and Mayor Greenlee for this opportunity to speak to the people of Louiston.

"I have with me my Board of Directors. I want to make them available for any questions anyone might have." He unleashed his most charming, disarmingly friendly smile, then went on to explain that he meant the citizens of Louiston no harm. He reminded them how local jurisdictions, and states nationwide, benefited from his redevelopment efforts.

"I'm a businessman. In my projects, everybody makes money. I've improved the lives and prospects of thousands of people, and I'd like to do the same here."

Lamont came across as arrogant and unsympathetic. As he droned on, the atmosphere in the room grew tense. They could smell the condescension on his breath and hear it in his voice. The grumblings were few and muted at first. Then came the outbursts.

"Aw, c'mon man!" came one cry from the gallery. "You suits and ties are all the same."

Despite the deterioration going on all around him, Lamont seemed unaffected, as did his Board. The four sat there, unmoving and wordless, like monuments; monuments to excess. When Lamont finally ended his pitiful appeal, the floor was opened for questions. Inquisition was more accurate. The confrontational and mercurial Stanley Payne was seething throughout Lamont's entire bogus appeal. He fired the opening salvo.

"First of all, Mr. Hughes, nobody here is hypnotized by your money. We're all aware of your corporation's track record. My question to you is, why, after this body told your representatives that no one was interested in selling, did your people continue to tempt our citizens by throwing money around like Halloween candy?"

"They knocked on my door a couple of times after I said no," came an angry voice from the back.

Lamont, who had returned to his seat after giving up the floor, stood up.

"Like I said previously sir, I am a businessman. I believe that each property or business owner deserves the right to make his or her own decisions."

"Well, how's that working out for you Mr. Hughes?"

Lamont could only manage an embarrassed smile. Mamie Johns, the hat shop owner, rose from the other side of the room.

"Mr. Hughes, my shop is all I have. I've owned my business for thirty years and I have no interest in being bought out and starting over somewhere else. I'm too old for that. A lot of the people you see here are in the same predicament. Whatever you offer, it means starting over and maybe having to leave Louiston. We simply aren't going to do that."

"That's right," came more shouts from all over the room.

"We're appealing directly to you, Mr. Hughes," said Velma Duhon. "This community doesn't want what you're offering. Do you plan to ignore our wishes and bulldoze over us anyway?"

"Well, Miss Duhon, to be honest, if I feel it's worth my time and effort, I will pursue my developmental objectives until I get what I want."

There were audible gasps throughout the gallery. The temerity to actually admit to his mercenary nature, his complete lack of concern or empathy. Wilson stood up and addressed Lamont's stance.

"So, let me understand exactly what it is you're saying Mr. Hughes, so that everyone here and those watching from their living rooms throughout the county won't misinterpret what you just said." For effect, he walked around to the front of the council table to engage his neighbors directly. He went up on his toes, then back down to the floor. "You're saying that no matter what *our* wishes are, no matter how many times we tell you and your corporation no, you will simply proceed with your plans to turn Louiston into some kind of luxury, seaside getaway for the rich. All at the expense of everything we hold near and dear."

Suddenly, one of the monuments snapped to his feet.

"Excuse me sir, if I may interject here. My name is David March, and I am the Vice President of the Hughes Corporation. I want to assure you and everyone here that our wish is not to disrupt the lives of the residents of Louiston."

A woman in the crowd rose, an infant in her arms, and pointed directly at the still standing Lamont. "That's not what *he* said!" she shouted.

"Please, allow me to elucidate on what our President said. Our most important objective is to work with communities and find alternatives that are mutually beneficial. We want to avoid any obfuscation. We don't wish to decimate any municipality."

Another citizen rose. "You suits come through here all the time, spewing your big words and smiling in our faces and the bottom line is that you want what we have and we ain't selling."

More raucous shouts of agreement emanated from the crowd. Henry Wallace deliberately exhibited sparse control of the contentious meeting. He wanted the Hughes Corporation officers to get a good dose of unfiltered local resentment. Lamont gave his V.P. a gentle pat on the shoulder, as if to say nice try, but I'll handle it from here. He obediently returned to his seat.

"That's not entirely true sir," stated Lamont. "I know for a fact that one among you has already sold a plot of land. Isn't that right Mr. Willoughby?"

Bert was surprised by Lamont's outing of his sale to Freda

Parks. Even though it was a matter of public record, it once again demonstrated the degree of scrutiny the Hughes people paid to what was going on in Louiston. Wilson spoke up.

"Everybody here knows about Bert selling a piece of his land. That's not news. It's his land and he can do what he wants."

"My point exactly, Mr. Davenport. He and any other landowner can do what they want. I just want to give people options."

Henry Wallace came to Bert's defense. "You're overlooking one important thing Mr. Hughes, individual homeowners don't disrupt the fabric of our peaceful community. Gaudy, seaside condos will."

Farmer Bert then stood, as he always did when he wanted to speak, and, in his calm and direct manner said, "Let me ask you something, son. Does your family own your corporation?"

Lamont proudly responded yes.

"Then you already know that the only source of true wealth in this country is based on ownership. Take a look around this chamber and you will see a room full of owners. We don't own a corporation like you, but what we have we own. That's all any of us ask, to remain owners just like you and just like those that came before us. Why do you want to take that away?"

After Bert spoke, the chamber went mausoleum quiet. Everybody wanted to hear his response.

"Like I've said previously Mr. Willoughby, I'm first and foremost a businessman. I scan the country for opportunities that enhance my corporation's profitability. The potential here is immense and I plan to share much of that with your citizens. I didn't choose Louiston, on the contrary, Louiston, with its location and existing infrastructure, chose me."

Once again, Lamont fell miserably short of endearing himself to the populace. He made it obvious he was driven strictly by profit, with little or no compassion for the plight of the locals. Stanley Payne had heard enough. He stood and lashed out.

"You haven't heard a damn thing anyone has said tonight. The fact that we like our town just the way it is didn't register with you at all. You keep repeating that you're a businessman.

Well, almost everybody in this room is a businessperson. And we care more for this town than we care for you! Louiston is a living, breathing symbol that the dreams and aspirations of our ancestors still exist, that their sweat and sacrifice was worth it. The same way they left something for us, we plan to leave this town, intact, for those that follow." Stanley took a moment to wipe his bearded mouth free of spittle. "As rich as you are, you don't have enough money to buy our legacy, our history, our children's inheritance."

There was a boisterous outcry from the gallery. People stood and shouted and drowned out any response Lamont attempted. Identical outrage spilled from the adjoining two rooms. Henry, for the only time all evening, used his gavel to bring the room back to order. He had never had to bang so hard or for so long. With order finally restored, Lamont decided to cut his losses. He signaled his Board it was time to go.

"Thank you, Mr. President, for this opportunity to address the council."

As he led his entourage toward the exit, LaVern made her way across the back row of chairs to the aisle. She stood there, her stare burning holes into him. Then, without muttering a word, their eyes met. The impassive, passionless countenance that he wore all evening faded away. It was the only time that night he was caught off guard.

"LaVern?"

She was unmoved. "So, you're the one responsible for all this misery. You ought to be ashamed of yourself bringing all this chaos to a town of peaceful hard working Black people. You are and always have been a loathsome and contemptible creature!"

Lamont regrouped quickly. He ignored her remarks. "You've done well for yourself since I last saw you. You must live in this town."

Just then, Wilson approached. "Anything wrong sweetheart?" he asked as he put his arm around her shoulder. Lamont shifted his eyes from LaVern to Wilson and back to LaVern. The gears in his devious mind began to grind.

"No sweetheart." She squeezed Wilson. "I'm fine."

Lamont turned and exited without a word. Just before he

entered the hallway Velma's voice could be heard shouting above the clamorous din.

"Mr. Hughes, are you considering implementing eminent domain procedures against us?"

He and his retinue exited without responding. People spilled from the auxiliary rooms and booed and harangued them all the way down the hall, out the double doors, and back to their awaiting limos, where the crowd outside picked up the baton and gave the execs a deafening and profanity-laced send off.

Later, after the bulk of the townspeople had left, Wilson and LaVern descended the marble steps and headed for their car. "I never thought," mused Wilson, "that we'd be in the position of fighting for our lives, protecting everything we've ever owned, from a Black man. But that's where we find ourselves. That's what it has come down to."

It was during this same spring season that Freda finally moved into her new house. Just like LaVern, she was instrumental in its design and filled it with expensive new furniture and the latest gadgets. And, just like LaVern's home, this house was architecturally light years from the cozy, clapboard cottages of her neighbors. Freda and Clancy decided to pay Mary Scales a visit to thank her for her past hospitality, and warm, generous treatment.

"I'll miss having you as guests" she said, "but I'll enjoy having you as neighbors."

As they headed for the door, Mary called out.

"Oh, by the way. After y'all left the last time, I started getting reservations from Los Angeles. Do you two know anything about that?"

"Who made the reservations?" asked Clancy.

"The first one was for someone named Vance Greer."

"Vance is *my* agent," said Clancy. "I bragged about you, and I guess he did some research and decided to book a room. You have a true heavyweight of the industry coming here Mary. Who else?"

"Javon White. I never heard of him either."

"Oh, my goodness," exclaimed Freda. "Javon White has

two books on the New York Times best seller list right now. He's coming too?"

"He'll be here in June for a week."

"Vance represents him too," said Clancy. "Word about your place sure got around fast."

"Wow, you have some very high-profile people coming here," said Freda.

"They won't be treated no different," Mary declared. "I take good care of all my guests."

Mayor Cornelius Greenlee had spent over two months traveling back and forth between Louiston and the state capital in Columbia lobbying on behalf of his constituents. His report to the council would be disturbing. Attendance had returned to its normal, paltry few as he rose and adjusted his round, gold, wire rimmed frames beneath his bushy eyebrows. He wasn't smiling.

"I have good news and bad news to report tonight."

There were moans and groans.

"Give us the good news first, Mayor," urged Bert.

"The good news is that, like I said at the community meeting, we're on solid legal ground. The State recognized our ownership of our shorelines and the established land use rules granted through our incorporation in 1900. The city must agree with any outside use of our property."

"Thank you, Armistead Louis," said Velma as she joined her palms together and looked up to the ceiling.

"And the bad news," stated Wilson.

"The Hughes Corporation is not giving up. They've been known to stop at nothing to get what they want. Their only recourse now is through the courts and if they're successful, we'll be offered 'just compensation' for our land and we can be bought out."

There were gasps of disbelief. The mayor continued.

"To prepare for any possible court proceedings, we should, as I mentioned before, prepare a defense centered on our city as being historically significant. State laws draw a clear distinction there."

To add insult to injury, Cornelius informed Velma that her

application for funding would probably be approved once the Hughes Corporation received permission from the courts to proceed. It was the ultimate slap in the face to her, her efforts and her community. The council's first preemptive strike had mixed results. The fight was still on. But the cunning Lamont Hughes was in no hurry. It would be many months before he would make his move.

By June, the beaches were crowded, and the town was vibrant and alive when Javon White checked into The Home Away From Home. He acclimated immediately. He wandered contentedly among the shops and along the shoreline and the boardwalk, engaging both vacationers and locals alike. One sultry and warm evening, Javon was sitting on Mary Scales' wooden steps taking in the late evening street activity. Vacationers, clad in shorts, sandals, sunglasses and tee shirts, meandered slowly, just happy to be out. Citizens, in contrast, walked with a single-minded purpose, in their work clothes, with bags of groceries, destined for home and family. Javon looked over his shoulder to where Mary idly fanned herself while she slowly swayed back and forth in her porch swing.

"You know Mrs. Scales, this is really quite a town you have here. I had trouble believing that a place like this existed for Black folks, but here it is. I can't believe I never heard of Louiston before."

"I wish I had a nickel for every time I heard that one. We've been here for over a hundred years. I just hope we'll be here for a hundred more."

"Why wouldn't you? This place is ideal."

"Not being a local, you wouldn't know about this but, there are forces out there trying to ruin everything that you see."

Javon moved to the other side of the wooden steps to face her. "Ruin? What do you mean?"

"You don't have to worry about these things, young man. These are strictly local issues. I shouldn't have even brought it up."

"Well, it's too late now. What do you mean by ruin?"

Mary heaved a sigh, then began. She touched on the Hughes affair and how all their development plans would destroy the

Louiston that everybody knew and loved. She talked about the Hughes Corporation's condescending and offensive efforts to sway public opinion and pointed to Lamont Hughes as the main culprit, his lack of compassion and his arrogance, his deceitful efforts to undermine the city council's authority and about the public rejection of his buyout efforts.

"What has Louiston done about it?"

Mary recalled Mayor Greenlee's valiant attempts in the state capital, the vociferous and confrontational meetings at City Hall, the undaunted, unified community spirit that compelled everyone involved to not give in, and the fact that it will come down to a battle in court.

"If he gets his way, I'll lose this place. Where am I supposed to go? I can't start over. I've put in too much hard work." Mary paused before she continued. "You know, Mr. White, we don't ask for a whole lot out of life. Everyone in Louiston is satisfied with being able to run our businesses, provide for our families and educate our children. We don't crave millions of dollars like a lot of folks. We don't want their glitzy hotels and their oceanside luxury apartments. We just want our little piece of the planet."

As Javon listened, his journalistic juices started to percolate. He sensed something bigger.

"What's Louiston's next move?"

"The rumor is that those Hughes people will have the judge in their pockets when they make their move. I guess we'll find out at next month's council meeting."

"There's a city council meeting next month?"

"Yes. I guess that's when Lamont Hughes will drop the sword on all our necks."

"He's going to be there?" said an even more intrigued Javon.

"Yes, and he's going to enjoy it too. He could've done it months ago, but he takes pleasure in watching the whole town wriggle like a worm on a hook."

Javon was convinced that the public outside of Louiston needed to know what was going on here. This was a story about survival versus corporate greed, the deliberate eschewal of a town's sovereignty and its right to exist. Before his week in

Louiston came to an end, Javon spoke with all the city council members, including the incendiary Stanley Payne.

"Those sons of bitches want to take our town," he declared one afternoon while sitting in a golf cart on his golf course. "We told them no repeatedly and the State sided with us. Now, they're going to buy off a judge to get what they want. That Lamont Hughes is scum. He should be ashamed, a Black man doing this to Black people."

Javon talked with Velma Duhon and came away with the identical character assessment; a dispassionate, profit driven and unsympathetic corporate raider. In talking with Wilson, he found the stubborn determination that flowed through the veins of every resident.

"We're not going to roll over Mr. White. It looks bad, but everybody here knows that Louiston is worth fighting for."

Javon interviewed shop owners and farmers and vacationers, anyone with an opinion. He decided not to approach the Hughes Corporation. He wanted to attend the council meeting and gauge for himself the state of the relationship between the two parties. In the interim, he pitched his idea for the story to his editors at the New York Times. They seemed as captivated as he was about this "David vs Goliath" story and gave him their wholehearted endorsement.

One month later, Javon was back in Louiston. The council members were aware of his journalistic reasons for being there, as was LaVern, who took her customary seat in the corner, in the back. No one else in attendance had a clue that an award-winning author was among them.

Javon placed himself in the main chamber and observed the fast-gathering crowd as they entered and seated themselves in an orderly but clearly irritated fashion. He also noted the overflow that quickly filled the two nearby auxiliary rooms, two groups just as testy and aching for a fight as the group he sat amongst. Mayor Greenlee was his typically tardy self. He worked the packed room as usual but this evening the response from his constituents was tepid at best and he soon found an empty seat in the front.

Everyone seemed to be in survival mode, closing ranks and formulating a single cohesive game plan. They knew their solidarity was key against such a formidable foe. A head poked itself into the room from the hallway.

"They're here!"

On the street, the identical two black limos as before came to a stop. The angry crowd closed in. Police Chief Ransom assumed a position at the top of the marble steps.

"Everybody, back off! Let these people exit their vehicle and anybody who tries to lay a hand on'em, I'm taking your ass right to jail!" He directed his officers to form a cordon.

The moment the doors opened, Lamont and his Board emerged onto the sidewalk amid a thunderstorm of obscenities.

"You can go to hell, Hughes, you greedy son of a bitch!"

"You call yourself Black? You and all your ass kissers!"

The execs wordlessly followed the police line, climbed the steps to the courthouse doors and entered. Just inside was Fire Chief Albert Coates. In the council chambers, Javon heard his bullhorn-like vocals.

"You know the way gentlemen," he said. "Everybody else, stay back. We're at capacity."

Then came the thudding of the courthouse doors. Council members ceased their impromptu skull sessions and returned to their designated places. Within seconds, Lamont Hughes appeared at the wide-open entrance to the chambers. Javon finally got his first look at the "devil incarnate" and his Board. The mood of the room shifted instantly from mutual cooperation to mutual survival, as if a flock of sheep suddenly realized there was a wolf in their midst. Javon noticed a stark and revealing contrast in attire also. The Board looked like the prototypical corporate execs, tailored business suits, polished expensive shoes, silk ties and matching pocket squares. Louistonians were adorned in their working-class best, overalls, jeans or shorts, tee-shirts, summer dresses and sandals, work boots, and tennis shoes. Nothing could illustrate the economic and social disparity better.

Henry surrendered the floor to Lamont, and it was like pulling back the spring on a mouse trap; what scientists called potential energy. As Lamont addressed the township, the fluorescent light reflected mockingly off his diamond encrusted tie clip and matching cuff links. It was like flaunting his upper-class privilege right in their middle and working-class faces. *Either this guy can't read the room, or he doesn't want to,* reasoned Javon. He suspected the latter. The locals weren't listening, they were simply biding their time before the mouse trap, and all that potential energy was unleashed. Then, out of nowhere, it came.

"You either accept my terms and sell, or all of you will end up with nothing!"

Javon couldn't believe his ears. *Did this guy actually say what I thought he said?* The indifference and cold heartedness was appalling and the trap was sprung. The eruption was both instantaneous and vicious, and it came courtesy of the more volatile and hard-core members of the community.

"Fuck you! How dare you come in here and give us ultimatums you mother fucker!" yelled someone from the crowd. "I don't care how many judges you buy, we ain't gonna let you hijack our town!"

"Can you believe this shit?" screamed another. "You got the nerve to come in here and try to scare us with threats? The only thing you gonna get is a fuckin' beatdown!"

People stood and pointed fingers and bombarded the Hughes group with one vile epithet after another. Metal folding chairs were knocked over and clanged noisily against the tiled floor. Tennis shoes squeaked like there was a five-on-five in progress. People from the other two rooms flooded into the chambers to lend more physical and obscenity laced support. Chaos reigned. Police Chief Ransom and several of his officers rushed into the room, their adrenaline pumping, eyes wide with excitement. Henry Wallace tried to regain order by gaveling and pleading.

"Please everybody, let's show a little decorum."

Mayor Greenlee tried to appeal to the out-of-control crowd. He stood up and extended his hands over his head. "Please people," he implored, "we're better than this."

Stanley Payne shouted over the disruption. "No Henry. This moron and his overpaid flunky's have disrespected us for the last time."

The tumult increased as the mob edged closer to the Hughes group. The execs were now on their feet and looked worried.

They should have been.

Henry shouted out, "Art, you and your men get these people out of here before somebody gets hurt!"

The Police Chief pushed his way through the melee and managed to cordon off the fearful execs and Javon was right behind them. Amid all this turmoil, the writer watched Lamont, who seemed totally unaffected by everything, even after delivering his volatile ultimatum. As LaVern watched all this unfold, she managed to work herself through the swarm and closer to where the Hughes people were being led out. Wilson went to join her, his arm resting on her shoulder. Then, she and Lamont locked eyes. He leaned toward her and whispered,

"Nobody dumps me!"

Her mouth flew open and before she could respond he was whisked away.

"What was all that about?" Wilson asked.

"I'll tell you in the car."

Javon followed as Art and his officers managed to escort the Hughes group out of the chambers, through a crowded and noisy hallway, through the double pine doors and down the steps. He approached Lamont and had to shout to be heard when he identified himself as a writer for the New York Times and asked for a comment about what happened inside. He looked at Javon with surprise and said no, right before he ducked into his limo.

"Are you sure?"

Lamont stared daggers into him and, without blinking, raised his powered, tinted window.

On the short ride home LaVern disclosed everything that connected her to Lamont Hughes. They were both students at NYCPA, she said, and they dated briefly.

"So, you know this guy?" Wilson asked.

"I *knew* him," LaVern corrected, "but I haven't seen or heard of him in over fifteen years. Back then, he was just this jerk from a wealthy family who drove a used Toyota and wanted to be an actor. He didn't think I was good enough, so I ended it."

"Good for you baby," Wilson replied. "His loss is my gain."

The following week, Javon's article was on the front page of the New York Times. The headline read: "Small Town Fights for Survival Against Corporate Colossus." It caused little stir nationally. Javon promised to return and write follow-ups as events demanded. He was determined to see it to the end.

As June turned into July then August, Louiston's future remained in legal limbo, and all that anybody could do was carry on. People went back to their farms and businesses, LaVern concentrated on the joys of raising Wilson II, and the council returned to the business of running the city. But the people of Louiston never lost sight of their extremely tenuous predicament. They knew the sword of Damocles was still dangling over their heads. Lamont Hughes had not dealt his death blow.

A crucial part of running the city now included council member efforts to strengthen their potential court case. As Mayor Greenlee advised, their future depended on convincing a judge, under the Historic Preservation Laws, of Louiston's historical and cultural importance.

Their gathered evidence included town ownership of the land and beaches, written testimonies from relatives of the original settlers, Louiston having been a Black incorporated township since 1900, and having been a vacation spot for Blacks for generations. Velma's petition for a local historical museum, and the artifacts on display at Mary Scales' place as well as others scattered all around the region, were all to become exhibits in the planned museum.

There was also the environmental impact. Wilson's research revealed that South Carolina's coastline was primarily salt marshes, most of any state on the east coast, and was an important ecosystem for wildlife like birds, sea turtles, snakes and fish. Even though there were state laws protecting these areas from development, there have been exceptions made. A greedy and conniving Hughes Corporation would be expected to exploit every legal loophole available, and Louiston would use every weapon in its arsenal.

The vacation season was winding down, but at a time when bookings normally slowed, business actually picked up. Javon's article eventually brought national attention to Louiston. Black America suddenly discovered this ideal vacation spot that had retained its easy-going, down-home identity, and its much sought after location right on the South Carolina shoreline.

The streets became dotted with roaming camera crews seeking sidewalk interviews and public feedback on the whole Hughes affair. Every evening news outlet broadcasted the story of the battle of smalltown Louiston valiantly warring against the mighty corporate giant. Council people gladly sat for interviews. The image conscious Cornelius Greenlee held court in his city hall office daily and reveled in seeing himself on that evening's national newscasts. But it was Stanley Payne, whose fiery rhetoric during an interview on his golf course, who earned his unintentional fifteen minutes of fame. He singled out Lamont Hughes for his total disregard of the city's wishes, his profit above all else approach, the unethical interference of Velma's application for funding, and the upcoming court proceedings.

"We refuse to let these Hughes SOB's march in here and annihilate everything we have ever known."

Stanley was ratings gold. The public loved his fierce, sometimes profane defense of his city. In their eyes, his position was justifiable. Lamont and his corporation's favorability in the court of public opinion plummeted like a shot pheasant.

It's a Rat Problem
Chapter Eighteen

LaVern's phone played a familiar ringtone. It was Shaundra.

"Girl!" she screamed, "What the hell is going on in Louiston? I found you this perfect, quiet, peaceful town full of quality Black folks and the next thing I know, the whole city is in the middle of a public fight and they're on the national news. I can't take you nowhere!"

They both cracked up at that last remark.

"Shaundra, you wouldn't believe all that's happened since you were here last."

"Really? Talk to me."

"Do you remember the guy I dated back at NYCPA? His name is Lamont Hughes."

"Oh yeah. The rich, snotty brother who wouldn't even let you meet his family."

"Yes, him. Well, he's behind all this turmoil."

"Whaaat? You have got to be kidding me."

"I kid you not, and the town is fighting back like a mama bear defending her cubs."

"That dude is twenty-four carat crazy. Has he seen you, Peaches?"

"I made sure he did. You should've seen his face."

"I don't know if that was a good idea, girlfriend."

"You may be right, but you didn't see how he treated the people here. I had to tell him what a scumbag he was."

"That does it. I'm on my way. I haven't gnawed on somebody's ass in a long while."

"Shaundra, please don't come here and throw gasoline on the fire. We have Stanley for that."

"Now Peaches, you know me better than anybody. Would I do something like that?"

Yes I do, and yes you would.

In his Boston home office, Lamont knew he and his company were losing the PR battle. The Board convinced him to correct the repugnant image affixed to him by the Javon White article and the national media, by doing a television interview instead of a printed article, assuming that his smile and good looks would win over the viewing public.

"You need to show you're not the ogre they think you are," they said.

Lamont suppressed his apprehensions about publicity and agreed. They suggested that Javon White conduct the interview because, if he confronted the same person who wrote that ruinous article, he could shift public opinion. Javon was quick to accept. A conference room in the Hughes Corporation Headquarters was selected and Javon and his crew, along with the Board, were the only witnesses to the proceedings.

Things began on the friendliest of terms. Lamont flashed his brightest and most ingratiating smile and Javon started with the traditional softball questions. As it proceeded, the atmosphere and the questions became more intense.

"The State of South Carolina has sided with the city of Louiston and decided against implementing eminent domain procedures. Are you contemplating continuing your efforts through the state courts?"

"Company policy prohibits me, or any other employee, from commenting on any possible court actions, real or imagined."

Javon continued. "I have it on good word that your company is working behind the scenes to obstruct Louiston's request for museum funding. Is this true?"

"No," Lamont lied. "We have nothing to do with that."

Javon reminded him of his attempts at intimidation with comments like *"either you accept my offer, or you will wind up with nothing."*

"I was there," Javon said. "I heard you."

"It was a regrettable choice of words."

"But surely you understand the effect your words must have had on those citizens who were there that night."

"Of course I do, Mr. White. Many of those in attendance

were businesspeople just like me. They know how business works. It was just business."

The board members could be seen off camera, in the shadows, whispering among themselves. They had reason to be worried. In his warped mind's eye, Lamont was convinced his likeability was shining through. He failed to realize that his appalling lack of human compassion shone through more. It was as if a huge skull and crossbones covered his face for the entire interview. In what he thought would be the icing on his public relations victory cake, he decided he would get his revenge on LaVern by dropping a bombshell.

"Besides", he continued, "they're just trying to protect their celebrity friends."

"What celebrity friends?"

"Oh, LaVern Whitaker *lives* there. You didn't know that?"

"No," replied an astonished Javon, "I didn't."

"So does Freda Parks. They both have houses in Louiston."

Based on his wrenched and twisted logic, by making Lavern's presence in Louiston known, and the inevitable deluge of publicity he knew would follow, people would come to realize that Louistonians weren't as concerned about their privacy as they led everyone to believe. They would be the bad guys, not him.

"If they can sell to movie stars, why can't they sell to me? Those stars aren't going to make them any money, but I will."

After Lamont's disclosure, the race was on to find LaVern Whitaker, the movie superstar who had successfully avoided the limelight for several years. Hordes of paparazzi descended on Louiston within days. Citizens were stopped everywhere, coming out of their houses, walking with armloads of groceries, in the fields, it didn't matter. These were nosy and impolite strangers, and their presence made the locals wary and uncooperative, and at no point did anyone disclose the location of LaVern's or Freda's homes. They had given their word, and they would not renege.

At one point, a veteran paparazzi wandered to the outskirts of town and stumbled upon a large, out-of-place brick mansion sitting back from highway 17. In this landscape, it stuck out like a tuxedo at a barn dance. He whipped out a pair of binoculars and scanned the property. A Porshe 911 Carrera sat in the driveway. This had to be either LaVern Whitaker's, or Freda Parks' home, he reasoned. He decided to wait.

Victor Tolson was a well-known, much detested member of the Hollywood paparazzi game. Despised by every actor in the business, his arrival anywhere was confirmation that all rights to personal space and privacy would be blatantly ignored. Word of his stakeout reached the other paparazzi and within hours, an assortment of cars and vans had collected, facing in both directions, along the shoulders of the road, one quarter mile outside Freda Parks' residence.

LaVern's home, unlike Freda's, was not easily spotted. Situated atop a small rise and behind the original house on a residential street, it turned out to be ideally concealed. She was free to roam around her property unseen with baby Wilson, but the public disclosure had rendered her housebound. She could no longer chit chat with Mary Scales on her front porch, or Velma Duhon behind her pharmacy counter. She couldn't stroll slowly through town and bask in its countryfied coziness. The hounds stopped in Cora Valentine's beauty salon, Mark Williamson's barber shop, Leo Durbin's bakery and Mitchell Tresvant's hardware store. But nobody betrayed anything.

Into this cauldron of confusion stepped Shaundra.

This was her first visit in over a year and a half. So much had taken place; Wilson II was now one and a half and learning to walk, Freda's house, which was under construction then, was now her completed home, Brittany was a mature eleven-year-old who adored and doted on her little brother, and Shaundra had earned her real estate license. The following day she announced she was going to venture out to reacquaint herself with Louiston.

"I think I'll pay my respects to Mrs. Scales first."

"Please give her my regards. I miss seeing her," said LaVern.

"I sure will."

As she pulled up to The Home Away From Home, a lone woman was lazing peacefully in the porch swing, reading a book. Shaundra was about to utter a polite hello and continue inside when she stopped abruptly and looked closer. She removed her sunglasses and gasped.

"You're Sylvia Ferguson. I've read your books."

"I'm flattered to hear that young lady," replied the author. "And to whom do I have the honor of speaking?"

A voice answered from behind the screen door. "That's Shaundra Jackson, Mrs. Ferguson."

Mary Scales came through the squeaking screen door clad in her omnipresent apron and wiping her hands with a kitchen towel. *It's good to see some things have not changed*, reflected Shaundra.

"Come here and give me my hug," Mary cried out.

The two embraced.

"How have you been Mrs. Scales? I really have missed you."

"That's so nice of you to say, darlin'. How long have you been in town?"

Shaundra ignored her question. "Mrs. Scales, do you know who this is?"

"I certainly do. She's Sylvia Ferguson and she's written over a dozen books that empower Black women."

Shaundra was impressed. She didn't know that ever since Mary began receiving bookings from notable people, she researched and familiarized herself with their histories. When she stepped inside The HOME AWAY FROM HOME for the first time in eighteen months, Shaundra was relieved to see that the lobby was as inviting and comfortable as she remembered. All the historical artifacts were still on display, along with newer ones. Mary returned from the kitchen with a platter of homemade chocolate chip cookies and a pitcher of tea. They returned to the porch and began to talk.

"First of all, LaVern wanted me to tell you how much she misses you."

"It's such a shame," said Mary, "all these media people looking for her, keeping her indoors all the time. I miss seeing her too."

"This is my first stop, but is it really that bad?"

"Oh girl," said Mary, "you just don't know. They've been hanging around like a low fog, just pesterin' people and trying to find out where LaVern lives." She paused to bite her cookie.

"They even came 'round here snoopin', bothering my guests and even camping out front for a couple of days. But what I'm really upset about is this Hughes thing. It's got everybody worried. We've never had to fret about our future…until now."

Shaundra left The Home Away From Home full of dread. She embarked on a walking tour and to her dismay, there were wandering bands of camera toting men everywhere. They were like an occupying army. As Shaundra rounded a downtown corner with a just purchased cherry snowball, coming toward her was Victor Tolson. They had a tormented history that always ended with both spewing profanities at one another. She had her shades and big straw hat on, but if he recognized her, it would be irrefutable evidence that LaVern was here somewhere, and the search would intensify. To keep her nerves in check, she repeatedly chopped into her cup of flavored ice with the plastic spoon. He stared straight at her, and she stared down into her cup. They passed without a word. As she rounded the nearest corner, the treat was tossed in the trash, and she started walking hurriedly toward The Home Away From Home. She jumped into her rental and drove to the Davenport compound. By the time Shaundra closed the door behind her, she was an emotional wreck. She came in and flopped clumsily onto a leather recliner, kicked off her sandals and with unsteady hands, removed her hat and shades. LaVern was there alone.

"Peaches, you won't believe who's in Louiston this very minute."

LaVern furrowed her brow. "Who?"

"That low life, nasty assed Victor Tolson."

"Really? Are you sure?"

"He walked right past me, but I had on these shades and my hat, and he didn't recognize me."

"I hope he didn't follow you back here."

"Peaches, you would've been proud of me. After he was out of my eyesight, I hustled back to the car. I was looking around, double checking everything that moved. I even drove around the block to make sure nobody was following me." Shaundra closed her eyes and rubbed her forehead. "It's been a long time since I had to do anything like that."

"First Lamont and now this scavenger." LaVern shook her head. "This is not good."

She realized events were closing in around them again. Despite the good intentions of her neighbors and friends, it would be a matter of time before their whereabouts became public. She was determined not to give that sleazebag Tolson the satisfaction of finding them first. As a family, they must once again decide on a course of action.

After his interview with Lamont Hughes, Javon began his quest to verify or disavow his claims that LaVern Whitaker and Freda Parks, or any other celebrities, lived in Louiston. He already had a major advantage over the paparazzi. He was known and trusted and was granted the kind of access the cameramen could only dream about, and he was invisible to them. He started with Mary Scales and asked her if what Lamont Hughes said was true. Her deflection spoke volumes.

"Look, Mr. White, everybody in town is grateful that you've placed our fight in front of the whole nation. It's clear you're in our corner and because of that, you've earned a tremendous amount of trust and respect. But I just don't see how revealing that kind of information is going to do any good."

"I understand your reluctance Mrs. Scales and believe me, I value the trust and respect this community has bestowed on me. If there's one thing I have come to realize, it's that you and your neighbors don't trust easily."

"You're right about that."

"But, thanks to Lamont Hughes, the information is out there, and the result is that your town is now crawling with people who haven't earned, nor do they deserve, a modicum of your respect."

"But, Mr. White, these people came here for the purpose of avoiding publicity."

"You're right, Mrs. Scales. Celebrities have a right to a private life just like you and me. But, if that wolf pack gets a hold of the story first, it will turn into a media feeding frenzy, the very thing they came here to avoid. On the other hand, if I can talk with them, they'll get their story out there first, in their own words. No hype, no surprise photos. And, if they tell me to get lost, I give them and you my word that I'll respect their wishes."

Mary was truly torn. "Give me a couple of days. I'll have an answer for you."

As Freda and Clancy neared the entrance to her driveway, they got their first sight of the gaggle of press stationed along highway 17. LaVern had warned them ahead of time. They reminded Freda of a pride of lions at rest. They look harmless, until they aren't.

"Well, there they are," she moaned. "I guess it had to happen sooner or later."

As the car pulled into the driveway, all the press boys were suddenly on alert. Field glasses were yanked out of jackets and off the front seats of cars and quickly affixed to their faces. All eating and conversation ceased. The car came to rest at the front door. The couple began unloading their luggage.

"Bingo!" shouted Victor Tolson. "That's Freda Parks and Clancy Morgan. I was right. I knew either she or LaVern Whitaker had to live here."

Clancy looked up at the paparazzi in the distance and waved. "They'd better keep their sleazy asses off this property."

That extra acre of land Freda bought was paying off now. After they unloaded their gear, they disappeared into their sanctuary.

After a sleepless night, a burdened and unnerved Mary Scales sat in the Davenports family room.

"Are you alright Mary?" asked Gloria. "You look so stressed. I don't like to see you like this."

LaVern, Wilson, and Shaundra looked equally concerned. The unburdening commenced.

"Do you remember the newspaper article about Louiston that was in the New York Times?"

"Yes," was the group reply.

"Do you remember who wrote it?"

"I sure do," answered Wilson. "His name is Javon White,

and he interviewed me and the rest of the city council for his piece. He did a great job."

"Well, he's at my place and he wants to meet you and LaVern."

"Does he know where we are?" inquired LaVern.

"No. He saw that Lamont fellow's interview and he's poking around. He doesn't know I'm over here talking to you. I didn't want to betray your confidence."

"Mary," said Gloria, "don't ever torture yourself like this again. Just come to us. We'll understand."

They promised to get back to her with their decision. LaVern had Galloway and Green check into Javon's background. They reported back with glowing terms and the Davenports gave Mary their approval to share their location.

The following evening, Wilson answered his doorbell and, at first, Javon thought he was at the wrong house.

"Hello Mr. Davenport, I'm looking for LaVern Whitaker. I was told she lives here."

Wilson smiled wryly. He understood Javon's bewilderment. "You have the right place Mr. White. Come on in."

Wilson led the writer through the house and into the family room. Javon stared in disbelief. It really was her. She really did live in Louiston. And he was the only journalist who knew where. She rose and approached the still befuddled writer.

"Good evening, Mr. White" she said as her hand reached out. "Welcome to my home."

"Good evening, Miss. Whitaker. It's good to finally meet you."

Miss. Whitaker. I'll address that later.

"Please, have a seat. Are you hungry? Do you want something to drink? I must warn you, no one in this house drinks alcohol."

"A glass of juice would be fine. Thank you."

Sitting in a chair by herself was an older woman with a toddler in her lap. Javon noticed another woman and an adolescent girl hunched over a scrabble game. The young girl stood and headed for the adjoining kitchen. He had no idea who these people were. He assumed the women were part of her personal staff. He couldn't figure out Wilson nor the teenager's connection. The toddler stumped him completely. After he found a place to sit, he watched as LaVern sat beside Wilson and tucked her legs underneath her, as if they did this all the time. Brittany returned with a glass of apple juice.

"Here you are, Mr. White. Enjoy."

"Thank you so much, young lady."

Brittany rejoined Shaundra at the board, but neither was interested in the game anymore. After taking a sip from his glass, Javon pulled out his notepad to prepare for the interview.

"You probably won't need that tonight Mr. White," said LaVern. "But that will be up to you."

"Okay," said the unsure Javon.

"I'm sure you're wondering who these people are sitting all around you," said LaVern. "It would be my pleasure to introduce them." She looked up into Wilson's eyes and rubbed the side of his thinly bearded face. "This handsome man is my husband, Wilson Davenport."

Javon's eyes lit up. *She's married? To the city councilman? The same guy I interviewed a few months ago? I was that close to LaVern Whitaker, and I had no idea.*

"So, from this point forward, I would appreciate it if you referred to me as Mrs. Davenport."

It would take a serious adjustment to peer into that famous face and remember to say LaVern Davenport, Javon presumed.

"You keep a secret well Mr. Davenport," observed Javon.

"Just protecting my family Mr. White. I'm sure you can understand that."

"To my right," continued LaVern, "is my mother-in-law, Gloria Davenport. And, on her lap, staring suspiciously at you, is my son, Wilson Davenport II."

A baby! Javon was flabbergasted. Nowhere had he read about LaVern Whitaker having a baby. He had only been in her house a few minutes and he was already blindsided with blockbuster news.

"I have to admit Mrs. Whit...I mean Davenport, I didn't expect any of this."

"There's more Mr. White. That young lady who brought you your juice is my daughter, Brittany. We don't use the term stepdaughter. That's just for your benefit."

At this point Javon started scribbling furiously. There were just too many bombshells going off to trust just his memory.

"And, last but not least, over there at the board game, is my childhood friend, Shaundra Jackson.

"Nice to meet you, Javon." said Shaundra. "I've read your work. I'm impressed."

"Well, thank you very much Miss Jackson. I don't always get such positive reviews."

"And that's it. That's my entire family, my support system...except for my parents. You're the first journalist Wilson and I have trusted to meet my family."

Wilson waited while Javon finished his notetaking.

"Mr. White, we realize we've given you access and information that no other journalist has, but every journalist wants. There's a very good reason for that. We chose you because you've shown yourself to be an honest and trustworthy journalist, unlike the vultures circling around our town now."

Wilson didn't mention the background check.

"I'm glad you feel that way Mr. Davenport. I always strive to earn and maintain the trust of all my interview subjects."

"We wonder if you would agree to a television interview instead of writing an article."

So, that's what LaVern meant when she said, "you probably won't need that notepad."

"We have managed to avoid public exposure of our family life, but, because of Lamont Hughes, that's no longer possible."

Javon glanced around the room and every head was bobbing up and down in silent approval.

"What we hope to accomplish with this television interview," continued Wilson, "is steal the thunder from the paparazzi, and they will leave us and Louiston alone."

There was momentary silence, then Shaundra piped up.

"It's like having rats."

Javon, and everyone else in the room, was perplexed.

"Rats?" he responded. "I don't get it."

"If you have a rat problem", she explained, "there's a very simple and inexpensive way to get rid of them."

"How's that?" asked Javon. He had to hear the logic behind this.

"Rats hang around because there's food to eat. Eliminate the food supply and they'll leave on their own. By doing this interview, we cut off the paparazzi's food supply, and there will be no more reason to hang around."

Little Wilson was becoming irritable in the arms of his grandmother, so LaVern quietly rose to relieve Gloria, and returned to her place beside Wilson. She cuddled and kissed him lovingly and he settled down in the familiar embrace of his mother. Seeing a star of LaVern's stature being so spontaneously nurturing left an indelible image on Javon.

"I must admit I wasn't expecting to be offered a TV interview when I came here, but I don't think an article would do your story justice. America needs to hear and see what I have heard and seen tonight. I have to work some things out, but I don't see a problem."

"Oh," said Wilson, "I have one more request of you Mr. White."

"Sure, anything you want."

"We want the interview to take place here, in our home. You know…familiar surroundings and all."

"That's a great idea. I think that would make the decision even easier."

"Good," said Wilson. "I guess we'll wait to hear from you."

The two men rose to leave.

"I should know something in a couple of days," said Javon.

As they worked their way toward the front door, LaVern followed closely behind, her arms full of a now sleeping Wilson II. As Wilson opened the front door, Javon had one last question for him.

"If you don't mind me asking, Mr. Davenport, what do you do for a living?"

"I own my own HVAC business here in Louiston."

"Thank you, sir," was his reply.

As Javon slowly made his way to the driveway, he turned around for a final look, and, still standing in the back lit entrance of the doorway, was a smiling and waving HVAC business owner, his Hollywood movie star wife and their one-

and-a-half-year-old son. He thought to himself, this story was made for TV.

The evening of the interview, with the media still swarming all over town, numerous precautions had to be undertaken; the camera equipment was smuggled, under the cover of darkness, in Wilson's company vans, the custom drapes were velcroed together to prevent any light seepage, and Wilson couldn't tell his fellow council members until after it was completed. The interview began when LaVern verified her location to a curious nation. She introduced Wilson as the love of her life and unveiled the identities of the rest of her family. She discussed the back story of how and why she ended up in Louiston and why she and her family felt this interview was necessary. Soon, Javon's questions moved to the sticky Hughes Corporation affair. Both LaVern and Wilson stated their case against the Corporations' redevelopment efforts and how it would adversely affect, not only their lives, but the lives of everyone in their peaceful, cohesive community.

"I'm trying to preserve my sanity and my city," she said.

Wilson described Lamont as a "backward walking" person.

"That's an old Native American term that describes someone who is different, but not in a good way. It's someone who is not to be trusted."

LaVern admitted to having dated Lamont briefly in college, she feared things would look worse if he made it public first but noted they hadn't seen each other since then. During the hour-long talk, Javon was fair but uncompromising. He pointed out that a celebrity of LaVern's status could expect just so much privacy, no matter where she lived.

"You have a point," said Wilson, "but, after this interview, we're hoping that we can resume something resembling the life we had before Lamont Hughes exposed us. What he did wasn't fair to us or the citizens of Louiston."

Javon wrapped up the talk and thanked the Davenports for their time. "I think it went very well. What do you think?"

"We can't be more pleased, Javon," said LaVern. "You were the right choice."

"Thank you. I think this interview will be a public relations goldmine for both of you. You deserve it."

"Thanks again... and please, call me Wilson."

"And call me LaVern."

"I'm honored," replied the writer.

The ratings for the interview were off the charts. The public, who for many years had little to no knowledge of LaVern's private life, were delighted at the sight of such a tight-knit, charming family. They loved the fact she found true love with a regular working man. America adored that she found peace and tranquility in a small town where its citizens banded together to protect her like one of their own. And America fell in love with the energetic and cute baby Wilson. One unexpected consequence of the interview was the reference to Lamont as a "backward walking man." Within hours, the internet was flooded with disparaging memes of Lamont, or Sasquatch, or a caveman, all walking backwards.

The Hughes Corporation, on the other hand, remained the enemy, and Lamont Hughes was the devil in the details. How could he justify his effort to undo a century of flourishing achievement? It was an unconscionable stance in the eyes of America, especially Black America. Lamont and his company were once again the targets of national derision. The most welcomed result of the broadcast was that it took all the wind out of the paparazzi sails. The scourge of cameramen slowly drifted out of town, their food supply having been severed.

One afternoon, after she exited Cora Valentine's Beauty Salon, Shaundra spied Victor Tolson packing his car in front of The Armistead Hotel, obviously preparing to leave. Shaundra walked right up to the back of the trunk loading paparazzi.

"What's the matter Tolson?" she shouted, "mad you didn't get the chance to spring out from behind some dumpster like the rodent you are?"

He whirled around and stared at Shaundra. "You!" he screamed. "I should have known your sorry ass was somewhere nearby."

"Not only was my sorry ass nearby," replied Shaundra, her head shimmying from side to side, "but my sorry ass will still be nearby long after your sorry ass leaves here empty handed."

"Get the hell away from me," he shrieked. "I got better things to do than waste my breath arguing with you."

"I bet you do, like finding another dumpster to jump out of!"

"You're a real bitch, you know that?"

"Yeah, I know it! I just want to make sure *you* know it!"

Shaundra turned on her heels and sashayed her way down the street. Her East Baltimore brashness had served her well on this day. Victor Tolson shouted something unintelligible from behind her, but she didn't know or care what it was because, just like she predicted, the rats were fleeing.

At the next council meeting, Harvey gaveled the members to order for what was expected to be just another humdrum evening of civic obligations. The mayor's attendance was disconcerting. Why was *he* here? the council wondered. Council President Wallace rose.

"Mayor Greenlee has an announcement to make."

He wanted to apply salve to the upcoming open wound, everyone assumed. Stanley furrowed his brow, Bert sat impassively, with legs crossed, Velma bit a painted lip, Wilson nervously twiddled his thumbs, and Ruth Van Meter covered her mouth.

"This concerns our pending court case," he began.

Oh no, everyone thought. *Here it comes.*

"It's over!"

It was as quiet as fog in the council chambers. Just addled looks of confusion.

"What are you talking about, Mayor?" asked Stanley.

"Those rumors about a bought judge were just that...rumors. The Hughes people never intended to go to court. They knew they couldn't win there so they disseminated that hearsay in a last-ditch effort to intimidate us into surrendering. It's over. We won."

Spontaneous shouts of jubilation and joy erupted. Papers were sent airborne, where they fluttered weightlessly before slowly, gracefully, settling on the linoleum. Council members jumped around and cried and hugged and stomped like they had won the world series, which, in their minds, they had. The only thing missing was bottles of Veuve Clicquot yellow label to pour over their heads. One arm of Mayor Greenlee's glasses still clung to his ear. The other arm hung free at a 45-degree angle across his smiling face. Little Louiston had fought for their survival against Goliath and won. Stanley Payne, amid the pandemonium, approached Harvey.

"We beat those sons of bitches," he shouted as he put Harvey's short, thick neck into an arm lock that would make The Rock proud. After disengaging from Stanley, Harvey banged his gavel repeatedly before the members resumed a semblance of decorum.

"There's more business to conduct."

Harvey removed from his leather portfolio a document clearly embossed with the seal of the State of South Carolina.

"I would like to read this official notification from the State to the City of Louiston."

He got as far as "an offer of matching funds to be used to begin the construction of the Louiston Historical Museum." More jubilant outbursts. Velma could only put her face in her hands and sob uncontrollably at the table. Her long valiant battle was over. Every member made their way over to her and offered consoling, heartfelt hugs and congratulations.

After their nationwide public relations beating, the Hughes Corporation made a quiet, wound licking exit from Louiston. It was their very first defeat. Lamont continued to be a successful, but scheming real estate juggernaut, but after his single foray into the national limelight, he returned to his comfort zone of wielding power from behind the scenes.

The Wilson and LaVern Whitaker Foundation held its first Board meeting in the family area of the Compound. A Baltimore area work training program for teenagers, proposed by Freeman and Jackie, was chosen as their first recipient. It was renamed the Earle Jackson Project. Shaundra was especially moved by the Whitakers' thoughtful gesture to honor her now deceased brother. Young men like him who weren't college material should have been taught a skill. This project was designed to fill that void.

Louiston returned to its homey, welcoming self, but now, the country knew about them. In addition to their regular vacationers, an influx of Black elites, educators, athletes, entertainers, politicians, wanted to build homes there. This was their Cape Cod.

LaVern and Wilson rented their old house out to vacationers. They watched with bemusement one summer day, a renter's reaction to having a famous actress as a neighbor. LaVern encountered the female in the rear of the old house.

"Hey!" the woman said, "are you LaVern Whitaker?"

LaVern admitted that she was.

"No, you're not!"

Caught by surprise, LaVern countered, "Yes, I am."

"No, you're not!"

There was momentary silence. LaVern decided to turn the tables. She asked the woman for her name.

"My name is DeLisa Curry," she said.

"No, you're not!"

After the nightmare that was Lamont Hughes, LaVern was having fun again.

THE END

Author Bio

Eric Grandy was born and raised in Baltimore City and graduated from City College. After he graduated from Essex Community College he was drafted by the Chicago Cubs and played six years for that team. He went on to a variety of jobs: photographer, lab manager, driver for DHL and warehouse manager. After retirement, he decided to devote himself to writing, producing several short stories and Accidental Paradise, his debut novel.

Grandy still lives in Baltimore with his wife Rhonda.